THE LAZARUS WAR:

ORIGINS

Jamie Sawyer

orbit

www.orbitbooks.net

ORBIT

First published in Great Britain in 2016 by Orbit

1 3 5 7 9 10 8 6 4 2

A CIP catalogue record for this book is available from the British Library.

ISBN 978-0-356-50549-7

Typeset in Stempel Garamond by Palimpsest Book Production Limited,
Falkirk, Stirlingshire

Printed and bound in Great Britain by CPI Group (UK) Ltd,
Croydon CR0 4YY

Papers used by Orbit are from well-managed
forests and other responsible sources.

MIX
Paper from
responsible sources
FSC
www.fsc.org   FSC® C104740

Orbit
An imprint of
Little, Brown Book Group
Carmelite House
50 Victoria Embankment
London EC4Y 0DZ

An Hachette UK Company
www.hachette.co.uk

www.orbitbooks.net

To Jake and Benji – my best buddies

"The UAS *Endeavour*'s mission remains of interest to all Alliance military agencies . . . It was the first and only time that any meaningful dialogue has been established between humanity and an alien race. Exactly how this was achieved, and whether it can be replicated in the future, remains unclear. All files pertaining to the *Endeavour* operation continue to be protected by Congressional Code Alpha-9, a rarely invoked secrecy clause which permits Alliance agencies to withhold disclosure of materials said to be prejudicial to state interests . . ."

Extract from Secret Histories: Conspiracies within the Alliance, *by Professor Frederick Boswell, published 2279*

"Everyone has heard of the *Endeavour*, right? She's the modern-day *Mary Celeste*. She went missing with all hands, never accounted for. Probably the greatest mystery in space-faring history. Not just her, but the rest of her fleet as well – sixteen starships in all.

"Ships go missing all the time. We're at war – whether the Pentagon wants to admit it or not – but a fleet of that *size*, that *magnitude*? No, that doesn't just happen. Someone knows where the *Endeavour*, and her sister ships, went. We're not being told the whole truth.

"Either that, or they weren't being honest about why she was really out there. Governments have a history of lying to their people. History has shown us that the bigger the government, the more likely they are to lie. And the Alliance government? Well, that's just about the biggest Gaia-damned government that the human race has ever seen . . .

"Not counting the Asiatic Directorate, of course."

Interview with Azra Asami, head of the Anti-War Coalition, broadcast by Core News Network, 27 July 2281

"The *Endeavour*'s mission was nothing but an unmitigated success. What's to hide? She went out into the dark, settled the Treaty, and that led to the longest period of peace the Alliance has ever enjoyed. The Krell threat was neutralised overnight. Sure, we lost some people out there. Sure, that's a shame. But it's a cost exercise, and from where I'm standing the books balance."

Extract from speech made by President Francis to
Alliance Congress, 29 November 2281
(prior to his assassination by Directorate forces)

AFTER ACTION INTELLIGENCE REPORT

*** EYES ONLY ***

CLASSIFICATION: TOP SECRET (RED UMBRA)

TO: **SECTOR COMMAND, CALICO BASE**

FROM: **CAPTAIN T. OSTROW, MILITARY INTELLIGENCE**

SUBJ: **OPERATION PORTENT (DAMASCUS), FURTHER ACTION REQUIRED**

OPERATION DATE: **10/08/2283**

The primary objective of Operation Portent was to harness an Artefact located in an area of space known as the "Damascus Rift". It was intended that this Artefact be used against the Krell Empire, to slow or otherwise disturb War-fleet 856. This operation was, to a large extent, a failure, leading to the loss of numerous Alliance warships, and several thousand personnel. Notable survivors are Major Conrad Harris' squad (the "Lazarus Legion"), as well as the considerable fleet asset UAS *Colossus* (with her attendant crew). Major Harris and his squad were recovered by a passing security patrol, on their return to what remained of *Liberty Point*.

I write this report to draw Sector Command's attention to several live intelligence leads in the aftermath of Operation Portent.

Firstly, "Williams' Warfighters" remain at large. There have been as many as sixteen unconfirmed sightings of the Warfighters in the last six months. If the *Colossus* managed to escape the Damascus Rift, then it remains possible that the Directorate warship *Shanghai Remembered* did the same. The relevant members of Williams' Warfighters must be terminated with extreme prejudice, and all sightings logged with Military Intelligence.

Secondly, both the Helios and Damascus Artefacts remain insecure. Alliance forces have not been back to either site. These sites may be in Directorate hands, and we must assume that any technology located there may be used against the Alliance [see also Tysis World, and other Shard holdings, in linked documents X-996 onwards]. It is my view that the Shard technology is a significant war-asset, which should be exploited wherever possible: that these very significant sites could be under

Directorate control is of particular concern [see Science Division files - REDACTED - INSUFFICIENT CLEARANCE].

Thirdly, and in my submission most importantly, the whereabouts of the UAS *Endeavour* remains of crucial importance to the war effort. Her mission to [REDACTED] may be the answer to our current predicament. If the [REDACTED] can be used against us, this may prove to be the tipping point for the Alliance military. It is my recommendation that this should be prioritised and pursued as soon as resources become available.

Following his return to active duty, Major Harris has been the beneficiary of a promotion to the rank of lieutenant colonel. Several members of the Lazarus Legion have similarly been promoted; the surviving members are on active duty. Their current activities revolve around operations on the Directorate Rim. This is not a satisfactory use of resources.

It is my final recommendation that the Legion be reassigned, and that Command considers [REDACTED].

Captain T. Ostrow, Alliance Military Intelligence
Universal calendar date: 1 October 2284

CHAPTER ONE

RIGHTEOUS FURY

Six months after the Damascus operation

We deployed out of the Jaguar's aft ramp.

Rounds slashed the air, pinging against the dropship's hull, ricocheting around inside the cabin. That and the snow made it hard to see where we were, let alone who was out there, and we were greeted with a wall of white: cold and impenetrable.

"We're taking some serious fire," Lieutenant James said. He was piloting Scorpio One, our designated transport. "I can't stay on-station much longer—"

The dropship swayed in the high wind, undercarriage grinding against the roof of the building on which we had landed. Quite frankly, that James was able to keep the boat in the air at all was impressive.

I zoned out: had more important things to worry about, such as staying operational. My null-shield lit – creating a miniature lightning storm in reaction to the incoming fire. The heads-up display on my tactical helmet flashed with warning icons, the communicator-bead chiming as bodies went down. Simulants were dropping all around me. Three greens on my left flank bought the farm before we'd even got out of the damned dropship: bodies cut to ribbons by armour-piercing, depleted uranium rounds.

And it wasn't just Scorpio One. My ear-bead was filled with panicked reports from the other squads, officers calling in casualties across the theatre.

"Lazarus Legion!" I yelled. "Form up on me!"

As some asshole once said, no plan ever survives contact with the enemy.

Six hours earlier, the briefing room aboard the UAS *Independence* was filled with personnel. Mostly, not simulants but real skins – troopers dressed in fatigues waiting for the drop. It was a big turnout: the Lazarus Legion, of course, but three other simulant teams as well – Hooper's Raiders, Baker's Boys, and the Vipers. They were all good outfits, squads that I'd specifically picked for this operation. Together with James and the flyboys of Scorpio Squadron, the *Independence*'s briefing room was packed out.

"We're currently six hours from the objective," I said. "Welcome to Rodonis Capa; a star system unremarkable in the extreme, located on the Rim of Asiatic Directorate territory."

Faces were bathed in the soft green glow of the projected graphics, as the display powered up and the briefing began. We were sailing in-system, moving on the singular point of interest in this sector. The star was faded and bitter; a G-class sun that had been in decline since before Neanderthal man had left his caves. Six whittled nubs of rock, any atmosphere they had once possessed long bled off, circled the star. Those worlds were largely inhabitable and long dead. The exception: that was our target.

"This is Capa V," I said, zooming in on a muted white ball. "This is where we're going."

Capa V was a world barely within the circumstellar habitable zone, a planet that clung to the heat and light of its distant mother-star.

"I'll bet it's lovely in the summer," Martinez said, with his usual dryness. He yawned; from the look on his face he hadn't long been awake. "Someone wake me up when we get there."

"Bottle it, padre," said Jenkins. "This is it."

Martinez had been acting as unofficial chaplain to the platoon, offering sermons of damnation and damnation in equal measure. There was even a rumour going around that Martinez had been ordained. Sperenzo's team were of the Creed – Latter Day Catholics, proper fanatics – and it was open for debate whether the Venusians would disobey an order from me if it were at odds with one of Martinez's. The Venusians, identifiable by their tanned skin and Latino features, watched Martinez expectantly.

He raised a dark eyebrow. "For real?"

Lieutenant Keira Jenkins looked to me, the prickle of anxiety about her lean face. "I got a feeling. Now settle down, people, and listen up." There were murmurs around the table, but no one spoke out of line. "The floor is yours, Colonel."

Jenkins was harder, angrier than I'd ever seen her. We'd been conducting raids like this for the last six weeks: searching for anything that might lead us to Vincent Kaminski or the survivors of the Damascus operation. The result was that Jenkins, more so than the rest of the team, had become an over-coiled spring. Long hours aboard the

Independence waiting for intelligence to come in had been filled with zero-G gymnasium sessions. She was more than ready for this.

Looking at her, then at the image of Capa V, I suddenly felt very tired. I couldn't take another false lead, not when we'd had so many already.

"You take this one," I said to Jenkins. "I want to see how you'd do it."

"Copy that."

Captain Baker, commanding officer of Baker's Boys, jabbed me in the ribs with his elbow. "Won't be long before you lose her," he said. "Sooner or later she'll want a team of her own."

Baker was probably the oldest Sim Ops officer on the Programme – certainly the oldest survivor of the *Liberty Point* Massacre – and had been a veteran of the Alliance Army long before induction. His Boys, on the other hand, were all fresh faces – barely a handful of transitions between them. The eager look in their eyes was unnerving.

"Later rather than sooner, I hope," I said.

"Pay attention, people," Jenkins said, and the room fell silent. "As the man says, our destination is Capa V. Known to its Directorate residents as 'Cold Death'."

A briefing file opened on the display.

Capa V was a uniform, brilliant white: a world in the grasp of an ice age from which there would be no return. Great ice shelves claimed half of the planet, frozen seas the rest. Only very occasionally were there breaches in the ice: blue streams indicating liquid water down there, streaks of black where rocky plateaux broke through. Empty, featureless plains were the order of the day.

"Looks cold," Baker said. I knew exactly what he was trying to do: to test Jenkins, to push her to the limit. But on an op like this? I already knew that wasn't a good idea. Regardless, he went on, "And you know how my rheumatism plays up in the cold."

"Stow it, Baker," Jenkins said. "Local weather is a pleasant minus twenty, but expect it to feel even colder with the wind chill." The image magnified. "At your age, you'll probably want to stay buttoned up."

Sufficiently cowed, Baker went quiet.

Jenkins continued. "There are three settlements on Cold Death, and our target is here."

A small outpost – labelled QUIJONG BASE – lay in the south, nestled at the foot of a titanic mountain range. The base specifications rolled over the display and I quickly took in the relevant details. Several kilometres squared, over a hundred buildings and hangars of unknown purpose: arranged in a neat network, interspersed with work-yards and open areas, gridded by roadways with the occasional concrete barricade. Numerous communications towers and potential HQ locations. Lots of surface vehicles, but no visible air support. A single landing bay sat on the edge facility, suggesting that the compound had at some time been air-capable, but this was currently empty: dusted with a thick layer of snow.

"Six days ago, an M9 Sentinel surveillance drone captured a data-feed from this outpost. This contained an embedded security key known to be employed by Directorate forces when handling the movement of captured enemy combatants. Command believes that there are POWs down there."

"Prisoners of war?" Sperenzo said. She was a small, compact Venusian woman – one of Martinez's kin, her face claimed by a mess of gang-tattoos, hair cut short to her scalp.

Jenkins nodded. "Like I said, this is the shit. What's more,

Command has been able to identify that these POWs are from the Damascus incident."

"Fuck me," Baker said.

I fought the urge to smile.

"How'd they find that?" Martinez asked, his eyes narrowing as he inspected the intel. "Seems too good to be true . . ."

"Maybe it is," I said.

Whatever the truth, Jenkins was more than sold on the idea. "The Directorate might have people in deep," she said, "but we have people in deeper. An intel source has identified this as a prison facility. The source has so far proved reliable."

"About those maps," PFC Dejah Mason said. "What are those things?"

Always with the questions, I thought. Dejah Mason was the youngest member of the Lazarus Legion. Whether her inquisitive nature was as a result of her age or her disposition was hard to say, but she was a damned good soldier. Young, blonde and Martian, I feared for any man or woman who dared underestimate her.

She pointed out a circular formation in the middle of the map; as big as a dropship, glazed with ice but not snow. It was made of metal: like a concealed missile silo or the entrance to an underground facility.

"It looks like a pit," Mason said. "Or a covered shaft."

Jenkins scrolled over the site, magnified the image. "Possible mine," she said. "Limited heat detected, no radiation."

Mason frowned. "So we don't know?"

"No," Jenkins said. "We don't. That a problem, Princess?"

She was using Mason's new callsign; the tag by which she'd become known since dropping the label "New Girl". Mason pulled a face as she looked down at the holo.

"Not necessarily," she said. "But it doesn't look ... right."

"Christo," Baker said, rolling his eyes. "We know all we need to. Let's get down there already!"

"What's the mission plan?" Captain Hooper of the Raiders asked. He was Tau Cetian, and the youngest officer on the strike force; right out of officer training. The holo-badge on his lapel flashed "99": indicating the number of transitions he'd undertaken. Not bad numbers for a kid only five years on the Programme. If he made it, I predicted good things for Hooper.

"Objectives will be uploaded to your suits before we drop," Jenkins said. "But in short, we'll make planetfall together and spread out once we get dirtside. Primary targets are these buildings." Flashing indicators marked the sky-eye view of the settlement. "Live capture and retrieval is our goal. Like I said, I've got a feeling about this place."

I hope that you're right, Jenkins. I really do.

"What's the predicted level of resistance?" Mason asked.

Jenkins sighed. "Mili-Intel suggests minimal. There's a garrison down there, but they don't know that we're coming."

Sperenzo whistled. "So far as we know."

"In any event, consider enemy forces secondary," Jenkins said. "Repeat: objective is retrieval of personnel. We're coming in-system dark, and Intel hasn't heard any Directorate chatter concerning our presence. *Independence* has already knocked out their communications satellite, so they won't have the chance to call for help."

The *Independence* would be anchored in high orbit; observing the objective and our progress. She was fitted with the best in stealth tech – hopefully enough to evade the Directorate's counter-surveillance. The orbital comms rig – the satellite to which Jenkins referred – had been blasted to space junk an hour ago. There was plenty of debris circling Capa V, and so the ground forces were unlikely to have read much into the loss of their comms.

Even so, I scrolled over the global map of Capa V. Our objective was in the south, and a few thousand klicks north was another base: largely uninhabited, according to surface scans. Further still was a refinery platform, protruding from a frozen sea.

"Going to have to watch for activity from those outposts," I said. Something about them made me feel uneasy. "The idea that they could mount a response to our incursion can't be ruled out."

Jenkins pulled a face. "Apparently both are automated. Command says that they aren't of tactical significance."

"I've heard that before." I keyed a command on the console, updated the tactical brief. "I want *Independence* to keep eyes on those outposts at all times."

"Affirmative," Jenkins agreed. "As we're expecting this to be a live exfiltration operation, Scorpio Squadron will be providing air support and pilots."

She glanced over at the flyboys, across the tac-display. Lieutenant James and his team were already skinned up, looking every bit the part of Alliance Aerospace Force pilots. They were using next-generation simulants. Those were gene-engineered skins designed to be lived in, replicas of human bodies with enhanced capabilities and response times. The trade-off to looking real was that the bodies were not as strong or durable as combat-sims. Even now, I'd never actually seen James' real body.

"We'll be dropping in MX-11 Jaguar heavy dropships," he said. "Lazarus Legion and Baker's Boys will be on Scorpio One; the Vipers and the Raiders on Scorpio Two. The third and fourth Jaguars – Scorpio Three and Four

– will be empty. They'll be available for evacuation of any recovered personnel. Once the ground pounders drop, all dropships will remain on-site for close air support." He waved at the station map. "The Jags have anti-personnel rockets and heavy slug-throwers. That should keep the Directorate heads down until you search those buildings."

Air support was likely to be the key to the success of this mission. In the event that we found prisoners, it would allow us to get people off Capa, but also provide some shock-and-awe. If the Directorate were caught by surprise, a couple of dozen Banshee anti-personnel missiles would cause quite a stir: persuade them that a much larger strike force was inbound.

"Just try not to leave us behind this time," Jenkins said. James looked affronted.

"What?" Jenkins said, in mock-ignorance. "You have form, jockey. Just sayin' is all . . ."

"All right, people," I said, ending the discussion. I didn't want this briefing to be derailed. Over the last few weeks, Jenkins had vociferously argued that James was the only reason we were out here. Maybe she was right, but dwelling on it didn't change things. "Let's do this—"

Captain Ostrow burst into the briefing room, jostling himself into a place at the tactical display. He scowled bitterly.

"I'd rather that you hadn't started the briefing without me," he said.

"Sorry," Jenkins said, "but we've finished without you too."

Ostrow was the Military Intelligence officer assigned to the *Independence*, and as such he was technically supposed to sanction every operation that we conducted in Directorate territory. According to our mission parameters, we needed him to endorse that we had "just cause" for each mission: that we weren't acting outwith our military authority. He was a genuine pain in the ass.

"Funny how that worked out," Mason said, smiling.

"I've been looking over this intel," said Ostrow, "and I've got to say, I'm not convinced. This is the third target you've identified this week—"

"The third *potential*," I said, firmly. I could use their own language against them, if Mili-Intel wanted to play it that way. "Which means that it could be an actual."

"It could be a mining station," Ostrow countered. "It's just as likely. And this supposed intelligence chatter could be explained by movement of contraband, of arms or warheads . . ." He shook his head. "The board is a no-go on this operation. It's a red signal."

The room settled into an agitated quiet, troopers waiting for my response. Their concern wasn't necessary. I had absolutely no intention of backing down; not on this or any other operation in Directorate space. The bastards were going to pay for what they'd done to us, and we were going to get our people back.

"I've read the intelligence files too," I said, "and *I'm* approving this mission. I'll answer for it if I'm wrong."

"Which is exactly why you shouldn't be conducting these operations yourself. You're too damned close. He was your man. This is Directorate space, for Christo's sake. Just our presence here is violating so many treaties that I don't have time to list them . . ."

I heard the pinch in Ostrow's response as he trailed off. He knew that he had gone too far. I saw Martinez's face drop across the display, and held up a hand to warn him not to react.

"They killed thousands of servicemen and women in

Damascus," I said. "Did that violate any of your goddamn treaties?"

"I realise that," Ostrow said, reading the anger that his comment had generated around the table. Even so, he gave it one last try: "That aside, this operation is not sanctioned by Command or the Pentagon. Resources are tight enough as it is; with the losses at *Liberty Point*, you should be on the frontline! This could trigger a major diplomatic incident—"

"*Another* major diplomatic incident," I corrected.

"We're already at DEFCON one—"

Jenkins looked at me expectantly. Eyes are windows into the soul, the old cliché went. When I looked into her eyes, I saw hurt and sadness: a combination of emotions that I knew only too well. There was no way I could add to that. Kaminski and Jenkins had been together, for what it was worth, and she had taken his loss worst of all.

"The mission is a go," I said, ignoring Ostrow. "On my approval, if no one else's. Strike force proceed as briefed."

Every soldier in the briefing room slammed a hand to their hearts.

I looked down at my missing left hand.

Both hands on my plasma rifle, I faced the snowstorm. It was blindingly bright outside, and although I was wearing a full tactical helmet I fought the very human urge to put a hand up to my face to shield my eyes. The sky was a brilliant white – Rodonis Capa nothing more than an ineffectual blur on the horizon – and the snow was so intense that it was disorienting.

"Everybody out," Jenkins yelled over the comm-net. Sealed inside our powered combat-suits, this was our only method of communication. "Go, go, go!"

I kicked off my boot-magnetics and armed my M95 plasma rifle. The Trident Class V suits were insulated and carried full life support, but even wrapped in that battle-tech the cold hit me immediately. The Directorate's nickname for the world – Cold Death – seemed more than apt. I felt the pull of Capa's gravity: the dropship had been gradually moving into the world's gravity well since we'd broken orbit. A surge of combat-drugs – a cocktail especially designed to keep me killing – hit my bloodstream.

As planned, Scorpio One had landed on top of a low, flat building – a hangar of some sort. The other teams started to call in to Jenkins; meeting the same level of resistance. The Raiders were pinned down a couple of hundred metres south, in one of the open yards between structures, and the Vipers were taking heavy fire beside a garage in the east—

Blam!

A lucky round breached my null-shield and I felt the slug pop against my shoulder. It bounced off my combat-suit armour plating, but it still hurt.

"Fuck!" I yelled, gritting my teeth.

The ablative plate was good but, as demonstrated by the three dead sims underfoot, given enough kinetic fire eventually we'd go down like any other skin.

"You okay, sir?" Mason asked.

"Try not to get shot," I said. "Hurts like a bitch."

"*Area is hot,*" came the voice of an *Independence* observer, watching our progress from orbit. "*Advise immediate relocation from that site, Lazarus. Multiple hostiles closing on your position.*"

"Lazarus Actual copies."

To describe the theatre as "hot" was a significant understatement. Fire slid by all around us, from both the roadways below and guard-posts liberally sprinkled throughout the compound. Most of it was small-arms fire – I guessed assault rifles and machine guns – but it was hard to tell in these conditions.

Barely visible through the half-light of the snowstorm, my tactical helmet identified the three other dropships. The Jaguars were big and heavy: hulls a dark grey, with bloated crew cabins and stubby wings. They were lifters, not fighters, and carried only light armament. The precise, planned formation in which they were supposed to land hadn't survived contact with Capa V, let alone the enemy.

I took a decision. "Make for safe altitude, Scorpio Squadron."

"Baker's Boys have been assigned the landing pad," Jenkins said. "If the Raiders take the—"

In my peripheral vision, I saw a flash of light. Immediately, I identified it as a laser weapon: a mounted cannon of some sort, big enough to generate a searing beam of ruby energy.

Scorpio Three was a couple of hundred metres to my left. She'd been skimming low over a concrete block, empty and ready for evacuees, access ramp grazing the roof.

The beam panned, like a searchlight, and hit the ship's underside.

"*Down!*" I shouted.

The wreckage of Scorpio Three went down fast, VTOL engines failing, and the shock of the exploding Jag dropship made the hangar shake. It landed somewhere in the middle of the compound, throwing up a plume of black smoke. Directorate troops – identifiable only as flashes of heat in the storm – began to move on the site.

James cursed over the comm. Scorpio One fired off a couple of Banshee missiles, unsuccessfully seeking to chase the source of the attack, and lifted skyward.

"*Scorpio One pulling out—*"

"Copy that. Two has evaded further anti-air fire . . ."

". . . Tagging multiple tangos on east wall. Looks like a laser cannon—"

The other ships started to do the same: hulls occasionally flickering with incoming small-arms fire.

If we wanted to stay operational, we needed to get moving.

"Legion, move on that satellite dish," I ordered. "All other squads, take immediate cover."

I hunkered down behind the light cover and started to plan our next move. Spy-feeds from the stealthship that had scoped the outpost were superimposed onto the interior of my helmet face-plate, demonstrating where we were supposed to be.

"Looked a lot smaller from orbit," Martinez said, gruffly. "And when there weren't people firing at us."

"Do you get that a lot?" Jenkins asked, ducking back as a grenade exploded on the other side of the dish. Hot frag showered the area, sparked against our shields.

"They weren't supposed to know that we were coming . . ." Mason said.

"Devil's eyes are everywhere," Martinez said with a shrug.

"Doesn't matter," I said. "Getting these buildings pacified and searched; that's what we're here for."

The outpost was situated between two mountains, criss-crossed by gantries and metal catwalks that provided numerous defensive posts. The scant overground constructions were all snow- and ice-covered; metalwork made brittle by constant exposure to the elements.

Mason knelt beside me and reached into the deep snow with her gloved hand.

"So this is snow . . ." she said, almost wistfully. Although Mars was mostly terraformed, it was a planet without such a weather system. "I never thought that I'd get the chance to see it. Almost pretty."

"If it wasn't so fucking cold," Martinez added. "Not like home at all. You ever heard of a simulant getting frostbite?"

"No," said Mason, "but I think I'm about to be the first."

"Not this again," Jenkins said. "And for your information, *this* is most certainly not snow. This is an impression of snow. Check your wrist-comps for the chemical composition. There's barely any H_2O in it."

"She's from California," I whispered, as I tried to get my bearings, decide where we should be heading. The cold was numbing, seemed to slow my thought-processes. "I guess she knows all about snow."

"Better than these two off-worlders," Jenkins said.

A stream of hard rounds hit the snow beside me.

"How many shooters we got out there?" I asked.

"I'd bet less than a hundred," Jenkins said. "Fifty on it."

"I'll take that bet . . ." Martinez said.

"Button it, troopers," I said. "We need to act fast. Drones away. Directive: identify and flag hostiles."

The Lazarus Legion deployed their surveillance drones. A dozen autonomous flying units detached from our backpacks and sailed out into the snow. Even as I watched, two were caught by gunfire, exploding in a hail of sparks. The others began painting hostiles. Almost immediately, ghostly green figures appeared on my HUD. *Ah, that's better: I can see them.* The drones sent back heartbeat, heat signatures, the whole deal. The info-streams combined with those of the rest of the strike force.

Martinez, back against the dish, clucked his tongue. "You owe me fifty, Jenkins."

At least two hundred bodies were circling the compound, converging on our location.

Jenkins checked her plasma rifle. "Tell you what, I'll pay you in Venusian dollars. That suit?"

"Fuck you, Jenkins," Martinez said. The Venusian dollar wasn't worth the unicard it was stored on. "You know I only bet in American notes."

Mason sniggered. "Unmarked, so I hear."

There . . .

Something on the drone feeds wasn't right.

"You see that?" I asked the Legion, broadcasting the feed to their HUDs as well.

"It wasn't on the orbital images . . ." Mason said.

The edge of the compound was a ragged, snow-bitten fence, studded with towers. One of those overlooked the landing pad: a tall, skeletal structure, with an armoured booth at the top. The sky illuminated as something up there activated, accompanied by a whip-crack every time that it fired. I magnified the image. A handful of Directorate troopers were manning the booth, firing a multi-barrelled laser weapon into the sky. I panned the drone's position, took in the rest of the security fence. The other sentry towers were only half-completed: this was the only anti-air weapon that worked.

"No way that the flyboys will be able to pick up with that thing covering the strip," said Jenkins. "That cannon will bring down anything approaching the landing pad."

"Plan has changed," I declared. "We're moving on that tower before we commence the sweep."

I opened the general channel. "This is Lazarus Actual; do you read me Baker?"

"Affirmative," Baker said. His suit transponder placed his team somewhere on the ground, but it was difficult to say precisely where. "We're pinned down. Where's our air support?"

"Fucked, is where," I said. "You saw that ship go down. Intel was wrong. They have anti-air."

He grunted. "Figures."

"Keep your heads down and stay alive. We're going to solve the problem."

"Copy."

I keyed the channel to Hooper. "Hooper, I want you to stay on overwatch."

"Solid copy, Lazarus," he said.

Hooper's Raiders were already in position. The five-man team were equipped with M-23 Long Sight plasma rifles: a proper sniper's weapon. That was their speciality, and the team was known for it. I saw the flash of rifles from the tallest structure of the outpost; firing almost incessantly. Hooper's team would provide covering fire to the other teams as they moved across the base.

Finally, Sperenzo's Vipers.

"Sperenzo," I said, "run harassment. Move towards your objective and wait for a lull in the fighting."

"Not expecting that any time soon," Sperenzo managed. "But we'll try."

"The Legion is going off plan. We're taking out the guard tower so that Scorpio can provide air support. Lazarus out."

CHAPTER TWO

RETRIBUTION UNREALISED

We dropped from the roof and made double-time across the compound.

Squads of soldiers materialised out of the snow: equipped with assault rifles, wearing snow-camo hard-suits. There were Directorate soldiers everywhere. Resistance was far heavier than we'd anticipated.

I vaulted over a concrete barricade: a tank-trap that had been set up in the middle of the road. Two Directorate troopers knelt behind it, hooked to a missile launcher. One acted as spotter, the other as operator. As we ambushed their location, the soldiers fell back, abandoning the launcher and firing pistols at us. Martinez caught both with his plasma rifle, slicing their hard-suits open with precise energy pulses.

I cursorily inspected the nearest body. The emblem of the People's Army was printed on the soldier's chest-plate. These were regular militia; a stock Directorate military garrison.

"Perimeter is ahead," Jenkins declared.

A ragged black line rose out of the snow: a simple chain-link fence topped with barbed wire.

"Use those snow-crawlers as cover," I ordered. "Move on my mark."

We dashed as one. I slid into cover behind the crawlers; pumped my grenade launcher and fired two frag grenades out into the snow. I caught a Chino soldier, but several others retreated back into cover at the other end of the road.

"Everyone intact?" I asked.

"Affirmative," Mason said.

"I have eyes on the target," Jenkins said. She poked her head from behind the crawler, looking to the fence and the guard tower.

"We've got to bring that thing down," I said. "Lay down frag grenades, move up to the foot of that tower."

"I'll take the right," Jenkins replied.

My M95 plasma rifle – now ancient by military standards, performance far surpassed by the later upgraded M110 model, but still my preferred long-arm – illuminated the area.

I dashed for another snow-crawler, took up a position behind it. Mason and Martinez hunkered down beside some cargo drums: from the fence, a heavy automatic weapon of some description began to fire, throwing rounds against those. I saw Jenkins from the corner of my eye, moving fast between burning crates. More Chino troopers were flanking us. Her null-shield lit as she moved.

"I'm on this," she panted.

"Stay in cover! We'll take the tower from the eastern ridge, move back around—!"

"I said that I'm on this," she hissed.

The guard tower anti-air weapon swivelled on its mount,

slowly sweeping over the compound. *Fuck*. That was a big-ass laser: if it hit Jenkins, combat-suit or not, she'd be wasted.

"Get back into cover!"

Brazenly, Jenkins pumped her grenade launcher.

The volley of grenades traced a clear, delicate trajectory; barely slowed by the wind. The tower was supported by four thin legs, planted into the snowy ground, and one of those was caught by the exploding ordnance. Jenkins kept firing. Her face, behind the visor of her helmet, was contorted in abject rage. Rounds hit her torso, bounced off her chest-plate. The combat-suit camo-field failed, illuminating her outline very precisely. It was as though sheer determination was repelling the enemy.

The structure wobbled.

From my position, I could just see the tip of the sentry tower: could see the soldiers crewing it yelling and waving below. They began to drop from the nest; to jump rather than fall.

Jenkins charged her underslung launcher again and again. The grenades whistled as they fired, peppering the foot of the guard tower.

"She's bringing it down!" Mason said.

The tower slowly toppled into the snow. It was tall enough to catch a series of gantries as it went; throwing the scream of metal-on-metal to the wind, the pleasing concussive boom of another explosion. The gorge around me echoed with the sound. Snow began to slide from the steeper mountainsides, cascading against the perimeter fence.

Jenkins just stood there for a moment. The Directorate troops had ceased firing and started to fall back – moving inside the compound.

"You okay?" I asked, as I jogged over to her position.

She nodded at me grimly. "I'm fine. I just needed to work out some stress."

Martinez exchanged a glance with me but said nothing. This was Jenkins now. She was different; had been changed by what had happened in Damascus.

"This is still a military operation," I said. "Follow orders."

Jenkins looked irritated behind her face-plate; as though she had forgotten that this wasn't personal, that this was supposed to be a rescue operation rather than some opportunity to vent our anger on the Directorate. The expression was fleeting though, and she nodded in agreement.

"Solid copy that."

Scorpio One flew low overhead. The Jaguar fired a volley of Banshee missiles from hard points under each of its stubby wings, and various positions inside the compound ignited in brisk blooms of yellow light.

"James has the airspace under control, at least," Mason said.

"About time," said Jenkins.

The dropships conducting strafing runs over the compound did wonders to suppress the Directorate. Meanwhile, the Raiders stayed on overwatch – keeping hostiles off the rooftops and picking out RPG placements. Baker's Boys and the Vipers began calling in their objectives, securing buildings and searching the compound. Assisted by the drones, they made swift progress through the overground structures.

Seven minutes on the mission clock, the Legion assembled in an abandoned barracks.

"Nothing so far," Martinez reported. "Whatever this place is, it isn't a POW camp."

27

Jenkins marched two captured Directorate troopers into the barracks. They had been disarmed but still wore battered hard-suits, and had been identified as officers. Tan-skinned, much older than most of the Directorate troops, both men were speaking at the same time.

I nodded at Jenkins. "Keep them covered. Suit: run translation."

My combat-suit obliged. Selected the relevant dialect and began a translation.

"*We know nothing!*" they said collectively, my suit speaking in stilted electronic tones. "*We are overseers of the mining facility . . .*"

It went on. They both sounded very convincing. Had it not been for the couple of hundred Directorate troops that had just tried to kill us, I might've even bought it.

"Put them with the others," Jenkins ordered Mason.

Mason prodded the two men with her rifle, encouraging them outside. Both remonstrated about being made to go out in the cold without full headgear, but Mason barked orders in broken Chino – using her suit translation package – and the two men quickly decided that their chances of survival were better outside than in.

They should be scared, I thought.

There was a yard in the middle of the compound, partially sheltered from wind and snow by a configuration of large buildings; overlooked by Hooper's sniper team. Mason lined the men up with the rest of the prisoners. There had been ten or so soldiers with sufficient intelligence not to throw their lives away; with enough common sense to lay down their arms. Most were kneeling in the snow, fingers locked behind their heads.

"They aren't Swords," Mason said to me.

She was referring to the Swords of the South Chino Stars;

the elite Special Operations unit that was responsible for the Damascus incident. And she was right – none of the prisoners were Swords. They were better equipped and more dangerous than the People's Army, and would probably have put up more of a fight.

"Not every Directorate agent wears a uniform," Martinez said. "We should watch them, *jefe*."

If nothing else, we'd take them back with us. It was scant justification for the military operation, but it might please Ostrow. Mili-Intel could milk these people: see if they had any useful intel.

Jenkins prowled between the lines of kneeling prisoners, and we watched as she did her thing. By now, I'd seen the show so many times that it'd lost its impact on me.

"You know who we are?" she asked, her suit-speakers turned up to maximum volume so that they could be heard over the wind.

At least a couple of the prisoners understood Standard, and they nodded anxiously. Jenkins stood at the end of the line; her rifle stowed, her PPG-13 plasma pistol cocked. She waved it at the prisoners. As one now, the group quivered. The cold did nothing to reduce the hate-heat emanating from Jenkins.

"Then you will know not to fuck with us. We're the Lazarus Legion, and we came here to get our people back. I want to know where they are."

"We know nothing!" one of the solders shouted in Standard. "We only work here – guard the mines!"

The prisoners began to babble all at the same time.

"Bullshit!" Jenkins spat. She bolted towards the nearest prisoner and slammed her plasma pistol into the woman's face. "We've been listening to your transmissions. You have Alliance prisoners down here!"

This one was less easily shaken. The woman was slim, muscled, with long dark hair and almond eyes. For the briefest moment, the prisoner reminded me of Elena. I shook my head and buried the thought. Face collecting snowflakes, the woman gave no response.

"I mean it," Jenkins said. "Start answering questions if you want to live."

Mason stood beside me. She looked unimpressed by the display. "Do we have to go through this again?" she asked.

Jenkins pressed the muzzle of her pistol against the woman's head and the weapon's arming indicator flashed. The man beside the endangered prisoner recoiled – probably glad that it wasn't him that was about to get wasted.

"Unless someone starts telling me what is really going on down here, I'm going to blow this bitch's brains out. Then I'm going to kill someone every minute, until I get some answers."

The male prisoner said something in Chino. Spoke too fast for my suit to translate.

"Don't fucking mess with me," Jenkins hissed at her prisoner.

The woman's eyes remained steely cold and she stared at Jenkins. Snow had begun to plaster her hair.

"We have nothing for you here," she said. "We have nothing."

Jenkins kept the gun pressed there for a long second. Martinez and Mason watched her, an air of uncertainty hanging between them—

My ear-bead chimed.

"Lazarus!" came a gruff voice. It was Baker.

I held up a hand to stay Jenkins' wrath. She paused, eyes still boring into the female prisoner's head.

"I read you Baker. What is it?"

30

"We've found something," Baker said. "You should come down and see. I'm uploading my coordinates."

My HUD flashed with Baker's location: his surviving team had collected in a garage near to our position.

"Inbound," I said. "Lazarus out." I waved at Jenkins. "Stand down."

With marked reluctance, Jenkins lowered the pistol.

"I really thought that she was going to kill that one," Martinez said.

"Wouldn't be the first time."

Mason sighed. "And probably won't be the last."

"Mason, Jenkins; with me. Martinez, get those prisoners cuffed, then join us at Baker's position." I couldn't trust Jenkins out here with the prisoners. "Keep watch on them, padre," I said. "None of them dies unless I say so."

"Affirmative," Martinez said. He sounded more than a little relieved with my decision. He shook his head. "Retribution unrealised is a terrible thing."

Baker cracked open the enormous shutter-style doors, and by the numbers we entered the depot. My drones flitted around me like fat flies – taking readings and reporting – but Baker's Boys had been the first personnel on-site. The storage shed was a hulk of a building, a vast garage filled with industrial vehicles: ore scoopers, snow-crawlers and tractors, all arranged in neat lines.

Baker's squad had been depleted to only three simulants. They squatted beside a snow-crawler, faces tight behind their illuminated face-plates.

"We're not quite sure what we have here," Captain Baker said. He nodded at one of his troopers; a green with the name ROBINS printed across his chest.

"I keep getting readings inside the shed, sir."

Jenkins tutted. "We came all the way cross-compound because someone got readings? Jesus."

Robins swallowed but stood his ground. "Bio-scanner readings, ma'am." He held up his wrist-comp: pointed out the sensor grid shown on the vambrace unit. "Lots of readings. They're coming and going."

"There's nothing else in this area," Baker said. "Hooper has visual on the roof. Nothing above us, nothing outside."

I patched into the kid's scanner results. Blips appeared on my HUD. There were several life-signs – the micro-throb of possible heartbeats, the flush of heat signs. That could mean nearby bodies, but the readings were erratic and unclear.

"See?" Baker said. "Something isn't right."

"Could be a scanner malfunction," Mason suggested.

Robins shook his head. "I don't think so. We've all been detecting the same readings—"

"Listen!" I insisted.

I heard a noise over the comms.

A soft wailing: an intrusive spike of static at the back of my mind. It was strong enough that I winced, put a hand to the side of my helmet.

"You okay, Colonel?" Mason asked.

"Fine," I said. "Anyone else hear that?"

Mason and Jenkins looked back at me with blank faces.

It sounded like distant moaning. I looked to the open depot doors. It was easily explainable as the sound of the wind moving through the structure, but the wind had dropped.

I swallowed.

I knew that noise. It was the Artefact.

This can't be happening again. It had been a long time since I'd last heard the sound, and these days it rarely ever happened while I was awake: tended to come in dream and nightmare, mostly. I'd managed to repress it with my own brand of self-medication.

This is different . . .

It was coming, I realised, from beneath us. I slammed a foot on the ground. The combat-suit was heavy; that and the simulant inside made for a big weight. The metal decking produced a metallic *thump*. I did it again, producing the same echo: loud enough to be heard even inside my armour.

"There's something underneath us," I decided. I pointed. "Get that crawler out the way."

Mason clambered into the cabin, activated the engine. With a low grumble, the big crawler pulled forward. The Legion and Baker's Boys circled where it had sat: looked at the patch of floor that had been uncovered.

"Well I fucking never . . ." Baker said.

There was a circular hatch – big enough to accommodate a man in armour – set into the ground. The frost-covered metalwork was worn, had recently been used, and the nearby area had been disturbed with a series of footprints. My HUD glowed with heat markers. They had a power supply down there. Beneath us, probably unaware that they had been found at all, the bio-signs disappeared off my screen. Either moving deeper underground, or fooling the scanner. I'd come across Krell that could do that – could manipulate their biological processes to avoid detection – but I wasn't aware of any such human tech. Still, the Directorate were full of surprises.

I prised open the hatch set into the ground, grunting as it came free, and the moaning sound became more precise. *Something is calling me down there . . .* Jenkins gasped. Baker started barking orders to his team, to give me room and provide covering fire.

33

I dipped my suit-lamps. Half-expecting to be met with a face full of flechettes, I peered into the shaft. A vertical shaft: precisely machined, made to accommodate human proportions. A series of metal rungs had been sunk into the compacted ice – forming a long and precarious ladder to whatever was beneath.

"There are lots of scanner returns down there," Jenkins said. Her voice quivered with excitement.

"How many?"

She swallowed. "A hundred? Hard to say."

"It's like they're on top of each other . . ." Mason whispered.

The shaft was deep enough that it disappeared into darkness. I unclipped a flare from my suit webbing. Flicking the activator, I tossed it down. Listened to the gentle *chink* as it hit the floor.

"You want to send a drone down first?" Mason offered.

"No," I said. "I need to do this myself."

I could see the flare at the bottom of the shaft now. Fizzing, throwing ragged light over a grilled floor plate. There was a facility of some sort below. My danger-instinct insisted that this was a *very bad idea*, but I needed to know what was down there.

"I'm going in. Jenkins, watch my six."

"Affirmative," she replied.

As I went, the moaning got louder and louder until I couldn't dismiss it any more.

It took me a couple of minutes to clamber down the shaft. One hand on the ladder rungs, the other clutching my PPG-13 plasma pistol: half-aimed at the segment of tunnel directly beneath me. The ladder was glossed with ice but as I climbed I realised that there were also fresh markings on the rungs – as though they had recently been used. Boot prints.

"How's it going, sir?" Jenkins asked.

"Fine. Any movement up top?"

"Nothing so far. You want me to come down and help?" she asked, with painful eagerness.

"No. I'm good."

It was a tight fit in full armour. My shoulders grazed the tunnel walls, and the expectation that I would be shot on the way down the shaft never left me. The flare light gradually diminished until I was alone. My left hand began to shake as I descended.

I reached the bottom of the shaft and panned the corridor with my plasma pistol; let the targeting software analyse for potential targets. This deep underground, the tunnels had been bored out of the ice: chemically treated to retain stability. The floors were decked with metal plating. Glow-globes were strung from electrical cabling in a line along the ceiling. Meltwater *drip-drip-dripped* from the ceiling and huge transparent icicles had formed overhead—

A hand brushed my combat-suit. Stained, bone-thin fingers.

I instinctively pulled away.

Then the noise hit me. A hundred voices, rising in a ghostly choir: individually quiet, collectively devastating. I couldn't hear actual words but the overall impression was undeniable. Cries for help, for salvation.

"Shit . . ." I said, the word escaping my lips unbidden.

I'd seen war. I'd seen horror: alien, human and even – with the discovery of the Shard – machine. There was little that could move me, that could genuinely shake me. But what I saw in that tunnel did just that.

"I'm at ground level," I said into my comm. "They have people down here." I swallowed. "Lots . . . lots of them."

Metal cages lined the corridor on either side of me, and skeletal hands were reaching from within. The cages went on for as far as I could see – as far as my suit-lamps would penetrate the dark – and each was crammed with bodies.

We'd found the prisoners.

Maybe I'd been stunned by what I'd seen, or maybe I'd just grown sloppy. Either way, I missed the prison guard until she fired the pistol.

She was facing me, but retreating – arm outstretched, firing again and again. I recognised the snap of a semi-automatic slug-thrower: a heavy calibre weapon firing at close range.

My null-shield failed to respond and two rounds hit my shoulder. There was a sharp spark of pain as the bullets impacted. AP rounds, I guessed: high-density anti-armour. Warnings flashed across my HUD, suggested immediate defensive action.

For a second, I was as frozen as the world around me.

Seeing one of *them* again, after so long . . . It was almost as debilitating as the pain.

She was Special Operations: a Sword of the South Chino Stars. Clad in full combat-armour; a hard-suit black as space, segmented like an upright insect. No helmet: her face made pale by the cold, bald head pocked by tattoos and kill-markings. She fired again and again, weapon flashing as rounds discharged—

Before I could react to the gunfire, she reached out with her other hand. Slammed it against the wall. The tunnel was suddenly bathed in red light, accompanied by the ring of an emergency siren—

Plasma fire erupted behind me and the Sword collapsed to the floor.

"Thank me later," Jenkins said, at my shoulder. "You're getting slow."

The spell was broken and I snapped awake. "I told you to wait upstairs."

"And I knew that you'd need back-up . . ."

Jenkins' voice trailed off. Her face slackened with a mixture of fear and astonishment. Hands reached for her, like they had for me. They were animals on auto-pilot: that was what they had been reduced to. Filthy, dying and exhausted, some of the prisoners were nothing more than eyes embedded in flesh-wrapped skulls.

"We . . . we need to get them out," said Jenkins. "They need suits, water, food . . ." She amplified her suit-speakers. "We're here to get you out, people. It's going to be okay. There are transports up-top. Follow us and embark as quickly as possible. If you cannot walk, make yourselves known and we will assist."

The cage doors opened with the groan of ill-maintained gears. The prisoners let out a half-hearted cheer. Some had started weeping, others rattling against the prison bars. There was no telling how long they'd been down here. Those in the worst condition recoiled further into the caged alcoves, covering their ears as the siren rang out.

This should've been a victory but something felt wrong here. The dead guard's body had fallen at an absurd angle. There were three gaping holes in her chest, caused by Jenkins' plasma fire. The guard was wild-eyed, nerve-staples across her naked scalp. Her time and place of birth were tattooed in universal code across her cheekbone: together with the name of the cloning-vat from which she'd been birthed.

Before she'd been shot, the guard had been reaching for something. I traced her actions and identified an unmarked control panel on the wall. Now activated, buttons glowing red in the dim light. The purpose of the unit wasn't immediately clear to me but I considered the possibilities. There were no other soldiers down here: had she been trying to summon help? I checked my comm, watched the vid-feed from my surveillance drones. They were currently circling the overground hangar, and had reported no new movement. Nothing had changed in the compound above.

"She opened the cages . . ." I whispered to myself.

Why did she do that? Why set off an alarm anyway? The Directorate commando was a top-of-the-line gene-enhanced soldier; no doubt her head filled with metal. She'd have an in-line communicator – a device that would allow her to communicate with the rest of her squad – somewhere in there.

Events overtook me before I could explore any of these doubts. Prisoners flooded from their cells and Jenkins was organising them, lining them up. There were servicemen and women from every agency here – Navy, Marines, Army – identifiable by their faded and torn uniforms. They responded sluggishly, zombie-like.

"Vincent Kaminski!" Jenkins yelled. "Any survivors from the Damascus expedition make yourselves known to me!"

For a long, fraught moment no answer came. Could we come this far not to find them? I felt Capa's cold grasp my heart: felt my tired bones aching despite the simulant body.

"What took you so long?" came a broad Brooklyn accent, from the back of one of the cells. "Whenever you're ready, we should get the fuck out of here."

PFC Vincent Kaminski, lost legionnaire, stood among the prisoners. A wide, inane grin was plastered across his face.

"'Ski . . .?" Jenkins asked. "Is it really you . . .?"

"It's me," he said.

Jenkins' reaction was immediate and unprofessional. She pushed her way through the dazed prisoners, and flung her arms around Kaminski.

"By Christo," he said, burying his face in her armoured shoulder. "I wondered whether you'd ever find me . . ."

Kaminski was in bad shape. His face was dirt-stained and bruised, head shaven. He wore a yellow vacuum-suit, the type used in evacuation pods: the words UAS COLOSSUS printed on his arms, in faded white print.

"We never stopped looking," Jenkins said. "Not for a second."

Beside a simulant in full combat-suit, Kaminski's emaciated form looked even smaller. He winced as Jenkins wrapped her arms around him. The bruising to his face made it obvious that he had taken a beating: a narrow line of studs in his head indicated where he had been nerve-stapled. I started to wonder how long he'd been down here, what the Directorate had done to him, but knew those questions would have to wait.

"Steady, California," he said. "Watch the ribs. Think I've got cracked something . . ."

Jenkins stepped back, evaluated Kaminski with wet eyes. "Thinking again? Isn't that what got you in trouble in the first place?"

'Ski smiled, but the reaction was muted and weak. "Lesson learnt. I'll try not to do that again." He ran a hand over his chin; through the rugged beard that had grown there. "I need a shave. Good to see you, Harris."

I felt almost as much emotion in the moment as Jenkins. Kaminski was my oldest friend, and we'd grown through the ranks of the Alliance Army – and then Simulant Operations – together. We fist-bumped, but gently. Kaminski's hands were blackened and blood-encrusted; poking from the cuffs of his torn vac-suit.

"And you, 'Ski," I said. "Jenkins is right; we never stopped looking for you."

"I don't doubt it," 'Ski said.

My tactical helmet had started a medical analysis of Kaminski's condition: he had borderline malnutrition, with a repressed heart rate. The spiral of his body consuming fat reserves had already started, would probably have become fatal in a few days – weeks at best.

"Looks like we got here just in time," I said.

"Not just for me, either."

Another thin and dishevelled figure hobbled towards us. A man with a black-and-grey beard, dressed in the same style of suit as Kaminski.

"Professor Saul?" I asked.

"Harris," he said. "I am most glad to see you. Yes, yes."

Saul was gaunt, tanned skin pulled tight over his cheekbones, and his beard was patchy and irregular. The vac-suit hung off his frame, pooled at his booted feet. He hadn't eaten in a long time, and hadn't seen proper sunlight in even longer.

"You aren't here to accuse me of being a terrorist again, are you?" he asked of me.

"Not this time," I said. "I'm glad to see that you made it out alive."

"Only just," Professor Saul said. He tapped a hand to his leg; flinching awkwardly. "The Directorate haven't been kind to me."

Saul's eyes were sunken into his head, one milky orb glaring at me blindly. He too had been beaten; face lacerated, both cheeks swollen with purple contusions. From the way that he moved – slowly, imprecisely – I guessed that he was even closer to death than Kaminski. His left leg dragged uncomfortably as he walked.

"We have a strike force," I said. "Lots of simulants and dropships, ready for evac."

"I hope that it will be enough," said Saul.

CHAPTER THREE

SAME AS US

"Holy Christo and all that is Venusian," Martinez said.

Mason was just speechless as she took in the line of shivering bodies; with the same horrified expression as Jenkins. It was pretty much a universal reaction to what we were seeing.

"Hello works just as well," Kaminski said, as he clambered out of the hatch, Jenkins grabbing his arm. "But maybe you don't know the words in Standard or something . . ."

"Ever the asshole," Martinez said. "Good to have you back."

"There was no one left to ride on you," Kaminski said. "I could hardly leave the job to Mason." He nodded at her, a little of his old self returning. "Glad to see you got your stripes, New Girl."

"No one calls me that any more," Mason said.

"Not to her face, anyway," Jenkins said.

Kaminski reached out, fist-bumped with Mason. He frowned as he read the nameplate on her chest. "I'm not sure that PRINCESS is much better . . ."

"She picked it herself," Martinez said.

"Save the chat for later," I said. "We've got prisoners down here."

Baker and his troopers stood back as the ragged column of POWs filed into the hangar. The prisoners were silent, following whatever commands we gave them.

"I hate to ask the question, but are we going to have enough ships to get these people off Capa?" he asked over our closed comms.

"No one gets left behind," I said. "We'll make return trips if we have to."

"Of course, sir," Baker said. "We haven't heard from—"

My ear-bead chimed.

"Lazarus!" came a panicked shout: I immediately recognised Hooper. "We've got renewed resistance out here!"

I heard gunfire over the comm-link, Hooper yelling an order. Distant thunder was audible through the hangar walls. Kaminski and the prisoners seemed to shrink in response to the noise.

"Hooper – you need to lock that down," I said. "We've got prisoners, moving to the landing bay."

"Something—"

Hooper's bio-signs vanished from my HUD. Not just his, but those of his squad as well. The comm-line went dead.

"Overwatch is down," I said. "We need to move fast."

"Copy that," Jenkins said.

I called up a map of the compound on my HUD: plotted a route cross-facility. The most direct path was beneath the tower that Hooper had been using as a sniper's nest, and around the covered mine shaft that we'd discussed during the briefing. About a klick through the snow.

I turned to the survivors. "Follow the Legion and stay

down. We'll go through the central yard and to the landing pad."

The compound had come alive again: the lull in activity well and truly broken. Gunfire poured down from every roof parapet and gantry. Mortar rounds exploded overhead: made the ground shake. Hot frag peppered the sector, forced us into cover behind some stacked cargo containers.

I took point, holding the Directorate back with plasma fire. Jenkins' null-shield flared, and prisoners hid behind her armoured bulk. Martinez and Mason carried those most badly injured or malnourished; scooping them under armoured arms like children. Baker and his remaining soldiers took up the rear, throwing whatever ordnance they had left at the enemy.

"The mortar shells are to suppress us," Mason said.

"I know," I said. "We've got to keep moving."

The wind had picked up again, with enough force that I had to brace against it. I dreaded to think how the survivors felt without proper survival gear. The centre of the compound was ahead, the comms tower reaching up through the storm. One of the circular structures – the pit or shaft, whatever it was – lay a hundred or so metres north. We were getting close.

"What's the latest on Scorpio Squadron?" I asked Jenkins, as we advanced. "Have they touched down yet?"

I couldn't see much above ground level, and with the Directorate active again the ships would be running dark.

"ETA three minutes," Jenkins said. "They're experiencing heavy resistance."

"Do we have anyone else left down here?"

Jenkins shook her head. "Sperenzo is off the grid, and Hooper is long gone . . ."

The remains of Hooper's squad lay in the snow. They'd probably fallen from their posts, high on the tower. The simulated bodies were riddled with rounds, pouring crimson blood into the snow – weapons and equipment sprawled around them.

"Move up on the mine shaft," I ordered. My M95 user display flashed with LOW AMMO, and I only had one power cell left. Hooper's team carried compatible ammunition: the Long Sight used the same cell. I waved at Mason and Martinez. "Get the survivors into cover. I'm restocking."

The rest of the team moved up, and I dashed to the bodies of Hooper's Raiders. All five of them had crashed out here, their armour already sinking into the snow. I stooped beside a soldier called REIKER – the name flashing on my HUD, stamped onto the combat-suit chest-plate. I pulled the body towards me, using the strength-augmentation of my own armour to shoulder the weight—

Reiker had been hit by a gunshot to the chest. Not a big wound, but noticeable by the extreme blood loss that it had caused. Something made me pause, for just a moment: my intuition screaming, causing me to examine the body in a little more detail.

For the second time that day, I questioned myself. I reached out and touched the ruptured armour. A piece of something black and blood-wet was stuck inside; and beyond the shattered face-plate Reiker's face was necrotised and withered. Hurriedly, panic rising inside like the storm out, I scanned the other bodies. Each of Hooper's Raiders had been killed in exactly the same way: armour breached by a handful of black spines, punching cleanly through the ablative plate.

But how can they . . .?

Something enormous and heavy hit me side on, with

tremendous force. Splinters of pain erupted all over my torso and I sprawled into the snow, rifle slipping from my fingers.

Then I was falling.

I reached out with my open hands for something to grip on to. Found nothing. The white sky spiralled above me.

The pit. I'm falling into the pit.

The drop was brief but brutal and I hit the ground hard. My breath was knocked from my lungs with intensity. I'd landed on my back, and despite the Trident combat-suit I felt the armour plating buckle around my neck and shoulder. I snarled as pain exploded across my left leg: knew that it had absorbed a good deal of the fall, that it was as good as broken. Medi-alerts flashed over my HUD. A blot of pain spread across the back of my head: a dull ache that probably signalled a fractured skull.

But I was still alive. The sim was made of sterner stuff.

NULL-SHIELD DAMAGED, my suit insisted. TAKE CORRECTIVE MEASURES.

I focused on my surroundings, on the immediate threats that I had to surmount in order to survive for the next five seconds.

I was underground. The covered shaft that Mason had noted on the orbital maps – the silo or pit – was now open: the mechanical hatch agape like a trap door, exposing the chamber beneath. The pit was dark, fetid, and something like fish guts were plastered to every available surface. The beginnings of coralline formations sprouted from the walls, providing artificial cover and possible handholds. Steam rose from the walls as the pit was exposed to the frosted air. The shaft was maybe twenty metres deep, and as many round.

Through the miasma of pain – quickly diminishing, becoming controlled by the advanced simulant metabolism and the combat-suit's medi-suite – I pieced together what I was seeing. *I'm in a viper's nest*, I told myself. The events of the last few minutes snapped into place: made perfect sense. The Directorate guard had deliberately let the prisoners out, but not to save them. She wanted to open the pits, because the Directorate had brought more than just *human* POWs back from the Maelstrom. Something had been imprisoned down here: but what had started as a prison, had become a lair.

Fuck. Fuck. Fuck.

"Jenkins!" I yelled into the comm. "Keep your eyes on—!"

A Krell xeno-form lurched over me.

I scrambled onto my elbows. I'd lost my rifle, either overground during the initial attack or when I'd fallen into the pit, and there was no time to search for it. Instead, I unholstered my PPG-13 plasma pistol with numb fingers, brought the heavy pistol round to aim. In the same smooth action I fired.

The alien was probably affected by the temperature. By human standards, it was still fast, but the Krell didn't like the cold. It was infinitesimally slower than would otherwise be the case, and I managed to shoot before it reached me. A volley of plasma bolts hit the alien's armoured chest and the corpse flew backwards, twitching with bio-electric feedback.

I got to my feet. The servos in my left knee-joint buzzed angrily in protest.

The primary-form was emaciated: muscled frame atrophied, shrivelled by exposure to the cold. The Krell's skin was blasted, had turned grey to an unhealthy white in places. The skull was pocked with metallic studs, and most of the alien's bio-tech enhancements had been torn out. It wore the remnants of a bio-suit – I always found it difficult to

47

decide whether the things were actually wearing armour or not, so closely grafted to the skin were their protective suits – but no helmet. Insignia that looked like scars stitched its chest. I wondered, briefly, whether that was some sign of allegiance to a particular Krell Collective, or perhaps birthing aboard a specific warship or fleet.

There was babbling over the comm-link from the rest of the Legion.

"Sir!" Mason asked. "What's happening?"

"We've got Krell down here, and in numbers!" I yelled, as I backed into the middle of the pit: in vain, trying to cover every angle of the nest.

Primary-forms bounded across the covered walls with renewed vigour. I clocked a handful of primary- and secondary-forms slithering over the edge of the pit, into the compound. How many had been kept in here? A hundred? Two hundred? Were there other nests like this, hidden elsewhere on the surface of Cold Death? Those questions ran through my mind, but I had no opportunity to consider them. My bio-scanner was quickly filling with signals. There were other, shadowy tunnel-mouths leading into the pit. *Things* were stirring inside those as well. Leader-forms, or something else?

Mason appeared at the lip of the shaft, helmet bobbing as she looked over the edge. "Oh, shit!"

Flame erupted from my flank as a secondary-form fired a shrieker; the Krell equivalent of a flamethrower. The bio-gun was loaded with a phosphorescent fuel: licking the ground with bright light.

That was it. The Collective was awake. Hissing poured from all around me.

I ducked beneath another gout of flame and ran for the nearest wall. Had to get out of there.

"Go, go!" I shouted to the Legion. "Pull out and run!"

I reached the wall and vaulted up it. An intense blossom of pain spread through my left leg – eye-watering, exquisite – but the leg held. That was the combat-suit in action: the leg joint supporting a limb that was for all intents now useless. The armour stayed rigid, and my toe slammed into the bio-coral. The porous, honeycombed material might've looked delicate, but it was far from it, and the structure took my weight. I scrambled up the wall, using the strength-aug of the powered armour to just get me out of—

"The colonel is trapped down there!" Mason shouted. "Covering fire!"

Mason started shooting. Plasma pulses rained, dropping Krell primaries as they lurched out of their prison. Martinez jogged into view, picking off bodies as they crawled up the wall after me. My fingers tore into the coral, found purchase on whatever surfaces I could, and I climbed rapidly. A claw grabbed my injured leg, but I lashed out: felt the pleasing connection of an armoured boot with a Krell skull—

They were more interested in getting out of the pit than in taking me down, I realised. The awakening Krell bio-forms rushed past me – gills flexing as they adjusted to the frozen air – and dashed out into the snow. I'd seen behaviour like this before. They had no leader-form to guide them: were reverting to feral instinct to stay alive.

"Take my hand," Mason said, reaching out with an open palm.

"I told you to go!" I said, but did as she asked. Even simulated, I felt a flood of relief to be out of the nest. "Keep that pit covered!"

As she dragged me over the edge, from one perilous situation to another only mildly less so, I reached for the combat-webbing across my chest. I unclipped a frag grenade. Twisted the activator and tossed it back the way I'd come.

"Fire in the hole!" Martinez yelled, already pulling back from the danger zone.

Krell pouring out behind me, secondary-forms firing all manner of bio-weapons into the storm, the grenade went off. The explosion shook the snow, threw up a yellow flash. It was probably futile – would only anger the nest – but it felt good to kill some of them at least.

Jenkins and the remainder of Baker's Boys were at the end of the road. The prisoners were in abject terror, harried by gunfire from both the Directorate and the Krell escapees.

"Well isn't that just great," Jenkins barked. "As if we don't have enough to worry about."

I dragged my injured leg behind me. "Just get out of here! Those things are pissed, and I don't think that they can tell the difference between us and the Directorate."

"Dropships are here," Martinez said, pointing ahead.

The sky brightened as three ships descended on the landing bay, the glow of the Jaguars' engines visible through the swirling snow. The landing bay was barely a hundred metres away – an elevated platform lined with ladder-shafts.

"Move, move!" I yelled. "Get through there! Ships are waiting!"

The ships immediately deployed their rear ramps. The air crews disembarked, waving handheld beacons – guiding us through the storm.

A Krell launched itself from between two buildings as we passed, and tore through our column.

"'Ski!" Jenkins screamed. "Stay down!"

The alien reached one prisoner, and ended him with a snap of the neck. Several others scattered in the xeno's wake, but it was faster. The unaugmented humans seemed to move so slowly – so painfully slowly – and the alien lashed out with claws and talons.

"What the fuck is that thing?" Martinez shouted.

This was a Krell, but much bigger. Six-limbed, more heavily armoured than the primaries: eyes set so deep inside a bio-helmet that it looked almost blind, a pair of pincer-like claws replacing its frontal limbs. The thing was fucking *enormous*. It looked more like a lobster than a fish. A tertiary-form.

I ran for Kaminski, hauled him aside. He was paralysed with fear, pale as the snow around him. I tossed him towards the landing bay—

The Krell brayed, throwing aside the bodies. It moved onwards through the storm, past us. Directorate troops emerged from the other end of the street, firing everything they had on the Krell. The Directorate Sword might've been trying to sow confusion by releasing the Krell prisoners but the xenos were indiscriminate in their slaughter. The ground beneath us shook as the horde advanced.

"More incoming!" Jenkins shouted. Her plasma rifle was on full-auto, her null-shield flashing intermittently.

More of the enormous, up-armoured tertiary-forms erupted from the pit. They stormed ahead of the massed Krell, absorbing enemy fire with their bodies.

"Up there, *now*!" I shouted at Kaminski. He and Saul clambered ahead of me, up the landing bay ladder-shaft.

As prisoners followed me onto the platform, James went rigid. His usually cocky demeanour shattered, what little of his face I could see behind the mirrored aviator helm sagging.

"What are you waiting for?" I said. "Get them on those ships! Start moving!"

"Yeah, s . . . sure . . ." he said. He dropped his baton,

scrambled for it in the snow. The rest of Scorpio Squadron waited for orders, just as disturbed by James' behaviour.

"What the fuck is wrong with you?" Jenkins screamed. "There are tertiary-forms down there!"

"Nothing," he said. "I just – well—"

A volley of heavy gunfire slashed the air and James ducked back. His co-pilot stood next to him – a woman I only knew as Michaels. Even in a sim, she was wasted: her body exploded in a red haze and hit the deck, lifeless.

"Directorate are still firing on us!" Jenkins said.

Flashes of light from the rooftops of nearby buildings indicated that they were deploying their own sniper teams now. Several prisoners collapsed in the snow, heads and bodies stitched with hi-ex rounds.

"Shit!" James said. "Michaels is dead!"

"Fuck Michaels!" I said. "She's a sim. *These* people aren't!"

I grabbed James by the shoulder, shook him hard. In my combat-sim, I was much bigger and stronger than his next-gen. "Get with it, James! I don't want to know what's wrong with you, only that it's fixed!"

"Yeah," he said, nodding. "Sure, sure."

I let him go, and he turned to his crew. "Move it, move it! Get these people onto the ships!"

The firefight was intensifying rapidly. Another of Baker's squad bought it. More Directorate troops were surging from the destroyed compound. Krell shriekers and stingers poured the area, almost randomly. A clutch of primaries clambered onto the landing bay as we loaded up – launching at us.

"Fuck 'em all!" Baker yelled. "I didn't sign up for this shit!"

Thump, thump, thump went his grenade launcher: explosives hitting aliens as they advanced.

Survivors almost crawled into the bellies of the waiting dropships.

"Get the ramps closed!" I shouted into the comm, unaware of whether anyone could actually hear me any more. "We'll take care of these assholes."

The nearest dropship, Scorpio Four, began to lift before it had even been sealed. Sheets of snow and ice expanded from beneath as it went.

My combat-suit successfully up-linked to the *Independence*'s communication-net. The icon indicating a secure comm with our ship flared across my HUD, and my ear-bead chimed incessantly. This was the sort of priority communication that I couldn't ignore, that I had no choice but to answer.

"This is Lazarus Actual," I started. "We are attempting to evac numerous POWs."

"You've got something big inbound on your location," Navy command said.

"Scramble some Hornets, get some air cover—"

"Too late," the officer replied. "They're already on you." She paused, then with a hint of contrition added, "They came in from the south, behind the storm."

"The other settlements?" I queried. *The ones that we were told were of no tactical significance? Fucking marvellous.*

"Affirmative. You need to move—"

The link died with a whine of static.

Scorpio Four didn't get far. The Jag dropship lifted off, VTOL motors whining, and crossed the perimeter fence. There was some small mercy in that, because almost as soon as the ship had left the proximity of the landing bay it exploded.

A direct hit from something else in the sky.

"Fucking hell . . ." Mason said. "This cannot get any worse."

"I think that it can," I said. "I think that it can get a *whole lot* worse."

The dropship went down in the snow, still burning. There had been no opportunity to activate the defence systems – the bells and whistles that flyboys so love to rely upon. The ship hit the mountainside hard, flashed once, and then died. Although the weather was fucking with my tech big time, I still had partial comms with the downed ship: was able to glean enough information to tell me that there was no one left aboard. *Like that's something I need to be told*, I thought.

"Where the hell did that come from?" Jenkins asked. She breathed in ragged, angry gasps: I hadn't even noticed that she was bleeding all over. Stingers poked from her breached armour like thorns.

In answer to her question, three streaks of light appeared on the horizon, moving so fast that even with simulant-senses it was hard to track them.

"Down!" I managed, as I realised what I was seeing.

Three Wraith attack ships scorched overhead. They were fast-response gunships: delta-winged, plated with radar-baffling black armour, commonly used as air-support for Directorate covert ops. They flew low – dangerously low – and unleashed a volley of missiles on the compound. Multiple plasma warheads dropped from the black ships; fell onto the centre of the outpost. Exactly where the Krell prisoners were being held.

"Containment?" Martinez asked.

Dealing with an asset out of control. Maybe the Sword had alerted reinforcements in the southern settlements after all; but sought to release the Krell in a terminal act of spite.

"Who gives a fuck," Jenkins threw back, "if it keeps them off our backs."

The resultant explosion illuminated the base, threw razor-sharp debris across the open areas of the compound. Although the strike was half a klick from our location – the warheads had probably been low-yield – I could still feel the shockwave that it produced. The landing bay creaked under the stress. That moment when you realise that there is no plan any more – that all tactical intelligence is gone? I was there, and the very real feeling that we might not escape Capa V, that the prisoners might die down here, suddenly hit me.

"Thanks for trying," Kaminski said. "I appreciate it, even if we don't make it . . ."

"Lock that shit down, 'Ski," I said. "We didn't come this far to get wasted."

"You're going to make it, 'Ski," Jenkins said. "You have to make it!"

Kaminski nodded. He dragged Saul to his feet; the professor appeared incapable of walking on his own. His features were snow-blasted but also empty. I'd seen the look before: the noise, the constant risk of death, the anxiety . . . Those things took their toll on a man. I hoped that he would come back from the edge, because if he went over, there was no medical technology in existence would bring him back.

Scorpio One and Two were the only transports left. They were filled with prisoners, bodies caught by the flickering red emergency lamps of the passenger cabins. Kaminski and Saul were the last in, scrambling up the aft ramp.

"Lazarus, get in if you're coming!" James said.

Gunfire strafed Scorpio One, and Kaminski flinched. A stray Krell launched itself towards the undercarriage. The dropship lifted off with the ramp still open, wobbling in the high winds.

"Come on!" Kaminski yelled.

The Legion stood on the landing pad and I took in the team. They were in pitiful condition: bodies stitched with Krell stingers, armour damaged, face-plates cracked. Jenkins swallowed at me, nodded. Her face was already turning blue, skin reacting to whatever Krell bio-toxin this Collective produced. Around us, the base was filled the screams of the Krell prisoners; the chatter of returning Directorate fire.

"Go, James," I said. "Permission to launch."

"Y – you're not coming with us?" James stammered.

"We're already dead," Jenkins said. "You stupid bastard."

"We're expendable, James," I said. "As ever."

Kaminski stood at the closing ramp. He waved at Jenkins, his face solemn. "See you on the other side, girl."

Jenkins tried to smile. "Too fucking true."

As the ramp shut, I caught sight of Professor Saul as well, huddling with a clutch of other prisoners.

The Directorate were on the landing bay now. Kinetics spanked against the hull of Scorpio One and Two, sparking. The dropships began to lift off and the enormous metal frames clunked and plinked with more gunfire. James fired smoke launchers, sending out a skirt of white mist as he went.

"I . . . hope that th . . . they make it," Jenkins said. She could hardly speak; I knew that she would be pleading for release from the skin. I'd felt that sensation myself.

Martinez nodded. "So long as the prisoners make it out, I'll sleep well tonight, *jefe*."

Mason slammed a hand to her chest. "For the Legion."

The ships were just visible on the horizon. Rising in altitude, slowly – so slowly . . .

"We have clearance," James said over the comm. "Scorpio One is sky bound . . ."

"What's that?" Mason said.

A silo in the middle of the base – a structure that was inside the Wraiths' target zone, but that had obviously escaped the worst of the destruction – began to rumble. I frowned, focused on the building. Snow tumbled from the roof, and the metalwork was deforming with intense stress.

Jenkins started to laugh. "Not more. Please God, nothing else . . ."

The building roof split open.

Something erupted from inside, began to rise above the compound.

The silo collapsed, and a Krell bio-ship emerged. In a bizarre parody of what we had just done, Krell primaries and secondaries lurched to get inside, clambering into every available pore and orifice that lined the ship's flank. Blue light poured from the engines, and the ship pivoted on the spot, beams playing over the surrounding structures.

Jenkins kept laughing. "The . . . they want to get away from here as well . . . Same as us . . ."

"Let them go," I said. My own voice was alien, slurred. "There's no point."

The clouds had parted – just enough to allow a splinter of sunlight to stab through . . .

The Wraith ships were coming back around, engines producing a noise like ripping fabric as they accelerated.

The Krell ship rose. Alien bodies fell from it as it did so, and I noticed just how badly damaged the ship was. The vessel was half-dead, hull speckled with breaches, bone-like protrusions erupting from the belly. She wouldn't be a threat to the *Independence*. From what I could see, the bio-ship was unlikely to get off-world, let alone pose any danger to our ship. But there was an undeniable majesty to the Krell bio-ship, and in her actions. This was impossible. She was out-matched, surely dead, and yet she would never give up. The Krell were tenacious, if nothing else.

Jenkins just laughed on and on and on.

The Wraiths dropped three specks of light from their bellies.

"Prepare for extraction," I said to the Legion.

The stars fell, scarring the sky. Accompanied by a shrieking noise: an otherworldly wailing.

We all knew what was coming. Mason closed her eyes. Martinez dropped to one knee in a classic prayer pose. I just stood and watched; let the incoming missiles burn my simulated retinas.

The Krell bio-ship's engine fired blue, fin-like appendages fanning from her aft: lifting higher, following the trajectory of our ships—

But too slow – obviously too slow. The ship was damaged and could never outrun the missiles.

When the missiles hit, they exploded immediately. The energy release was intense and overwhelming – expanding to consume not just the compound but the surrounding airspace. A wave of cleansing heat washed over me, so hot that it was all-consuming. My armour was no protection from the heat, force and radiation, and it was peeled away in an instant. Inside, my simulant was obliterated. The pain was extraordinary, but so much that I couldn't process it properly.

It'll pass, I told myself.

Death was nothing more than an inconvenience and I'd experienced it too many times to concern myself with the novelty. The last thing I saw – as my eyes were boiled away, my simulated brain eradicated – was that bio-ship, her black outline framed by the intense release of energies. She was caught in the explosion as well, and torn apart just as easily as my simulant.

Death two hundred and thirty-six: by nuclear detonation. If nothing else, it was new.

CHAPTER FOUR

KNOWS YOUR NAME

We extracted back to the *Independence*.

The starship's exact astronomical coordinates were unknown, at least to me, but we were somewhere beyond the reach of any orbital response that the Directorate ground forces could muster. We were somewhere safe. Had the fact been otherwise, we'd have been smeared across real-space by now.

And Kaminski?

Through ears that barely functioned – a second ago, that hadn't even existed – I heard a response over the comm-network.

"That's a confirm on the evac. We have two birds in the roost."

"Nice work, people. Another one for the Legion."

There were cheers of triumph, probably from somewhere on the bridge, but they were irrelevant to me. That Kaminski was safe and aboard the *Independence*: that was what mattered.

Back in my real body, I peeled open my eyes. It hurt – a

lot. My skin was scalding hot. The marrow of my bones was boiling. The light was so Christo-damned intense that I knew when I looked down that the skin on my arms, chest and legs would be blistered black—

Except that when I did, through the sanitising haze of amniotic, there wasn't a mark on me. At least, nothing that hadn't been there before the operation on Capa V. Only scars, welted flesh: reminders of a lifetime of military service, and not all of it simulated. Once I would've rankled against the pain – screamed, yelled as I rode it like a wave, got it all out. Now, I let it ebb from me. Let the sensation sink through me, evaporate.

The same chamber beyond the glass. A different starship, different technicians. Even different squad members, but the same chamber. Another anonymous Simulant Operations Centre – aboard another anonymous starship. I ignored the voices over my comm-bead: knew the questions that were being asked, the responses that I should give. Maybe I was talking; maybe I gave the right answers.

This gets harder every time. I clambered out of the simulator-tank. I knew that the pain of my simulated death would soon be gone. All I would be left with was the ache of not knowing; the cold void of indifference to real life. *This* was what was becoming harder: not dying, but coming back to reality.

The Legion each had their own post-extraction rituals.

Elliot Martinez: kneeling naked on the floor, crossing himself. Mumbling a prayer in pigeon Spanish; looking to the view-port to thank God Almighty for his resurrection.

"He's getting worse," said Jenkins.

Keira Jenkins: the Californian lieutenant of my team. She'd been with me for longer than I cared to remember; had seen the evil that men do and the horror of the Krell Empire.

She, too, was changed. Harder faced, leaner bodied, more muscled. Her own naked body was becoming cluttered with scars. The worst was the gunshot wound she'd acquired from the operation in the Damascus Rift; even stitched up, and months later, the healed scar on her stomach still looked vivid.

Martinez finished his prayer, then rose from the deck with an irritated expression on his face. "Fuck you, Jenkins."

Jenkins stumbled across the SOC. Threw her arms around me, breathing ragged and emotional.

"We have him," she said. "We have our man."

Mason was still in shock from the last extraction.

"They nuked their own colony," she said, shaking her head – her long blonde hair dripping with blue amniotic gel. Repeated: "Those bastards nuked their *own station*."

Dejah Mason: I'd been with her during her early transitions, when she had joined the Legion as a probationer. That seemed such a long time ago – an impossible age. She was a machine now. Her eyes were the worst part: cold, hard, wonderless. She still kept a souvenir of the Damascus mission close to her tank – a mono-sword, recovered from a dead Directorate commando aboard the UAS *Colossus* – just in case.

"Only the Directorate," Jenkins said. "'Ski's back; that's all I care about."

"But what was the point?" Mason asked.

"Either to stop us, or the Krell, from getting off-world," I said. "Plain and simple."

"But we did it anyway," Martinez said. "God's work is done, and Kaminski is back in the fold."

"If you ask me," Jenkins said, "those assholes got what they deserved."

"Would you have shot that woman?" Mason said to

Jenkins. She had started to fend off an army of medical technicians that had descended upon us; taking their readings and blood samples, logging the results of the transition.

Jenkins didn't answer for a moment, then called back, "If it would have helped us find Kaminski, then of course I would have done."

An officer pushed his way through the circus of medtechs and approached me. It was Captain Ostrow: dressed in an immaculate khaki uniform, short-sleeved fatigues exposing his muscled arms. His normal eyewear – dark glasses, proper spook apparel – was missing, and his flinty grey eyes fixed on mine.

"Well done, Lazarus," he said. "That was excellent work."

The science team ignored Ostrow. If any of them had served with me before – and I genuinely couldn't differentiate one fresh-faced science puke from the next – then they would have seen the same show recently. It was nothing new. I righted myself. Let the crick in my back ease itself out. Because that was a real pain, it was somehow worse than the nuclear wind I'd just endured down on Rodonis Capa V.

"I seem to remember that you were unwilling to sanction that drop," I said.

Jenkins let out a false laugh in support.

"It's more complicated than that—"

"I'll bet it is," I said.

"I'm going to retrospectively sanction it. Command will buy that."

"Like I give a shit," I said. "We got our man back. That's all I care about."

"And Professor Saul as well," Ostrow said. "Sector Command will be very pleased with that."

"I take it that your opinion has changed because the raid was a success?" Mason asked.

"It's not that straightforward, Private," Ostrow said, defensively. "And please do not refer to it as a 'raid': that was a dedicated exfiltration operation, based on a solid intelligence lead."

Mason shook her head in feigned disbelief, and pushed past Ostrow into the corridor towards the showers. She was still naked from the tanks and he watched her go. She was a pretty girl; it was a response most men would've shown in the circumstances.

"How many did we get out?" I said.

"Eighty-three," Ostrow said. "The infirmary is crammed with them. This is very good news. Psych Ops is going to be all over it."

That was Psychological Operations: the propaganda limb of the Alliance military, responsible for feeding the masses news from the frontline. I didn't like them much.

"I'm sure that CNN will love it," said Jenkins. "I just hope that those poor sons of bitches make it. It was cold down there."

"They're getting the best medical attention that we can give them. For most of them, frostbite and hypothermia are the least of their worries."

There was a hitch to Ostrow's response; one of his many tells. Ostrow had been assigned to the *Independence* as a sort of overseer – supposedly, as the final arbiter of whether an operation could or should be conducted in Directorate space – and we'd been working with him for several months. In that time, I'd learnt his tells. For an MI man, a spook, he had enough of those. The wobble in his voice? It meant that there was more to this.

"Go on," I said.

A medtech was helping me get dressed into duty fatigues now. The simulated pain lingered on in my bones. I'd noticed that recently: how the pain seemed to last longer, would sometimes wake me in the night. It never really left me.

Ostrow tongued the inside of his mouth, crossed his arms over his chest. "The news isn't all good."

"Is he . . .?" Jenkins asked.

"PFC Kaminski is fine," Ostrow said. "He'll need some surgery for those nerve-staples, but he's going to pull through."

"Then what is it?" I said.

"Ahh . . . Sector Command is requesting your immediate recall."

"Where are we going?"

"We're going to Calico Base."

Ostrow couldn't have known the effect that would have on me; surely didn't know *why* I hated Calico. I found it very hard to conceal my reaction though, and Ostrow swallowed hard – took an unconscious half-step away from me.

Anywhere but Calico . . . I thought.

Ostrow regained his composure. "The orders just came through. Captain Qadr is plotting a course directly out of Rim space, and we'll be leaving Directorate territory within the next six hours."

I couldn't actually remember having even spoke to Qadr. He, or she, was another interchangeable Navy captain; another face assigned to ferry around the Lazarus Legion. I recalled, with a pang of self-condemnation, what had happened to so many Navy staff under my command.

"Tell him to cancel the order."

"I'm not going to do that. She has her orders."

"And I'm ordering you."

Ostrow smiled. His skin was a deep olive, hair neatly slicked back. He'd once told me that he was from Mainfall,

Proxima Centauri III; where apparently the sun-baked American ideal lived on.

"I'm Military Intelligence. Under the joint military charter, you can't give me orders. We're currently moving under FTL drive past the last world in the Rodonis Capa system."

I stormed out of the SOC, through the *Independence*'s narrow corridors. She was a littoral combat ship, made for operations close to the shore, and she had seen better days. Most of her belly had been torn out and refitted, to accommodate the multiple Sim Ops bays. The place stunk of amniotic and electrolyte fluids; of data-port lubricant and sweat. Operators were gradually drifting from their bays, stumbling about in a semi-daze: troopers from Baker's Boys, the Raiders, the Vipers. Although some deaths had probably been kinder or faster than others, every single one of them had just died on Capa V.

Ostrow followed after me, his boots tapping against the deck. "You want my advice?"

"No," I said. "But I'll bet you're going to give it to me anyway."

Ostrow did just that. "This has to stop. You've got to put what happened in the Damascus Rift behind you."

I can't do that, I thought, *because I don't want to put it behind me.* The Rift had changed everything. I'd been so close to finding Elena – so close that I had seen her damned *ship!* – but it had also cost me Kaminski. I'd spent the last few months trying to right that wrong.

"You should start leading," Ostrow said. "You're a lieutenant colonel now. You have responsibilities. You should be back on Calico – taking your place on the security council—"

"Don't talk to me about Calico."

Ostrow shrugged. "The Joint Chiefs are demanding your

return. There aren't enough starships to keep policing the Zone."

Since the Massacre at *Liberty Point*, as it had become known, that was too often the case. A good deal of the Alliance Navy's resources had been lost during the battle . . . And I hadn't been there to do a damned thing about it. The Massacre had been the worst atrocity in Alliance history. Given that we had been at war against both the Krell Empire – and in a more covert sense also the Asiatic Directorate – for the last generation, that was quite some laurel. The Massacre had claimed millions of lives.

"Don't talk to me about the Zone either," I barked.

For all intents, there was no Quarantine Zone any more. The phrase was a misnomer, because the quarantine had been well and truly broken. There weren't enough ships, Army infantry or Sim Ops teams to police what was left: and week by week, month by month, we were being pushed back. If we'd had the resources invested in the *Point* at our disposal, maybe we would've had a fighting chance. Now, with all that lost? We were losing this damned war. The Krell were claiming more and more territory.

We reached the main bridge bulkhead. There were Marines and Navy officers standing ahead, and all parted as I approached. Conversation stopped: heads bowed. The face of every man and woman we passed was filled with irrational hope.

"You get us some payback, sir?" a particularly keen sailor asked. "We heard that you brought some of our boys back."

"Lazarus Legion all the way . . ." another said.

Not this shit again.

They didn't want Conrad Harris, ageing colonel of the Alliance Army. They wanted Lazarus, legend of Sim Ops.

The *Independence*'s bridge was small and cramped. A

couple of dozen Navy staffers rose from their workstations; gave me brisk and prideful salutes. Most were young, fresh from the Ganymede Naval Academy. A slightly older female officer – with rank badge and shoulder epaulettes of a captain – jumped to attention as well.

"Lazarus on the deck!" she declared.

"Please," I said, with barely disguised irritation, "as you were."

As the bridge crew gently settled into the idea of working while I was present on the deck, I manipulated the main view-screen.

"Get me a visual on Capa V's surface," I said, waving my right hand – my only hand – at the monitor.

"You heard the man!" Qadr said.

I watched the surface of Capa V – Cold Death – and focused on the location of the prison outpost. Where once it had been concealed by the snowdrifts and angry local weather, now it was painfully visible to anyone who cared to look.

To one of the Navy officers, I said: "Pull a closer magnification on that quadrant."

"Yes, sir."

The outpost had been annihilated in the detonation. Only an ugly, blasted crater remained: a basin with a kilometre radius, superheated by the nuclear explosion. The bare ground beneath a millennia of snowfall was heated to a glassy residue. Numerous sub-explosions had coursed over the mountain range, burning a violent spider-web into the landscape—

The image suddenly fuzzed with static, then collapsed to blackness.

"We've lost the Sentinel spy probe," an officer replied, "and our local scopes are out of range."

"Did the Krell bio-ship make it?"

The officer shook his head. "No, sir. It was caught in the blast."

Ostrow followed me to the hatch. "Maybe a few weeks on Calico will do you some good," he persisted. "You can get that hand replaced."

The stump of my left arm was pinned inside my fatigue cuff, a constant reminder of Damascus. I could've had the missing hand treated months ago, but had chosen not to do so.

"I don't need it replaced," I said. "I'm fine as I am."

I am Lazarus. I always come back.

"Just a thought," Ostrow said. "You might need it, is all."

What with four Sim Ops teams and Scorpio Squadron stationed on the *Independence*, the ship had started cramped: with the additional POWs now aboard it was packed to the gills. Looking for Kaminski, I went down to the Medical Deck. Every available bunk was filled, with the walking wounded milling around between medical stations. Harried medtechs oversaw the new arrivals, administering medical assistance as best they could. A row of black body bags, neatly arranged on the infirmary floor, reminded me that some were beyond help.

I snagged one of the nurses and asked him where I could find Kaminski.

"That one has been causing us some trouble," he said, shaking his head. "He's on the Observation Deck, despite advice."

The Obs Deck was almost as busy as Medical. Those survivors that could walk and talk seemed to gravitate here. This was the most open deck aboard the *Independence*, and I reasoned that perhaps the ex-prisoners wanted to revel in their freedom. The windows provided a view of the void – Rodonis Capa dwindling to the extent that it was now barely visible against the curtain of stars.

I found Kaminski sitting in the corner of the deck. He'd exchanged his vacuum-suit – garb that he'd been wearing for the last few months, since Damascus – for hospital fatigues. I'd never seen him look so tired, exhaustion showing through the new stress-lines on his face. His hair had been shaven during his incarceration and the nerve-staples – implants, Directorate neurosurgery – appeared more pronounced: silver studs across his cranium.

Jenkins sat beside him, her hand in his lap, and they talked softly. Everyone else on the deck seemed to give them a wide berth: as though they realised that this was a long-earned moment of intimacy. I couldn't help it, but I felt a pang of jealousy. This was what I wanted with Elena. The tender expression on Jenkins' face communicated more than words ever could. As she saw me approaching, Jenkins sat a little more upright. Now that she had been promoted to lieutenant – a commissioned officer's rank – the relationship between her and Kaminski was going to be more problematic. He was a PFC, and had been for years.

"At ease," I said. "This isn't a formal visit. I just wanted to see how things were."

"All good," he said, with his familiar grin. "I've nothing to complain about."

"You should be down on Medical," I said. "The medtechs don't sound happy that you discharged yourself."

"That's what I keep telling him," Jenkins said, "but he won't listen."

"Like I said, I'm all good," 'Ski insisted. His smile dropped just a little. "There are people down there that need the bed more than me. How's the Prof?"

"Professor Saul? They say that he'll pull through, too. Physically, at least."

I'd been updated on his medical status via the mainframe: Saul was being treated as a priority patient. The truth was that Command viewed Saul's survival as of far greater tactical significance than Kaminski's, or any other survivor's. Saul was irreplaceable; a specialist in Shard linguistics and tech. The idea that his intel could've fallen into enemy hands was unthinkable. But what good he'd be, after this experience? I couldn't say.

"I'm glad to be off that frozen shitball," 'Ski said.

Jenkins nudged him in the ribs; playfully, delicately. "You've had enough of being behind bars, eh?"

"That was nothing like Queens," he said.

I noticed that Kaminski involuntarily put a hand to his head, rubbing the nerve-staples, as he spoke. Although the flesh around the studs was mostly healed, the surgery looked harsh and brutal: as though conducted by a backstreet medico.

"Military Intelligence will have a lot of questions for you," I said, "when we get to Calico Base."

"Is that where we're going?" he asked.

"Those are our orders."

Jenkins shook her head. "I expect that Command will approve you some downtime, 'Ski. Maybe you can go to Fortuna for a few weeks, if not longer."

'Ski laughed. "I don't need downtime, Jenkins. I need a decent drink and a simulator-tank."

"I'm sure that you'll be recertified in good time," said Jenkins.

Fortuna was a pleasure world, but it was also light-years from the frontline. If Kaminski went there, his posting with the Lazarus Legion would be over, and the time-dilation would surely end any relationship he had with Jenkins.

"Have you told him about the *Point*?" I asked her.

She nodded. "I've told him everything: the *Point*, the Warfighters, the Krell . . ."

Although 'Ski had only been gone for a few months so much had happened. He would have to be formally briefed on the situation if he was ever going to get back to active deployment.

"Damned fish heads," Kaminski said, with some fervour. "The *Point* was home. Un-fucking-believable."

"You better believe it," I said. "The Krell have made it as far as Barnard's Star."

"You're shitting me?"

"I shit you not. They're spilling out of their tank and they've already taken a dozen systems on the border."

"Then we need to get out there and do what the Legion does."

"Easy, trooper," Jenkins said. "Take your time. The Krell can wait."

The truth was that the Krell could not wait, and Jenkins knew it. The situation along the Maelstrom border was dire, and it had taken all of my clout as a lieutenant colonel – as Lazarus – to resource the operation into Directorate territory. We were running low on everything; even simulants, the most basic of commodities required to keep the Sim Ops Programme going. I didn't tell Kaminski, but one of the territories just ceded to the Krell had been a farm: a geno-facility dedicated to harvesting sims.

"Why were they down there?" I asked. "The Krell, I mean."

"It's too early for a debrief—" Jenkins protested, protectively.

"It's okay, girl," Kaminski said. "I'd rather tell the Legion what happened before the MI." He gave a sharp intake of breath, started the story. "After we bailed out, the Krell turned up. We – Saul and I – saw the *Colossus* going through the Rift, then everything was chaos. The evac-pod didn't have scopes or sensors, and next thing we knew the Directorate had picked us up. They weren't in much better shape. There were lots of survivors in near-space – lots of crew evac'd their ships – and the Directorate took them all. And not just human crew: Krell too. We saw some of them aboard a Directorate ship. That's how they must've gotten to Capa."

"But what did the Directorate want with the Krell?"

"They never told me," Kaminski said. "But I'd guess the same as us: intelligence. After they captured us, they put us in the freezers. I woke up on Capa." He rubbed his head again, the nerve-staples there. "They knew who I was, and they wanted intel from me."

"They picked the wrong trooper there," said Jenkins.

Kaminski smiled. "Sure did, girl. When I didn't tell them anything, they started to use the staples."

"That shit been scanned for tracking tech?" I said.

"Of course," Jenkins replied. "None of it is traceable."

Even so, we couldn't rule out the possibility that one or more of the POWs had been implanted with a tracer. Although over interstellar distances it would do the Directorate no good, the Chino played for the long game: I didn't want this to be something that they could use against us on a future occasion. The nerve-staples would have to come out once we got to a proper medical facility.

"Did they tell you anything?" I asked.

"That isn't how an interrogation works," Jenkins said. "And this is too early, Harris."

I knew that I was pushing it too far now, that I should leave this. Debriefing of a POW was for Mili-Intel, and Jenkins was right – it was far too early – but I had to know.

"It's okay," Kaminski insisted. "They didn't so much as *tell* me anything, but we talked among ourselves." 'Ski raised his shoulders; still muscled despite his ordeal. "We heard things."

"Such as?"

He sighed, and his reaction made me all the more eager to hear what he had to say.

"Go on."

"We heard that they had the Key," Kaminski muttered. "They said that they had the Shard Key."

"How is that possible . . .?" I started. "I saw it destroyed . . ."

Jenkins gave me a hard look. "I've read your debrief," she said. "You left it aboard the Artefact. You never actually *saw* it destroyed."

I rubbed my chin, let that thought bounce around my head. In Damascus, I'd used the Key to activate the Artefact – to open the Shard Gate – and then I'd extracted. I'd left it there, confident in the knowledge that it could never be retrieved and used against us . . .

"I don't know why they'd want it," Kaminski said, "but it's Shard, and the Directorate seem to want pretty much anything Shard. But listen, don't read too much into it. For all I know, it might be wrong."

I nodded, although it was hard not to. "Anything else?"

"Just that the Asiatic Directorate really hates you," Kaminski said. "They told me that Director-General Zhang himself knows your name, and that he wants you dead."

"I'm flattered, but I'm still waiting."

Zhang: premier of the Asiatic Directorate, leader of over two-thirds of the population of explored space. His counterpart – President Francis – had been assassinated at some point while we were away in Damascus. We still didn't

74

know whether there was any connection there, but the Directorate had assumed responsibility for the incident.

"That was all they said," Kaminski added. "Thanks for coming back for me."

"You should never have been left out there in the first place," Jenkins said. "You can thank James and Loeb for that."

Kaminski didn't react, and his face was accepting. That was the lot of a soldier: the risk that a man took when he went into the Maelstrom.

"What about the Warfighters?" I asked. "Did you see them on Capa?"

Kaminski pulled a face at Jenkins. "I told you that I never trusted Williams."

"That wasn't the question," she said.

He shook his head. "I don't think so. But, if what Jenkins tells me is true, they could be anywhere now. Until Command and Sci-Div let you in on the Next-Gen Project . . ."

Next-gen simulants were almost indistinguishable from human bodies. Wearing those skins the Warfighter's could be anywhere, and *that* did spook me. I shivered involuntarily and scanned the Obs Deck again, fought the dizzy sensation in my head. My data-ports began that steady throb, promising release and a sense of invulnerability that I could never feel in my own skin. My missing left hand gave off a phantom itch.

"Sorry to hear about what Williams did to you," Kaminski said.

"It could've been worse."

"I just want to get back into the tanks," he said. "I can almost count the days since my last transition." He nodded at the chest of my fatigues, at the holo-badge that read "236". "I need to catch up with the boss."

Although there was a captain somewhere on the Askari Line who claimed to have topped two hundred and thirty successful transitions, I still held the record. It was a dubious honour and one that I wasn't necessarily proud of, but it was another aspect of my legend: a statistic for the greens to look up to.

"It's not the number that counts," Jenkins said, "it's what you do with it."

"We'll be back on Calico in three days, provided we don't meet resistance," I said. "Take it easy until then. Anything you need, just let me know. There are some perks to being a colonel."

"Well done on the promotion," Kaminski said.

I shrugged. "They had two choices: court-martial me or promote me. Glad to have you back, 'Ski."

I turned to walk away, but Kaminski kept talking. "They know you, Harris, and they're scared of you."

"They should be," I said, with all the conviction that I could muster.

My mind was elsewhere. I found myself wondering whether the Asiatic Directorate would fear me if they knew who I really was.

What I really was.

Old, exhausted, lost.

By the time I'd finished with Kaminski, and checked on the progress of the other prisoners, it was late in the *Independence*'s day-cycle. Mess had finished, and the ship was quiet: exhausted Sim Ops teams and flyboys sleeping off the short trip back to Alliance space.

So I found the mess hall dark and largely empty. I grabbed a hot coffee and some stale bread from the servery, and hunkered down in one corner of the hall.

"Do you find that dying makes you hungry?" came a voice.

I snapped awake and realised that I wasn't alone. Lieutenant James sat at the other end of the room, and stalked over to sit at my table. He looked dejected and shaken: a similar expression to that I'd seen him with on the surface of Capa, when he'd hesitated on the landing pad.

"No," I said, swallowing a mouthful of bread, "but dealing with fuck-up flyboys who lose it when I need them most: that tends to make me hungry."

"Yeah," he said, "I'm sorry about that."

He had a small bottle of Martian vodka, already uncapped. It was plain and unmarked, but seemed to emit a psychic beacon that called out to me.

"Next-gen sims don't get drunk," I said. "We've been through this before."

That wasn't quite true, because I'd seen James inebriated when he drank at speed. But this was a single bottle of vodka and I didn't think that it would be sufficient.

"I'm not drinking to get drunk," he said.

"You get permission to bring alcohol aboard?"

He raised an eyebrow. "Why? You going to tell Captain Qadr on me?"

I didn't answer but took the offered bottle. I'd been resisting it for a while – trying to do my best, hoping to avoid the other simulant teams seeing me in an impaired condition – but I couldn't resist any more. That ache in my bones, the sensation that could only be relieved by a good drink . . . I couldn't hold out. The spirit tasted hot and calming as it went down.

"What the fuck happened out there today, James?"

"Nothing," he said, sighing. "I . . . I just . . ."

This wasn't like James, not at all. He was everything that a space jockey should be: handsome, cocky, a devil with the ladies. *This* James – simulated as he was – just looked frightened. He leant back in his chair, the rubberised flight-suit creaking. I had never actually seen him in his real body, and in the months we'd been stationed together I couldn't recall ever having seen him out of the flight-suit either.

"Kaminski was lucky," he said.

I gave a hoarse laugh. "Try telling him that, but I wouldn't do it when Jenkins is around."

He swigged the bottle, wiped the back of his hand across his lips. "I'm sorry. I fucked up. It was just seeing those prisoners. It was too close to home."

"What do you mean? You never said anything . . ."

He grimaced. "You ever wonder why you don't see me in my own skin, Harris?"

"Not especially. Your next-gens are made to live in, aren't they?"

"Some of us don't have a choice. What happened on Capa . . . It brought back memories."

There was more to James than I'd realised. He'd mentioned family, mentioned previous postings, but not much else about his background. Scorpio Squadron had their own Sim Ops bay; that was pretty much protocol now, whenever Aerospace Force crew were attached to a sim operation. There were sixteen pilots on James' wing, and he was commander of the airgroup.

"How long did you do?" I probed.

"Six years, real-time," he said. "Nothing like Cold Death, but just as bad. Jungle world; real hot, real sticky. I never even found out the name."

"You should've told me. You could've run support—"

"That's not what I'm here for."

78

"You jeopardised the mission, James. There were real skins down there."

"It won't happen again," he said. "We've all left people behind, Harris. We've all got guilt."

Those words hit a nerve within me and I swigged deep at the bottle, wished that I had a whole case of the stuff. There was a real, bona fide war going on with the Krell. Not just a cold war, the likes of which I'd endured since the Treaty, but the real thing. The Krell were invading Alliance space again. I knew that I had responsibilities on the frontline.

All of those things were true.

But that didn't mean that I'd wanted to hear them.

I was feeling survivor's guilt.

I felt guilt because I hadn't been there when *Liberty Point* had gone down. I hadn't been there and hadn't been able to stop it. I felt guilt because over a dozen Alliance Navy starships had been lost in Damascus Space, with all hands. But if I dug really deep – painfully so – I knew that the real reason for my melancholy was Elena. At Damascus, I'd been so close to finding her: found a simulated copy of her aboard the Artefact. When the UAS *Colossus* had travelled through the Shard Gate, I had even seen her starship – the *Endeavour*. We'd witnessed the Shard Network; the grid of planets, stars and gateways that the Shard had left behind. The *Colossus* had been damaged by the journey; her sensor-suites and telemetry modules fried, her data-core burnt out like the neural synapses of a man driven into insanity.

So, Elena's location remained unknown. And try as I might, I hadn't been able to secure backing for another operation into the Maelstrom. The Alliance was too busy defending the new frontier to risk sanctioning another offensive. That wasn't good enough for me. The war wasn't going to be won by retreating, by gifting real estate to the Krell and hoping that they would be satisfied. For the Krell, it was *never* enough.

I pulled myself back to the conversation, realised that I'd finished the liquor. James didn't complain as I passed him the empty bottle.

"Did you hear what happened to the Buzzard?" he asked.

That was Admiral Joseph Loeb's nickname; earned from his appearance and his nature. He had been commanding officer of the *Colossus*, during the Damascus mission. I didn't answer: Loeb's situation was another source of guilt.

"His wings got clipped," James said, drolly. "He's been permanently grounded, awaiting court-martial."

"I know," I answered. "I hear that he's on Calico now."

James nodded. "I got new orders, too," he said. "The whole of Scorpio Squadron got a recall notice."

"Maybe that's for the best," I said.

"Maybe," James replied.

The conversation ended and James left a short while later.

I sat alone in the dark, the heave and sigh of the ship my only company.

It wasn't long before my mind turned to thoughts of Calico . . .

CHAPTER FIVE

SHE'S ALREADY GONE

Ten years ago

Thirty-four years old, I was a captain with the Army's Simulant Operations Programme. The day that I had a chance to change my life, but didn't take it.

The last time that I saw Elena for real was on Calico.

I jostled my way through the crowded passageway, cursing as I nudged elbows with miners, colonists and corporate employees. Every outpost, even ship, had its own scent and aura: that instantly recognisable smell that comes with a home territory. Calico Base had it in force; a sweaty, grimy odour that reminded me this whole planet was basically one big mine.

Before the First Krell War, Calico had been a very profitable mining outpost. The original colonists were practitioners of some bizarre Hindu-Gaian sub-sect. Big on peace, small on war: despite the outpost's location close to the frontline, the Calicans had successfully avoided much involvement in the hostilities. They earned a living by mining raw materials from the rock, processing them in bulk, then hurling them Corewards. The planet wasn't much bigger than Old Earth's moon, and there was no atmosphere outside to terraform.

Closed ecosystems like this were always the worst for smell, and the off-worlders and tourists seemed to have swelled the population to double normal capacity. There were people everywhere: crammed into doorways, leaning from overhead railings. Every public space on Calico had been turned over to the procession, to the pomp and cere-mony that would mark the launch of the UAS *Endeavour*. As I fought my way through the crowds, I even saw banners and flags printed with HAPPY LAUNCH DAY! It made my stomach turn.

Months prior, Elena had told me – when she left Azure, when she left me – that the launch details for the *Endeavour* expedition were classified. That had remained the case for several weeks, but when the Alliance media machine had got their teeth into the project everything had changed. The last few weeks had seen the mission made public.

I stared down at my wrist-comp. Thirty minutes until the launch. An avalanche of ideas occurred to me. I had to see her one last time. I had convinced myself that if I saw her – *if she saw me* – things would be different somehow.

"Where you headed, stranger?" a teenaged boy asked me, blocking my path.

"Shuttle bays."

"Same as everyone," he said. Shook his head. "It's a walk. You cutting it fine, soldier."

I had cut it fine, and I knew it. I'd come down on the utility docks on the other side of Calico. That had cost me more time than I'd appreciated.

The boy shrugged. "But I can get you there, through the shafts, before a launch. You want, that is."

"Yeah," I said. "I reckon."

The kid wore a bright orange vacuum-suit, his head comically small poking from the ring collar. I hadn't been on Calico for long – I'd taken a shuttle in, used my Sim Ops credentials to get a free ride – but I'd already noticed that everyone here wore vacuum-suits around the clock. While the base was fully pressurised and atmo-rated – you could go anywhere without a suit – some traditions were long in the tooth. The kid's suit looked as though it had been passed down several generations – worn and frayed, covered in a variety of neo-religious symbology. I doubted that it would actually survive exposure to vacuum.

"Gonna cost yous," the boy said. "Ten credits get you there and back. No touch by gangs. Me see to it."

"Nice try, kid. I'll just take directions, and those for free."

The boy was mixed Indo-Asian stock; maybe thirteen or fourteen. A small gang of them were arraigned about the corridor, ducking and diving between the tourists. Making a little on the side, pick-pocketing and making do. Like most of the children running amok around the base, this one was strangely stunted – his face much too old for the rest of his small body. Whether that was a lifetime of living among the grav-generators, or old-fashioned malnutrition, it was hard to say.

The boy rolled his eyes. "I can do it for five, sees. But no less. Gotta lotta business today. Launch day, see? I know these corridors."

Reluctantly, I realised that the boy was probably right. I'd already got lost twice on the way here, and the passageways were tortuously labyrinthine. There was an enforced no-fly zone in effect. That meant no air-cars, no inter-base transport. I needed to make up lost time if I was going to stop her . . .

"All right. Five credits."

"Up front, yes?" the boy said, flexing an open palm in my direction.

I rifled in the pocket of my fatigues. Found a credit chip and dropped it into the boy's palm. Despite his full vac-suit, he wasn't wearing gloves.

"Name's Vijay," he said. Pocketed the credit chip in one of the many pouches lining the outside of his suit. "I be your guide today. And you?"

"Conrad. And if I get robbed on the way, Vijay, I'm promising you that I *will* kill you."

"Me no scared of death, soldier," Vijay said, flashing a yellow-tooth grin. "I born a bred Calico Base, see? Death walks here."

Vijay started off down the corridor.

"When you get down, Soldier Conrad?" Vijay asked.

"Conrad is just fine. And I came down a few hours ago."

"Me copy," Vijay said. "Me like real military, sees?"

"Mmmm. I see."

We passed through public halls, through big expanses with domed roofs. Calico had that slightly out-of-control feeling about it: of a plan gone awry, the hallmarks of a hundred changes in administration. Buildings were planted atop buildings. Structures sprouted from other structures. There was probably some architectural significance to the design work – this was, after all, a civilian facility, and how things looked was apparently as important to the builders as what they did – but it was lost on me. There were temples here and there, breaking up the monotony of grey buildings and metal scrapers. Those were painted in more exotic and

84

enticing colours, as though to ensnare new followers. Lots of images of Old Earth, looking far greener and bluer than when I'd seen her last.

"I been a here since the start," Vijay said. "Start a me, at least."

"I follow that. Your folks first-generation colonists?"

"Or something. I no know 'em. No matter. I get in a Guild, get me accredited. Get me a rig, go a mining like the rest 'em." He nodded in determination. "Get me a good life. Why you wanna come a Calico, anyhow? We no see so many soldiers a these days."

"They're building a station," I said. Although I could give the kid the exact details, because none of it was classified – not any more – I thought better of it, and summarised what I knew. "A few star systems out. A big base called *Liberty Point*. It'll divert traffic away from here."

"That good a bad," the kid said. "Probably mean less war a here, but maybe also less tourists. You sound American."

"I am. That a problem?"

"Not for me. For lots out here, it is though. Maybe you should a get something else a wear?" He pointed out a clutch of tourists wearing bright orange, faux-Calico vac-suits. "You want one a these suits, I can find someone who can get you one. Rated for the vac and all."

"I don't need a suit. My uniform is fine. I don't want to miss this launch."

"You seem awful keen to get there. You got a girl aboard or something?"

"Something," I said. "Are we far?"

"No," he said. "I can even get you into a press pit, for a little extra. It'll be one a the best places to watch a launch."

I don't want to watch the launch, I thought. *I want to stop it.*

"Do that," I said. Didn't even ask about the credits.

For his faults – mainly, that he wouldn't stop talking about the history of Calico, about where he was from, and about the various items that he could acquire for me for just a few more credits – Vijay proved to be a reliable and decent guide. We carved our way through the passages and conclaves until we reached the transport sector. All the while, the timer clicked down. Anticipation was mounting inside of me. I'd already faced multiple simulated deaths by then – and started my meteoric rise within the Sim Ops Programme – but this was anxiety of an entirely different calibre.

If I didn't do something now, then Elena would be gone for good.

Through the transparent domed ceilings, I saw that the sides of star-scrapers had been dedicated to the celebration as well. The faces of the lead crew cycled through: in fifty-metre glory, each of them smiling towards the camera. It was sickening.

"Don't they know what they're doing?" I said aloud.

"They want a peace, see? That's what you military types don't understand. They want a go see a Krell and talk to 'em."

"It'll never work."

"But if this Treaty," Vijay said, wagging his finger in a sage fashion, trying to appear far more knowledgeable than he actually was, "works out, then we'll all be winners. They talk about a Quarantine Zone or something." Vijay ducked between two men wearing blue and green robes, swinging incense burners. "Shuttle bays a this way."

It was there that Elena would be boarding, using the

Calican shuttle terminals to reach the *Endeavour*. The actual expeditionary fleet was far above us, visible only as a collection of blinking lights, lost to the sea of stars.

"We start a build a space elevator," Vijay told me. "It gonna be real good for finances."

A metal beanstalk grew from the transport sector, surrounded by a series of industrial cranes and scaffold structures. Only a few hundred metres long at present, the unfinished elevator would connect Calico Base to the orbital docks: would allow for faster transport to and from the surface. Right now, the shuttles were the fastest option. That, and it gave the Alliance media machine plenty of opportunities to parade the crew before the cameras.

"Where's the press pit?" I asked.

Vijay pointed. "Down a that a way. I got a pass."

The boy led me to a gangway. Sector security – men dressed in big blue vac suits, with white lettering across their chests and backs – milled among Alliance Military Police; identifiable by their black flak-suits and the carbines slung over their chests. Vijay waved his wrist-comp at the nearest guard; a man with a head and face of tattoos, and missing front teeth. The guard raised an eyebrow in disbelief that a station rat would have a press pass, but was obviously too lazy to bother making the necessary checks.

"Go a through," he said. "Enjoy a show."

"We will, sir. Thanks a much, see."

The shuttle bay had been completely given over to the launch and thousands of people were piled into the chamber; doors currently sealed, sixteen staunch transport shuttles on the apron, surrounded by launch scaffold and steps to the passenger cabins. Mostly unnecessary, but all part of the show. In the midst of the hangar, a military band paraded up and down the apron: fuckers in dress uniform playing their songs, barely audible above the combined cheering of the crowds. Civvies were blowing horns, waving flags, chanting.

I was glad that the press pit – despite its name – was elevated, overseeing the civilian onlookers. To my surprise, there was a mixture of press and military in the pit. The area above and around me was abuzz with news-drones – tiny cameras and microphones recording everything for posterity.

An enormous LED countdown flashed with TIME UNTIL BOARDING – 45 SECONDS AND COUNTING! SPONSORED BY DELAT ENTERPRISES!

There were no seats, but Vijay secured us a place near the front of the pit next to a female military reporter. I jostled my way forwards. I could see right down into the landing gantry from here: would be as close as I could get to Elena. Directly beneath us was a clear corridor, policed with security staff: a cordon holding back the swelling civilian masses.

I can't let her go, I told myself. *She can't do this.*

"Great! You're Sim Ops, huh?"

A female reporter stood beside me. Flame hair spilled over her shoulders, and a tight smart-suit clung to her body.

"What gave it away?" I said.

"Your uniform, actually." She smiled at me with full red lips. It was an award-winning smile. An expression designed to make the recipient feel at ease.

"I was being sarcastic," I said.

The woman shrugged off the implied insult. Two small news-drones circled her head. "How many deaths for you, Captain?"

So she could read rank insignia as well, huh? "Too many."

She smiled that Pulitzer-winning grin again. I vaguely recognised her from one of the news-feeds that the Alliance military regularly put out; Cassi Something? Her deep green eyes flashed; data dancing across her pupils. I guessed she had an uplink with the Calico Base mainframe.

"Captain Conrad Harris, one hundred and twelve transitions," she said. "Impressive."

"That's a dangerous toy. Lot of intel could get into the wrong hands like that."

"Core News is careful," she said, tapping the holo-badge on her chest. The name read CASSI BROOKE, CORE NEWS NETWORK. Brooke nodded at the hangar. "Looks like you're just in time, soldier-boy."

The countdown flashed: BOARDING! BOARDING! BOARDING!

The crew were protected by a military cordon, and were now being hustled to their waiting shuttles.

Shit. This is it.

Faces projected on to massive billboards, holos of the brave men and women of the Alliance expeditionary force.

Brooke began her spiel, speaking not to me but the news-drone in front of her. "Ten minutes to launch, people! The atmosphere here is incredible. The festivities have to be seen to be believed. The UAS *Endeavour* is currently kilometres above us, in Calico's galaxy-famous orbital docks."

I gripped the safety rail of the pit. Far from being incredible, the atmosphere was dizzying. Beneath me, flags of a hundred colonies, of tens of nation-states, were being flown. Representatives from pretty much every colony, outpost and national body had gathered here.

"The *Endeavour*'s mission specs are staggering," the reporter said. "She's one of the largest non-military vessels ever built by the Alliance. Capable of prolonged faster-than-light flight, with the most sophisticated quantum-space disruption drive ever installed in a ship of this size."

I fought to see the gathered crew. Everyone wore the same deep-blue vac-suit, carrying black boxes on hoses connected to their chests. Again: part of the show. Parodies of earlier explorers, of the first astronauts that had probed the dark of outer space.

"She is, we're told, equipped for any eventuality," the reporter continued. "Made to counter whatever the Krell Collective have to throw at her. But we mustn't forget that the *Endeavour* is one of several starships tasked with this mission. There are in fact sixteen ships on this expedition."

Their names were known all across Allied space: had already captured the public's fickle imagination. The AFS *Lion's Pride*, HMS *Britannic*, UAS *Ark Angel* . . . Many of the vessels were multi-nationals, each differently constructed, with a dedicated role on the expedition.

"And here comes the crew!" the reporter gleefully squealed.

I panicked. Here she was.

This was a photo opportunity, and nothing more. There was no functional purpose in boarding the crew in this way. One by one, they climbed the scaffold towards the outer shuttle doors.

"Commander Cook!" someone declared. "Christopher Cook is the expedition leader, as well as the captain of the *Endeavour*."

He turned, paused, waved at the crowd. His face – middle-aged, wise, smiling – appeared twenty-storeys high on the billboard. I felt like I knew the man already. I'd read multiple interviews in *Dispatches*, in the *Alliance Daily*. His face had been plastered over every publication that Psych Ops could put out.

"One of our own," Vijay interrupted, nodding proudly. "He a Calican, you know."

Cook was a family man: three wives and sixteen kids. That was supposed to be some sort of reassurance to the public, a subliminal suggestion that the mission would be coming back – that he wouldn't be abandoning his family.

"Cook's second-in-command, Lieutenant Reji Ashwari!"

Another familiar face, another cheer. Another practised walk up the gantry, into the waiting transport.

"Sergeant Thomas Stone!"

The faces went on and on. Almost all of the crew had military, or pseudo-military, titles. That had been a deliberate conceit; to get the public onside. I'd already dug into the files, tested my sources. Only Stone had any actual military experience, and he'd been assigned a five-man simulant team to provide security.

"You a okay there, see?" Vijay said. "Look a pale."

I swallowed hard. "Five men for all those ships."

"Dr Elena Marceau!"

I leant into the rail. Waved a hand at her, shouted. Of course, my voice was drowned by the sea of noise around me: the jubilant, senseless, pointless cheering.

Then Elena's face appeared on the billboard and it took all of my strength not to pass out. I teetered on the edge as she took the walk towards the waiting transport. There was only a couple of hundred metres between us, but it may as well have been light-years. Soon, once she had commenced her mission into the Maelstrom, it would be.

I'd never forget the way that she looked that day. The vac-suit was fitted, not as puffy as the older-style EVA gear, and her lean figure was evident as she strode the gantry.

The French flag on one shoulder, the Alliance on the other. Because she was a pretty face for the cameras, Elena's inner suit hood was lowered. Her long dark hair was pulled back in a semi-utilitarian style; her red lips glossed, cheeks blushed. She had never looked more beautiful.

She paused at the end of the gantry. Framed by the open shuttle hatch. Scanned the crowd. None of the other crew had done that. Dallied at the access. Was she looking for me, or was that just my imagination?

"She's going to be putting the schedule out . . ." Brooke muttered to me, *sotto voce*. "She's only the fucking shipboard psych, for Christo's sake . . ."

There were a lot of people between her and me. I felt her gaze turn in my direction. Those dark eyes lingered on the press pit. Did she see me? We made – or at least, I thought that we made, fleeting eye contact.

Don't go. Please; don't go.

The second – that was probably all it was – passed, and Elena disappeared into the ship.

I can't let her do this.

I leant forward, tested the safety rail. It was firmly attached, would hold my weight. There was an open security corridor beneath me, only a five-metre drop.

"What you a do, boss?" Vijay asked, as though the cogs in his brain had started to whirr. "That's not a good idea—"

"Fuck it," I said.

I leapt over the railing. The crowd was still cheering, still yelling like the bunch of idiots that they were, and hardly anyone noticed me. I landed hard on the floor, went into a roll. Knew that I had to think and move fast: that to reach the shuttle I'd have to get past security—

"Hold it!" someone shouted, moving at the end of the cordon. "Stay where you are!"

Vijay and Brooke were watching me from the press enclosure, leaning over the railing. The Mili-Pol reacted faster than I'd predicted and moved on my location. Supporting security-drones flitted over the heads of the civilian crowd.

"I can't let her go!" I yelled, tearing towards the shuttle.

Two figures appeared at the end of the open corridor, storm batons drawn and shock pistols at the ready. Big MPs wearing full flak-suits focused on me. Others were closing in too, circling the closest approach to the shuttle boarding gantry.

I swung a solid punch at the first MP. Connected with his nose; sent the brute sprawling backwards in a spray of red. He yelped, dropped his baton, cursed at me. I side-stepped the second, moved on towards the shuttle—

"No you don't!" the soldier yelled. "This is a restricted area!"

"You don't understand!" I shouted back, feeling hands grasping at my collar, dragging me back. "She can't do this!"

"Yeah, well, she's already gone," the MP growled.

I slammed an elbow into the trooper's ribs, felt a solid connection with bone. The man gave an angered groan in response, but didn't go down like the first. He fought back, pulling me further from my objective, the open boarding hatch of the shuttle suddenly seeming an impossible distance. I struggled some more, lashed out with fists and feet—

A storm-baton slammed into my back. The device was made for exactly this purpose: a non-lethal, but extremely painful, method of detaining suspects. Electrical discharge danced up my shoulder as I slumped to the floor. Soon I was incapacitated, a pair of MPs were above me, slamming the batons into me again and again, until I couldn't fight back any more.

I caught a glimpse of the press area as I went down. The

reporter watched on with intrigue in her eyes. As I rolled onto my side, and consciousness began to evaporate, I saw the shuttle boarding hatch. Elena was inside that transport, and very soon she would be leaving for the *Endeavour* and the Maelstrom.

That was the last time I saw her.

I blacked out.

CHAPTER SIX

CALICO

Cruising at FTL speed, the *Independence* grazed the edge of some Japanese space holdings – technically, for now at least, still Alliance territory – and moved through French airspace. The trip took three days; no need for a quantum-space jump, so no need for the damned freezers. En route we lost several prisoners to miscellaneous medical conditions, and the tally of stable survivors dropped to sixty-two.

Kaminski made a fast recovery. Hot food and Jenkins did wonders for his constitution, and over the days he became more and more like his old self, despite the metal in his head. Professor Saul remained bed-bound, but I had reports that he was conscious and lucid.

As we entered Alliance space, we began to receive updates on the war. Virulent as the plague, scuttlebutt raged throughout the ship. The news wasn't good: another two star systems purged by the Krell, and still they kept coming. Several new war-fleets had entered Alliance space in the last six weeks, and we'd lost three battlegroups across the old QZ. The Navy had taken a pounding at Askari and the latest prediction on reinforcements was another two years. Those were the real effects of time-dilation from the Core; the currently insurmountable realities of running an inter-stellar war.

I returned to the Observation Deck on the approach, but found that it wasn't as empty as I'd expected.

"Morning."

There was the Legion, including Kaminski. He was even dressed in full uniform. Eyes glued to the long armour-glass window.

"Morning, Legion," I muttered. "I thought that this would be a good place for some privacy."

"You want us to go?" Mason asked.

"No," I said.

I was suddenly glad of the Legion's presence: their re-assuring aura. I realised that I didn't want to face Calico alone. Having Kaminski back, the team being together: it felt like old times. It felt good.

"You know why they want to see you?" Jenkins said.

"No, I don't know why they want *us*," I said. "It's not just me: the Legion goes where I go."

"You think Ostrow knows?" Mason said.

"I doubt he'd give me a straight answer even if I asked. I don't trust spooks. Never have."

Below, Calico bloomed like an enormous grey flower. It had been growing steadily for the past day, larger and larger until it filled every view-port. The wave of memory that the world evoked irritated me.

Post-Treaty Calico had enjoyed a period of relative calm, but corporate investments had never quite returned to pre-War levels. Ore seams had dried up and fortunes had waned. Nervous company men in their glass towers back in the Core had decided that Calico Base wasn't such a safe bet any more. The result was Calico, 2284: a mess of half-abandoned mines and refineries, of haunted hab-domes and empty dom-blocks.

"I've been here before," I said, absently. "Ten years ago."

Watching her go: boarding the shuttle, leaving human space behind . . .

Mason pulled an intrigued face. "Isn't this where the *Endeavour* expedition was launched?"

I saw Jenkins give her a determined frown, shaking her head *not to go there*. But Mason was always with the questions, and she wouldn't be deterred.

"Yes," I said. "I was here when the ship launched."

"Must've been quite the occasion," Mason said, with genuine interest.

"It was. But Calico was very different then."

The resurgence of the Krell threat – what the media was now calling the Second Krell War – had, perversely, led to renewed interest in the outpost, but for all of the wrong reasons. The Krell had already destroyed several border systems, and that put an enormous strain on the resources available to Calico. As of now the place was experiencing a migrant crisis. Air, water, heat: those things were finite quantities in space. The population was crippling the outpost.

"There must be something to enjoy down there," Jenkins said.

"Maybe the open air?" Mason suggested. Her tone was playful; sarcastic even. "The plant life?"

I groaned. Calico Base had neither of those.

"What would a Martian know about open air?" Jenkins said, frowning. "Your cities are almost as bad as Earth's."

"Except they're red," Martinez said.

"Let's not get started on who has the best planet," Mason

said, backing away from the obs window. "Because we all know who will win that one . . ."

Kaminski interrupted the conversation. "What's that?" he asked, pointing to a structure in space.

Calico's orbital dock – a boxy conglomeration of workshops and hangar bays – was just visible at this distance. Several warships were either docked with the station, or moored in close proximity. The gathered fleet was substantial; comprised a variety of different starship patterns. The dock sat a few thousand klicks from the surface, tethered to Calico Base by a long metal girder that glinted in the muted starlight: a space elevator.

"The Spine," I said. "Locals were proud of it, once."

"That didn't work out so well," Mason said. "Whole thing is locked down, so I hear. Only military personnel and cargo can use it now."

"Not that," Kaminski said. His face had grown pale, and I noticed that his hand was shaking as he pointed. "I mean the ship."

The UAS *Colossus* was moored at Calico Base, so big that she filled several berths in the orbital dock. She dwarfed all other ships, her profile and pattern unique.

"I'd heard that she was here," Jenkins said, with more than a hint of annoyance in her voice, "but nothing concrete . . ."

"You need new sources," Mason suggested.

"When the great Keira Jenkins' scuttlebutt is unreliable . . ." - Martinez sucked his teeth - "you know things are FUBAR."

It had been six months since any of us had seen the *Colossus*, and like Calico she had changed since we'd parted ways. We had been through a lot with the old warship. She had almost been put down in Damascus; had suffered debilitating interior and exterior damage. The injury to her left flank – a ripple in the ablative plate – had been enough to puncture one of the engine nacelles, and most of her essential sensor-suites had been critically damaged by the journey through the Shard Gate. I'd heard a rumour that her data-core and stacks – the thinking elements of her AI – had been seized by Science Division. They could refit her, repair her, but she wouldn't be the same ship any more. *And not without Admiral Loeb*, I thought.

"You okay?" Jenkins asked Kaminski.

"All good," he said. "It's just . . . Kind of weird seeing her again."

The *Independence*'s shipboard PA chimed. "All hands, prepare for arrival at Calico Base. All hands, prepare for docking procedure."

I sighed, turned away from the obs window. "Come on, Legion. We better get down there."

"Has James arranged transport?" Mason asked.

"Jesus, girl," Jenkins said, rolling her eyes, "you want to wear that interest any more blatantly? Have some respect."

"Fuck you, Jenkins. I'm not interested in him; I'm only asking."

"We're going down the Spine," I said. "We can get a nice view of Calico Base on the way."

"This day just keeps getting better . . ." Jenkins moaned.

The Legion were given priority disembarkation orders and the docking procedure went as smoothly as could be expected, considering that the space lanes around Calico were choked with starships. We didn't ride alone – a dozen space jockeys from Scorpio Squadron took the cart down with us – but it was a nicer ride than for the rest of the Sim Ops teams. They were assigned to dropships, and subsequently parked in holding patterns in high orbit. Professor Saul and the other prisoners were being held aboard the *Independence*; they would be dropped to the surface once appropriate medical facilities had been secured. Captain Ostrow had stayed with them for the formal debriefing procedure, and I was glad to be temporarily rid of him.

The Spine was a mutant tree searching for sunlight. An enormous structure erupting from Calico Base, metal vertebrae lined by a series of elevator carts: glass-sided, affording a panoramic view over Calico's surface. The Lazarus Legion were sprawled across the insides of the cabin, variously lolling against bulkheads and padded drop-couches.

"No weather, no sunlight, no nothing," Jenkins added.

"That's not quite true," Mason said. She was, tourist-like, pressed up against the armour-glass window: looking out at the approaching city. "They have Spiders."

Beyond the confines of the crater-base, there were small dark figures on Calico's surface. At this distance they looked like spiders crawling on cheese but I knew that was just perspective playing a trick.

"Those, my friends," said Mason, "are Spider mechanised mining rigs – 'MMRs' for short."

"Check out New Girl," Kaminski said. "She's a regular bookworm."

The rigs were actually two or three times the height of a man, just as wide – massive, multi-limbed walking machines used to extract ore from surface seams. Except for the base itself, Calico had only micro-gravity, and the Spiders used their many legs to anchor themselves to the surface.

"Creepy . . ." Martinez whispered. "I don't like them much."

"Me neither," I said.

It so turned out that real spiders were regular survivors, having been transported to most corners of the galaxy by the human race. Arachnids existed in almost all human-friendly environs and stirred the same reaction in most varieties of humanity. As the cart glided towards the terminal, several of the Spiders paused and watched us go. Although I knew that there were men in there – that the mechs were nothing more than strength-amplifiers for the drivers inside – it was easy to believe that they were big arachnids. There were hordes of them, scraping the grey surface of Calico. They were equipped with paired lasers and other industrial operating tools, all mounted on the front of the machine under the cockpit – positioned so that they looked like an open maw. Lots of the machines had graffiti and other personalised logos on the outer hulls.

"Three minutes to touchdown, sir," Lieutenant James said.

There were some sighs from the Scorpio Squadron as the elevator made descent. We were close enough to the surface now to see every detail of the base.

"The hospitals have been busy," Mason whispered.

Vacuum-tents were pitched out on the grey. Huge red crosses – meant to be visible from space – marked most of the structures as infirmary domes. In the distance, just beyond the Alliance base proper, were the refugee camps: of a more haggard and mismatched nature, a patchwork of oxy-tents, shanties and temporary dwellings.

"How many do you think there are down there?" Kaminski asked. His voice was low, sullen. He hadn't been speaking much, I realised.

"Millions," Mason said, "at a guess."

Set on Calico's frozen surface, they were maintained by temporary life-support facilities – leaching off the central heat-sink. Mobs wearing tattered vac-suits had gathered around the base of the military outpost.

"This isn't a nice place for a trooper," James said, absently. "Even the Legion should watch itself down here."

"I'm not scared of your bullshit, James," Jenkins said.

"I'm not bullshitting you, California. Way I hear it this place is on the verge of civil war."

"I do not want to be around when this place goes off," said another of Scorpio Squadron.

James nodded along enthusiastically. "They're saying that the Alliance governor, Tarik Al Kik, is a puppet of Congress. He's trying to broker terms for an increased military garrison, but all the Workers' Union want is better working conditions. That's not easy when the life support is carrying twice the number of colonists this place was designed to hold."

"There was a riot in the industrial sector last month," another pilot said. "The Workers' Union holds a lot of power out here."

"You guys are worse gossips than Jenkins," Martinez said.

There were six million colonists on Calico, and about a million Alliance personnel. Those odds, if they ever became relevant, weren't good.

"This isn't living," I said. "This is surviving."

"Sometimes surviving is good enough," Jenkins responded.

"But fighting is better," Kaminski said.

The Legion fell quiet as the elevator commenced final descent.

The base – a carpet of glowing lights – came up to meet us.

The Spine ended in an enormous terminal; a space with the look and feel of a starport departure lounge. Concession stands lined the walls and glowing advertising holos dominated the domed ceiling, but things weren't right down here. The departures and arrivals board displayed a single message: ALL CIVILIAN TRANSPORTS ARE SUSPENDED UNTIL FURTHER NOTICE. Columns of civilians – from their appearance, not indigenous to Calico – were lined up at the gates for processing.

Kaminski looked daunted by the presence of so many people. Jenkins moved to his side, protectively, but he waved her off.

"I'm good," he said. That was his mantra: as though, if he said those words often enough, they might even become true.

"Do you want us to call a transport to the military sector?" Mason asked. "I'm sure that we won't have to push our way through this mob."

"No need," Martinez said. "Someone leaked that we were coming."

There was a welcome party gathered at the gate: four young officers in Army fatigues, and a clutch of Sci-Div personnel with a grav-stretcher.

"That'd be for you, 'Ski," Martinez said.

Kaminski shook his head. "Fucking science pukes."

"It is my pleasure to welcome you to Calico Base, sir," said the lead Army officer, face beaming with pride. "*Independence* commed us with an update on the prisoner situation."

Another young aide cut in: "Five hundred soldiers, sir? They're saying that it's the biggest haul in military history, since hostilities with the Directorate commenced."

Jenkins sighed and activated her wrist-comp. She frowned as she read the news-cast, and waved it under my nose. LAZARUS LEGION RESCUES FIVE HUNDRED PRISONERS FROM DIRECTORATE PRISON, the headline read. Beneath, there were images of the Legion – all service shots that were years out of date. The story claimed that the Directorate prison had been bombed by the Alliance during a dawn raid, and that it had been declared incompatible with the Geneva Convention.

"Baker isn't going to be happy," she said. "The Boys didn't even get a mention."

"Baker is never happy," I said.

This was the Alliance propaganda machine in full effect, and whether we liked it or not the Lazarus Legion were a key weapon in Psych Ops' armoury. Our names were known throughout Alliance and, increasingly, Directorate space.

"Private Kaminski? Serial code 561892?" the aide asked, reverently, despite being several ranks above that which 'Ski had or ever would achieve. "I'd like to welcome you back to Alliance space. You are due a full medical evaluation; Science Officer Delores here will make you comfortable."

Kaminski grinned at the small brunette beside the stretcher. "Where I come from, that means something completely different . . ."

Jenkins jabbed him in the ribs. "Quit it, Private."

"PFC Dejah Mason; you are also due a full assessment."

Mason rolled her eyes. "Can't a trooper get a break?"

The female science officer ignored her protest, and moved briskly on to me. "I have orders to see to your hand—"

Simultaneously, all five of our wrist-comps chimed with updates as they linked to Calico Base's mainframe.

"Great," Martinez said. "And this is why I prefer field-work . . ."

A series of messages flowed across the small panel mounted on the stub of my left wrist. One update caught my eye, and cancelled out all of the others:

```
*** REMAIN ON STATION ***
ALL OTHER ORDERS ARE RESCINDED WITH
IMMEDIATE EFFECT
LAZARUS LEGION MUST BE READY FOR
REASSIGNMENT AND DEPLOYMENT
```

"You just get the same message?" Jenkins asked me.

"Yeah," I said. "Real cryptic."

"Even me . . ." Kaminski added.

"You're still Legion," Jenkins said.

"Let's get moving," the lead aide interrupted. "If you will all just follow me—"

An MP grunt broke the line and approached the Legion.

"Welcome to Calico Base, Legion," he said, going to salute. "Please submit to security procedures."

"It's fine," the aide said. "The Lazarus Legion doesn't need to be checked."

There were several Mili-Pol on the clearance gate, all armed with short-pattern carbines – security-issue models, M400 kinetics. A couple started to deploy handheld scanners, sweeping the new arrivals.

"Standing orders, ma'am," the MP said. "All incoming personnel to Calico Base have to be checked."

"Check us," Jenkins said in support. "And make sure that you check everyone coming in, whether they want to be or not."

The aide looked hurt as the security detail ran their checks; scanning us and our luggage with negative results.

"You need more dogs," Jenkins muttered, under her breath. "You can never have enough dogs."

An assortment of combat dogs – big, ugly bastards with bionics grafted to their skulls – milled around the terminal. They occasionally stopped to sniff the air; circled around us but took no particular interest. Science Division had found, as a result of our mission in Damascus, that dogs were able to differentiate simulants from real skins. The exact science wasn't yet known, but so far this was the quickest way to detect next-gen and combat-sims.

Just then, James clambered down from the elevator cart.

"Steady!" I shouted. "He's skinned!"

The dogs went berserk: mouths wide and slathering, eyes glossy with rage. Their MP handlers fought to hold them on heavy chain leashes. I was surprised by the vigour of their reaction.

"Aerospace Force Sim Ops," James said, pointing out his shoulder patch. The rest of Scorpio did the same.

"Stand down," the lead officer said.

The security team did their thing, employing DNA scanners over any patch of exposed skin. The machines flickered affirmative reads, and the dogs almost immediately desisted. I guessed that those bionics were direct cranial interfaces – allowed their controllers to somehow alter their behavioural impulses. The dogs became docile, retreated from the sim pilots.

"They didn't work so well with Williams . . ." Martinez said.

"New tech," a handler said. "They won't get past us again. We're supposed to check everything and everyone inbound."

"You find anything yet?" I asked.

He shrugged, tapped his chest. "Not yet, but I'll keep trying. Get me a bonus that'll pay for a nice plot back on Proxima."

There were four oversized playing cards taped to his chest. Each card had a name on it, with a reward figure in bold type beneath. The faces on the cards had become almost as well known as those of the Lazarus Legion.

CAPTAIN LANCE WILLIAMS. Leader of Williams' Warfighters, and the arch-traitor. Now the Ace of Spades.

CORPORAL DIEMTZ OSAKA. Second-in-command to the Warfighters; a big Martian bastard of a man. Now the King of Clubs.

PRIVATE ALICIA MALIKA. Just another soldier in an army of millions. Now the Queen of Diamonds.

PRIVATE REBECCA SPITARI. The Queen of Hearts.

Each card had been annotated with sighting details. Some – particularly those of Osaka and Malika – had been striped with tallies, indicating alleged deaths that associated simulants had suffered. The locations spanned Alliance space, as far as Alpha Centauri and as wide as Barnard's Star.

"It's the gift that keeps on giving," the MP said, making a gun out of his forefinger and thumb. "You kill them, and they just keep coming back."

"Sir," the aide broke in, "an escort has been arranged—"

"I can't even be trusted to get down to Medical on my own now? I'll see to the hand later." I looked back at the team; noted the slightly frenetic expression on Kaminski's face. He needed out of here. "See to the Legion; get them settled."

"Whatever they need," the aide said.

I nodded at Kaminski. "'Ski; go with Delores. No touching." To the aide, I said, "You can help me with some directions. I'm trying to track down an old friend . . ."

We walked together into the main archway that marked the entrance to Calico Base, beneath an enormous security holo that constantly barked the message SUBMIT TO SCANNER SEARCHES ON REQUEST – TERRORISM: TOGETHER WE'LL BEAT IT.

*　　*　　*

I didn't want to spend any more time on Calico Base than was absolutely necessary. The place had changed in the ten years since I'd been here; since I'd seen *Endeavour* and her fleet off into the darkness. All the dusty vaults and tight corridors held for me were ghosts, unfulfilled opportunities.

But I had to do something while I was here; had to salve my conscience. The decision was against my better judgement, because I knew that I would not be able to help – knew that decisions had been taken far above my head – but even so I had to do it. The aide gave me directions, and even arranged an air-car for transport. Then she fucked off exactly as I'd ordered; leaving me alone in the dirty and desperate area of Calico Base. Suited me fine.

This was a prison by any other name. An area to which the dead and dying were relegated, to stop them spreading their pernicious diseases. Except that the diseases here were not physical ailments; the contagion that required quarantining was a mindset. The Alliance, and in particular Command, did not want those stationed here to pollute the rest of the outpost.

A single Military Police guard was posted at a junction.

"Sir," he said, saluting. "This is a restricted area. I can't let you go any further."

"You know who I am, trooper?"

"Yes, sir. You're Lazarus."

"Then you'll know that I have clearance to go wherever I want."

That was, of course, a lie. I was a lieutenant colonel now, and I was Lazarus, but there were restrictions on my movements just the same as with any other trooper. The difference was reputation.

"Of course, sir."

"I'm looking for a particular officer. You know where I can find him?"

I pulled up the details on my wrist-comp, placed it under the MP's nose. His eyes widened a little and he nodded.

"Yes, sir. Cell – I mean room – 11-B. End of this corridor."

A figure sat alone at a desk in the corner of the room, manipulating a tri-D, the glow of the projection dancing over his face.

"Yes?" he yelled, without looking up. "Come to check I'm still breathing? You take away my bloody dog—"

"It's me, Joseph."

Admiral Joseph Loeb, former commanding officer of the UAS *Colossus*, turned to look at me.

The old admiral – the Buzzard, to those crews fortune enough to have served under him – had a rugged, angular face, but his features instantly softened as he saw me. When he smiled, it looked as though he had not done so in a long time: as though the expression was alien to him.

"How the damn are you, old bastard?" he said. "Come in."

Despite everything that had happened – everything that was going to happen – Admiral Loeb still wore his duty uniform: pressed, parade-ground fresh. Chin clean-shaven, greyed hair cut close to his scalp. His service cap sat atop a stack of printed plastic sheets. Just waiting for that call to arms.

"Sit, talk," Loeb said. "As you can probably guess, I don't get many visitors down here."

I looked around the chamber. There was little furniture, and the room was in darkness save for the glow of the ships coming and going outside, visible through the obs window. Loeb cleared the stacks of reading material – hardcopy as well as data-slates – from the small couch, and we took up some seats.

"How have you been holding up?" I asked.

"Well enough," Loeb said. "This is no way for an officer to live, but I'm making do."

Since our return from the Maelstrom, Loeb had been under what the Navy still rather quaintly referred to as "house arrest". He was a man used to travelling on starships – as his gaunt, thin appearance demonstrated. Without a command, without a ship, he was a man without a purpose. This – being planet-bound, confined to a small room – was hell for him.

"I've been keeping up to date on the news," he said. "Watching the casts; there's little else to do in here. Five hundred POWs? That's quite a result."

"The feeds lie, Loeb. There were eighty-three, and some of those didn't make it, but we found Kaminski."

Loeb's face illuminated. "Gaia be praised!" he exclaimed.

"And Saul too," I said. "'Ski is in a better state than the Professor, but they say he's going to make it." I sighed. "I want you to know that I don't blame you, Loeb, and I don't think that Kaminski does, either."

"Is he going to be operational?"

I smiled. Loeb knew Sim Ops well by now: knew that being operational, getting back into the tanks, was all that mattered to a proper operator. "Sci-Div will do their tests and we'll see, but I hope so."

Loeb settled back into his chair. "I have some news of my own: I ship Corewards next month. They've fixed a date for the court-martial."

"That has to be a good thing."

"I'm not sure any more. Is hell any better than purgatory?"

"That's a question for Martinez," I offered.

Command wanted someone on whom they could pin the blame for the Damascus incident, and Loeb was an easy target. He was a spritely sixty-seven Centaurian years – not much older by Earth-standard measurements – and pushing the door on retirement. Hell, he probably only had a few years of desk service left in him.

"Don't be like that," I said. "It could go your way."

Loeb shook his head. "I severely doubt that, Harris. They'll want to make an example of me. They've reassigned the *Colossus*."

The Spine traced a silver thread to the orbital docks and the *Colossus* was clearly visible up there, poking from the metal sheath of the docks. Loeb wiped his hand against the inside of the window, then – as though he'd only just realised that I was watching – quickly drew it back.

"The new captain is a Proximan," Loeb said. "If you can believe it. They've even stripped out all of her original scanner-suites; replaced them with cheap Proxy shit."

While I had no particular animosity towards the descendants of Proxima Centauri, Loeb was an Alpha Centaurian. There was rivalry between the sons of those two colonies: each claiming that the other was inferior in some respect. The idea of a Proximan – even a Proximan American – manning the *Colossus* clearly had Loeb riled.

"What's this?" I asked, pointing to a stack of printed plastic sheets on the desk in the corner. I was trying to change the subject. "Looks like some good tribunal prep."

There were schematics, maps, photographs. The stack fell open on a particular image; a low-res, tri-D capture of a woman's face. Her features were a mass of miscellaneous scars; some recent and blotchy, others angular and almost ritualistic. Like a cancer, a black network of veins seethed beneath the skin of her left cheek: moving with a life of its own. Her black hair was cut short, an arc of metal studs reaching her temples. Strangely, she seemed almost impossible to age; her features so unusual.

"It's research," Loeb said. "Quite a looker, isn't she? Reminds me a lot of my ex-wife. She's the commanding officer of the *Shanghai Remembered*."

The *Shanghai Remembered* had been the flagship of the Directorate fleet sent to intercept us at the Damascus Rift. That explained the weird black shit beneath her skin: the result of a symbiotic graft with her starship. She felt everything that her ship felt, could react faster and with greater efficacy: was equipped with a full range of in-head comms apparatus. She wasn't quite human, and yet so much more – an engineered soldier, created for a purpose.

"She's a clone," Loeb said. "But she's not like the line troops. She's worse: a custom-made job, sanctioned by the Executive." He scowled. "Her name is Director-Admiral Kyung, but they call her the Assassin of Thebe . . ."

Loeb's voice trailed off, and he suddenly seemed a very long way away.

I was alone. I felt my hand trembling, the shake in my chest that told me I needed a drink, and needed one *now*. Thebe was a moon of Jupiter: a world many, many light-years from Calico Star. A world that had once housed an Alliance science station known as Jupiter Outpost . . .

"What's wrong?" Loeb asked.

"She was at Thebe . . ." I whispered. A heady mix of hate and remorse welled within me.

"That's what I just said. A lot older than she looks, that one, and the *Shanghai* has been refitted more times than I'd care to say . . . But it's the same ship. Scuttlebutt is that the *Shanghai* made it back from Damascus," Loeb said, quietly, conspiratorially. "And if your man, Kaminski, came back as well: that confirms it. The ship is still out there."

Maybe it was a coincidence that the *Shanghai* had been dispatched by the Directorate to take us on in Damascus. Odds should've been that time-dilation, and the distances involved, threw Kyung and I to different fates: to paths that would never dissect.

"Except that God doesn't do coincidences . . ." I whispered.

Not my words, but Martinez's. They seemed to have taken on some significant import: looking at the stylised globe that represented Jupiter Outpost, at the campaign badge worn by the Assassin of Thebe's crew.

I stood from the couch, abruptly. "I have to be going. I'm expected in Medical."

"Good to see you, Harris," Loeb said. "Take care."

"And you," I said, and I turned to leave: Kyung's mutilated face scorchingly precise in my mind's eye.

CHAPTER SEVEN

WHEN THE WAR'S DONE

Almost as soon as I'd left Loeb's quarters, I was apprehended by two fully decked MPs.

"Are you lost, sir?" the lead trooper asked. Both wore imposing black flak-suits that completely covered them. The helmet visor was flipped shut, making their appearance a mystery. "The infirmary is in Sector Ninety-Eight."

I doubted that these two had found me by chance. They were probably watching my movement via the security systems; via the surveillance drones that populated the tunnel junctions.

"I was just on my way," I lied. I'd been intending to catch a drink, to do something to blot out Loeb's disclosure about Kyung.

The lead MP tapped his shoulder badge. "I'm Sergeant Nico, part of base security. Dr Hunt is waiting for you in the Medical Sector. The elevator shaft is the quickest way down there."

"This way, sir," the other trooper said. He was much bigger than his colleague; a hulk of a man.

"Let's walk," I said. "I could do with the exercise. Dr Hunt can wait."

"Yeah, man, sure," the trooper said.

Calico's main infirmary was filled with a mixture of personnel: military – Army, Navy, and lots of maintenance crews – but just as many mining staff. They sat in despondent groups in the concourses, always in their vac-suits; crowded the corridors.

"Move aside, citizen," the MP from my escort said. "We've got a genuine VIP coming through."

He nudged his carbine into the chest of a miner who had blocked our passage. The civvie stood aside, but I could feel his eyes boring into the back of my head as we passed.

"These guys never learn," the other trooper said. "Dumb fucks. Always getting caught in rockfalls . . ."

I saw a lot of crush and impact injuries. I guessed that this was a common ailment among the miners – a risk that had to be managed but couldn't be eliminated.

"Hey, Nico," I said. "You want to take it down a level? We're guests here, and I'm sure that these people don't take kindly to me queue-jumping."

"Yeah, sir. Sorry."

A small man in a white coat pushed in our direction. He carried himself with an air of certainty that suggested he was in charge down here, and his name-tag – DR HUNT: CHIEF MEDICAL OFFICER – confirmed it. He read from a data-slate, continually running a hand through his bright blond hair. I didn't know the man, but remembered that *Liberty Point*'s last chief medico had told me a new recruit was due to take his place.

"I guess that you must be Dr Viscarri's successor?" I asked.

"Hmmm," he answered. When he looked up, he appeared almost angered by our presence. "I've been chief medico for over two years."

"I've been away," I said.

"Command has sent orders for a refit," Nico said. "This is Colonel Harris."

Hunt shook his head. "We already have one of your troopers down here."

"That'd be Private Kaminski," I said. "How's he doing?"

"Hmmm," Hunt said, commencing to read from the data-slate. "He's got elevated neural readings and the data-port in his right forearm might need replacing. After what he's been through, he'll need a full psych-eval. All tests. He's not getting certified before I can look at his results."

"But he will be," I said, forcefully.

"He's broken," Hunt said with a shrug. "Just like you. Come this way, and we'll talk about that hand."

Hunt led the way to a quieter area of the infirmary, away from the civilian crowds.

"You're lucky that Alliance forces fell back to Calico," he said. "While this facility doesn't have a regeneration pod, it does have an extensive supply of cybernetics. In reality, I doubt that a man of your age and disposition would survive a week in a regen pod: with a blood pressure like yours, it'd be a risky proposition. There's every prospect that you'd develop an immune reaction. You could end up with a failed graft."

"Thanks for the vote of confidence."

"Just saying it like it is. But there is an alternative. The miners here; they aren't exactly a careful bunch. This is the safest course."

A female medtech wheeled a table into the room. A glass

tube sat on top, and inside was a metal hand, tapering in a trail of bio-organic cabling. The digits were multi-jointed but crude, whereas the upper limb was graphite-coated and armoured.

"It's a combat model," Hunt said. "Made from a reinforced plastic-titanium compound. The grip response is far improved over your original model."

"My real hand?"

"Your real hand," Hunt said back at me. "I know that it's not pretty, and it won't win you any friends, but it's one of the better military models." Without waiting for my consent to operate, he added, "Do you want to use the auto-doc for the surgery, or for me to arrange a surgeon to do it manually?"

"Manually. I prefer the old ways."

"Why did I already know the answer to that question?" Hunt grumbled. "This really would be easier if you'd trust the damned machine instead."

"I have a problem with auto-docs."

Just over six hours later, I was awake on a treatment couch with my new bionic hand attached. The neural rethread was done via a nanite injection, which was the easiest part of the process, and I was asleep through the rest: the reweaving of titanium-composite grafts to the existing bone network, the reconnection of the surviving nerves. I felt groggy from the anaesthetic, but it was a fast-acting version and I knew that I'd be up and about within minutes.

I examined the hand. A complex arrangement of attenuators and semi-concealed hydraulics, the exposed metalwork glimmering softly under the treatment-room lights. It's amazing the number of individual bones, the variety of muscles, in the human hand: each of those natural occurrences had now been replaced by a man-made alternative. Palm up, I clenched the hand and watched the fingers move. The action caused an involuntary wave of revulsion in me. No matter how advanced the appendage was, it was still foreign. Not my own.

Dr Hunt swept into the room, the female tech chasing after him.

"Up already?" he asked. "Surely that wasn't so bad, eh? I bet you wish that you had come to see us sooner."

I sighed and said nothing.

He went on, "You'll need to take it easy for a while and you'll need to get to know that hand. It'll be easy to over-grasp to begin with. You won't know your own strength."

"Don't go shaking anyone's hand," the medtech said, dryly. "Or anything else."

"It'll take several months to bed in," Hunt insisted. He prodded the line where flesh met metal with the tip of his pen. I could feel where the item touched flesh, but not where it contacted the prosthetic. "I'm ordering limited use of the hand to begin with."

I flexed the hand again, noted the delay in response time. It felt clumsy. The physical operation was only one half of the undertaking: there was also a lot going on under the hood. Medical nanotech worked on the inside; fusing neural pathways to enable my nerve impulses to be interpreted by the new hand. The nanites were self-assembling an electrode array inside me, and I knew that over time their integration with my body would improve.

"It'll get better," Hunt said. "Try light, simple activity at first; the more regularly you use it, the faster it will become. We run twice-weekly sessions down in the Bionics department. Lots of veterans attend – they can teach you some useful exercises."

"Looks like it'll have to do," I said.

Hunt's face softened a little. Not so much that I'd venture that I liked the man, but enough to let me know that he was human. "You ever think about taking some downtime?"

"No," I said, brusquely. "I have too much to do. There's a war to fight, Doctor."

"And don't I know it. I'm not talking about removing you from operational duty. Perhaps taking a rear post for a while."

"Become a REMF?"

"That's what you troopers call them, isn't it? 'Rear echelon motherfuckers'?"

I nodded. "I'm no REMF."

"Maybe a few months running a battalion administratively, watching the war from the sidelines, might be a good idea. You're a colonel now, Harris. Colonels don't go to war on the frontline, last I checked."

"This colonel does," I said. "I'm Sim Ops, and I'm Lazarus Legion."

Hunt sighed. It was the sound of a man used to giving advice, but in the knowledge that it would be ignored. "I know all about Lazarus Legion, and I know about Dr Marceau. Your story has become more than common knowledge." He turned the data-slate to me; showed me what he'd been reading. LAZARUS LEGION LIBERATES A THOUSAND PRISONERS FROM DIRECTORATE LABOUR CAMP, the headline read. "I won't remove your certification, Harris, because people out here need someone to believe in."

"So what's your point?" I said, swinging my legs off the end of the bed, readying to end the conversation.

"You're burnt out. This is a young man's game, and you're not getting any younger."

"So people keep telling me. Look, all I need to know is can I get back in the field?"

"You keep getting into the tank, sooner or later you're not going to be coming out. It's as simple as that." He paused, meaningfully, tightened his lips. "The results of your most recent medical examinations aren't good. We're talking synaptic damage – extensive – and degradation of the tissue around your spinal port."

"Then put a new one in," I said. "That's not a problem. I just need you to recertify me and my team. All of us."

"Private Kaminski?"

I nodded.

"By my oath as a doctor, I should medically discharge him. The Directorate have put so much metal in his head there isn't room for much else in there."

There wasn't much in the first place, I thought to myself.

"You can take it out," I said. "He's an essential member of the Legion."

"He needs a long-term psych-eval, and even more than you he qualifies for some shore-leave."

"But you *will* recertify him," I said. My tone made it plain that this was not a question: that I expected Kaminski to be back on the force. "We look after our own." I looked to the data-slate in front of Dr Hunt: at the glowing icon that said CERTIFICATION: YES/NO. "I just need your bio-print on the dotted line, and I'll be getting out of your hair."

For a fraught second, I thought that he might press the NO icon, but just as he seemed to veer in that direction he keyed YES.

"I'm doing this because Viscarri told me that you were a good operator. I'm doing this because I want to leave this shit-forsaken outpost . . . But I'm serious about one thing.

You'll need to let that new hand bed in. Nothing strenuous for at least six weeks, while the nerve-connectors do their thing."

"I'll be careful."

"I mean it!" Hunt rebuked. "You could cause serious damage to the remaining skeletal-muscular structure, and I doubt that a man of your age can take another implant—"

"I'll rest when the war's done, Hunt."

"I think that your rest will come a lot sooner than that," Hunt said. "Gaia's praises be on you."

Dejah Mason was waiting for me in the room outside. A couple of miner kids, dressed in diminutive orange vac-suits plastered with a combination of corporate badges and religious iconography, chased around her feet. She flipped them a credit chip, tousling their hair. When they saw me approaching, with my metal hand, their eyes went wide and they both scrammed towards their waiting mother.

Mason smiled. "That new hand has some benefits, at least."

"You were recertified, I take it?" I said.

She activated her wrist-comp and waved it in my direction. "Borderline test results, but they'll do. I would've asked for a certificate, but I guess they were all out." Mason's eyes narrowed. "And Kaminski too, surprisingly. They said that he's going to be fine, that he can get back in the tanks whenever he wants."

"Good," I said.

"He seems happy with the decision. Did you have anything to do with it?"

I ignored the question. "Let's move. I don't like it down here."

"What's to like?" Mason said. "Colonists, injured servicemen, whining kids . . . Where are you headed now, sir?"

"Thought I'd go and get a drink," I said. "I can't do much else, what with this 'remain on-station' order in effect. Care to join me?"

Mason sighed. "No thanks, sir. I'm going to ring home—"

My wrist-comp chimed, noisily. The screen filled with a priority alert. This was the first time I'd ever received such a message.

```
*** ORDERS *** ORDERS *** ORDERS ***
EYES ONLY
REPORT TO COMMAND SECTOR FORTHWITH
IMMEDIATE ATTENDANCE REQUIRED
```

"Christo, they don't mess around out here!" Mason said.

"There's a war going on," I said. "No time to waste."

"Good luck," Mason called after me, as I hailed a transport.

The Command Sector was located on the outer edge of Calico Base. It was the current centre of tactical operations in the region: the beating heart of the war effort. Admin staff hurriedly dashed between their posts, jostling stacks of paperwork and data-slates. Officers were plugged to holo-consoles, plotting troop dispositions. Sci-Div xeno-specialists argued with tacticians over potential Krell invasion patterns.

Two MPs met me at the security entrance and I noted with amusement that they had been my escort from earlier in the day.

"Not hassling any dumbshit colonists this afternoon, Private Nico?"

"No, sir," Nico said, through his speaker grille. "Better things to do this shift."

"Good."

The second MP guarded the main gate through to the command chambers. He held out a gloved hand.

"Sidearm, sir," he said.

"Is that necessary?"

"Sorry. Regulations. Only MPs are allowed to carry weapons in the Command Sector."

I unholstered my sidearm from the webbing on my chest. It was my only weapon, but it wasn't much of one: a standard Berringer M-5. I felt a twinge of uncertainty as I removed the gun, but overrode the impulse and handed it over. That was what I'd become – hardwired to expect the worst. The idea of being unarmed *ever* . . . It felt uncomfortably alien to me. The big MP didn't seem to notice my reaction and placed the handgun into a lockbox beside the security arch.

"Your appointment is through here," Nico said. "Follow me."

The room had been converted into a dining hall appropriate for the senior officer cadre: several tables meticulously laid with metal cutlery, real ceramic plates and napkins. There were even stirrups to anchor the tableware, in the event of the loss of gravity – a layover from when Calico Base's gravity generator was less dependable. The empty lunar plains were visible through the windows that claimed one wall, and in a glorious display of bad taste an enormous fish tank occupied the opposite aspect: replete with multi-coloured aquatic life-forms that reminded me a little too much of the Krell.

An aide met me at the door, feet seeming to slide across the carpet as though he'd made a profession of moving around senior officers without causing disruption. *What a skill for a soldier to have*, I thought.

"This way, sir," he said, leading me across the chamber.

Although the dining hall could probably accommodate a hundred personnel, there was only a handful of occupants. Several fully uniformed senior officers were sitting around a single table. The scent of proper hot food lingered in the air; the clatter of cutlery against plates. As I reached the table, proceedings paused. Eight pairs of eyes stared up at me. The brass evaluated me, and I could almost see the gears working behind their ancient eyes. Asking whether I was really the legend about which they'd heard so much, or whether they'd been sold a lie.

As they assessed me, I did the same to them: asked myself whether I had any allies in here. I found one possibility at the head of the table: General Mohammed Cole, looking every bit as exhausted as the last time that I'd seen him. That had been two years ago, during my briefing for the Damascus mission. Now he wore his formal uniform, but it was skewed and he looked uncomfortable in it.

The other occupants of the table were from a variety of military branches. Two Army, two Navy, a Marine, a Military Intelligence officer and a Science Division representative. All were high ranking, their uniforms carrying the insignia of generals, admirals, commandants, chief science officer. I swallowed. Realisation dawned on me. Faces and names tumbled through my memory: I knew these people, had seen their likeness on numerous military bulletins and holo-feeds.

What have I walked into?

The brass said nothing, because they didn't need to. This wasn't a normal briefing. This was High Command: the apex of the decision-making tree for the war. As I stared into the face of Command, I wished that I had come better prepared. For a grunt like me, it was like staring into the face of God.

"Welcome to this special assembly of the Council of War," one of the officers grumbled. To the aide: "Thomas, commence recording and ensure that the door remains locked."

"Of course," the aide replied.

"Do sit, Colonel," came a voice from the table.

The speaker was an elderly male dressed in the long white smock of a Science Division officer. He waved at the aide, who had appeared ghost-like at my shoulder.

"Serve the colonel some food," the Sci-Div officer said, adopting the persona of a kindly old man, his quaffed silver hair falling in strands over his balding scalp. "Calico might not be known for its delicatessens, but this is mostly imported. The steak is really quite good."

I was too stunned to turn down the offer of food, and, although I didn't see what, the aide served me with something. Everyone else sat over plates of steamed meat and vegetables. Not substitutes, by the smell, but real food. Given that food was fast becoming a scarce commodity, acquiring anything that wasn't out of a ration-pack was an impressive feat.

"You don't need to know everyone's name," Cole said gruffly, "because several of High Command are here in a purely observational capacity." He glared around the table, and a few of the attendees shrank back, obviously primed that they would take no part in the discussion at hand. It seemed that not all members of Command were created equal. "I'll introduce those that matter." He pointed out the science officer. "Dr Storemberg, head of Science Division."

With my track record for destroying Artefacts and Shard tech, I predicted that there would be friction here, but Storemberg gave a restrained nod and said, "It is a pleasure to finally meet you, Colonel. I am most grateful that you managed to retrieve Professor Ashan Saul from the hands of the Directorate." His smile hardened. "His presence will be important to the war effort in the coming days."

Cole pointed across the table at the next officer. "Fleet Admiral Sunsam."

Sunsam was a bona fide five-star Naval officer, and the chest of his Naval dress uniform was weighed down with a plethora of medals and other rank insignia. He'd been recruited from Azure, had been in service when I'd lived on that planet. This man alone commanded sufficient firepower to obliterate most of the Milky Way Galaxy. He said nothing in greeting.

"Commandant of the Marine Corps," Cole said, "General Leonovich."

Leonovich was middle-aged with a bad haircut, maybe in the fashion of the moment for whatever Core World she'd crawled from. She was smoking, ethereal swirls rising from an ashtray in front of her.

"Good evening, Colonel," she said. "I too am glad to meet with you."

Cole waved a hand at the rest of the gathered personnel. "I'll introduce you to the others as necessary. As I said, many of our members are here to listen rather than participate."

"Understood, sir," I said.

"We have been reviewing your recent debrief material," Dr Storemberg said. He spoke with a Germanic lilt, his intonation difficult to follow. "What happened in Damascus Space has us all very concerned. Would you say that the operation was a success, Colonel?"

"No," I said. "I would not. There are numerous intelligence leads that remain live."

"You mean the discovery of the *Endeavour*?"

Just mention of the name set me on edge. "Yes, sir."

Leonovich leant forward, feeding herself a sugar beet from her plate. "What you found in Damascus – what you did there – might be the key to ending this war."

"And that is why we have called you here today," Cole suddenly broke in. "You're obviously aware of the loss of *Liberty Point*; and you know that it went down due to a Krell war-fleet."

A holographic projection sprang to life in the middle of the table. It was a bizarre effect; cutting through plates of steamed vegetables and rapidly cooling meats. Military aides jumped from their hiding places around the dining hall and quickly moved aside the plates.

"This incursion," Admiral Sunsam picked up, "is the end of things. The end of us."

There was silence as all parties absorbed the imagery. What the map showed was far worse than we'd encountered during the First Krell War: the Krell were moving in a ragged mob – disorganised, unpredictable – into Alliance systems. As the animation progressed, glowing markers disappeared beneath the tidal wave. Each represented an outpost, a world, a star system: billions of lives lost to the Krell.

"This map demonstrates the movement of Krell forces across the Quarantine Zone," he said. "As you can see, we have lost substantial territories in the Van Diem Straits and several star systems bordering the Asiatic Rim. The Krell seem to be attacking in far greater numbers, with greater ferocity, than was previously the case. They have no clear line of attack. This has made anticipating their advance difficult. Impossible even, in some instances."

"That," Dr Storemberg said, "and the obvious fact that the Krell seem to be evolving at a hitherto unknown rate.

Their ships are becoming faster, their ground troops more resilient, their weapons more effective."

I'd been a first-hand witness to that. There had been a time when the hulking tertiary-forms were a rarity – employed only when the Collective needed a hammer to shatter resistance. Now, as on Capa V, they were appearing with most Collectives.

"We have even received unconfirmed reports of so-called 'quaternary-forms'," Storemberg said. "Quite what they are evolving into, and why, is anyone's guess." He shrugged. "For another time, perhaps."

Markers shifted across the map. Red represented Krell forces, and green Alliance. Calico sat on the new frontline; probably just months away from the Krell advance.

"Putting it bluntly, we don't have sufficient forces to repel them," Sunsam said. "We've already evacuated several of the more remote listening posts, and we have started moving non-essential personnel back to the Core." He sounded less than happy about that. "All available resources are being fed into the war effort. As I'm sure that you can appreciate, Colonel, time-dilation is a significant issue when synchronising an operation of this scale."

"There are additional, political considerations as well," Storemberg said. "I am, technically, a citizen of the nation-state once known as Germany, a constituent of the European Confederacy." He tilted his head. "Of course, my family connections are with Tau Ceti, but that is hardly the point. You may be aware that certain elements within the Alliance wish for another peace treaty. The Confederacy has been most vocal in expressing this intention. There is much discussion in Congress as to the possibility."

Cole sighed and shook his head. "It's tearing the Alliance apart, Harris. This war is fracturing what we have left, and the politicos and pen-pushers can't decide on our response."

"So I'd heard," I said. It was hard not to pick up on these things; the civilian news-feeds were filled with hackneyed opinions on the Alliance's continued viability in the face of the Krell threat.

"Here we are," Leonovich said, sucking hard on her cigarette, "facing extinction – or some reasonable facsimile of it – and all we can do is argue."

Storemberg gave that saccharine smile again. "Such it is now, such has it always been. General Cole has touched on the loss of *Liberty Point*, and the Krell's involvement, but what else do you know?"

"Only that it was destroyed by the Krell," I said.

"And?" Storemberg probed.

"I hear a lot, Doctor. Not all of it is reliable."

Cole cut to the chase. "The Asiatic Directorate appear to have launched a raid on *Liberty Point* in the hours before it went down. They had people inside our structure. We've been compromised, and with access to the Next-Gen Project, they could be anywhere."

I was hardly surprised by any of this. Rumours were rife as to Directorate involvement, but it was the sort of scuttle-butt Jenkins peddled and none of it had been officially confirmed. The idea that the Directorate had somehow caused, or encouraged, the fall of *Liberty* was certainly consistent with their actions at Damascus.

One of the unnamed Military Intelligence officers slipped a plastic sheath from an envelope, slid it across the table in front of me.

"You've probably heard of Director-Admiral Kyung," he said. "The so-called 'Assassin of Thebe'."

It was a moving tri-D image; a long-distance spy-cam shot of Kyung, taken from some unidentified warzone. The woman wore full ghost-plate, specially adapted anti-detection armour. I noticed that her face was marble-like, features unblemished. Whatever had caused the horrific scarring to her face – as I'd seen from Loeb's files – must have happened recently.

"It has been confirmed by multiple intelligence sources that Kyung is currently working with the Swords of the South Chino Stars," the Mili-Intel officer said. "She heads their Xeno-Tech Acquisitions Division." He looked over at me, eyes fixed on mine with peculiar intensity. "She was Dr Kellerman's handler on Helios, Colonel. She orchestrated the attacks in Damascus. The attack on *Liberty Point*? We believe that was her doing as well."

"It started with Thebe," Storemberg said, "but if this woman gets her way – if the Directorate gets its way – then she will see the Alliance burn."

Did they know? I wondered. My connection to Kyung was far more personal than any of this. The imagery on the holo-desk shifted. Displayed something bone-chillingly familiar, something that I hadn't seen for a very long time. *The Shard Key.* A tri-D graphic, spinning, analytical data scrolling alongside.

"We have unconfirmed, largely anecdotal, reports that the Directorate may have seized the Key from Damascus," another anonymous officer said. "Quite how that is possible," he continued, shrugging, "is currently unknown. The cost in blood must've been phenomenal."

Another officer leant across the table. "To think of it: you've beaten Kyung the Assassin twice now, without even knowing it. That's quite some achievement, Colonel."

Cole snorted. "Although it's not much to be proud of. She's purpose-built, a slave-organism, and her kind don't take kindly to failure. We've multiple reports that she has been driven to the edge of insanity."

The Mili-Intel man nodded. The ghost of a smirk played on the corner of his lips, as though he found it funny that the pinnacle of Directorate bio-tech could experience madness. "The official line is that she has overstepped her authority within the Directorate, that she's gone rogue. Notwithstanding what the diplomats have to say, we believe that she is in fact acting with the full authority of Director-General Zhang himself."

The backing of the most powerful man in human space, I considered. *That's some currency.*

"You said that the Assassin was linked to the Massacre of *Liberty Point*," I said. "How so?"

"An intelligence package was due to be delivered to Mili-Intel in the hours leading up to the fall of *Liberty Point*," said Dr Storemberg.

"Are you telling me that the Directorate were after this intelligence package?" I asked, putting the pieces together for myself. "That this was the reason for their attack on the *Point*?"

Cole nodded. "That's exactly what we're saying."

"I'd be very interested in knowing what was worth that loss," I said, without thinking about my words.

Cole just laughed. It was an expression about as pleasant as Storemberg's smile. "I'd say that it was worth it," he said.

Ah shit.

A lance of hope speared me, and I felt my pulse beginning to race.

"It's the whereabouts of the *Endeavour*, isn't it?" I asked.

"We would probably have figured it out anyway," Storemberg said, between mouthfuls of steak. His knife noisily scraped across the ceramic plate, pulled me back to reality. "The UAS *Colossus* has been thoroughly examined by our technical teams, and her data-core has been of specific interest."

"Although it wasn't exactly easy," Cole said, "because it appears that the journey through the Shard Gate caused significant electromagnetic damage to several of the flight systems."

"Loeb did tell me," I said. "More than once."

"This will be your greatest gift to the war," Storemberg said. "You have discovered a network of gateways that will allow instantaneous travel between the stars. It will allow us, given the appropriate access to the Shard Network, to stab into the very heart of the Krell Empire."

"Which is exactly what we are going to do," Sunsam said.

The map shifted again, green indicators popping up as a tide of Alliance Navy assets sailed in from the Core Systems. Despite myself – despite the revelation that I could actually *Christo-damned follow Elena!* – the soldier in me was excited by the plan. My mechanical hand clamped shut, noisily, as the animation progressed. The Navy moved through the old QZ, jumping through flashing icons that I assumed represented Shard Gates: other relics left over by the machines when they had abandoned the Maelstrom.

"This will be the largest counter-attack that we can muster," Sunsam said. He was smiling, the jittering light of the tri-D throwing his unhandsome face into a strange rictus. "We will destroy the Krell once and for all."

"How does the *Endeavour* fit into this?" I asked.

"We'll get to that," said Storemberg.

"From what data we could recover, we've been able to plot the course trajectory – which has allowed us to see exactly where the *Colossus* went," Cole said. "By triangulating the acquired military intelligence package with the flight path taken by the *Colossus*, we've been able to pinpoint the coordinates of the *Endeavour*."

Finally. This was the biggest, most certain breakthrough

that I'd ever been privy to. Elena was still out there, and now we had the data to follow her.

"This is probably the single most important mission of the war," Cole interrupted. "You need to know what is at stake here; that you simply cannot fail to do what we are about to task you with. This attack will not succeed unless we have some assistance."

In the distance, somewhere out in the corridor, a dog began to bark.

CHAPTER EIGHT

CHAOS BREEDS

The room was quiet and still, and the dog's lonely howl cut through the background hum of the air-recycler.

Where have the serving staff gone? Previously so attentive, they were nowhere to be seen. *And only the security force on Calico have dogs . . .*

"To answer your question," Cole said, "as to how the *Endeavour* fits into this . . ."

His words trailed off and he frowned at me, aware of my change in presentation, misunderstanding the reason for my alert status. The rest of High Command were oblivious. Leonovich sipped at her glass of red white; Storemberg sat with a ceramic coffee cup poised between both hands, tendrils of steam climbing up his face.

They were all old, too damned old.

All caught in time.

Frozen.

About to be shattered.

The two Military Police officers – Nico and his associate – circled the table. Both were still dressed head-to-toe in their flak-suits, completely anonymous. Nico moved behind Cole, the other beside me.

Where did the MPs come from?

The dog barked on and on and on . . .

The MP behind Cole started to speak. "We're experiencing a security alert, sir," he said. "For your safety, this room will be going into lockdown."

But Sergeant Nico's words didn't fit his actions. He had something in his gloved hands: a spider-web cord, so thin that it was only visible by the light that it reflected. Drawn tight. Ready for use.

Mono-filament, a memory screamed to me. *A garrotte.*

The storm was about to break.

"Down!" I yelled at Cole.

The MP behind him moved inhumanly fast.

The cord was over Cole's head in a heartbeat – now frightening visible against the flesh of his neck, just above his collar. The general reacted in slow motion, hands to his neck. His expression still spoke of a minor inconvenience – the temporary interruption of an important briefing – rather than what this was: an assassination. The mono-filament made a tiny sound – a sickening *click* – as it sliced through the tips of his right index and forefinger. When it met his neck, the wire glowed red with blood. Gore splattered the tablecloth and the plates, sprayed across the face of the nearest MI officer. All in silence: happening too fast for any of them to respond.

Cole – general of the Alliance Army, commanding officer of the combined military forces ranged against the Krell Empire – was *out*. Not just extracted, but really dead.

Every molecule of my tired body screamed to me that I had to *move move move!*

The tall MP beside me had a pistol in his hands. The

barrel was extended, fitted with a silencer. He aimed the pistol at me—

Assassination. Planned. Directorate. Here.

No time to think.

I arched my back, knees against the edge of the table. My chair toppled backwards, and I went with it: away from the weapon's arc. I rapidly considered the gun's capability. A kinetic, a semi-automatic service pistol. Limited range and clip size, but at this range – and in my real skin – as lethal as a nuke.

The traitor-MP fired. Three shots, just to be sure. *Phut-phut-phut.*

Missing me, the volley of shots stitched Leonovich's body. She looked surprised as her chest ruptured across the table, and she too pitched forward.

I scanned the room in a split second. Considered possible escape routes, potential cover, items that I could use as a weapon.

Weapon. Need weapon.

My holster was an empty weight across my chest; useless. The MPs – whoever they really were – had taken my pistol on the way in.

"Oh dear . . ." Storemberg said.

The pistol fired again, and Storemberg was ended. He collapsed, arms sprawled over the table, sending tableware crashing. The remains of his plate went the same way: meat rind, gravy, his fork and—

Knife.

I lurched for it. The dead scientist was to my left, and I swiped with my bionic hand—

Delay. Not my hand.

The metal fingers closed around the hilt of the knife. It was a silver steak knife, the blade slightly serrated.

Certainly no mono-knife, not powered, but it would have to do.

Cole crashed. Almost decapitated by the mono-filament garrotte, he slid back into his chair. Blood bubbled at the slit in his throat and he let out a gasp: the autonomic expulsion of air from deceased lungs. The MP threw the used mono-filament to the floor, and swung an M400 carbine from over his shoulder. Unlike the pistol, this was a proper weapon.

Got to get out of here.

The door was metres away from me – sealed, the red MEETING IN PROGRESS lock flashing.

"Pl . . . please no!" an officer wearing Military Intelligence uniform stammered.

"Yeah, man," the MP who had just killed Cole said over his suit speaker. His voice reminded me of someone's, but I couldn't quite remember whose. "Just a security issue."

The officer – a man whom Cole hadn't even named – threw his hands up to his face. "I know things!"

"Sure you do. Just not enough."

A horrifying, precise calm descended over me.

I rose from my crouch. Less than a metre from the nearest MP, I flipped the knife blade down. Felt the motors of the bionic hand flex. The knife handle deformed with the force of my grip. I recalled Dr Hunt's words: "You won't know your own strength."

Let's hope.

Metal trays and cutlery clattered to the floor. Another of the female officers started screaming, pushing back across the room. It would do no good. These people were used to fighting wars on view-screens, hiding behind those with dirty hands. Well, I was the man with dirty hands, and I wasn't going to die in here. Not while Elena and the *Endeavour* waited in the Maelstrom.

The bigger MP had his pistol up and was already shooting across the room: picking off the stunned officers. He fired again and again. Every shot hit a target. Bodies bloomed like red flowers.

I doubted that I could measure my continued existence in much more than seconds. I had to think fast. There was a seam between flak-plates on the soldier's thigh. The suit was meant to protect the wearer from frag and debris, and I reckoned that a cutting edge would pierce it. I aimed there in the hope that it was the weakest point. A downward stabbing motion.

The blade sank into the MP's leg.

I heard the servos of the bionic hand whining, and planted the knife with all of my strength. Blood welled from between the flak-plates.

The MP let out a gut-wrenching yelp.

"He fucking shanked me!" he yelled. He spoke with a deep Martian burr; the accent of a Marina Valley low-lander. "Lazarus got me!"

Which meant . . .?

"Didn't I tell you to do him first?" said the Nico MP.

The injured MP stumbled back, dropped his pistol. Both hands were to his leg, clutched around the shattered hilt of the steak knife.

"I'm bleeding out!" he yelped. He dragged his leg back with him, away from the table, crimson dripping freely from the wound. I hoped that I'd hit an artery, but doubted that I'd be so lucky.

"Quit making such a meal out of it," said Nico. Nice to see that the murderer still had a sense of humour. "I'll see to it."

"No! I can get it out—"

"You started this with the malfunctioning collar, Corporal."

Nico discharged the carbine. A single round punched through the second MP's head, his helmet no protection at this range. The contents of his skull made a quick evacuation, plastering a nearby table, and he crumpled to the floor.

I'd finally placed that voice.

Captain Lance Williams.

I reached several conclusions from what had happened. None of them good, all of them terrifying. The Directorate had a simulant-farm – a facility to produce more sims for Williams' Warfighters. There were none left, that I knew of, from the *Colossus*. I'd destroyed most of the Warfighter's skins myself, and the remainder had been seized by Military Intelligence.

And yet here Williams is.

High Command: Cole, Storemberg, Leonovich – every other non-combatant asshole who had directed this war from start to finish? They were all dead. Gone. Snubbed out. Really dead. The will to survive drove me on; stopped me from dwelling on that fact and the implications that flowed from it.

Williams brazenly unclipped the lower portion of his face-mask, let his respirator dangle loose at his throat. He looked exactly the same as when I'd seen him last, down to the sprinkling of blond stubble on his chin. Exactly as he did on the playing card at the immigration gate. Service record clean.

The Ace of Spades.

He was using a next-gen simulant – a copy of his real body – rather than a combat-sim. A combat-sim was physically much bigger, wouldn't be passable for a normal human. A next-gen sim would've been much more difficult to detect;

suited up, he would be almost undetectable. What about the security dogs?

"Long time no see, man," Williams said.

"Not long enough," I said. "I killed you once, and I can do it again."

"You got lucky, was all," Williams said, setting his jaw.

The next-gen sim moved fast. Carbine up, fire stitched the room. Cutlery, plates and other irrelevant shit was scattered. I darted beneath a nearby table, the carpet igniting behind me. I was now reasonably sure that the second MP – the bigger, stockier one – had been the Martian.

Diemtz Osaka: the King of Clubs—

He had a gun, I remembered.

His service pistol lay beside his body. Though it was only three metres away, it might as well have been back in the Core. It was an M4 – a peashooter – but a damn sight better than no gun at all.

Moving again, I was under another table. Williams sprayed the room with gunfire, his back to the obs window. I tipped the table up, rolled behind it and grabbed for Osaka's pistol—

"It's no use running," Williams said. "Like I said, Damascus was a fluke."

Rounds punched a line of fine holes in the far wall. The fish tank set into it exploded: spilling enormous aquatic life-forms and alien coral-formations. Water gushed across the floor.

I filtered out everything non-essential to my survival. Noise, light: everything fell away. Getting that gun, shooting Williams, escaping the room. Those were my objectives. I was now a metre from the service pistol. Williams stalked on through the room, crunching debris underfoot . . .

I braced against the floor with my left hand, reached for

the gun with my right – fingers ready to close on the pistol grip . . .

Williams swivelled around, pounding towards me.

He fired his carbine – not the disciplined reaction of a soldier, but frenzied and uncoordinated.

My hand closed on the pistol, my real palm touching the warm plastic grip. I brought it up. Gunfire slashing the air all around me, I returned fire.

How many shots did the gun have left? I didn't know. In truth, I didn't care. The probability of me escaping this chamber was zero, or a fraction near enough. The game was stacked phenomenally in Williams' favour. He was bigger, faster, just plain better than me. I almost envied the speed of his reactions.

The pistol was a muted jackhammer in the enclosed environment. A round hit Williams in the shoulder: a neat hole right through the flak-plating. Another hit him in the chest; failed to penetrate his armour.

But he kept coming. He just damned well kept coming. Inside a simulant, he didn't care. I could probably have emptied the whole clip into him, and it would have barely slowed him down.

Zero odds.

"Don't you get it?" Williams roared. "It's over, Harris. This is the part where I smash your fucking face in, and the Alliance gets what's coming to it."

He crashed into me, and we collapsed into another table. The simulant was much heavier than a man, and in his armour Williams was even more cumbersome. The carbine and service pistol were lost somewhere between us – bodies rolling across the floor.

I felt a heavy, gloved fist impact with my head. My vision wavered, and the dissociation that comes with cranial injury swept over me. Williams grabbed my head with both hands, slammed it into the floor again and again—

Shit. I'm going to pass out.

He was getting the better of me. *Not getting; he always had it.* I would've liked to think that in our real skins, I could've taken Williams on. But even that was optimistic: he was younger, fitter and just as hungry as me. Who knew what drove the traitorous bastard? Was there an Elena for him out there somewhere, some motivation for his betrayal of the Alliance? Blow after blow connected: my face, chest, abdomen, everywhere. The force of each impact was thunderous. My hands scrabbled against the floor, searching for a weapon – *anything* – that I could use against him.

"See the black, Harris," Williams said, wet spittle lining his lips. "Go for it. Don't fight it any more—"

There was a noise from somewhere behind me. The hum of the door opening, boots against the deck and carpet—

Rescue?

"Jesus, sir! What's happening in here?"

Ostrow. I recognised the voice: an annoyance in any other circumstance, an opportunity for survival, a sudden reprieve, in these.

Williams' eyes flittered past me, to the chamber door. They flared with anger and surprise.

"Fucking shoot him!" I shouted. "Do it!"

Williams went to roll sideways, faster than Ostrow could shoot.

Pistol shots rang out across the chamber, aimed at Williams. Some may even have hit him, but not enough to put him down. He was an alert, moving target: a head shot was too much to ask for.

I stumbled to my feet, and felt the wave of anger and hate crashing around me, the white noise building in my

142

ears. I summoned it, let it come to me. The rage was just waiting to be released.

Let that hand bed in. You won't know your own strength. The bionic hand.

I flexed it. There was pent-up motive force in the new joints, the gentle *click-clicking* as the fingers closed into a fist. I pulled my new hand back and launched a punch squarely into his face—

Williams pulled back for another round. I grappled with him, managed to close the hand around his throat. He struggled, but I held on. It felt so good. Williams' Warfighters had killed Elena, even if it had only been simulated. He had to pay for that. They all did. Behind me, soldiers yelled for back-up – Ostrow issuing orders. They couldn't get a clear shot at Williams, not without hitting me.

That didn't matter any more: Williams was a dead man.

Bone and cartilage and flesh crunched, and the metal hand just kept closing. There was a plastic collar around Williams' neck, carrying a metal device no bigger than my thumb. *Pheromone collar*, I guessed: used to fool the security dogs. That was what Williams had been referring to. Osaka's collar had malfunctioned, called in the dogs. Accelerated the execution of their plan.

They wanted the Endeavour's *location. That's what they came here for.*

"V . . ." Williams gasped.

"I'm done with listening to your shit."

The sim's face began to turn a shade of blue, veins raising on his temples. Williams bucked beneath me and I fought his resistance. He was bleeding all over, I realised. Some of Ostrow's shots must've hit home.

"V . . . view . . ." Williams said. He was struggling to breathe now.

I flexed the metal hand. Hunt had been right about one thing: I really didn't know my own strength. I felt bones in the simulant's neck pop as I tightened my grip. A bubble of pink fluid burst on Williams' lips. His eyes – becoming bulbous – shifted to the back of the room.

He was smiling.

". . . por . . ." he completed.

View-port.

I broke eye contact. Looked to the windows.

A Spider mining rig loomed massive at the view-port, so near to the module exterior that it was almost on top of the room. It was ramming the outside of the chamber: about to breach the outer skin.

"Out of the room!" I shouted.

Williams' body went rigid.

I recoiled from the window. Started back towards the chamber door; barely took in Ostrow and a Marine squad looking on in amazement, as though unable to process properly what they were seeing. I couldn't blame them for that.

"What—?" Ostrow managed, but reached his own conclusion before he finished the sentence.

The Spider MMR raised one of its enormous, multi-jointed legs – tipped with a claw, used to grapple the lunar surface – against the port, and tapped the glass. The action appeared almost gentle, though the consequence would be anything but. The MMRs carried powerful man-amps: I knew that the machine would be capable of smashing its way through the window. As I watched, where the tip connected with the glass, it immediately hazed. There was vacuum on the other side of the window. If the room breached, the doors would seal, trapping us in the compromised sector. No simulant to save me, no tank to hide inside.

Ostrow was already up and at the door—

Though the Spider was behind me, and I couldn't see what it was doing, I could hear it. The room around me shook with the force of each impact, the glass screeching as the metal claw hit the window again and again. Jagged shadows were thrown against the walls either side of the door, the stark outlines of more Spiders advancing on the chamber. Those things had cutting tools: my panicked mind began to consider whether they might employ the laser mandibles to cut through the glass—

The briefing room door hummed open, panels receding into the walls. Ostrow, the Marines and I piled out.

"Get that door shut!" I yelled.

I barely had time to register the disaster in the corridor outside. A dead dog on the floor, in a pool of viscous blood. Another MP, propped up against the wall with his or her throat cut.

There was a crash behind me. The window to the briefing room gave way, and atmosphere began to rush from the inside of the facility. The Spider rig had broken through, clawed legs slamming into the deck.

Pressure dropped, and the temperature plummeted.

My ears popped, noisily and painfully: the instant reaction to vacuum. I felt my heart rate rising rapidly, my blood pressure dropping, the rush of gas from my lungs. All the typical, lethal signs of a decompression incident. I stumbled against the wall, lurched away from the door—

Close, goddamn it!

The lead Spider scuttled across the room. It brushed its black canopy against the ceiling, multi-jointed legs smashing aside tables and chairs. The machines were not made for use inside the base, and the MMR was so big that it only just fitted inside the room. Through a screen of tears, I saw the face of the operator inside the rig.

The Queen of Hearts: Private Rebecca Spitari.

She wore a hijab over her head and a full vacuum-suit, a respirator plug dangling loose from her neck, but her face was unmistakable. Snarling, she gunned the controls of the walker, sending it lurching onwards, front legs rearing up like a metal praying mantis. There were three more of the rigs in convoy behind her; partly tangled in the remains of the window, but advancing into the room.

Ostrow slammed a hand against the emergency door control – again and again – and the briefing room door slid shut, seeking to seal off the leak. The only defence the facility had against this sort of disaster was to shut the sector and call it a day.

I stumbled away from the briefing room, through the amber-lit corridor. Before I'd gone into the briefing I had barely registered the layout of this area of the base. There had been no need to do so: I hadn't expected to be fighting down here. *I'm getting old and slack*, I rebuked myself.

The dead MP on the floor had an M400 carbine across his lap. Still moving onwards towards the end of the corridor, I grabbed the rifle and slammed the SAFETY OFF stud. The weapon's laser sighting holographic popped alive; painted the floor with a red targeting beam. I checked the ammunition clip on the reader. Sixty shots left: half full. Not good.

"You're hurt," Ostrow said. I realised that he was grabbing my shoulder, trying to shake me.

I whirled about, the carbine aimed at his face.

"It's me!" he said.

Four Marines in vac-rated Alliance combat gear stood around us. Armed with carbines like mine, helmets clipped to belts.

"Get away from me!" I shouted.

My immediate instinct was to fight him off. I couldn't trust anyone, not any more. But my options were limited. Behind me, the Spiders were thumping across the deck: beyond that door, there was only hard vacuum. Breached, this whole sector would go into shutdown. I had no suit, no protection against the void. These troopers had armour, and there were more than enough of them to kill me if they were traitors.

Captain Ostrow was dressed like the Marines, but wearing dark glasses that were completely at odds with the vac-suit and made him look like a tool.

"We don't have time for this," he said. "We need to get you out of here."

I kept my rifle trained on the four-man team, though they took no offensive action. The Marines just paused, uncertain as to what they should do. At my back, the wall vibrated violently. Wouldn't be long before the Spiders either burst or cut their way through the wall, door, or both.

"I'm not going anywhere," I said. "Not until I know that we're on the same side."

"I tried to shoot Williams, didn't I?" Ostrow still had a pistol in one hand and a small black graphite case in the other. He flipped the pistol up, defensively: pinched between palm and thumb. "There's no time to explain what's happening, but we need to leave – right now."

The walls around me shuddered. I was running on adrenaline and fumes. My whole body was trembling, riding the endorphin highway. The laser-dot holographic danced as my hands began to shake.

"I have someone with me," Ostrow said. "Maybe she'll convince you."

A small blonde-haired figure appeared behind him. Mason, dressed in her service uniform, sidearm held in both hands just like they taught you in Basic, her Directorate trophy-sword hanging from a sheath on her belt. She looked shaken but uninjured.

"Sir?" she said, frowning at me as she evaluated my condition. "You all right?"

"Command is dead," I said. Reluctantly lowered the carbine. Wondered whether Mason had seen the inside of the briefing room, the carnage that Williams' Warfighters had caused. "But I'm alive. I killed Williams." I swallowed. "Again."

Mason's expression dropped. She'd killed him on the *Colossus*, when he had revealed that he was a traitor. "For real?"

"Simulated," I said. "I'm pretty sure, at least."

"This place is compromised," said Ostrow. "You'll have to trust me. I need you to commence your mission." He patted the black case that he was holding. "This is an intelligence package. *The* intelligence package. I was supposed to deliver it to you after the briefing. Please, you have to believe me."

The pounding behind the sealed door reached a crescendo.

I could die in this corridor from vacuum, or I could take my chances with Ostrow and the Marines. There was hardly a choice here.

I lowered the rifle. "Let's go."

We ran through the Command Sector, and Ostrow sealed every door that we passed: blast-sealed, leaving the Spiders trapped behind six-inch-thick sheets of reinforced plasteel. The immediate risk that they posed was quickly fading, but there were other dangers lurking on the outpost.

The evacuation siren sang out overhead.

"This station is under martial law," the AI declared, first

148

in Standard then in Hindi. "Sectors Eleven, Eighteen, Sixty-Eight and Ninety-Five have been breached. Proceed to the nearest shelter, and remain on-site until Alliance forces confirm that the emergency has passed . . ."

Whatever had happened in the briefing room, it wasn't contained: it was happening across Calico. Ostrow and the Marine escort pushed their way through corridors choked with personnel. We rapidly cleared the military sector, but things only got worse as we entered the civilian districts. This was a coordinated assault, with the singular purpose of destabilising Calico Base.

Chaos breeds, I thought. *Given the right conditions.*

And what conditions these were. As I fell in step with the rest of the team, I watched the scene unfold through the mounted scope of my carbine. I expected the bullets and beams to start flying at any moment. Dissident elements – hidden in the shadows while the Alliance military were on-station, while they retained some semblance of control – had risen to the top. Graffiti so fresh that it looked wet had been sprayed onto a tunnel wall: TARIK OUT! CUT HIS STRINGS! FIGHT THE REAL ENEMY! An anti-grav mule – one of the universal transport buggies – lay overturned at the nearest junction.

"Are the other sectors like this?" I asked.

"Most are worse," Ostrow said. "The whole of Calico is up in arms. Riot, rebellion; call it what you want." A rifle started firing in the distance. Someone was screaming, someone else cheering. "It was only a matter of time. This place was a nuke waiting to be detonated."

"And the Directorate keyed the countdown . . ."

"Exactly," Ostrow said. "That wasn't just Sector Command in there, Harris. That was *High* Command – the War Council."

"So they said." Ideas began to occur to me. I turned to

Mason. "We should get to a comms room. I can make an address to the station—"

Ostrow laughed, briefly and bitterly. "I've read your debrief on the *Colossus* incident. Getting you on the PA is literally the last thing that we need to do. Getting out of here: that's what matters."

"I need to get skinned up," I insisted. "We need simulators, an operations centre—"

"I have it all taken care of."

"Then where are we going?"

"Up the Spine, to the *Colossus*." Ostrow didn't face me, instead waved his squad on down the corridor. The four Marines covered one another, battle-signed that the area was clear. "I've already overseen the loading procedure; you have simulants, armour, weapons. The ship was supposed to be ready in three days."

"I guess that this has changed things," Mason muttered.

"Events have overtaken us," Ostrow agreed.

"I'll need a crew and a captain. And I'm not going anywhere without the rest of the Legion."

I'm not leaving them, I thought. *Not again.* I thought of Kaminski: of his reaction in the Spine's terminal. Where was he? Had the Directorate sent simulants or Swords after the rest of the squad?

"Taken care of on both counts," Ostrow said. "You're dealing with Military Intelligence here, not a bunch of amateurs."

I decided not to make any comment about how Mili-Intel had failed to predict the disaster that was enveloping Calico. Mason raised an eyebrow, acknowledging that she recognised it as well.

"The Legion are meeting us at the Spine docking terminal," he said. "All necessary equipment is onboard. Saul too, if my plan has worked."

Ostrow's shades were for more than just appearance. The insides of the glass lenses were painted with graphics: targeting reticules and shot acquisition data, like that we used on our combat-suits. I looked over his shoulder at info-streams flooding the small screen. Security camera footage, stuttering images reflecting against the sheen of sweat on his cheek.

"I'm tapping into Calico's mainframe," he said. "They're almost there. We need to hurry."

"I don't even know what I'm walking into yet," I said. "Command hadn't finished briefing me."

"That'll have to wait. I can give you specifics once we're aboard the *Colossus*. This is highly classified shit, Harris; war-winning material." Ostrow patted the case. "This box contains intel on your mission. Again, when we aren't under fire, I'll explain everything."

We passed through another open bulkhead. Emergency lights flashed in the corridor ceiling and there were view-screens set into the walls. Lots of them had been smashed, but some jittered and jumped with safety warnings: SEEK SHELTER NOW! RETREAT TO LOWER HAB LEVELS FOR LOCKDOWN! The seven of us formed a tight unit, guns trained in front and behind.

"The Directorate have just breached the control rooms," Ostrow said. One hand went to his ear, tapping a bead there. "They'll have full control of life support – heat, atmosphere, gravity – within the next fifteen minutes."

"But we'll be long gone by then, right?" Mason asked, hopefully.

Gone, or dead.

"Sure," I said.

The emergency siren was interrupted by an announcement chime. View-screens along the tunnel walls flickered to life, in sequence, all displaying the same image. A face appeared on the screens, projected in high-res tri-D: crystal-clear. It was a face that I knew; that I had seen only twice, but that I'd never forget.

After what she had done, what she had caused.

CHAPTER NINE

PAYBACK

"I am Director-Admiral Kyung."

The voice was almost preternaturally calm and barely accented, marking Kyung as a well-practised speaker of Standard. From the scene behind her, she was on the bridge of a starship. Poised, coiled, in the command throne: dressed in an immaculate black uniform. Behind her, Directorate officers manned the ship and tended banks of glowing consoles. We were seeing, I was sure, exactly what Kyung wanted us to, and her message was clear: *I am armed and dangerous. I am in control.*

As if to reinforce the point, she declared, "I am commanding officer of the Asiatic Directorate vessel *Shanghai Remembered*, currently in orbit around Calico. I want no part in this war, people of Calico. It is a matter for you whether you wish to be governed by the Alliance military complex. I wish to make clear that my mission is not with you."

"Bullshit . . ." Mason whispered.

"I expect that they funded the rebellion," Ostrow said.

Kyung continued. "I come to Calico Base seeking your

assistance. I am looking for a person who has done great harm to the Asiatic Directorate. Most specifically, he has inflicted injustice upon me, my starship and my crew. His conduct cannot go unpunished."

Kyung's face dissolved on the screen and another took its place. An image from my service record. Probably from Azure, shortly after my promotion to captain.

"I will not call this man a soldier, because he is not. He has no honour and has no right to bear the title. He is a war-criminal, and that is why we come here. We require immediate surrender of this man; the man that you know as Lazarus. I urge your leaders to deliver him to us, and forthwith."

Kyung paused, looked into the camera. I could swear that she was looking at me, and I felt my heart freeze. Every bit the Assassin of Thebe. She'd left no one alive on Jupiter Outpost, and I had no doubt that she would pick Calico clean too.

"That will be all," she said, and the announcement ended. My mute picture remained on the viewer-screen.

I breathed out slowly. Turned to face the survivors. "You want me to hand myself in," I said, "I'll do it. If it'll save Calico – preserve whatever we have here, then I'll go."

"It isn't you that they really want," Ostrow said. "They've come here for the intel, and they think that capturing you will be the fastest way to acquire it."

"Which is probably true," Mason said. "Sir, you can't do it. You can't give yourself up to them. Whatever she – this Kyung – says, it isn't about you."

Ostrow tossed me a respirator, detached from his suit. Strapped around my head, the black plastic mask would cover most of my face. It was hardly a disguise but I'd pass a quick glance.

"No," I said, standing as upright as I could. "I'm not hiding."

"Have it your way," said Ostrow, scowling. "We have even less time than I thought and the Spine's dock is two sectors away. We need to move."

"Remember your CQB training," I said to Mason as we closed on the terminal.

"As if I'd forget that," she said.

CQB: close quarters battle training. But fighting your way through a city of corrugated training huts on Olympus, Mars? That was hardly the same as what we were facing down here.

The place was a write-off: beyond repair or recapture with what limited military resources we had on-station. There were insurgents everywhere. Men and women armed with mining gear, with industrial lasers and rivet guns, yelling battle-cries and warnings to leave the station. The chanting carried on the air, was audible above the crackle and pop of a hundred fires: "*Alliance go home! We don't want the war! Soldiers back to the Core! Alliance go home! We don't want the war! Soldiers back to the Core!*"

"Bastards," I hissed. "Don't they understand what's happening here?"

It's not whether you want the war, I thought bitterly. *It's whether it wants you.*

Clattering mêlée weapons against helmets – a percussive accompaniment to their chant – the mob disappeared through the smoke in a ragged column, onwards through the outpost. My team hid behind a cabinet that someone had dragged out into the corridor, Mason holding on tight to my arm Perhaps she thought that my natural inclination would've been to take the rebels on. She was probably right, but equally I accepted that it would've been a wasted gesture. Getting off Calico: that was a far more pressing goal than teaching some dipshit colonists the true meaning of citizenship.

The mob passed us by, their voices becoming more distant. "Move up," Ostrow ordered. "Terminal is through here."

I stalked on to the next corridor junction. My body ached from combat with Williams. Every minute, the throb in my face seemed to become more vibrant. My fatigues were sticking to my back now. I took that to mean that I was bleeding. The question was how badly.

The Spine's docking terminal sat ahead. The bars that had previously dominated this sector had been looted and abandoned. Signage had been torn down and windows had been broken. AMERICANS GO HOME had been sprayed across one fascia. Two bodies – headless – were bound up with heavy chains outside a bar door. Both wore Alliance fatigues, bloodstained to the point that their military agency was impossible to identify. As we passed by, I saw a metal flask on the floor; stopped to scoop it up. That, and a box of cigarettes poked from the pocket of a dead miner. I grabbed them both, slid them into a pouch on my uniform. Mason paused and watched me, but I waved her on.

"Thought I saw an ammo clip," I said.

"We should stay with the Marines," she said, unconvinced by my explanation.

Mason crushed glass fragments underfoot, and her laser sight caught smoke in the air, as she moved into the terminal. Overhead, dangling from lighting rigs, were crude effigies of Governor Al Kik: burning. Christo only knew where they had come from; whether the dissidents had prepared them in advance. It was scary how the atmosphere, the tone of the place, had changed so rapidly.

"The Directorate won't need to shut down life support," I said. "The fires will see to the oxygen long before."

"Maybe that's part of their plan," Ostrow said.

The Spine's terminal was in overdrive. All four elevator carts had been locked down, and they sat docked at the base of the shaft. The chamber was rammed with people – thousands of civilians, all clamouring for the middle of the terminal, for safe passage. The crowd produced an overwhelming wall of cries and shouts, echoing around the terminal.

Barely visible through the civilian mob, a military barricade had been established around the base of the Spine. The immigration gates had been reinforced: shoulder-high metal stockades bolted to the deck-plate to provide instant cover, arranged around the elevators. Dozens of Alliance Army soldiers and Marines were deployed in a tight circle inside the cordon.

Ostrow waved us on. "Weapons ready, people."

"Let us take this, sir," one of the Marines said. The four-man unit fanned out, pushed their way through the crowd. "It might get nasty."

"They want to get off Calico too," Mason said. "That's all they want."

"We can't help them, Private," Ostrow said, angrily. "Unless we get the Legion out of here, we can't help *anyone*."

I grabbed the cuff of Mason's uniform with my bionic hand, pulled her close. "We don't have a choice."

She nodded, mutely. It was hard not to be moved by the hungry, frightened eyes glaring back at us. So many were just looking for some peace, attempting to escape what Calico had become—

"Step away from the elevators!" an Army officer roared over a handheld PA system. Although his voice was amplified by the horn, it barely cut through the cacophony generated by the baying mob. "This area is in lockdown! Seek shelter per emergency protocol!"

"It's Captain Baker," Mason said. "He made it out too."

"And the Baker Boys," I said.

He was in hardcopy; this was the real Baker – I could tell from the weathering of his old face. His uniform was ripped at the shoulder and he held a service pistol in one hand. Many of the troopers manning the barricades wore Sim Ops badges, but none of them were in simulants.

The civvies surged forward. Soldiers raised rifle-butts, slammed them into faces. Some of the horde went down. Others tried to clamber over the blockade. All were eventually repelled.

"I will authorise lethal force if you do not stand back from the elevators!" Baker yelled. "This is your final warning—"

Someone in the crowd launched a bottle.

"Americans go home! Americans go home! Americans go home!" they chanted.

Baker got to full height behind the barricade. Looked angry. He had been hit, I realised: a red slit marked his left temple, claret smeared across his forehead. He extended his arm in the air, rigid. Fired a single round from the pistol. Speaker unit to his mouth again.

"Stand down! The Spine terminal is closed! I will not issue another warning! I'm not even American, for Christo's sake!"

The crowd retreated, cleared a perimeter around the barricade. Although I knew that it would only be temporary, they were cowed: their shouting dampened for a moment.

"Get down, and let military personnel through!" Baker shouted.

Baker panned his pistol across the crowd. His boys were armed with carbines and a couple of shotguns; itching to fire on the ungrateful civilians. The mob begrudgingly obeyed, either stooping over or crouching. That made it much easier for us to reach the foot of the stockade, and we started to climb over: Mason first, then me, Ostrow and his team following.

"This all for us?" I yelled at Baker.

"Lazarus?" he asked, smiling. The expression was tired but genuine. "We thought you'd never make it."

"It's me, Baker. Haven't you heard? I always come back. Where are my people?"

"I've been looking after them."

Jenkins emerged from the group, carrying a carbine, with Kaminski behind her. Martinez followed, also armed. They looked uninjured, though Kaminski's skull was a welter of fresh scars: flesh-grafts where the surgeons had removed the metal from his head.

"Thank Christo that you're alive," Jenkins gushed. "What's going on?"

I shook my head. "Shit. Fan. Hitting."

"You okay, Mace?" Jenkins asked of Mason.

The younger soldier nodded. "For now, but—"

"Where is Professor Saul?" Ostrow shouted. "It's imperative that he goes with you."

Jenkins nodded behind the barricade, to Saul. He stood near the elevator cart, so still that he had almost blended into the background. His face was completely slack: devoid of any emotion whatsoever. Physically, he was in one piece, but the damage went far deeper than that.

"Saul!" I called to him. "Stay with it. We're getting out of here."

He jumped to life, nodding. "I understand," he said.

"Who we fighting?" Martinez barked.

"Kyung's here," Mason said. "The *Shanghai Remembered* has come after us."

"Then let's bring God to the godless," Martinez said. He looked down at my hand. "Nice hand, *jefe*."

"We're not doing that," Ostrow declared. "We're bugging out, because you need to start your mission. We're going to the *Colossus*."

"We don't have a captain yet," I said.

"In position," Ostrow said, pointing to the sky. "Already gone up the Spine." He turned to Baker. "Is this all there is?"

Baker shrugged. "Everyone alive is here. I ordered all Sim Ops teams to the dock."

Ostrow exhaled. "Damn it."

"Why do we need—?" Jenkins started.

"Because this is so damned important!" Ostrow barked. He looked, suddenly, like he had lost his cool. I'd never seen Ostrow do that, had never seen a Mili-Intel man do that. He shook the black case at Jenkins, began to climb the barricade. "This mission could change everything."

Something rumbled around me again; the entire structure shaking. Could've been a bomb detonating, a collapse inside the base, even the Spider MMRs breaking through the walls. Whatever it was, the noise triggered another wave of panic from the civvies. Many got back up, began to charge for the barricade again. The soldiers manning the line gave each other worried looks.

"Go, go!" Ostrow yelled.

A woman holding a bundle of rags made it to the blockade. I watched her running the no-man's land between the civilians and the base of the Spine: closing it surprisingly fast. My sighting laser skated over her weathered vac-suit – patched up with so many emergency seals that the original suit was barely visible. She was on top of Ostrow before he could get fully over the barrier.

"My baby!" she wailed, thrusting a filthy package in our direction. She wore the full niqab over her face, only a pair of dark eyes peering from within.

Baker reached for her, his pistol lowered. "We can't help you, ma'am!"

"Get back!" another officer yelled.

Then there were hands everywhere, grabbing at us, dragging one of the soldiers across the barricade. It was inevitable that someone would lose their cool. A carbine started to fire, then another, bodies falling on both sides of the divide. The woman with the child continued her piercing wail, thrusting the limp baby towards us.

"Take her with you!" she shouted.

The niqab fell from her face, part of her cloak catching on another refugee's vac-suit. She was smiling beneath the covering.

I immediately recognised that face.

"Bomb!" I shouted, at the very top of my lungs. "Everybody down!"

The woman held out the bundle. "This is payback for Damascus!"

I grabbed for Ostrow—

The Warfighter known as Private Alicia Malika self-detonated.

For a long time, all I could hear was a high-pitched whine.

I wasn't on Calico any more.

I wasn't a lieutenant colonel in the Alliance Army.

I was a sergeant again – about to face promotion – and I was lying on my back among the wreckage of a monorail train, on a world called Azure.

I had no sensory perception save for the constant ringing in my ears. The sensation was excruciating: a demonic sine wave enveloping everything, becoming my only reality.

"Elena!" I shouted, searching the dark.

Her body was warm and wet. Soaked with blood, covered in frag.

Then the white noise all around me, obliterating everything.

It was not the sound generated by the explosion any more, but something much, much worse.

The Artefact's insidious signal: the Shard's call to arms.

CHAPTER TEN

I'LL BE SEEING YOU

I was close enough to the explosion to be in the primary blast zone.

The overpressure wave roared over me.

My already-aching eardrums became dense balls of pain and the air was wrenched from my lungs. I felt internal organs compressing, the bones of my ribcage crushed by the pressure. Bright splinters of pain lanced across my chest, through my shoulder. Those injuries, I knew, were secondary – likely to be less serious than anything going on inside, but they hurt all the same. My Army fatigues were no protection at all from the blast.

Then the calm: the terrifying tranquillity that comes after a life-threatening experience. I teetered on the edge of consciousness. Made my addled brain focus on the here and now. The ground beneath me. The pain in my chest. The feel of wet blood between my fingers. I grasped those details and focused on them.

Pain is good. It reminds you that you're alive.

The calm didn't last long.

"On your feet, trooper!"

It was Jenkins, screaming into my face. She grabbed the lapels of my fatigues and pulled me up from the floor.

I felt woozy, sick. The ringing gradually receded, so that I could register expanding pandemonium around me. My vision shivered, but I made out enough of the surrounding deck to know that this was FUBAR.

"Here they come!" someone yelled.

The terminal was shrouded in black smoke, and the air was thick with the unmistakable odour of roasting human flesh. The barricade was a mess of torn metal and body-parts, soldiers and civilians alike crumpled across it. There wasn't much of Alicia Malika left – most of the body had been incinerated by the blast, burnt rags and a few shreds of vac-suit lingering on the skeletal remains of her lower half.

A simulant suicide bomber. The perfect weapon.

Mason lay beneath me. She slowly got to her feet too.

"Th . . . thanks for the save . . ." she stammered.

"I didn't realise that I had . . ."

"Harris is hit," Martinez yelled, half-turning to me. He was firing into the indig mob, slicing bodies with carbine fire as they threw themselves at the line.

"We are *gone*!" Jenkins said. "Like, yesterday gone! Up, now!"

"Ostrow!" I started. "Where's Ostrow?"

He had the *Endeavour*'s intel. He knew what we were supposed to be doing, where we'd find the ship.

"I'm here," he rumbled, stirring beside me.

Several pieces of shrapnel had peppered his face; shattered one lens of his glasses. He was on his side, clutching at the black box – crawling back towards the Spine elevator entrance.

"Can you walk?" I shouted, over-compensating because of my trashed eardrums.

"I'm fine. Lieutenant Jenkins is right; we need to go."

I knew, from painful experience, that the most serious injuries caused by such a blast would be internal. But there was nothing that we could do to evaluate those down here. The *Colossus* would have an auto-doc and a medical bay – the best chance for any injured personnel was to get them onboard. Both Ostrow and I probably needed a full assessment–

"Fuck, fuck!" an Alliance soldier yelled.

A flaming object – a Molotov cocktail of some sort: crude but effective – sailed over the remains of the barricade. It smashed into the outer hull of the elevator cart. Flames licked over the area, caught one of the defenders. Dressed in only fatigues, the young Army woman's clothing ignited. She dropped her rifle, began to roll around on the floor, screaming.

"Get an extinguisher over here!" a trooper said. "She's on fire!"

Just then, a pistol began to discharge from the mob. Rounds spanked off the defensive barriers. Soldiers began to return fire.

"Get your shit together, troopers," I yelled. Not just at the Legion; at anyone manning the defences. "We're getting into that elevator."

"Go, go, go!" Baker shouted. "My Boys'll hold the fort. We'll take the next cart up!"

Baker began to randomly fire his sidearm at the crowd, slamming another clip into the feeder when the first was empty. The soldiers around him didn't move either, instead braved the hail of incoming small-arms fire. Too many of them were already dead or dying. It was only a matter of time before the indigs broke through the cordon.

The Directorate would know where we were going now. Alicia Malika's sim was dead, but once the neural-link was broken the *Shanghai Remembered* would know that we were going up the Spine. They might even have been monitoring her, watching her feeds via a simulator somewhere. I swept the sea of angry faces; wondered how long it would be before the Directorate sent more copies of the Warfighters after us . . .

"Just go!" Baker said.

The Legion and Ostrow backed towards the open elevator door. Another home-made explosive hit the Spine, more fire pouring over the barricade. The crowd dragged a trooper across the divide – he disappeared, flailing and shouting.

The elevator cart was heavily armoured, and nothing the indigs had done so far was capable of disrupting the machine. The interior looked a lot like a starship cargo deck. Sealed metal crates sat on the apron, in a state of organised disarray.

"Get this cart moving," I ordered.

Somewhere along the way, although in my current state I couldn't say when, I'd picked up a carbine again. Jenkins and I took up positions behind the crates. Picked off targets as some made a run for the doors, bodies splitting with red light. Kaminski did the same, firing with a handgun. Saul huddled behind a crate, covering his ears.

"Control panel . . ." Ostrow groaned. "Need . . . my clearance . . ."

"Do it!" I said.

Ostrow punched keys on the control panel, pushed his hand onto the DNA scanner. The cart lights began to flash amber, cycling in sequence. The enormous pneumatic blast doors rolled into position; years-old gears grinding as they did. More gunfire plinked against the armour-glass. The chanting reached a crescendo outside – so many voices, so disparate, that I couldn't even make out what the protest was about any more.

The doors slammed shut – *finally* – with a thunderous boom, and the cart vibrated as it mounted the magnetic rail. Inside, everything sounded muted: the ring of gunfire far away. Another improvised explosion chased us and hit the outer hull, but the elevator commenced its ascent.

I crept out from behind the crate. The cart was moving towards the upper dome, where it would enter a lock and then continue out into space. From where I crouched, I could look down on the battle below. Despite myself I involuntarily exhaled.

"Is it bad?" Jenkins asked, still hiding.

"It's bad," I said. "Really bad."

The dome was filled with civilians, all storming the barricades. Not just those looking for safe passage off Calico, either: now armed gangs, the groups we'd seen roaming the vandalised corridors. They had weapons – from improvised laser drills, through to carbines and pistols. It looked like some of the military armouries had been plundered.

"Baker isn't coming after us," Jenkins said. She spoke the words as a statement, not a question. "None of them are."

I nodded. "I . . . I think we're all that's left."

Ostrow gasped for breath. He lay slumped against the control panel. Martinez put his hand on Ostrow's shoulder. He made a horrible noise at the back of his throat, but waved Martinez away when he went to prop him up. His tanned complexion had gone grey as Calico's plains.

"We'll get you to the *Colossus*—" I said.

"I've shut down the other elevators," Ostrow interrupted, speaking fast, like he didn't know whether each word would

167

be his last. "No one else is coming." Both hands were suddenly on his chest, wrapped around the black box. "You need to get to the sh . . . ship, with this data . . ."

"Rest," Martinez said. "Just take it easy for a moment."

"I can't rest!" Ostrow barked. "And neither can the Legion. You need to do this, for all of our sakes."

"All right, *mano*," Martinez nodded.

The cart continued its progress, through the lock in the upper dome, and we danced between the gravity wells generated by the main base and the docks. Space opened above, Calico below. The entire outpost looked as though it had been under attack. Lights flashed and winked. Domes were breached. Some structures were blackened.

Above us was the orbital dock, the skeletal scaffold encasing several Alliance starships. Safety lights still flashed on the extremities of the mooring spars, warning pilots of the danger of getting too close. The *Colossus* was the biggest ship, but was in a state of repair. Large sections of hull plating had been removed, and the remainder was covered in robot maintenance teams like insects on shit.

"I can see her . . ." Kaminski muttered under his breath.

He wasn't talking about the *Colossus*: the *Shanghai Remembered* was coming into view. Martinez crossed himself, muttered a prayer under his breath. I even heard Saul – previously quiet, too stunned to say or do anything else – inhale sharply. Directorate warships had that effect on people, and especially ships as old and venerable as the *Shanghai*. She hung in low orbit, moored so that she could oversee the destruction of Calico, just as deadly as I remembered her. Whereas in Damascus she had employed stealth – had been reigning in her firepower – here she unleashed it in all her hellish fury. An armour-plated destroyer class, her hull flashed with laser batteries, discharging death into the void. There were Alliance ships around her in pieces.

"There goes the Navy," Jenkins said, matter-of-factly.

The *Shanghai* wasn't alone. Three more ships of the same pattern lingered in near-space, in the same orbit. A swarm of T-89 Interceptors and Z-5 Wraith attack ships were disengaging from the main Directorate fleet, descending on Calico Base.

We crossed beneath the shadow of the *Shanghai*, like a minnow beneath a shark, and made good our approach to the waiting *Colossus*.

"Weapons at the ready," I said. Nodded towards the cart bulkhead. "We don't know what will be on the other side of that door. Mason and Martinez, help Ostrow. Jenkins and I will cover the door."

The Legion rumbled agreement and got ready to move.

The engine chugged as it docked, and the cart slid into position. The amber strobe began to flash again, control panel chiming.

"Protect Kaminski, Ostrow and Saul," I said to Jenkins. I braced against the exit bulkhead and prepared to open it. "You ready for this?"

"Looks like it," Jenkins said. Her weapon was primed and trained on the door like it had personally offended her. "Just give me a target."

"On my mark . . ." I said.

As I dropped my hand, the bulkhead opened.

The Spine terminated in a main dock. It was a vast, work-like space, caught in semi-dark, lit by the occasional LED overhead lamp and an observation window at one end of the hangar. Scores of airlock-style doors provided direct access to the ships in port. Because so many workers were stationed here, the docks had their own gravity generator. That made for better battlefield conditions, if the docks turned out to be hot.

I battle-signed to Jenkins, and took up a spot behind a stack of crates. She nodded and followed suit on the opposite flank. Our carbines were trained on the hangar.

At the other end of the dock, beneath the sign that declared DOCK THREE: UAS COLOSSUS, I saw movement. Flashes of blue uniform were visible at this distance. *Navy crew.*

"Harris? That you?"

Admiral Joseph Loeb poked his head around the engine nacelle of a transport shuttle. He was clutching a pistol in an entirely unconvincing fashion, his cap pushed back on his head and sweat pouring down his face.

"It's me," I said. To Jenkins: "Stand down."

"What the hell is he doing here?" she asked.

Loeb grimaced and shook his head. From all around him – stowed in the shuttle cargo bays, behind crates, wherever else there was to hide – Navy crewmen and maintenance teams appeared.

"He's your captain," Ostrow groaned from behind us. "And you need to move. Are the pilots here?"

"I am."

James emerged from the group. He looked barely ruffled by what had happened; had obviously been up in the orbital docks the whole time. Aviator-helmet in the crook of his arm, he flashed a white-toothed grin at Jenkins.

I knew that she wouldn't be happy with the idea of going aboard the *Colossus* with James and Loeb, but she was a soldier first and foremost. Before she could argue, I said, "We don't have a choice."

She nodded with dour resolve. "Understood."

"These were the only officers that I could trust," Ostrow said. "I knew that the Directorate hadn't got to them."

Of James, I asked: "Your real body aboard the *Colossus*?"

"Sure is," James said. "Otherwise I'd be leaving it behind, and can't have that . . ."

"Where's the rest of Scorpio Squadron?"

"Coming up the Spine," James said, frowning. "You didn't see to them . . ."

"They're gone," Ostrow said.

"Hang on!" James insisted. "If my squad are down there, we can't leave them—"

Ostrow began an unpleasant-sounding cough. Sounded a lot like he'd dislodged something inside of him, and it wasn't a good something. "I'm not going through this again. They're dead: everyone is dead."

Still clutching the case, he stumbled at half-steam towards the dock, the Legion and the Navy crew in tow.

"Code red," the ship-wide address system demanded. "Repeat: this is code red. All hands to battlestations."

I hadn't expected the sudden and visceral emotional response that I felt as I stepped aboard the *Colossus*. The memories that I associated with the vessel were like caged demons – desperate to get out, to drag me back to what had happened here. They rattled at their bars as I stalked the corridors. I ground my teeth, locked the gate: fought to remain in the now. As I looked down the empty corridors, I could hear the voices of the invading Directorate Swords – could see their dark shapes lingering at the edge of my vision like ghosts.

If being aboard the ship was having any effect on Loeb or James, neither of them were showing it.

"CIC is this way!" Loeb yelled, taking off down a corridor.

He broke a security tape that had been strung over a junction; hustled the rest of us onwards.

"Will he even be able to fly this thing?" Jenkins queried. "He's awaiting trial for negligence."

"Court-martial," Loeb corrected. "And nothing has been proven yet."

"Ostrow isn't looking good," Martinez said. "He needs medical assist, immediate."

The Mili-Intel officer was strung between Mason and Martinez, in a semi-conscious state. His glasses had been lost at some point during the evacuation, but both of his hands were still wrapped very tightly around the black box, making it even more difficult for the Legion to support him. I didn't say it, but I suspected that Ostrow didn't have long, and I doubted whether there was much that we could do to help him.

Loeb waved at an officer. "Lieutenant Allaji, get that man down to Medical."

Allaji nodded, gathered another sailor with him, and took over the duty. As Ostrow was transferred between crew, he suddenly jerked awake. His eyes were wild, unfocused, and the abrupt activity sent a wave of pain across his face. The sailors quickly vanished with the injured man.

"He isn't going to make it," I said, under my breath.

"I didn't think that you even liked the guy," Jenkins asked.

"Doesn't mean that I want him to buy the farm," I said. "Not here, not like this."

Crewmen scattered in our wake. Loeb fired off orders at everyone we passed, from engineers to a handful of Marines that Command had stationed as a garrison.

"Get our systems warmed up for activation. But do not

– repeat *not* – initiate drive boot. Keep the mainframe AI off-line until I give the order."

Despite his predicament, no one challenged him.

"Aye, sir," I heard his comm crackle.

"Loeb out."

We hit the command intelligence centre at pace.

Just as the rest of the ship had been refitted, so too had the CIC. It was crammed with glowing consoles, with new scanner-units and weapons stations. The lower workpit – where the tactical holo-display was situated – was criss-crossed with gantries and suspended observation pods, making for a hectic and complicated working environment. The blast-shutters were open, and the tactical display hummed with a holo of near-space. Twenty or so officers were at stations, powering up what little tech would not be detected by the Directorate fleet.

"Get my command throne ready, now!" Loeb said.

"Aye, Admiral," a young-faced Naval woman replied. The command throne had been shrouded in a plastic sheet; the guts of Loeb's personal scanner-suite opened beside him.

"Do you want the scanner running passive, sir?"

"Of course I do!" Loeb said, settling into his throne. Someone offered him jacks to his data-ports, and he slammed them into his forearms. "Let's see what we've got . . . Get the weapons systems booted, but all modules are to remain on passive. Nothing that might let that bitch see that we're powering up."

James and the Legion chose posts around the CIC. Saul was silent, and took up a seat at the rear of the centre. There was more than enough space.

"We have a helmsman and a navigator, sir," an officer said. "The bridge is ready to go online."

"And now we have weapons . . ." Martinez said. He'd taken one of the weapons pods at the nose of the vessel; it hummed as the pod elevated inside the crew-pit. "I have the *Shanghai* in my sights, but I won't remember her."

"Don't fire!" Loeb barked. "Any of our weapons go active, and the *Shanghai* will read our identification codes and energy signature. She'll know that we're out here."

"How long until the *Colossus*' engines are operational?" I asked.

"Three minutes," Loeb said. He waved at the workpit, to any crewman who was listening. "Recall all robot engineers and anyone on the outside of my ship—"

The communicator beside me washed with air-traffic from surrounding space. *"Broken knife,"* an operator said. *"Repeat: broken knife."*

"What's that supposed to mean?" I asked, exasperated.

"It's the code word for general retreat," Loeb said. "It means that we've lost."

Already, ships in near-space were breaking orbit, pulling away from Calico, leaving multi-coloured smears of light on the blackness of space. Activating FTL drives. Far below, Calico Base was being consumed by a carpet of warheads. The collected, focused firepower of the Asiatic fleet was unstoppable. Intense white explosions claimed the precarious towers. Hab-domes lay open to the void. The mine shafts were collapsing in on themselves, consumed by the dust-plains of Calico.

"God have mercy on their souls," Martinez said. *"Gracia de dios."*

"I . . . I can't get the remote docking claws open," an officer said. "I'm getting a systems error. I need to make a link with Calico Space Control for permission."

"No way," Loeb said. "We'll have to pull away with them

attached. It'll do wonders for our hull plating, but it's a damned sight better than getting hit by a Directorate warhead."

"Null-shield is ready for activation," an officer said. "On your order, Admiral. The engine and thrust control will be two minutes and counting."

Loeb nodded. "Raise the shield."

This was it: the gamble. With the shield up, I seriously doubted that the Asiatic fleet would be able to ignore us.

"Raising."

Space outside rippled. The effect was just at the edge of my perception; a blue tint against the black. Something – probably a piece of debris thrown by the engagement between the Alliance and Directorate – hit the shield. It sparked brightly, marking successful activation.

"Thrust control is going to helm!" Mason yelled. The excitement in her voice was barely containable. "We're going to make this—"

"What are we going to do?" Kaminski asked. "We can't use the Q-drive in-system."

He was right; using the quantum-drive technology that allowed us to compress space and time wouldn't be possible in the gravity well of a local star or world.

"We'll use the faster-than-light drive," Loeb declared. "Pull away at full thrust, and hit maximum velocity. That'll get us out-system, and away from here."

"Good enough," Kaminski shrugged.

Outside, a stray Interceptor approached us. The frag wounds on my back throbbed in time with my pulse, willing the far smaller ship to *just fuck off!* Martinez was antsy, and I could see his holographic suddenly snapping to focus on the Interceptor.

"I could take it . . ." he said.

"You want to do the honours?" Loeb asked me. He flipped open the manual control unit on his command station. It housed an archaic but symbolic red button labelled SYSTEM BOOT. There was, no doubt, a good deal more to it than just pressing a button, but nothing felt quite so definite as pushing a DNA-encoded control.

I reached over, watched the incoming Interceptor – framed perfectly by her bigger sisters, the *Shanghai* and the rest of the Directorate fleet – and rested a finger on the button.

"Going online," I said.

I pressed the button.

"We have helm control."

"Patching to bridge."

"Activating inertial dampeners, internal and external."

"Engine is online. Thrust control ready."

"Gravity well is stable and holding. All life-support systems are active."

"Bring us ninety degrees starboard," Loeb said. "And break umbilical with the orbital dock."

"Aye, sir."

There was a loud, pained screech – metal-on-metal – as the *Colossus* repositioned herself. The hull ground against the landing spars attaching her to the dock: broke the shell in which she'd been encased. Parts of the deep-space facility broke away, floated in space around us—

The communicator chimed.

"Oh, shit," Kaminski said.

The simple, commonplace occurrence had taken on a sinister edge.

"We're being hailed," a communications officer declared.

Loeb turned to me. His expression was fixed. "You make the call, Lazarus."

176

"How long until we can pull away, make for FTL?" I asked.

"We'll need clearance from Calico's gravity field," Loeb said. He shrugged. Quickly calculated, based on data scrolling down his monitor. "Another thirty seconds."

Thirty seconds was more than long enough for a warhead to breach our shield. Not only that, but pulling away from Calico's gravity wouldn't guarantee our successful escape: the *Shanghai* or her sister fleet could pursue, send robot fighters or attack ships after us.

The chime sounded again.

Though our course continued, and the agonising groaning went on as we pulled from the dock, the CIC fell quiet.

"It's coming from the *Shanghai*," the same officer confirmed. "She's locking weapons on us."

"She's turning," Mason said. "Engine thrust at ninety per cent."

From down in the crew-pit, Martinez tutted with obvious annoyance.

"*Solo déjame tomar un tiro, por favor,*" he barked. *Just let me take one shot, please.* "It'd be for 'Ski; we owe him that at least."

Kaminski was white-faced with a combination of rage and nerves – being presented with his captors – but to his credit said nothing.

"Not yet," I said. "But be ready on my mark." I nodded at Loeb: "Respond. Open a comms channel."

The tactical display illuminated with a holographic of Admiral Kyung's face, and I looked on the Assassin of Thebe.

"Am I addressing Colonel Harris?" she said. That same tight, precise pronunciation of Standard.

"I am here," I said.

"You are the one that they call Lazarus?"

"I am."

Mason held up a hand to me. She mouthed words. *Twenty seconds.*

Across the CIC, displays began to illuminate. Green responses were coming back from each station. *Keep her talking*, I thought. *Give the crew time.* Loeb sighed quietly, no doubt willing the machines around him to work faster. His wish to train weapons on the *Shanghai*, to take out the woman who had caused his disgrace, was intoxicating, but I knew that he was too good an officer to let bloodlust get the better of him. I was wrestling with my own emotional response. Did Kyung know, I wondered, what she had taken from me?

Outside, the *Shanghai* described a tight arc. Thrusters fired along her aft and her black bulk initiated a turn in our direction.

"I am Admiral Kyung, appointed as battlegroup commander of the Third Asiatic Directorate Response Force—"

"Let me stop you there," I said. "That ship is Directorate Spec Ops, and I don't give a fuck who you are. I already know *what* you are: the Assassin of Thebe. A murderer."

The woman's face was unreadable. The nano-comms threads that etched her features glowed as she read her ship's systems, but her cheeks were puckered and swollen; a mass of keloid tissue that looked like the result of Krell boomer fire. *Injuries from Damascus?* I asked myself. That would make sense.

"Surrender," Kyung said.

There was an impassive coldness there: as though there was a huge void between this woman and the rest of the human race.

"Fuck you," I said.

I mentally counted down the seconds, but that gaze – the hard edge to the woman's eyes – was enough to put me off.

"Ten seconds . . ." Loeb whispered.

"There is no point in running," Kyung said. "We have more than enough firepower to put Calico Base down."

"I know what you want," I repeated, feeling the rage swell within me. "But what I want to know is why? This isn't about me. It's about the *Endeavour*."

"Is that what you think?" Kyung said. "I can assure you, it really isn't about her at all."

She was playing for time, I was sure, as well.

"Then what do you want? Why do you want me, Assassin?"

"I have my reasons." Kyung's pale-lipped mouth twitched at the corner. On another face I'd have considered the expression a smile. "The *Colossus* is an old ship; we can outrun her, and take what we want."

"Your FTL isn't hot. You're talking shit."

Loeb counted down the seconds on his hand – *five, four, three, two, one!*

"And we're good!" he yelled. "Systems online across the board."

Leaning into the display so that I was staring her down, had her in my sights, I said, "I'll be seeing you." I pointed to Martinez. "Do it."

Kyung went to speak again, but the image collapsed into the holo.

"*Vete a la mierda!*" Martinez yelled.

He hunched over the weapons controls, his holo indicating successful discharge of the railgun battery. Bright flashes signalled null-shield breaches, explosions racking the *Shanghai*'s flank.

Buzzard takes Assassin.

179

Loeb slammed a fist onto his armrest. "Go!"

The perspective through the ports changed and the wasted vista of Calico Base disappeared beneath us. I remembered fleeing Damascus Space, travelling through the Shard Gate. The *Colossus* had been in her prime then, but even then she'd been a bruiser, not an assassin. Speed was not her strong suit. Without any proper opportunity to calculate thrust, to predict course vector, all we could do was move. I collapsed into a crash couch, just as the *Colossus'* thrusters fired.

Martinez's volley didn't go unanswered, and the *Shanghai* responded immediately. The railguns on her spine charged, began to lay down a heavy curtain of projectiles through near-space.

"Point defences are operational," an officer said.

A bright matrix of light stitched space, dispersing lethal debris in our vicinity.

The *Shanghai* was poised in the distance. At least one railgun shot looked to have breached her hull armour, but it was difficult to tell. I squinted, watching the tactical displays and the logistic-engines flush with data. But even now, the *Shanghai* was dwindling, and as the distance between the two ships increased the flow of reliable intel trailed off. She'd been hurt but it was impossible to know how badly.

"Maximum thrust achieved! Permission to activate FTL drive?"

"You have it!" Loeb said.

The *Colossus'* FTL drive lit and space around us collapsed into a blur—

In that last instance – as the ship breached, broke and then rewrote Einstein's laws – I saw a spark of light where the *Shanghai Remembered* had been.

Could've been a critical hit, I thought: a lucky shot from Martinez's chance attack. *But just as likely it was her drive lighting.*

Before I could reach any conclusion, and long before we could do anything about it, the *Colossus*' CIC lights went out.

CHAPTER ELEVEN

BLEEDING EDGE

I sat in darkness for a moment, my own heartbeat – thumping in my ears like gunfire – my only companion.

Then the CIC slowly rebooted.

Beneath me, as though the *Colossus'* cardiac system had been resuscitated, the deck vibrated just ever so softly, life-support systems coming back online. The *Colossus'* thinking machines seemed to take a moment longer to recalibrate. The tactical display fuzzed with static, then holographic schematics began to rebuild. Overhead, the lights flashed on in sequence.

"Everyone all right?" I whispered. Corrected: "Everyone *alive*?"

"Affirmative," Mason said. "But I don't think that I will ever get used to that . . ."

She looked decidedly green around the jowls. It wasn't only her; the rest of the CIC staff looked on the verge of being sick. It was perhaps a miracle that no one had been.

"That's what, your third FTL jump?" Martinez said.

Mason nodded. "About that."

"Trust me, when you've done enough FTL travel, you won't feel a thing." He yawned, rolled his shoulders. The weapons pod in which he was mounted had lowered, ready for him to disembark. "We used to do them all the time in the Marine Corps."

"Fucking jarhead . . ." Jenkins said under her breath. She stirred beside me, still strapped into her crash couch. "But let's not do that again anytime soon."

"No promises on that one, trooper," I said. "Kaminski, Saul?"

Both were strapped into CIC workstations, alert enough to respond.

"That was pretty intense," Kaminski said, rubbing his newly patched skull.

"Intense doesn't really do the experience justice," Saul said. "At least the inertial dampeners held out."

"We'd be plastered across the bulkheads if they hadn't," Loeb muttered.

"And you, sir?" Mason asked me.

"I'm good," I said. "All good."

The Legion looked on with concerned expressions.

I was in a bad way. My stomach had finished somersaulting but I still had the iron tang of bile in the back of my throat. I unstrapped myself and clambered out of my couch – slowly, reacquainting myself with my own body: with the rheumatic aches in my knees, my shoulders, my neck. Though my insides felt pulverised – like I'd been in a high-G dogfight with one of James' Hornets – the sensation seemed to drill down to the cellular level. I held up my bionic hand: watched as the metalwork sparked with blue light, the finger-joints twitching erratically. Every muscle screamed, and my head pulsed with an intense ache. I felt something wet on my upper lip. Reached up to my face, with my real hand, and wiped a strand of bright red blood from my nose.

"I thought that the flying was pretty good," James said. He looked completely unruffled by the experience, almost as cool as Martinez. "I barely felt a thing."

"You wouldn't," Jenkins said. "We're not all skinned up, you know."

The CIC was soon a well of light and noise. Admiral Loeb, ever the taskmaster, leant forward in his command throne and surveyed his empire.

"Give me a damage report, XO," he yelled.

"We're green across all systems, sir," the executive officer responded. "All appear to be running at acceptable levels. No significant structural damage."

"Has every department called in?"

The officer paused, then read from his screen, nodding. "Engineering, life support, drive, bridge ... Everything looks good."

"Anything on the scanner?" I said. "Did they follow us?"

Loeb gave me a knowing grin. "This is my speciality, Colonel. Our destination is wilderness space. We're using the FTL engine, not the quantum-space drive. There's no tachyon wake to trace."

I consulted the tac-display. We were currently in the void between stars, teetering somewhere on the Alliance side of the Quarantine Zone, but I couldn't identify our location or destination. The Directorate weren't the only threats in this quadrant: there were probably Krell war-fleets out in the dark, roving for targets.

"This is dangerous territory," I said. "We shouldn't linger out here for long; at least, not alone."

Loeb sighed. "'Broken knife' is the retreat code for the Alliance fleet. Always has been, since I was a green. The ship's AI has a pre-programmed destination in such a scenario: a randomly chosen muster point to which all remaining fleet assets should retreat."

"How long will it take us to reach the muster point?" Mason asked.

"ETA is an hour," said Loeb. "We can't fly FTL for ever, but we can plan our next move from the muster point."

The faster-than-light drive was a crude device by modern spacefaring standards, and the *Colossus* wasn't made for unlimited FTL travel. Like most contemporary starships, for long-distance ops she relied on her Q-drive. The power required to fly a ship at FTL speed was phenomenal, and I knew that staying on FTL propulsion was out of the question. We'd have to plot our next course via Q-space; find a jump point and move on from there.

"We'll have to assemble what forces we have left," Loeb said, staring at the obs windows, "and then we can go back and take on the *Shanghai*. When we have safety in numbers, we can make uplink to Command and teach these bastards a proper lesson . . ."

"I hit her, for sure," Martinez said. His beard and dark hair were glossed with sweat. "She might already be gone."

"I doubt it," Jenkins said. "You aren't that good a shot."

"No telling what damage I did though," Martinez said with a self-assured grin.

"Maybe we took out the Warfighters," Mason said.

"I hope so," Kaminski said, with an earnestness that surprised me. "I really do."

That thought was darkly warming. It was likely that the real Williams' Warfighters had been ensconced some-where – in their own Simulant Operations centre – aboard the *Shanghai*. The suggestion that Martinez's chance oper-ation of the railgun had killed them, struck at the soft underbelly of the traitors' strike force, was certainly appealing.

"There's no point going back anyway," I cut in, "because there is no Command. Not any more."

Loeb paused for a second, unsure of how to take that comment. "We can try the tightbeam communications array, make contact with High Command — "

"They're all gone, Loeb. I was there. Williams and the Warfighters killed them all."

Loeb narrowed his eyes, unwilling to accept my explanation. "That can't be right," he said. "Not High Command. I knew Fleet Admiral Sunsam. What were they all doing on Calico?"

These were the very people who had insisted on charges being brought against Loeb. Perversely, he seemed to be clinging to the chain of command as though it was a life raft.

"They're dead," I insisted. "They came to brief me on an operation; a mission that General Cole said could turn this war."

Saul shivered from the back of the CIC. "By Gaia. This is worse than I thought."

Before I could ask Saul to explain that comment, there was a chime over the ship's PA system.

"Colonel Harris to the infirmary," requested the AI. "Your presence is required immediately."

I nodded at the Legion. "I want a full inventory check of what equipment we have aboard this ship, by the time we arrive at the muster point. Mason, check the simulant operations centre. Martinez and Jenkins, the armoury. Kaminski, see to Saul. And Loeb, anything out of the ordinary at all – Krell, Directorate or Alliance – inform me immediately."

*　　*　　*

A Sci-Div medtech appeared at the entrance to the infirmary, dressed in a smock that was so splattered with blood that it looked more red than white. A pretty middle-aged woman, with cold features and blonde hair plaited down her back, she looked seriously out of her depth. She bowed her head at me.

"Colonel, I am Dr Erika Serova. I received mission attachment orders this morning . . ." She trailed off. "Are you all right, Colonel? Your face – it looks like you need some attention yourself."

"Save the niceties," I said. "Where's Ostrow?"

Now we were away from immediate danger – away from the *Shanghai* and her sister ships – my mind had turned back to the mission. Ostrow knew what I was supposed to do, and he was my only link back to the *Endeavour* intelligence package.

"He's through here," the tech said. "He keeps asking for you, saying that he has to see you. You should be aware that he's in a critical condition. That he's conscious at all—"

"Is he going to make it?"

The woman pulled a noncommittal face. "He's suffered extensive blast injuries. Likely ruptured a lung, and with a grade-six hematoma on his liver. I suspect some form of spinal injury as well, although he won't let us examine him any further."

She showed me through to a small chamber. Inside, Ostrow lay on his back in a bunk. The doctor quickly retreated from the room, leaving us alone, and the door hummed shut behind her.

Ostrow was in a really bad state. His eyes were closed, and although the machine beside him beeped rhythmically – showed a holo-projection of what I guessed was his heartbeat – he looked a lot like he was already dead: his skin had that waxy pallor, and his closed eyes were sunken into his head. Other bio-signs were broadcast on to the terminal, and none of them were encouraging. He'd been stripped out of his body armour, and his undersuit had been torn apart both by shrapnel back at the Spine and the treatment he'd received in the infirmary. Cables and monitor pads ran across his chest; medical dressings were plastered over his left shoulder. As I came near, he jerked awake, eyes flashing open with surprising determination.

"Harris . . ." he started.

"Take it easy," I said, genuinely surprised by his reaction.

"Y . . . you need to know what to do . . ."

Ostrow still clutched the black metal box in a bloodstained hand. It attracted me like a magnet: made my heart beat that little bit faster. I quelled poisonous emotive responses that threatened to infect me.

"The *Endeavour* is the key . . . to this war . . . She's the origin." His face twitched, spasmed with pain. "And the war won't stop unless she's found . . ."

"You're not making any sense. Tell me what I have to do."

He pushed the case near to the edge of the bed, offering it to me, and I reached for it without a thought. The outer armour plating was battered and warm to the touch; Ostrow had been holding it tight.

"Ev . . . everything," he said, struggling to speak, "is on there. That's what they want; it's what they've always wanted. L . . . look after it. A lot of good people have died for what's in that box."

"Where is she, Ostrow? Where is the *Endeavour*?"

"In the Maelstrom," Ostrow said. "Her c . . . coordinates . . . the box . . ."

After years of searching, this case contained hard intel

on her location. I held it in my real hand, felt the worn safety catch. It was DNA-encoded but had been unlocked by Ostrow. I had to fight the almost irresistible temptation to open it here and now – to examine exactly what it contained – but Ostrow's ragged breathing drew me back to the room.

"You don't have long," he said. His lucidity seemed deliberate, as though he was really concentrating on telling me this. "Planning a c . . . counter-attack . . . All in package . . ."

Sunsam's counter-attack: reinforcements from the Core Systems. But High Command hadn't survived long enough to give me the details of the operation, and I only knew that they had – somehow – intended to rely on the Shard Gates . . .

"Tell me," he said, "did Professor . . . Saul . . . make it?"

"Yes," I said. "Saul is alive."

If what Saul had become – a frightened shell of a man – was actually living.

"He knows more than you can ever appreciate," Ostrow managed. "This will be the last time, Harris. You're finally getting what you want." He reached out, blindly feeling for my hand. "For God and the Alliance."

"I've never believed in the first," I said, "and I'm not sure there's much left of the other."

Ostrow's eyes shut. "I'm sorry, Harris. Sorry for what you will find out there."

The bio-signs on the machine next to him abruptly flattened, and Ostrow's breathing became softer and softer.

"Medtech!" I yelled. "Get in here!"

There was no death-knell – no last-ditch, desperate attempt to cling to life. He just faded, until the machines began their insistent chiming. The medtechs came, blustered around him.

Took their readings, logged it all down. Just as they ever did.

"He's gone," Dr Serova declared.

It struck me, as the medical team left the room, as they drew the bed sheet over Captain Ostrow's ravaged body, that I knew so little about him. We'd served together for months now, and despite the annoyance that he had caused me he had been a faithful servant of the Alliance. This was not a soldier's death. He had deserved more. I didn't even know his first name, for Christo's sake.

Despite all of that, I left the Medical Deck in a hurry. I told myself that it was because I wanted to make Ostrow's death mean something – because this was what he had died for – but the truth was closer to home. *Is this it?* I asked myself, as I clutched the security case. I could focus on nothing but what I would find inside. It had taken on near demonic proportions – felt as though it had grown heavier and hotter in the brief time that I'd possessed it.

I raced from Medical to Communications. There would be a closed computer suite there. The room was lit only by space outside: the view-ports in the open position.

Strength began to ebb out of me, as the after-effects of the massive adrenaline flood left my system. I felt the hard-wired chemical reaction that was my body telling me "thank Christo we made it out of that alive". The sims never suffered from that response; the combat-suit medi-suite countered the comedown perfectly. Things were very different in my own skin.

Light headed and giddy, I slapped the case down onto a workstation. My hands – flesh and mechanical – were actually trembling as I opened it. Inside, dwarfed by the case, I found a single data-clip. It was battered, scratched, dirty:

I guessed that the clip was the original that Storemberg had described during the briefing. It had come from *Liberty Point*, had survived attacks from the Directorate and the Krell.

I inserted the data-clip into the workstation. Holographics jumped to life in front of me; military-issue security warnings.

I sat back and watched, as everything was unlocked.

There were files on crew manifests, on equipment lists, and ship specifications for the *Endeavour*, her sister ships the UAS *Ark Angel*, the HMS *Lion's Pride*, and numerous other ships. I dismissed all of that information. While it was no doubt important, analysis of that material would require time and patience. I had neither of those qualifications right now.

Finding Elena's whereabouts: that was my objective.

A familiar map of the Maelstrom appeared in front of me. Coordinates were flagged; deep, deep within. Through the twisted web of black holes, quasars, spatial anomalies – into the eye of the storm. Other than the *Colossus*, during her fleeting jump through Shard Space, this was further than any Alliance ship had ever gone: far into the heart of the Krell Empire, within a cluster of suns called the Reef Stars. Every trooper worth their salt had heard of those stars, and the worlds that orbited them. The Krell's supposed home star – identified only through analysis of the Shard Key – sat in the middle of the Maelstrom, flickering softly. Around that system, unnamed so far as I knew, were numerous other stars bearing occupied worlds. These were ancient holdings; likely the first interstellar settlements claimed by the Krell. No one – not even the Lazarus Legion – had set foot on those alien worlds, but through repetition rumour had become fact. Troopers told of hell-worlds, of whole star systems driven mad by alien bio-technology.

"Why did you go there, Elena?" I whispered to myself. "Why did Command send you there?"

The briefing offered no answers. Quantum-space jump points had been identified, again as a result of the Shard Key that the Legion had recovered from Helios. In tri-D, I watched as the jump data was plotted – safely taking a starship to the *Endeavour*'s current location. Of course, the *Endeavour* and her fleet had done the journey without Q-jump data: had flown blind into the hazing stars of the Reef.

The briefing tagged a sector of space known as the Arkonus Abyss, but the computer overlaid the map with the words SHARD GATE. *Another wormhole.* The Abyss was a node of the Shard Network, and this was where we had seen the *Endeavour*, during the retreat from Damascus. There were worlds held within the crushing grasp of the Abyss – gathered in a vast accretion disc – but this was no simple black hole. The spectral and spatial analysis of the rent in time-space was a virtual copy of the Damascus Rift. I watched in wonder and horror as the two Shard Gates connected: felt my temples begin to throb and ache as it went on to show how the *Endeavour*, and later the *Colossus*, had crossed the Maelstrom in less than a second of real-time. It pained me to see how close we'd come – how we had almost grazed the *Endeavour*'s hull, during the flight through the Shard Gate. The computer glitched for a second, the portal between the Rift and the Abyss appearing to remain open—

A hundred Shard Gates suddenly appeared all across the Maelstrom. Markers throughout the region – glowing red, sometimes connected via glittering strands. The hairs on the nape of my neck bristled. I felt the Artefact's signal piercing my mind again – felt it lingering at the edge of my hearing. I shook my head, rubbed my neck; chased it away—

When I looked back at the display, it had refocused on the single Shard Gate: the Arkonus Abyss.

That was where Command wanted us to go; to find the *Endeavour*.

A stream of words were associated with the operation. CODENAME: REVENANT.

I punched some keys on the terminal, called up a comm-link to Loeb in the CIC.

"Loeb," I said, "I have news. I need to call a briefing."

"Copy that," Loeb said. "I have news of my own."

"How long until we reach the muster point?"

"We just did."

"And?"

"I'll explain," he said.

I cut the link. Stared hard at the maps of the Maelstrom that appeared in front of me; tried to ascertain why they were so important to the war effort. Ostrow's dying words had been insistent.

After a long minute, I ejected the data-clip and made off for the briefing.

By the time I arrived, the briefing room was already occupied by the Legion, James, Saul and Loeb. I took a seat and turned to Loeb. His expression was grim.

"This is bad," he said. "We're currently at the muster point. There's no one else here. As of now, *we* are the fleet."

"Christo . . ." Martinez said. "No one else made it out? You sure we're in the right place?"

Loeb nodded. "The Broken Knife code is fleet-wide – it generates the same muster point. I suppose that there could've been a mistake, but it isn't likely. We've run diagnostics on our AI mainframe, and it's functioning correctly. I think that we're in the right place."

"Fuck me," Jenkins said. "This really is the shit."

"Then what do we do?" Mason asked. She looked particularly shaken, her pale cheeks still crossed with smears of my blood.

"I say that we use the FTL drive back to Calico," Loeb said. "We can search for survivors, pick up any personnel who managed to get off-station. We can jump deep in-system, and surprise the Directorate."

"And you can get your pound of flesh from the *Shanghai Remembered*, huh?" Jenkins said. "Except it'll be a wasted gesture when the Directorate counter-attack wipes us out in return."

"We're a match for the *Shanghai*," Loeb insisted. Jenkins had obviously shone a spotlight on his motivation, and it had nothing to do with rescuing survivors: it was instead old-fashioned revenge. "We can go in with stealth systems engaged, and strike hard—"

"*Hermano*," Martinez said, "I hit the *Shanghai*, but she wasn't the only ship out there. I saw plenty of them. There was a fucking battlegroup. We go back, they'll ghost us."

James sighed and sat over the table, the plastic of his flight-suit creaking noisily. "I agree with Martinez. We don't have the aerospace support to fight a war against the Directorate."

"Rubbish," Loeb said. "We have a full complement of plasma torpedoes."

James shook his head. "Even if the *Colossus* has superior firepower, their fighters will bring us down. They had Interceptors and Wraiths; we have nada air support."

"That's not quite true," Loeb argued.

"All right," James said, exasperated. "We have two Hornet gunships. Sorry to speak out of turn, Admiral, but that's not going to cut it. Even if we had ships, we don't have pilots. As of now, *I* am Scorpio Squadron." He paused, looked around the table. "So believe me when I say I want to go back as much as anyone: my pilots are back there."

"How'd your real body end up on the *Colossus* then, James?" Jenkins probed.

"Good fortune," James said, caustically. "Because this was our next posting, and I was loaded in advance of the others. We can't do this; we can't go back to Calico and expect to make any difference."

James rubbed his face. Sim bodies usually coped with exhaustion and hunger very well, but I guessed that it was the emotion that was catching up with him. That came from the mind – currently floating in blue amniotic in the refitted SOC, somewhere at the aft of the *Colossus*. That was something that Sci-Div could never solve.

"Then we should make uplink with whoever is next in the chain of command," Loeb said. "The Navy yards at *Novo Selo*—"

"Those docks are gone," Mason said. She gave an involuntary bristle. "They fell to the Krell last month. And Command is gone."

"They'll appoint replacements," Loeb said. "We'll get new orders!"

"When, exactly?" Kaminski suddenly spoke up. "Admiral, I know this is hard to accept, but the structure is *gone*. We're on our own. It could be months, real-time, before we get new orders from the Core. Meantime, the Krell will be running rampant through Tau Ceti, through Alpha Proxima, through the Centauris."

Loeb tapped his chest, over his heart, at mention of his

beloved homeworld. "Then what are we going to do?" he asked, almost meekly.

I placed the intelligence package on the table in front of me, the data-clip still in its protective casing.

"Ostrow's dead. He died getting this off Calico," I said, indicating the data-clip. "It's an intelligence package on the *Endeavour*."

I called up the course projections, the route maps; showed the team where the *Endeavour* was located. The group sat in silence as I went through the intelligence, stunned by it.

I nodded at the projected map. "This was the mission that High Command tried to give me."

"Except they got bumped in the process . . ." Jenkins said.

"Because the Directorate wanted what we have," I said. "This is what they died for. Before Command was assassinated, General Cole told me that – in the hours before she went down – *Liberty Point* had been infiltrated by the Directorate. The Krell killed the station, but the Directorate let them in: disrupted the sensor network."

There were mutters around the table. Only Jenkins seemed unfazed by the suggestion. "I've been saying that since the start," she said. "My sources never lie."

"Nowhere is safe any more. The Directorate hit us at Damascus, *Liberty* and Calico. They will not stop until they have this information; until they have the *Endeavour*. Before he died, Fleet Admiral Sunsam told me that the Navy were planning a counter-attack, an offensive against the Krell."

The mission briefing had been scant, and I wished that I'd had just a little more time, just a little more intel . . . *This attack will not succeed unless we have some assistance,* General Cole had said. *What did he mean by that?* I knew nothing about the timing of the offensive, about the forces involved.

Loeb chewed his lip. "I'd say those course projections will take us almost nine months, objective, to get into the Maelstrom."

I hadn't checked the calculations, but I suspected that Loeb was right. Going into the Maelstrom, via a Q-jump, would take a decent chunk of real-time: for all I knew, even if we succeeded in acquiring the *Endeavour* – in doing whatever it was Command had expected of us – we might be too late.

But what's the alternative? I asked myself. *To just give up?*

"Did Ostrow tell you *why* the *Endeavour* is so important?" Martinez asked.

"He didn't," I said. "But this will be our target, and whatever is out there, it's the key to ending this war. Ostrow believed in this. And I know that the Directorate are putting everything into stopping us."

Martinez sighed. "It's not like we have a choice, *jefe*. We're Lazarus Legion. We stick together."

Mason nodded. "For the Legion."

"I might not be Legion," James said, "but I can't let the Directorate win. I got family back in the Core; I can't let them down either."

"Anything to add, Professor Saul?" I asked.

Saul had that same distracted air that he seemed to get when he was around Shard discoveries. He was still ghost-like – pallid, thin – but as he looked at the mission plan, something began to burn behind his eyes. I wondered where Ostrow had sprung Saul from, dressed as he was in a simple blue jumpsuit. Had he been detained in the infirmary, like Kaminski, or had Sci-Div immediately put him back to work?

The nerve-staples had been removed from his shaven scalp, and like Kaminski he had received unpleasant flesh-grafts, but he didn't look capable of going back into the Maelstrom.

Even so, he said, "There is nowhere else to go, and Command wanted this done."

"*He knows more than you can ever appreciate*," Ostrow had told me. Saul avoided eye contact as I watched him from across the table.

"Don't worry," Kaminski said. "We'll look after you, Prof."

"Or at least we'll try," Jenkins added, making the joint decision.

"Give me a full tac-analysis of our situation, Loeb," I said.

Loeb stared down at a data-slate in front of him. "Weapons systems and null-shields are operational. The munitions stores are full: we have plasma warheads, power cells for the laser batteries, slugs for the railguns. We have a dozen orbit-to-ground nukes, if we ever need them. Food and air for a long haul – years, in fact. All life-support systems are functioning optimally. The hypersleep bays are running. The engine systems have acceptable bleed.

"But there are less than a thousand personnel on this ship, and only a third of those are experienced hands. We were in orbital dock; having veterans do routine work probably didn't sound like a good idea at the time. We can cover the minimum number of watch standers, but you" – he nodded at me, as though deferring responsibility – "need to understand that this crew is mighty tight, and they're all on edge."

"The Legion will step up," I said. "We can cover whatever posts you need us to. We'll set a watch schedule. What about other equipment? Do we have simulators? Is the simulant operations centre functional?"

"The SOC is ready to run," Mason said. "We've got tanks, and they work. But no Science Division support."

"I never thought there would be a time when I'd miss those fuckers," Martinez said, "but it's finally come."

He was right. The Sci-Div complement was a requirement for a simulant operation; usually made up of fifty or so medical staff. I'd already checked the numbers, done a tally: the *Colossus* currently carried five medtechs. All were of the minimal operating grade for a sim op and one was injured. Dr Serova was the most senior, but she had seen only a single combat operation and wasn't sim-tech approved.

"We've got plenty of simulants," Mason said. "On last count, we've got enough for ten bodies a piece." She smiled at Kaminski. "Even 'Ski has some new skins."

"That so?" he asked, raising an eyebrow. "I'm itching to get skinned up again."

"Could've been an administrative error," Mason said, "or maybe Captain Ostrow planned it that way."

"What about other equipment?" I said, turning to Martinez.

"Good news on that front; we've got a decent supply of arms and armour," Martinez said. The Venusian's eyes glimmered for a second, and despite our current circumstances he looked enthused. "We got upgrades, *jefe*. Mili-Intel came through on this one. There are fifty suits of Ares battle-armour in the armoury."

Mason whistled. "I've read about that. It's bleeding edge."

"Believe me," Jenkins said, "it looks a lot better in person than it ever could on paper. It's some real nice shit."

Battle-suits were up-armoured and up-gunned versions of the usual combat-suits employed on sim ops; armoured units comparable with exo-suits or powered mechs in terms of their offensive capability. That Command had approved their use on this mission, or that Ostrow had managed to secure fifty of them, was impressive: given the current war-footing, it was a considerable investment of resources.

Kaminski cracked his knuckles. "If I get the chance to kick some Krell ass, all the better."

I stood from the table, took the intel data-clip again.

"I'll make an address to the crew," Loeb said. "After everything that's happened, it's the least they deserve."

"You do that. Those medtechs will need to get the sleepers prepped as well. We're going to be in Q-space for a long time – too long to stay awake."

There were some groans from the Legion.

"It'll take a couple of hours to conduct final flight checks," Loeb said.

CHAPTER TWELVE

SLEEP WELL

The hours before the sleep were filled with hurried, desperate preparations for launch. Those that needed it received medical attention from the limited sci-med crew. I insisted that they leave me until last, and Dr Serova oversaw the cleaning of the frag injuries to my shoulders and back, the wealth of lacerations to my face, the broken ribs. Far from them being the worst injuries I'd received, I was more than able to work on through them.

The *Colossus* sailed as quietly and invisibly as she could in an attempt to hide from both the Krell and the Directorate. No other ships turned up, and there was not so much as a single transmission received from the rest of the Alliance fleet. I was satisfied that they were gone: that the surprise attack on Calico Base had scattered, if not destroyed, the remaining Navy battlegroups.

We held a brief and impersonal funeral service for Captain Ostrow. His body was wrapped in a body bag and laid in the main hangar deck, surrounded by a handful of crew. No one knew enough about him to make any kind of comment on his passing, but Martinez said a few words: the Latter Day Catholic funeral rites. Then Ostrow's body was loaded into a firing tube, usually reserved for missiles, and we stood at salute. The body was launched into space, rapidly disappearing into the void, visible through the viewports as a quickly diminishing spot in the dark.

"I hope that doesn't attract attention from the Krell," Jenkins said.

Mason bit her lip and glared sideways at the older woman. "Have some respect, Jenkins. Please."

Jenkins shrugged. "When you've seen death as often as the rest of us, you'll understand. This is nothing new."

"At least it isn't one of our own this time," Martinez said, sighing and shaking his head. I knew that it wasn't meant glibly.

"It's an occupational hazard," I muttered. "And it'll get us all in the end."

"Let's not forget the passing of those lost at Calico Base," Martinez added, bowing his head. "We should pay our respects to Baker, Sperenzo; everyone else we left behind. They won't be forgotten."

The deck cleared very quickly, and the task was done. I followed Kaminski and Saul out into the corridor. Not quite friends, they seemed to stick together as though the time spent in Directorate detention had somehow forged a bond between them.

"You sure that you're up to this?" I asked Kaminski.

"I was recertified," Kaminski said, rolling his shoulder blades. "I can do this."

"You don't have to go in with the Legion," I said.

"Stop talking about me as though I'm not Lazarus Legion." He grinned boyishly. "I was gone for a while, that's all."

"I'm not going to ask you again," I said, "but you need anything, 'Ski, just say."

He paused, nodded. "Appreciate it, boss, but it really isn't me you need to watch. The rest of the team is just as strung out."

Saul lingered wordlessly nearby, wringing his hands with unrelieved anxiety. "Same goes for you, Professor," I said. "I know this is tough on you too."

Saul looked at me as though he hadn't realised I was speaking to him, blinking behind his enhanced-visual glasses. "Yes, yes. Of course."

"I guess that you were hoping for a break from the madness, Prof?" Kaminski jibed. "Somewhere warm and safe, eh?"

"Something like that," Saul said. "I'd rather keep my head out of this mess, if I can. What the Warfighters did in the terminal, it . . . it wasn't something that I want to see again."

"Did Command, or Ostrow, explain any of this to you?" I questioned.

Saul hesitated before he answered. "No. Nothing."

I don't believe you, Saul, I thought.

"What about the code word 'Revenant'? That mean anything to you?"

That same pause again. "No."

The *Colossus*' PA system gave a soft chime overhead.

"Last call for sleepers," came the announcement. "All personnel to the hypersleep suite for pre-sleep medication."

"After the sleep," I said, "you and I need to talk."

Saul repressed an uncomfortable swallow, his Adam's apple bobbing. "Of course, Colonel."

"All hands to the hypersleep bays . . ." the AI declared, repeating the order every couple of minutes.

The life-support systems cost power, and the starship AI was eager to conserve that wherever possible. By the time that Kaminski, Saul and I made it to the hypersleep suite, the *Colossus* had already started to put herself to sleep. The machine was taking decisions of its own accord, and had decided that several decks no longer required heat to operate at maximum efficiency. Given that we were surrounded by vacuum, the ship was quickly becoming cold. A plume of hot breath escaped my mouth as we made our way onto the crowded deck. The crew seemed to huddle together for warmth – or maybe safety – and there was only a single hypersleep bay operating for this operation.

Dr Serova patrolled the capsule banks, jotting things down on her data-slate as she went.

"All crew accounted for," she declared to Loeb's executive officer, nodding to herself. "Except for Flight Lieutenant James . . ."

"So we get to see flyboy in his real body?" Jenkins said. She had changed into a hospital gown, and a clutch of IVs and data-jacks dangled from the open ports on her forearms like extracted veins.

Just then, a metal casket with a glass front floated into the bay: a grav-sled operated by two medtech custodians. Both kept a respectful distance from the pod; a machine something like a simulant-tank, stamped with the Sim Ops Aerospace Force seal.

"The lieutenant is here," the nearest tech said. "Ready for decanting."

The outer canopy of the pod was semi-opaque, and when I looked inside – curiosity getting the better of me – I immediately regretted it.

There wasn't much left of the body in the tank. A vague outline of a terribly scarred torso; metallic plugs grafted to the chest, feeder-tubes penetrating the ribcage. No arms or legs that I could see, but plenty of mottled skin where they had once existed. The face was the worst part, because it was undeniably familiar: because without even being told, I knew that this was Lieutenant James. He slept, eyes shut, but somehow I doubted that this was chemically induced hypersleep.

"Maybe you ought to go easy on him," I said to Jenkins. She pulled her eyes from the tank. "Maybe I should."

I remembered James' explanation for his hesitation on Calico. His words: *Kaminski was lucky.* Seeing the thing in the tank – what was left of James – I realised that he had been right. The Directorate were capable of much, much worse.

The medtechs went about getting James into his hypersleep pod – thankfully, a unit away from the Legion – and we settled into our own machines.

I stripped out of my fatigues and struggled into a hospital gown. My bionic hand was performing well enough, but I still hadn't got used to it. The metal frame sent off harsh reflections. I stared down at the appendage for a moment.

Mason and Martinez were already loaded into their pods, and Jenkins was in the pod next to me. She had climbed into her machine and was wriggling against the cold plastic crash couch, making herself comfortable. I did the same, and soon the Legion were all hooked up and ready to be put under. The room around us had quietened down now. Medtechs were logging each pod, and some of the canopies had closed.

I felt the familiar rush of cryogen and sedative hitting my bloodstream. The dissociation that always came with the hypersleep was taking me more rapidly than usual. That might be, I considered, because I was already dog-tired. The attack on Calico had taken it out of me.

"Night," Mason said, her voice anxious.

"Sleep well, assholes," Jenkins replied.

"Always," Martinez mumbled, in his sleep.

"Good to be back," Kaminski said. He leant over to Jenkins' capsule, and the troopers kissed briefly. "Sleep tight, baby."

"Dream about me," Jenkins said. "But nothing slutty."

Kaminski tapped his scarred cranium. "My head, Jenk. My rules."

The pod canopy slid into place, humming as it descended. I closed my eyes, let the sleep take me.

I saw – whether imagined or real, I couldn't say – a prickle of light on the inside of my eyelid. A blue light: star-bright. Even without opening my eyes, I knew what I was seeing. It was a tenacious image that had burnt into my mind, and had been plaguing me since Calico.

Had the *Shanghai Remembered* fired her drive as we'd left?

I knew that I should've discussed it with Admiral Loeb. At the very least, I should've asked the Legion whether they had seen it. There had been officers on the CIC – sailors manning the bridge – and their sensor arrays might've picked up emissions from an activated drive.

I couldn't tell them, in case it turned out to be true, I thought to myself. *And if it's true, then I might lose the last chance that I have to save Elena.*

I filed the thought away and let the hypersleep pod do its thing.

CHAPTER THIRTEEN

NEED A NAME

Ten years ago

I spent the next couple of hours locked in the back of a
Mili-Pol meat wagon, cradling my bruised head with a medi-
pack. The only indication that the launch had happened
– that the shuttles had disembarked from Calico Base, left
for the waiting expeditionary fleet – was the eruption of
voices around me. The words "Launch! Launch! Launch!"
were repeated again and again and again, accompanied by
a tide of cheers and shouts.

This was not how I'd wanted today to go at all.

The inside of the van smelt of vomit and bactericide – a
contradictory and heady combination – and although there
were others caged nearby I was the only occupant of this
particular holding cell. It was best described as cramped: a
two-by-two with a metal bench on the cabin side, and a
heavy wire-mesh grille separating me from the van's rear
doors. No view-ports to the outside world, no way of stopping the mess that was unfolding in the hangar. I guessed

– from the noise and commotion – that I was either still inside the launch hangar, or in an adjoining corridor.

I wrestled with the urge to be sick. The MPs had done a proper job on me: enough to put me out for the afternoon but just short of causing any lasting damage. Assholes. I closed my eyes. Willed the throbbing in my head to subside just a little.

There was a thumping against the outer door. *Maybe something has gone wrong. Perhaps there's still a chance that I can save her.* The rear door opened, leaving only the grille between me and freedom. Light spilled into the darkened cabin.

"He's being held pending double assault charges," a gruff male voice said. "I got an officer willing to testify that he charged the cordon, ma'am."

"Puh-lease," a woman said in response. "He fell from the enclosure and got disoriented. Nothing more than that."

I immediately recognised the voice. The CNN reporter from the press pit: the Brooke woman. She stood at the door, watching over the shoulder of an armoured MP. The officer blocked her path but held the door open just enough that she could see me inside the cage.

"He isn't going anywhere. We've had several incidents like this today, lots of disruption. It's bad enough dealing with the dissidents and religios without fuck-ups in uniform. I'm going to have to lodge a complaint with his senior officer."

The reporter shook her head. The more I looked at her, the more recognisable her face became.

"This has been a great, momentous day for all of us," she said, stroking the officer's forearm. "It really has. So let's not ruin it. I'm sure that the captain is sorry. Is informing his CO really necessary? It'll probably be a bucketload of paperwork for you to process, and like you say: you already have lots of other prisoners to deal with . . ."

The reporter grabbed his hand – so quickly that I barely noticed it – and, like a pro, slipped something into it. She was good, but so was the officer. He kept his hand lowered. His eyes remained on me. *And that*, I thought, *is how you bribe an Alliance Military Police officer into releasing a suspect* . . . But if it got me out of the cage, who was I to argue?

"He's Simulant Operations," Brooke pined. "You know, officer, how difficult it is for them. They do such hard work – all that dying . . ."

The MP nodded. "All right. Just make sure that he stays out of trouble."

"I'll see to it," Brooke said. "He can be released into my custody."

"Well, that was interesting . . ."

Brooke walked with me through the passageways of Calico Base. The celebrations were still in full swing, and didn't look as though they were going to slow down anytime soon. It made me feel a lot worse than the injury to my head. I had already tried to lose Brooke several times, but that wasn't as easy as I'd hoped. The woman was pernicious and faster than she looked, always on my tail.

"Thanks for getting me out and all," I said, "but I have places to be."

She raised a pale eyebrow at me. "Really?"

I grunted. She was on her own now, without news-drones, and she looked about as lost on Calico as I did. At the first sign of trouble, it appeared that Vijay the guide had vanished, eager to avoid trouble with MPs.

"I have a shuttle to catch," I said.

"Funny how you weren't thinking of that when you jumped off that gantry . . ."

"I fell. You said so yourself."

"Didn't look like that," she said. "Didn't sound like that. Seeing a Sim Ops captain out here; it gets my news-senses tingling."

"What do you want from me? I'm not a story, Brooke."

She smiled. "I never said that you were. And call me Cassi."

"Thanks for getting me out, Brooke, and I can pay for the bribe if that's what you're looking for."

"That was on the house, Captain. But if you have the time . . ." She shrugged. "Maybe you can talk with me. Ten minutes. We can go for a drink." Her face brightened. "I know a good place, not far from here. I'll even buy."

I thought about it for a moment. Getting a shuttle off Calico Base would take some wrangling. It might be hours before I could get transport arranged, maybe even days before I could get out-system. Just the mention of a drink diminished the ache in my head, but exchanged it for a yearn in my gut. I hadn't appreciated that my hands were shaking until Brooke mentioned the drink.

What harm can it do?

"One drink," I said.

"One drink," she repeated.

The bar Brooke had suggested turned out to be the press lounge. It was barely recognisable to me: glittering glass frontage, a robotic piano player in one corner, chromed metallic floors and walls. Ordinarily, I would've avoided that place like the New Detroit heights, but today it wasn't an unappealing location. Every other bar, diner or club was packed with tourists and launch-celebrants: the press lounge, being reserved for Press Corps and associated Alliance staff, was far quieter. Granted, the launch had attracted press from all over, but we could get a seat and the bar hadn't run dry.

"This okay?" Brooke asked, pulling into a booth with glass walls and a transparent table.

"Fine," I said. "But you promised drink."

"That I did."

She ordered us some local spirit that I didn't recognise. The bartender was human – an androgynous-looking man in an orange vac-suit – and quickly served up the drinks.

"I don't usually drink in press lounges," Brooke said, "but today is an exception. That, and I've never been to Calico Base before. You?"

"First time for me," I said, sipping the drink. I scrunched up my face: it tasted sweet and foul at the same time. "But I thought you said that I wasn't a story."

"Those were your words, not mine."

"You didn't disagree with me."

She gave me a brittle, sympathetic smile. "I saw what you did out there. Everyone knows about Simulant Operations, what it could become. The new shit, the next big thing. Blah, blah, blah. I know what you troopers put up with, but what you did in the shuttle bay? It wasn't anything to do with Sim Ops. It was personal."

"It was private," I said. Staying and drinking was a very different beast from revealing what had happened between Elena and I.

Brooke tapped a cigarette from a crushed packet, offered one to me. I declined. "You had a thing for the girl, the doctor? What was her name – Marceau something or other?"

I sighed. "Elena. Her name is Elena Marceau."

"Right, right," Brooke said. "She was from Azure, wasn't she? Originally Old Earth, French origin? Am I right?"

I finished the sweet-tasting monstrosity but found that it had done nothing to quench my thirst. Without answering Brooke's question, I ordered another couple of drinks. My choosing this time: a basic Martian vodka, something crude but effective.

"I want to prove myself," Brooke went on. Her voice had lowered; she was a good actress. "I don't want to be doing stories about *virons* being stuck up trees on Tau Ceti IV for the rest of my career."

"*Virons?*"

"It's a native to Tau Ceti," she said. "A lizard with fur, like a cat."

"Does this act work on many soldiers?"

She shrugged, the veil of vulnerability lifting instantly. "Some," she said. "But not you?"

"Not me. I'll drink with you, and then I'll get my shuttle."

"Fair enough. Just tell me one thing: why were you so upset when you saw Dr Marceau leaving? Off the record."

Before I'd had a chance to stop myself, something broke inside of me. I blurted, "I told her that if she left me, it would be the last time she would ever see me. I promised her that." I swallowed back emotion. "That wasn't to be."

"I've read her personnel files," Brooke said, "such that are publicly available."

"By which you mean none," I said. All of our records were restricted. Sim Ops wasn't a secret any more, but that sort of data was still confidential. Even with Elena's posting to the *Endeavour* expedition, her civilian service record was classified.

"You'd be surprised what walls fall before a determined reporter," Brooke said, "so we don't need to play that game. She was Sim Ops, and she was one of the original psychologists attached to the Programme."

"That's true."

"She was also one of the very first proponents of the Programme. A very vocal supporter of it, although she suggested that it should have very precise limits placed upon it."

I said nothing to that: it was all painfully true.

"Look," Brooke said, "I got you out of that prison van. They were going to report you to your CO—"

"And you said that it was gratis."

"I'm not asking for a full interview or anything."

"She was my girl, and she left me for the Maelstrom," I said, as definitively as I could. "Let's leave it there."

"And today, I guess, was your attempt to stop her from leaving?"

"Yes, it was."

Brooke rolled her eyes. "That's some seriously romantic shit, Harris."

"Fuck you."

"You think that she will ever come back?"

"I *hope* that she will," I said.

But deep down? I was sure that she wouldn't. I thought of those starships – the expedition fleet – clustered in high orbit. All so fragile, all so weak. They weren't warships, and they shouldn't be taking the risk of sailing into the Maelstrom.

"So it was personal," Brooke said. "Fair enough. Maybe not much of a story in that. Here's to the Treaty."

She raised her glass. Several patrons nearby copied her.

I just drank hard and let it all go.

It turned out that I had more than a drink with Cassari Brooke – better known to CNN as Cassi Brooke, prime-time reporter for the Core Worlds. The evening rapidly spiralled into multiple drinks, until the table was filled with empty glasses.

Brooke got other information out of me, but – I was sure – not enough to make any sort of story. We talked about my father, although I studiously avoided the topic of his suicide, and then my grandfather. I was less concerned about talking about him, because there was so little to say.

"He was Section Eight," I said.

"Which means?" Brooke slurred.

"He was discharged from the Army by reason of mental instability."

"He went nuts?"

I shrugged. "You could say that."

"How does this, ah, Section Eight, work with Sim Ops? Aren't you all a bit crazy?"

"Not enough for a discharge," I said.

"Let me give you a name. A name for a man who doesn't ever die."

"I die all right. I just keep coming back."

"Is there a difference?" she asked, frowning.

"The simulation isn't real," I said. "It only feels that way."

This was basic textbook stuff; the material drip-fed to the media. Although the Sim Ops Programme was still young – was still a fraction of the size of the wider Alliance Army – we were already finding difficulties. More than enough recruits *had* gone full Section Eight: unable to tell the difference between what was real and simulated. The brain interpreted everything experienced in a sim as real, whether in a simulant or a hardcopy. The only difference was that simulated death wasn't final.

"My dear Captain Harris," she said. "Died one hundred and twelve times." She sat upright for a moment. "Do you guys all have, like, nicknames?"

214

"Call signs, you mean?" I said.

"Yeah."

"Some of us," I said. "Not me. Not yet."

"You should have one." She ran a hand through her red hair, massaged her scalp. "Men don't fear men. They're scared of monsters. That's what the Krell have up on us, see?"

"I see."

"Men needs myths. That's what you need to be, Harris. A myth. And with all those transitions . . ."

My attention was elsewhere, directed at the tri-D viewer beside the bar. It was getting late now, and many of the customers had moved on. The tri-D was still broadcasting a composite of news recordings from throughout the day, and the remaining patrons had gathered around it, eyes focused on the glowing graphics. Much of the material was pointless rubbish – overviews of the marching bands, detailed breakdowns of the starship specifications, further biographies of the crew. But this programme had caught my attention.

There were talking heads explaining what this mission meant to the Alliance. And not just the Alliance: Director-General Zhang, high executive of the Directorate, even made an address.

"He always looks so calm," I whispered. "Whatever he is saying."

Was that a learnt skill? I wondered. Whether he was declaring war on the Outer Colonies, suggesting trade embargoes against the Antarctic Republic, or naming his fifteenth son, there was never any malice in his tone. He never so much as *looked* angry. It was particularly disturbing.

Zhang was nearly a hundred years old, but didn't look much past forty standard: his rounded face, unlined by age or worry, bearing only the slightest hint of his ethnic Chino roots, was almost cherubic. Dressed in a black smart-suit, frame well-exercised. As premier of the largest power bloc in human space, he wielded the combined military weight of the Asiatic Directorate. Indisputably, Zhang was a dangerous man, but a man who didn't want you to *believe* that he was dangerous. He smiled to the camera, nodded and gesticulated – never staying still.

"*This mission represents the future of human–Krell relations, and as a spokesperson for the Asiatic Directorate, as a representative of over two-thirds of the human population in this galaxy, we wish you luck, crew, in your voyage.*" He paused, a warm smile playing on his lips. "*And we will be with you, in your hearts.*"

"You think that they wanted to go too?" Brooke asked me. "Into the Maelstrom, I mean."

"Yeah," I said. "I think that they wanted to go a lot."

The *Endeavour*'s mission was purely Alliance-backed, but that hadn't stopped Zhang and his senior advisers from requesting that the ship carry Thai observers. The Thai Kingdom was the least militarised nation-state of the Directorate; with colonies as far flung as Nebaris III, it was also one of the most advanced. Other elements of the Directorate had been less diplomatic about what they saw as proper involvement in the expedition. Unified Korea – Uni-Kor – had been particularly insistent that a Directorate ship accompany the fleet. They had even threatened military repercussions if their demands were not met, but intervention from the Euro Confed had talked them down before the launch.

"I interviewed one of his lieutenants, once," Brooke said. Her voice suddenly sounded very lucid – not very drunk at all – and her eyes were extremely focused. "It . . . wasn't a nice experience."

"I reckon," I said. I had the overwhelming urge to tell her about Carrie, about my sister: killed by Directorate Special Forces when she was barely out of adulthood.

Brooke waved a finger at the holo. There were marching rows of soldiers, dressed in all-enclosing black suits, hides as shiny as rad-ants. Those were called hard-suits: assisted exo-skeletons for use in hazardous combat environments.

"You know what they're doing, now?" Brooke asked me. Before I could respond, she was talking again: "They don't have mothers, and they don't have fathers. They're grown in vats, birthed from test tubes. Can you imagine it? A whole army of those bastards."

"I've heard the rumours."

Not all soldiers, of course, but the Directorate were resorting to cloning tech: creating Special Ops teams in crèches, out in Cambodia. Labs where all they did was build men and women, breed children that only cared about war. Command insisted that the Directorate were creating paler imitations of simulants, that their genetics programme was nothing to be afraid of, but I didn't see it that way. What the Directorate didn't have in quality, they would eventually have in numbers.

"Do you think that something grown in a tube has a conscience?" Brooke said, still staring at the screen.

"No, I don't."

"You did the right thing today," she said, suddenly changing the subject. "Trying to stop Dr Marceau, I mean."

"I know," I said.

"I don't mean like that," Brooke said. "The *Endeavour*'s mission . . . I've heard things. We've all heard things."

I froze. I suddenly felt very sober, very angry and very alone. Everything else in the room dropped away from me. "Such as?"

"Not everything is right with the expedition," Brooke said, leaning in to me. "Not everything is as it seems. There's a lot about it that you don't know."

"Tell me," I said. "Everything."

Brooke looked left, then right. She appeared genuinely frightened, her expression only slightly tempered by the fact that she was thoroughly drunk. Abruptly, she drew back from the table. I saw the barest flicker of intelligence-sharing across her pupils; that blue flash that indicated she was remotely consulting a database somewhere. Her eyes reflected on the mirrored table surface, but by the time she looked up at me – the false smile across her face again – the connection was gone.

"I've seen some of the manifests," she whispered. "There are weapons onboard. Plasma tech, kinetic carbines. She's carrying a big armoury."

"That's not news," I said, annoyed. "There's a whole simulant team onboard. Under Sergeant Stone; organised by O'Neil."

O'Neil was head of Simulant Operations; the asshole who had approved security for the mission.

"Why do they need weapons to organise a Treaty?" Brooke said.

"Because they're going into the Maelstrom: they need protection."

I was only repeating the official line, but the words left my mouth by rote: a single Sim Ops team wouldn't be protection enough for a whole expedition. *The crew are doomed*, my inner voice whispered.

Brooke swallowed down a mouthful of liquor, noisily, and gave me a broad smile: snapping out of whatever rut she had fallen into. Her mood instantly shifted, and the moment passed. As though she had decided against whatever disclosure she had been about to make.

"Sorry to get your hopes up, buddy," she said. "What will we have to report on, when the war is over? That's the real question."

"I'm sure you'll find something," I said. "Was that all you had to tell me?"

"Pretty much. I . . . I feel kind of sick. It's real hot in here."

The drunken look returned to her face. She had gone almost green. I stood from the table.

"I think that I'd better go. I have a hotel room in Sector Three. The Mumbai."

"Fine," I said. "Safe journey."

"You could say it like you mean it, trooper. It's real nice – old-fashioned – that you're waiting for her, even though you don't think she's coming back. It was good meeting you."

"Pity I can't say the same," I said, as Cassi Brooke left the bar.

I managed to secure a bunk down at the local barracks, playing up my Sim Ops position, and the night passed uneventfully but I slept little. I constantly relived Elena leaving on the shuttle, the fact that I hadn't stopped her. Had I been able to? Probably not, but that didn't stop me from feeling that I hadn't done *enough*. What plagued me most was the uncertainty. Had she seen me as she'd entered the shuttle hatch?

Mostly, I was tormented that she might've done so, and yet still boarded the transport.

I had come to Calico hoping to – in some way – interfere with the launch. I had naively presumed that if Elena had actually seen me, she would've changed her mind about leaving. I knew, deep down, that things were not that simple, but that had been my objective.

And then there was Cassari Brooke's disclosure that something was wrong with the expedition. What had she meant by that? Her explanation about weapons hadn't been convincing.

What did she really know?

The morning: maybe that would hold some answers.

The opposite was of course true, and the morning held just more frustration.

I left the barracks early and went straight to the Mumbai. Post-launch, it was busy with departing tourists, but slightly less hectic than the day before. Paying no heed to the queued off-worlders, I went straight to Brooke's hotel. Brooke wasn't the only person who knew how to give a bribe: I paid-off the door-staff for her room number, and took the lift to her floor.

Only to find that her room was empty. A cleaning droid was inside, stripping the bunk.

"You can't be here," the droid said immediately, singular security-eye flashing in non-recognition. "You are not a registered guest."

"I know," I said, "but I'm looking for one."

"This room is being prepared for the next occupant."

I looked down at my wrist-comp: it was only oh-eight-hundred hours. Still early by civilian standards. "What happened to the last guest?"

"Gone," the droid said, sterilely. "Checked out."

"When?"

"Early. How should I know? I only clean rooms."

I sighed with anger. "Did she leave anything?"

The droid shrugged its metal shoulders. "Your name Harris?"

"Yeah, it is."

"Then this is for you," it said, indicating.

There was a folded sheet of paper on the cabinet beside the bunk. I opened it, read the message inside. It was a single line, in scrawled block letters.

HARRIS, ABOUT THAT NAME: WILL "LAZARUS" DO? GOOD LUCK WITH THE GIRL. C X

I crumpled the paper.

"Fuck."

The droid paused over the bed for a moment. With robots, even hotel-staff bots, it's always difficult to read an expression or motive. I could swear that this droid was smiling at me.

"You read the news, Harris?" it asked.

"No, why?"

"You might want to," it said. "Now get out of here. I have beds to make."

I left the room in a hurry, blood thumping in my ears. As I waited at the elevator door, I opened my wrist-comp: called up the latest news-feed. There were, of course, multiple stories about the *Endeavour*'s launch, about the crew, on post-expedition analysis and the prospects of the Treaty being agreed . . .

And something else.

SIM OPS: THE MAN THEY CALL LAZARUS.

Reporter: Cassi Brooke, CNN correspondent.

CHAPTER FOURTEEN

GODS OF TECHNOLOGY

We awoke under the light of a different star, light-years from the Alliance.

I sat in the mess cradling a cup of hot coffee. It was surprisingly good; smelt real enough and tasted rich at the back of my throat. It was my second cup: the caffeine always helped to throw off the effects of the sleep. The Legion sat around the mess hall table, trying their best to shake off the post-sleeper hangover.

"We're inside the Maelstrom," I said.

Jenkins yawned. "There was a time when that would've shit me up . . ."

For the Legion, like death, the Maelstrom had lost its glamour, but the same could not be said for everyone aboard the ship. I noted the greenhorns and newly promoted maintenance staff eying us from across the hall. More than once, I'd heard the word "ghost-ship" and "government conspiracy" being muttered between crewmen.

Mason sat across from me with a plate heaped with breakfast items: fried eggs, cornbread, potatoes and more. The look of the massed Navy food – so soon after we'd come out of hypersleep – made me feel vaguely queasy. She was almost rabidly consuming the food.

"Where do you put that stuff, Mason?" Jenkins asked. "I've never seen a girl eat as much as you."

Mason barely looked up from the plate. "It's the freezers," she said. "They always do this to me."

"Right," Jenkins said. "That's your excuse, and you're sticking with it."

"Let the girl eat," Kaminski said. "Nine months is a long time." He smiled, gave a bitter laugh. "No telling what's happened to the rest of the Alliance. Maybe the Krell have given up, and the War's over."

"We're in the dark," I said. "No comm-link, no news-feeds. But I severely doubt it."

Any contact with the outside world could summon the Krell, and surrounding space was likely filled with fish heads. We were in a sort of perfect isolation; unaware of the progress of the Second Krell War, the hostilities with the Directorate, or any other fate that might've befallen the Alliance.

"Maybe we've lost," Jenkins said. "I mean, for all we know, the Krell might've reached the Core Systems by now." She waved a hand in the air. "All of this might be a waste of time."

Just then, Lieutenant James breezed past our table – took up a seat with some of the Navy crew in the corner of the room. He'd obviously been decanted directly into a simulator, and was back in a next-gen sim, ignorant of the whole incident in the hypersleep bay.

"Jesus," Jenkins whispered. "How does the guy live like that?"

What other choice does he have? I asked myself.

"Same as everyone," I said, keeping my voice low. "Does what he has to."

223

"I heard that he has a kid and wife, on Tau Ceti," Jenkins added. "I wonder if he goes home in his real body."

"Not like that, he doesn't," Kaminski muttered.

Mason suddenly stopped eating. She pushed her plate, only half-emptied, away. "I don't feel like eating any more," she said.

I sipped down another mouthful of coffee. "We've got a mission to execute out here," I said, "and you can all stop with the theorising. I want everyone on point and frosty; not thinking about what could've happened back home. The real work starts now. We don't know what we're going to find on that ship."

Martinez sighed. "The new battle-suits are going to need some prep work," he said. "They need to be marked up and stamped for duty." He looked around the table. "You haven't seen anything until you've seen these bad boys. They are *absolute* bad ass. Nothing going to stand in our way with that armour."

"I want those suits tested," I said, finishing my coffee, "as well as complete weapon drills and equipment checks. No corners cut."

"Affirmative," Jenkins said. "Where are you going?"

"To see Loeb," I said.

The CIC was populated by newly defrosted staff, mostly gathered around the tactical display. A projection of what I guessed was the local star system was shown there: glittering in green wireframe tri-D. I paused to examine the data.

As we drew nearer to our objective, the star system was being detected with increasing clarity. A wilted red star sat in the middle of the map, its light blurred but still strong, and a collection of rugged planets orbited the sun. The

Arkonus Abyss sat among the network of planets, devouring any planetary debris that came too close: a blue rent in time-space.

"The readings are off the charts," Admiral Loeb said, as he approached. "I was just about to call for you, Harris."

He stood at the head of the table, hands behind his back: already completely alert and awake. That was the benefit of being a regular spacer; despite his age, he had the constitution to throw off the hypersleep with ease.

"Morning, Loeb. What have we got?"

Loeb waved at the tri-D. "We made Q-space translation exactly as planned. There's a lot of debris out there, but we're taking it slow and easy."

"Debris?" I didn't like the sound of that.

"Nothing we can't handle," Loeb said. "A lot of chaff, but not enough to provide cover for a fleet. A quasar on the edge of our sensor range, a couple of black holes nearby." He sounded almost blasé about the whole thing, but I could understand why. He shrugged. "For the Maelstrom, none of it is unusual. Well, except for *that*."

The Arkonus Abyss.

"The energy emissions are very similar to those recorded from the Damascus Rift," Professor Saul added. He stood across from me, peering down at the display. "I'm certain that this is another Shard Gate. It's emitting a fairly regular stream of tachyon particles, as well as flooding near-space with exotic radiation."

He magnified the map; focused on the blue rift in space broadly in the middle of the star system. It flickered, writhed with energy, as though it was a living entity, appearing as an area of non-space, visually very similar to the phenomenon we'd encountered at Damascus.

"Far as we can tell," Loeb said, "this one isn't active."

He nodded at Saul. "The Professor has been lending his scientific expertise to our technical team."

Saul gave a tepid smile. "I'd like to help where I can, and it keeps me busy."

The Abyss had a hypnotic quality to it, and I felt some tiny triumph at proving its existence. Elena was really out here; she'd used this Gate to contact me at Damascus.

"How close do we have to get to it?" I asked.

Loeb sighed. "Nearer than I'd like. Ostrow's coordinates take us further into the system," he said. "Almost half an AU out from the gas giant." A flashing beacon appeared on the holo, slowly looping around it. "Going to be a while before we can get proper eyes on the target."

That planet was designated by a string of numbers. Electrical storms coursed over the surface, spreading like cracks on a sheet of ice. It was encased by multiple bands of rock in almost geometric shapes, and without even consulting the scanner I knew that it would be projecting a decent volume of background radiation. Probably nothing down on the surface, I concluded – the giant was too similar to Sol's Jupiter, and not even the Krell could make their home down there.

"What about the other planets, Loeb? We got eyes on them too?"

"Such as we can," he said, shaking his head. "The chaff the Abyss is putting out is making it difficult to build a proper picture."

I pointed out a blue and green world, closer still to the Abyss, held in the sway of the deadly Shard Gate. The name DEVONIA flickered along the display. *Strange*, I thought, *that no other world out here has a name . . .*

"That looks like surface water," I said. As I absorbed the imagery, it became undeniable: Devonia was the only nearby world with active surface water, and it was locked in an orbit that could even give it life-sustaining temperatures. "Water and Krell . . . They go together like shower and shit."

"That's where the Krell will be," Saul agreed. "And a fitting name, too."

He laughed, but the reaction had a forced and almost manic quality. When no one else joined in he quickly stopped. I didn't probe that response; so far as I was concerned, unless the world was an immediate threat it wasn't my problem.

"We're watching near-space for any activity," Loeb said. "Stealth systems are at full deployment."

"How long?" I said.

I couldn't wait for this. The tang of excitement was thick in my mouth. That, but also fear: the horror that this could all be torn away from me.

"Twelve hours, at sub-light," Loeb said.

"Good," I said. "If we can make it any faster, then so be it."

Loeb nodded. "Understood."

That veil of focus that always came before a drop fell across the Lazarus Legion, and the squad dispersed across the *Colossus* readying for the mission. There was much to be done: weapons loading, equipment prep and simulant-checking. I ordered the Legion to assimilate the tactical database on the *Endeavour* and her fleet – shipboard schematics, projected entrance and exit routes, potential hazards. There was a lot to absorb, given that we didn't know exactly what we were going to find on the ship. In other circumstances, with more time, we'd have run a simulation on the search. It could be a combat-op, a rescue mission, or something in between.

With less than an hour to go, I sought solace in the starship's hangar bays. They were vast, depressing chambers. Made to hold wings of fighter ships, with the two Dragonfly gunships as cargo they were now cavernously empty. I walked the elevated gantries and watched the deckhands work – supervised by Lieutenant James – on the primary Dragonfly. It was being loaded with Banshee anti-personnel missiles, the two door-guns equipped with kinetic assault cannons.

I fished two items from my fatigue pockets: the silver flask and the packet of smokes that I'd picked up as we left Calico. Automatically, I unscrewed the cap – did my best to ignore the inscription on the outer case, words from a loved one to a partner or child who was now long dead – and smelt the contents. *Malt whisky.* I swigged it back hard, felt my eyes burn with the taste. *Jesus; that's good.*

"They work fast."

Professor Saul stood further down the gantry. I'd been so enraptured with the liquor that I hadn't even heard him approaching. Almost cautiously, he edged beside me, leant on the railing to watch the loading process. The Dragonfly looked like a drab green bug – enormous wings spread, each racked with red-tipped missiles. The hull gave off a vague sheen, but it had seen action and there were scorch marks and patched scars along the flanks.

I ignored Saul's comment, and grudgingly offered him the open flask.

"No, no," he said. "I don't drink."

"Of course you don't," I said. "A religious thing?"

Saul's jumpsuit was open, exposing a large blue and green emblem at his chest: a pendant of the Gaia Cult. The Cult worshipped some far-out ideal of Old Earth, back when it had been green and beautiful and something to hold on to.

"Something like that. Unless food or drink comes from Earth, it isn't sanctified."

I laughed. "Sounds expensive, but for all you know, this might be Earth-produce."

"If it came from Calico, I doubt it."

I decided it was best not to ask him how he'd fared in Directorate custody: I doubted that his captors had shown much reverence for his religious beliefs. Instead, I swallowed the liquor and stared at the unopened packet of cigarettes. They were some cheap Calican brand, produced on-base, and there was a smear of blood across the plastic wrapper.

"I didn't know that you smoked," Saul said.

"I don't," I said, clutching the packet carefully. "They're for *her*: for Elena. She's been gone a long time, Saul, and I think she'll appreciate a taste of home."

By home, I meant humanity. Elena and her team had been out of circulation – isolated – for a decade. That'd be tough on anyone. Saul nodded, but it was plain that he didn't really understand.

Just as I was about to ask him why he was here – why he had searched me out – he said, "Before we left for the Maelstrom, you said that you wanted to speak with me."

I nodded. "I did. I saw the way that you reacted when I mentioned the Revenant. Anything you want to tell me, Saul?"

He let out a long sigh. The deck was consumed by the clanger of munitions being loaded into assault cannons, and Saul cringed. When the noise cleared, he spoke again.

"I haven't been entirely honest with you, but my reasons are genuine."

"Go on," I said, swigging the bottle again. "Treat this as a confessional, if you will. A clean slate."

"Whether you believe me or not, I don't know anything about the *Endeavour*'s mission," he said. "But in this case,

229

the absence of knowledge is perhaps more telling. The entire project was only ever accessible to echelon-four Sci-Div staff."

I raised an eyebrow at that. "And you're not echelon four?"

"I'm three," he said. "And there are, to my knowledge, only fifteen such staff across Alliance space."

"All right. Then what about Operation Revenant?"

He shook his head. "It's not an operation, but I'm not sure exactly what it is. The word was attached to a series of glyphs found on Tysis World."

"Tysis World?" I asked. I recognised the name as a planet on the border of the old QZ, a planet within the confines of the Maelstrom. Saul had mentioned it once before, I suddenly recalled: during his interrogation aboard the *Colossus*, in Damascus. "Enlighten me."

"We found ruins there; Tysis was the first world which proved the existence of the Shard. Nothing as useful as the Artefact on Helios, but we were able to use what we could find. There were starship components, elements of a factory complex . . . Many years ago, before the end of the First Krell War, the Sci-Div team on Tysis managed to access some of the machinery left behind. I call it machinery, but it was far advanced beyond anything we have available to us now. A thinking machine: a true intelligence. I was instrumental in accessing the machine's central core."

Saul watched the loading process with a certain intensity, although it was surely of no interest to him. I let him speak, chose not to interrupt or ask questions. His hands were trembling on the safety rail.

"The Shard are an ancient race, Harris. No longer a race, even. They have transcended the flesh – become something better. They are true gods of technology."

"You sound like you admire them," I said, involuntarily. I'd been here before.

"I admire what they represent, of course. Immortality, an opportunity to escape the confines of our mortal bodies. The Shard once had incredible, world-building technologies on Tysis." He stared sideways at me, and I noticed that he was looking at the data-ports in my forearms – the connections that allowed me to operate a simulant. "Much of what we found there we reverse-engineered. A lot of it was, obviously, beyond our comprehension, and probably remains so."

"So what is Revenant?" I asked. I had no time for Shard worship, and the clock was counting down.

"Shard linguistics are not the same as human language," Saul said, shaking himself out of it. "It's difficult to explain, but it was a name given to a piece of machine-code. Broadly, it means 'world-engine' or 'planet-killer': a machine capable of stripping whole planets, or building them."

"Which was it?"

He laughed, but the sound was forced and hollow. "The nature of their linguistics – their code – suggests both. It's probably just a myth, and even if it did exist, it's impossible to say whether it still does."

Saul had been lost in Damascus Space at the time, with Kaminski, but when the *Colossus* escaped through the Shard Gate – into the Shard Network – I remembered the malignant intelligence that I'd felt lingering there. Something slumbering; something vast and malicious, slowly awakening. I didn't know whether that was linked to what Saul was telling me, but it immediately came to mind.

Saul continued: "The Shard sailed the stars when the human race was in its infancy. Their war with the Krell lasted millennia, so far as we can tell, and they were capable of blasting the fish back into the primordial ooze that birthed them. The best chance of our survival is to go under their radar, to escape their notice."

"Why are you telling me this now?" I said.

Saul rubbed the circular flesh-welts on his head. "Because the Directorate have been inside my head, Colonel. They know whatever I know, and I can't keep things from you any more."

"I appreciate it," I said, even if I didn't really buy it. Despite what had happened, despite what he'd been through, I didn't trust Saul. After Helios and Damascus, I'd never again trust Sci-Div or Command. By comparison, maybe I should've questioned the intel that Ostrow gave me, but the need to find the *Endeavour* – to find Elena – induced a wilful compliance in me.

"You should consider—"

Saul's words were cut off by a piercing siren, rising above the clatter of the gunship prep.

"Fire on Deck A-76," the AI declared. "Fire detected on Deck A-76. Emergency sub-routines have been engaged."

Saul jumped back from the railing, looked to me for guidance. The deck crew were shouting orders, rapidly filing out of the hangar.

"Get to the Crew Deck," I barked. "Follow the Navy."

I thrust the cigarettes back into my pocket, and tipped the whisky on to the gantry. I didn't, I decided, need it any more.

By the time I'd reached Deck A-76, the emergency siren had ceased and the crew had dispersed: gone back about their usual business. I suspected what had happened before I even reached the hold concerned. A-76 was a storage unit attached to the main armoury: an old gun-range. As I approached, the air smelt of halon gas – a fire repressant used on starships – and I could hear the Legion laughing among themselves.

"What's going on in here?" I yelled.

"Sorry about that, *hermano*," Martinez said, smirking. "We had a little difficulty with the new suits."

Jenkins was at the hold environment controls. "Martinez got over-excited. There was fire involved."

I shook my head. "Everyone is jumpy as hell out here. Try to be more careful."

Kaminski sat on a cargo crate, watching the proceedings. "It was worth it. Show him the suits, Martinez."

There were several hulking sets of armour racked on the walls around him.

"This, my friends, is the Ares battle-suit," Martinez said. He operated the storage rack, and the armour slid out, allowing him to inspect the back of the unit and the other hidden features. He ran a hand over the matt-grey plating. "The successor to the Trident armour; fully upgraded."

These were undeniably of the same heritage as the Trident combat-suits, but so much more. Almost twice as large as the regular suits; up-bulked and armoured. Thick, heavy-looking plates covered the torso, shoulders and all four limbs. The helmet looked like a vast progression of that found on the regular kit; the face-plate smaller, the neck joints concealed by further armouring. The suit's overall profile reminded me of an armoured bear. Martinez activated a control, and the armour opened like a clamshell, allowing the operator to quickly disembark.

"Give Harris a run-down," Jenkins said.

"For sure. The plate is lighter, but also stronger: an impact-resistant plastic-metal fusion. Seven days of EVA capability, thanks to the life-support unit in the backpack, and it carries a jump jet and thruster pack too." He tapped the oversized backpack mounted on the battle-suit. "For use in or out of an atmosphere."

The armour was equipped with a thruster pack, fitted with short-use propulsion jets. It couldn't exactly achieve flight, not in an environment with standard gravity, but it was close enough: the wearer could move around in zero-G with virtual impunity, or jump a limited distance in gravity. The outer plating was finned and sleeker looking, more aerodynamic than the combat-suit.

"You get stuck in space, or go into a zero-G spin," Martinez declared, "then you can activate the harpoon."

A metal barrel was mounted on the right forearm and the tip of a wicked-looking harpoon was just visible in the tube. A complex arrangement of metal cabling sat at the rear of the suit, above the jump jets.

"It's got plasma tech," Martinez said. "The blade carries a charged explosive; capable of penetrating starship armour, so the field-test notes say. Carries a reel with almost a kilo-metre's worth of cable."

"It doesn't have any recon drones," I noted.

"Who needs surveillance when you've got this much fire-power?" Martinez said. He pointed to two weapon mounts – like those I'd seen on Directorate-class mechs – that sprouted from the shoulders. "Pods here and here can take anti-personnel missiles. Ostrow – Christo bless his soul – was kind to us, *mano*. He left us a crate of cluster warheads."

An open metal box sat beside the suit. Inside were a thousand tiny rockets, ready for loading.

"And that's not all . . . The fish heads get too close? There's a flamethrower on the left arm." Martinez patted that, reverently.

"Hence the alarm." Jenkins whistled. "I do so like to burn stuff."

The bulkhead beside her was scarred, partially melted. I could just about read the words FISH FUCK scrawled there: a crude bull's-eye drawn beneath.

"Someone is in love," Mason said, laughing.

I had to admit that it was an impressive piece of kit, but I had my doubts.

"It's flashy," I said. "Don't we have any combat-suits?"

Martinez raised his eyebrows in exasperation. "No, *jefe*, we do not."

"I just like what I know," I said. "And we've never trained in this armour before."

"No need for additional training; the battle-suit uses the same neural interface as the combat-suit." The armour shimmered softly with light-reflective coating, and Martinez did a lap of the harness in which it sat. "You want to fight a skirmish, you take the Class V Trident. You want to fight a war, on the other hand, then you take the Ares battle-suit. A finer fighting suit you will not find."

Jenkins smirked. "Just remember, a new suit isn't a substitute for a bigger dick."

"What other equipment do we have?" I asked.

"You're a hard man to please, Lazarus," Jenkins said.

"Usual shit," Martinez said, kicking a foot at another metal crate. He wasn't interested in the old toys. "Power cells, grenades – EMPs, phosphorous, frag, hi-ex – demo-charges, mono-blades . . ."

"A lot is riding on this," I said. "And I don't want an R & D fuck-up costing us the mission." *Costing me Elena*, I mentally added. "I'd have preferred a longer training time in this armour before we use it."

"Neural interface, *mano* . . ." Martinez echoed.

"Whatever," I said. "Briefing is in twenty."

CHAPTER FIFTEEN

WEAPONS OF MASS DESTRUCTION

I stood before the CIC view-port, the Legion, James and Saul at my shoulder, and watched the UAS *Endeavour* drift past.

Starships generally weren't much on the eye. They tended to be big, ugly masses of metal, made for travel through the cold and frictionless void, but the *Endeavour* was different. There was a majestic beauty to this ship, as though her designers had been aware of the important historic role she would play. She was no warship; that was apparent from the elegant lines of her flanks, the bulbous sensor pods and glassed observatory domes studding her stern. The *Endeavour* was an exploratory-class vessel, and one of a kind: made for a specific purpose. Her bridge and command module was globular and awkward-looking. That met with a thin, precarious midship that housed numerous scientific and habitat bays. The overall design wasn't aerodynamic, yet it had a certain perverse grace.

"No surface damage," Kaminski muttered. "She looks space-worthy."

"Where's the rest of her fleet?" Mason asked. "The *Lion's Pride*, the *Britannic*, the *Ark Angel* . . ."

"They're not here," Loeb said. "She's the only ship within sensor range."

"Minimal energy core and drive leakage," an officer said. "No reason she can't fly sub-light."

"Or squawk . . ." Jenkins said.

This was the culmination of years of searching.

This, potentially, was the key to end the war.

And yet, right now, it was *nothing*.

I wanted to feel exhilaration, excitement. All I could muster was disappointment. Crushing, enervating disappointment.

"She's not responding," said the lieutenant manning the communications station. "We've tried sending out a broad-spectrum hail, but she's not talking."

"Then try again," I ordered.

The comms officer looked past me, to Loeb. She was seeking his permission. Any transmission, no matter how short-ranged, ran the risk of attracting attention from the Krell. Loeb gave a tiny nod of approval and the officer keyed an open channel.

"UAS *Endeavour*," she said, "this is the UAS *Colossus*. Please respond. We are a rescue operation sent to provide assistance. Immediate recognition of this transmission is requested."

My heart hammered triple-time in my chest, but as the seconds passed, only the warm crackle of static greeted us. That was the gas giant's timeless voice, saturating near-space with background radiation.

"Bridge is initiating declaration," an officer declared.

The CIC washed with Navy chatter. The lidar and radar operators were chanting back declining numbers, the scanner-suite chiming regularly. The tactical display began to fill with new data as the *Colossus'* sensor systems received it.

The *Colossus* achieved synchronicity with the *Endeavour's* orbit, and such was the vastness of our elliptical orbit around the gas giant that the two ships appeared to barely move. The CIC – and, likely, most of the ship – held its collective breath. One false move, one misfire of the thruster engines: we'd collide with the *Endeavour*, and this mission would be over.

Outside, the *Endeavour* drew uncomfortably close. Unless they were in a combat situation, ships rarely got this near to one another. In the void, there was no need. A bead of sweat broke on my upper lip, and I licked it back.

"Distance?" Loeb barked.

"Two kilometres, sir."

"Take us in nearer. Low thrust."

The tac-display updated with new graphics. I could see every detail of the *Endeavour's* hull now: the numerous airlocks, the closed hangar bays. She was a true behemoth, but also an apparently dead one.

"Told you," someone whispered, "ghost-ship. Bad spirit."

I turned, searched the CIC for who had spoken, but only blank faces stared back: no one was willing to take responsibility for the comment.

I paced the tactical display. Unlike the plans we'd been using so far, this was a true pictorial: captured by the *Colossus'* sensor-suite and deep-space cameras. The actual ship was visible outside the observation windows of the *Colossus'* CIC; so frustratingly close that I could almost reach out and touch her.

"No hail, no significant energy emissions," Loeb added. "Whether we expected this or not, we're looking at a dead ship. Neither her engines nor her power core has been recently fired."

"There are lights on down there," I said. *That's it, Harris: cling to whatever hope that you can* . . . Large peaked glass domes were scattered across the ship's hull, representing observation points and comms stations. Several were still lit, and the interior glow stained the glass like small cathedrals. "Those stations are still operating. Have we tried running a bio-scan?"

"We've run long-range bio-sensor scans on the target," Loeb said, "but the unit hasn't been reliable since the refit. Damned Proximan workmanship." He shook his head in dismay. "The scanner isn't the same quality as the *Colossus'* original unit. That, together with the magnetic interference – generated by the gas giant – makes the results less than reliable. If we had some proper Sci-Div support, maybe we could counter it, but right now that ship is virtually unscannable."

"Maybe that's how she's managed to remain hidden for so long," Mason said.

"Possibly," Loeb replied.

Had the location of the *Endeavour* been deliberate? Her placement was almost perfect; difficult to detect for the Alliance, let alone the Krell and the Directorate. It seemed like more than a coincidence.

"Then there's only one way that we can get answers," I said. "We'll have to go over there." I couldn't let go of the possibility that Elena was aboard the ship. Not now, not ever. "Once we're aboard, we'll run local scans and get some proper intelligence."

"Boots on the ground," Jenkins said. "The only way that the Legion knows."

"That's not going to be easy," James suddenly piped up. "I don't mean to piss on anyone's parade, but unless we can get that ship's AI talking, we can't board her."

He stood beside me, indicated the ship's exterior on the holo. There were large hangar bays on her flank: big enough to accommodate multiple shuttles and smaller starships. All of the bays were sealed shut.

"She could still have atmosphere," James said, "and unless we can crack her safely, I wouldn't want to risk an assault. If we fly one of the Dragonflies over there – without knowing the *Endeavour*'s atmospheric condition, and whether her AI is functioning properly – there's every chance that we could cause a catastrophic hull breach."

"So what do you suggest?" I asked.

"We could move into close proximity with the *Endeavour*. Run a docking tube between the two ships. It's risky, but it's possible."

Before anyone could respond to that idea, Loeb jabbed a finger at the observation window: at the *Endeavour* outside. "Whoa, whoa," he said. "That starship is running a goliath-class energy core. She was made for long-term exploration." Loeb was referring to the anti-matter core; the energy drive that powered the entire vessel. "The *Colossus* has the same tech at her heart. She's got fire in her ass, that one. If we're parked next to her, she'll be inside our null-shields. That energy core destabilises, we'll be caught in one hell of a blast."

"Then we'll try not to blow it up," I said, definitively, "but we are going aboard that ship. I'll deploy the docking tube."

I took a tactical officer's post down in the well of the CIC. The plastic crash couch was warm to the touch, the cabling just as well-used. I plugged each of those cables into my data-ports. Slowly, methodically. With each new connection, my bond with the *Colossus* became stronger. Soon, I was inside the machine-mind: the vast AI that controlled the warship.

USER RECOGNISED, the mainframe system told me. My identification tags scrolled across my mind's eye, insisting on the limits of my authorisation. There was a wealth of junk machine-code in the *Colossus*' AI system. Fragments of former operating systems. The remains of previous network upgrades. The sensation of making union with something so powerful was daunting. The *Colossus* hungered for activity, and I was almost glad that I did not have access to her weapons systems. *It would be all too easy to get lost in here*, I thought.

"We're in optimum position to deploy the boarding tube," Loeb said.

Green activity indicators flashed across my terminal.

"Here we go," I said. "Probe away."

The *Colossus* launched the utility drone from her port-side flank. I watched through the drone's eyes: saw the doors peeling open, exposing the bay to outer space. The sector had been cleared of personnel for this operation, and the drone was a specialised unit used for just this task. Much bigger than a simulant, the machine was equipped with a limited-range anti-gravity drive. I felt the kiss of vacuum on its metal hide as it drifted out into space.

I navigated the drone using a combination of directed-thought and manual controls. Almost hesitantly, the drone adopted a course towards the *Endeavour*, the only other target in near-space. A concertina-packed boarding tunnel trailed behind as the machine moved. That would become rigid, eventually provide a safe bridge between the two ships.

"Six hundred metres to target," Loeb remarked. "Keep her steady."

The drone ponderously sailed across the void. The machine had no real intelligence of its own – just a fragment of the *Colossus'* operating system, sheared off to assist in the single-minded operation. I nudged it back on course, more than once, as it made the journey.

"Three hundred metres," Loeb called out. "I can see the *Endeavour*'s main starboard airlock."

"I have it," I whispered.

The boarding tube became a rigid structure – still open to vacuum, but the ribbed interior forming a recognisable shape. The tunnel lined up with the hatch.

"Contact is perfect," an officer said. "Good work."

The drone finally reached the *Endeavour*'s hull, deploying its utility claws. The airlock doors were standard-pattern and the drone used the outer control panel to breach the security system. Code flushed my screen as the doors peeled open.

"Boarding tube is holding," an officer said. "There's an atmosphere on the other side; still has reasonable oxygenation. Sending report on life-support conditions to intelligence."

"I have the reads," the intel officer replied. "We're good to proceed."

The drone activated a high-powered lamp, set into its spherical body, and panned it back and forth, illuminating the inner chamber. It looked like that of any other ship – dark and, judging by the other readings, cold. As the machine proceeded into the lock, it caught drifting particulate in the air. An age of dust was filtering through the interior atmosphere.

"She's got gravity," I said.

The drone disconnected from the boarding tube, began to fix the umbilical to the outer hull.

"Boarding successful," Loeb said. "Get ready to send the drone in—"

"No," I said. "I need to do this."

Loeb scowled at me, but nodded in agreement. "If you're sure."

I needed to be the first person aboard that ship. Not some machine: my flesh and blood, even if it was only simulated. I set the drone on a home course back down the tube, then withdrew from direct control of the machine. I couldn't help thinking that it was eager to get back to the *Colossus*.

"Job done," I said.

It didn't feel very satisfying though; rather, my brief and remote entry to the starship felt disconcerting. One by one, I unjacked the cables from my data-ports. I stood from the console, flexed my limbs. Although it felt like it had taken hours, the entire operation had actually only taken a few minutes.

"Are we getting any more scanner results now that the boarding tube is in place?" Mason asked.

Loeb frowned, watching feeds on his terminal. "The drone was able to examine the sector behind that airlock – a few decks deep. No signs of life." He shrugged. "I'm sorry, Lazarus."

I just stared down at the holo-display: at the image of the *Endeavour* and *Colossus* coupled now, starboard to port. We were so close that our null-shields were useless – they would be entirely neutralised at this range. Elena didn't want to make things easy for whoever had come out here to find her.

"Ready for transition, Legion. We're going in."

"What do you want me to do, Colonel?" James asked.

"You're coming with us, flyboy."

Transition into my simulant brought with it a sudden shift in my POV.

Out of my old, tired skin – shed like a piece of damaged battle-armour – and into my new, fresh simulant. There was a sensual rush of integration as hyperawareness took me, that exhilarating peak in my perceptions that I only ever achieved when I was in a simulant.

Our new skins were already mounted in the *Colossus'* airlock.

"This is some hella armour," Jenkins said. She grinned back at me from inside her suit, face just visible beyond the polarised glass of her helmet visor. She bashed Kaminski on the arm. "You ready, trooper?"

"Born ready, Lieutenant," he said. He gave Jenkins a wink. The worry lines that had been etched on his face since his rescue were absent from this new face, generated from a gene-sample taken before Damascus. "Just need me something to kill."

The space inside the lock was almost completely occupied by the five troopers in full battle-suits, standing shoulder to shoulder, now a species entirely apart from the squad of Alliance Marines stationed on the other side of the *Colossus'* airlock. In the new suits, we'd doubled in mass.

"This armour . . . it's amazing," Mason said.

She flexed an enormous, armoured hand. In her real body, she was small and slender. Inside the sim and the Ares armour, she was taller and broader than any example of the human race.

"You feeling inadequate yet, James?" Jenkins asked.

The flyboy wore a vacuum-suit, together with helmet. "I

prefer my women without guns, if that's all the same." He carried a standard PPG-13 plasma pistol on his belt, and slapped it. "You might be bigger, but I'm faster."

"Don't try me," Jenkins said.

The interior of my face-plate flooded with new data-streams. WEAPONS SYSTEMS ONLINE, the AI informed me. I weighed my M95 plasma rifle, checked the power cell for the fifth time. The underslung grenade launcher was stocked with high-explosives, and I had every type of muni-tion webbed across my chest: incendiaries, phosphorous, EMP charges. I glanced down at the harpoon gun on my right arm, the diamond-shaped tip just visible, although I couldn't imagine the circumstances in which I might use it.

"We are walking weapons of mass destruction," Jenkins said, with glee.

"Don't get too cocky, people," I said. "We don't know what we're going to find on that ship." I tapped my left gauntlet; the flamethrower unit there. "We have an oxygen-ated atmosphere aboard the *Endeavour*, and there may be survivors in there."

I hoped, at least. I stood at the *Colossus* end of the boarding tube and surveyed the long and lonely distance to the *Endeavour*. She still sat immobile, silent. Stars flickered over her hull. The range-finder on my HUD calculated that the distance between the ships was almost a kilometre. The Legion stood around me, all of us using the mags to remain locked to the deck.

"Suits sealed?" I queried.

"Affirmative," Jenkins said. "Locked and loaded."

The weapon mounts bristled on my shoulders, tracking the troopers around me. The suit had incredible strength-augmentation, and although I had two missile pods mounted on my shoulders I barely felt their weight.

"This armour might be new, but you're in charge. Don't let the AI run it. Priority one is to recover any survivors from that ship. That's where you come in, James. We might need a transport off this ship." The *Endeavour*'s flight assets had included several shuttles, and we might be able to use some of them. Right now, with the *Colossus*' hangars empty, we could easily accommodate more transport craft. I turned back to the boarding tube. "*Colossus* CIC, do you read?"

"We copy, Lazarus Actual," someone said: an officer, but not Loeb. "Green light for EVA deployment."

"Lazarus Actual out."

A face was visible through the view-port of the *Colossus*' interior airlock door: sergeant of the Alliance Marines. The Marines' armour was vac-proofed and combat-ready, but much less functional than the simulant battle-suits. There were ten soldiers, clutching laser carbines in gloved hands, wearing full respirator packages that covered their faces. The sergeant gave me a nod.

"We'll remain on-ship as ordered, sir," he said, over the comm. My HUD danced with his estimated bio-signs. They told of a man on the verge of panic.

"You do that."

The men were jittery. They probably felt inadequate in the presence of a simulant team, and I noticed that Jenkins and Mason were making particular efforts to stand at full height, enjoying the threat-aura that an armed and armoured simulant projected even when at ease.

"There's nothing to be afraid of until I say so," I said. "Just remember that. This is an extraction operation, nothing more." I turned to my team. "We ready to do this, people?"

"As we'll ever be," Jenkins said.

I activated the airlock door control panel. The small terminal screen lit green and the outer hatch door slowly opened. There was a brief hiss of releasing atmosphere as the airlock and the tunnel pressure equalised. I stepped out of the *Colossus* and began the slow walk across the docking tube. Within a couple of strides I was beyond the warship's gravity well. The boarding tube had a metal-strip floor, made to fix mag-locks, to keep users upright. Instead of using that, I used the ribbed walls of the tunnel to move – propelling myself along the distance with both hands. As I touched the tunnel walls, they sometimes gave just a little. The docking tube was disposable: made of transparent heavy-duty plastic, and would collapse in the case of an atmospheric breach.

The Legion adopted the same procedure behind me. We cleared the thousand-metre distance rapidly, using zero-G to our advantage.

"Coming up on *Endeavour*'s airlock," I said. "Legion is boarding."

"Copy that," the CIC replied.

With hands that were shaking with anticipation – despite being skinned, despite my powered gauntlets – I grasped the hull of the *Endeavour*. Felt the cold metal through the palm of my glove. I wanted to feel some spiritual awakening – some sliver of kinship with Elena, to finally be aboard her ship – but the only emotion I could muster was fear.

I gently propelled myself over the boundary, into the *Endeavour*'s interior airlock. The rest of the Legion followed me in.

I paused for just a moment, looked back down the boarding tube. The distance seemed incredibly vast. The Alliance Marines had piled into the open airlock and were visible as tiny black specs. My suit identified their weapons – down to make and model. I could kill them with a thought: the missile pods on my shoulders were almost

daring me to activate them. I switched to the Marines'
channel.

"Remember what I said, Sergeant."

"Copy that," the sergeant said.

"Let's hope that you won't be required. Lazarus out."

CHAPTER SIXTEEN

TOO LATE

"Everyone is in," Jenkins said. "You want me to do the honours?"

"Go ahead," I said.

Jenkins moved to the airlock controls mounted on the interior wall. She waved a hand towards the waiting Marine cohort, although at this distance and without improved sim-sense I doubted that they could see her.

"Later, boys."

The *Endeavour*'s outer airlock sealed shut.

"So far, so good," Mason said.

This was all as expected; nothing out of the ordinary.

"Open the inner lock," I ordered. "Martinez, run a scanner sweep."

Jenkins manipulated the controls. Atmospheric pressure between the inner lock and the corridor beyond – the real interior of the *Endeavour* – rapidly equalised. I felt tiny electrical shocks of apprehension run up my spine.

"Wide coverage on this corridor," I ordered. "Kaminski, watch our six."

"Copy that," he replied.

I took point and cautiously edged into the corridor beyond the lock. Suit-mounted lamps probed the dense dark like fingers. My HUD was painted with graphics, confirming that Kaminski and Martinez were moving behind me, Jenkins and Mason still waiting at the lock controls. James hung back in the lock as well.

"Area is clear," I said.

We were in a long, straight corridor section, much wider than those aboard the *Colossus* and not as utilitarian as a military vessel, with smooth ceramic panelling on the walls. I scanned the floor: found no footprints, no other marks to suggest inhabitants. The deck was clear save for a thick glow of dust. I could feel the cold and age of the ship around me, both pressing and depressing. My HUD illuminated with schematics and plans of the surrounding area, indicating key locations such as the bridge, crew quarters and the energy core.

"The bio-scanner has no reads," Martinez said. "No movement, no signals."

"What's the penetration?"

"Going through this deck. Density is too much for me to get a reading beyond that."

That feeling that something was wrong here returned to me, despite my attempts to shake it. *It's a trap*, the voice insisted. *And you've led the Legion into it.*

"A trap that hasn't yet been sprung . . ." I whispered back.

"Negative copy?" Kaminski said.

"Never mind."

I stalked on a few paces, rifle aimed ahead of me. I activated my suit speaker-system.

"Hello?" I called.

The noise echoed off down the empty corridor. A tense few seconds passed, but the greeting went unanswered.

"You sure that's a good idea?" Kaminski asked over the comm. "No telling what's in here with us . . ."

"Quit fucking with Mason's head," Jenkins said, but her tone wasn't very jovial.

I reached up for the catches on my helmet and blew them. My ears popped as they adjusted to the new pressure though the difference was minimal. The Legion did the same, glad to be free of their headgear. The crisp scent of antiseptic – of a well-maintained atmospheric system – filled my nostrils.

"Not exactly what we expected, huh?" Jenkins said.

"It isn't over yet," I said. "Not until we've searched the ship. Elena was aboard the Damascus Artefact. We all saw this ship when we travelled through the Shard Network. There must be someone here."

"Unless they're all gone," Mason said.

I surveyed the lonely stretch of corridor. The *Endeavour* was a vast starship; a maze of tunnels and dedicated modules.

"Drones would've come in handy," I said. "I guess these new suits aren't all they're cracked up to be . . ."

"You said just the same when they first brought the drones into service," Jenkins muttered.

"We'll split up and search the vessel. I want everyone using the bio-scanners and running sweeps in every corridor." I jabbed the controls on my wrist-comp; sent a mission plan to each of the Legion. "Martinez, you take the Communications Deck. Jenkins and James, hangars. Kaminski and Mason, I want you to search the Command Deck."

Jenkins didn't argue. She slapped James on the shoulder. In the battle-suit, the action was more of a threat than a reassurance. "Come on, flyboy. Maybe we'll find some ships down there."

"And you, *jefe*?" Martinez asked.

"I think you know that already," I said. "I'm going to the crew quarters."

My scanner was on passive mode, pinging softly as it ran on my wrist-comp. The Legion and James disappeared from my sensor net as their orders took them elsewhere and we left the vicinity of the airlock.

"*Main hangar deck breached . . .*" Jenkins declared over the squad comm-channel. She sounded as though she was whispering; as though she was afraid to wake the dead.

"*I'm on the Comms Deck,*" Martinez reported in. "*Real quiet down here.*"

"*Same here,*" Mason said. "*Scanner is empty.*"

I silenced the squad channel. If the Legion found anything, they could comm me direct. They weren't reporting anything that I wasn't seeing with my own eyes. With every module, hangar and crew chamber we cleared, my disappointment levels increased. Was this another dead end in my search for Elena? I needed more than this: some clue – an explanation, just a shred of evidence – to show what had happened to her.

Although life support was running, the transport network wasn't, so instead of using an elevator, I took the ladder-shafts to the upper decks. The corridors around me softly whispered as I went. The airshafts sounded like there was wind running through them, the structure sighing as I searched.

I eventually emerged into the crew quarters. There were hundreds of cabins on this deck; the ship had housed five hundred hands in all. Some quarters had been shared – those for the military personnel attached to the operation – but just as many were dedicated to the civilian staff. That meant separate berths for each crew member.

The stark, empty corridors were lined with doors, and outside each was a printed metal plaque. I stopped to trace the names on some of those doors. Felt the embossed name-plates through the second skin of my gloved fingertips. Such a quaint anachronism. I matched each with the faces I'd seen back on Calico, so many years ago. They could surely never have even suspected that their optimistic endeavour would end like this. I felt a pang of sadness as I saw each name.

The hydraulic hatches were unpowered, and I used the manual locking mechanism to open them. Each door came open with a nerve-jangling creak – the sound echoing off into the empty ship – but it felt good to be testing out the improved strength-augmentation of my suit.

"Hello?" I called again, as I entered the first cabin. "Commander Cook?"

Cook's rooms were plush, akin to the state rooms of senior Naval staff, and the largest on the ship. Equipped with a decent-sized bunk, walls filled with his accolades from years in the Alliance Navy, of his lengthy stint as a corporate merchant sailor. Photos of smaller versions of him – I guessed his children – lined the ultra-modern furniture; as I swept a hand over a cabinet, a couple of tri-Ds even came to life. A half-filled decanter of something green and probably alcoholic sat beside his bunk.

It was dust. All dust. The quarters felt and looked as though they had been unoccupied for centuries, rather than years.

"Moving on to auxiliary staff quarters," I said to my suit.

From my analysis of the schematics, I knew exactly where the room was, and I'd already planned my route. Anxiety – such a foreign emotion in a simulant body – gnawed at me as I closed on it. I'd never been so close to finding her as I was now, and I imagined her walking these corridors: tried to reconstruct her footsteps. The bulkhead hatch was shut, like all of the rooms, and I stood outside for a long moment. My bio-scanner was quiet: the gentle green glow of the holographic reflecting off the corridor wall. I stared at the printed nameplate.

DR ELENA MARCEAU (PSYCH SUPPORT).

Do you really want to know what's behind this door? the voice asked me. *Isn't she best consigned to memory; remembered how you want her to be?* Sometimes that was true. Sometimes people were better remembered than experienced, but not Elena. She had been my only motivation for the years since she'd left. I had to find her, and had to put this right.

As my gloved hand made contact with the outer hatch, the ridiculous notion that I should knock occurred to me. I shook it away, and began manually to crank the wheel. That was what Elena represented to me: normalcy. She was my anchor. This – the Maelstrom, the Shard, the Krell, all of it – wasn't real. As Elena had warned me, I couldn't allow myself to get lost in it, but that was exactly what I'd done by allowing her to go.

The hatch came open with a low groan, and I slowly pulled it wide.

"Elena?" I whispered.

The room was deserted. Four-by-four, with an adjoining head and a locker for personal effects on one wall. The other was studded with view-ports. Each of those was open, revealing the multi-coloured and shifting surface of the gas giant far below. There was an unmade bunk in one corner. I poked the tussle of bedsheets.

"Elena?" I asked again, louder this time.

The place smelt of her. The scent lingered on the air, just

beyond the ken of my perceptions. The sim's olfactory senses were as sharpened as the rest, and I doubted whether I'd have detected the aroma in my real skin. It was almost painful.

Damn it. This isn't right.

I grabbed at a bedsheet – clutched it in my gauntlet. Crumpled it.

"Elena!" I shouted. "Where are you?"

There had to be some sign of her. Some explanation.

The Legion and James converged in one of the *Endeavour*'s atriums. Located on the upper deck, the chamber was bright and airy; working glow-globes were interspersed with full-length observation windows. A series of huge gene-engineered plants sat in pots around the room. They were long deceased, reduced to withered brown husks. As we filed into the chamber, the layer of dead leaves and shed branches crunched underfoot. The impression I got of a civilian spaceport lounge was reinforced by the moulded plastic tables and chairs that were arranged in clusters around the dead plants.

Mason slapped her rifle down on the nearest table, and collapsed into a chair. It creaked beneath her simulated weight. Jenkins was less willing to give up her weapon but took up a position on one of the tables as well.

"What's the matter, LT?" Mason asked. "Frightened that we're actually going to get some action on this ship?"

Jenkins sighed. "I get plenty of action, thanks. And don't call me LT."

Mason nodded. "Got it."

Martinez sucked his teeth. "It's not the ship that we got to worry about. It's the dead, man. This place really is a ghost-ship."

"Maybe we should call in the Sci-Div techs," Mason offered. "Let them go over the ship."

"What Sci-Div?" Kaminski asked, prowling the edge of the room, looking up at the ceiling. It was entirely composed of armour-glass and ribbed with metal supports. "Who makes a ship with a glass ceiling? This is crazy. These people want to get hulled or something?"

"Didn't happen though, genius," Martinez said. "This ship has been out here for years, and she hasn't been hulled yet. Your time in the camp didn't help much with the smarts. Mason's right; we need forensics and that shit. This isn't Sim Ops work."

Jenkins froze a little at Martinez's reference to 'the camp', but 'Ski weathered the jibe well enough.

"You sound scared, Martinez," he said, grinning.

Martinez scowled. "Fuck you. It has bad karma."

"I didn't know that Catholics believed in karma," Jenkins said.

"There's probably a whole lotta things that you don't know about the Venus Creed," Martinez said. "And I haven't got time to tell you."

"Cut out the chatter," I ordered. "This place isn't right, and I'm not happy about it at all."

"Command Decks are empty," Mason said.

"Any bodies?"

"None. The bridge is fully functional."

"What about you, Jenkins? Did you find anything?"

"We've swept the main hangar decks," she said. "There are berths down there for maybe twenty shuttles and other short-range ships. But they're all empty. Whatever happened here, someone took all of those ships with them."

"The inventory says that the *Endeavour* wasn't carrying anything bigger than a shuttle," James explained. "Well, the files are wrong. I'm telling you that the hangars were holding a lot more than that. Those decks were made to hold a fleet."

Jenkins nodded. "I've got everything on my vid-feed. There are run marks on the decking, thruster burns on the mag-runs."

"They look like they were made by something a lot bigger than a shuttle," James said.

"Maybe it was some sort of exodus," Martinez offered. "The crew bugged out, decided it wasn't safe here any more."

Jenkins shrugged. "It's possible. There's lots of equipment missing from the hangars: EVA suits, breathers. Place has been plundered."

"The evacuation pods have been fired as well," James said. "Every last one of them."

I spied the *Colossus* in the distance outside the obs window, moving parallel to the *Endeavour*. Running lights blinked along the ship's flank, and a single beacon flashed on her prow, marking roughly the location of the CIC. The ship was still tethered to the *Endeavour*, the lifeline umbilical stretched out between the vessels, taut like a piece of string. Beyond, the pale glow of the Abyss was ever-present.

"Maybe Loeb has some ideas," I said. I tuned my wrist-comp to the *Colossus* command frequency, and opened the comm-net to the rest of the Legion. "Command, this is Lazarus Actual."

"We read, Lazarus." Despite the squall generated by the giant, the link was clear enough: we were virtually on top of the *Colossus*. "Loeb here."

"We've conducted a partial sweep of the ship. No signs of life."

"We've been reading your suit-feeds," Loeb said.

"Can anyone offer any assistance?" I said.

Loeb sighed. "What about the ship's data-core?"

Of course: that would hold the ship's virtual black box – her flightpath data. The core would also record almost every aspect of the AI's decisions, and justifications for everything that the ship had done since it had been abandoned.

"We'll make that the next objective." The task of retrieving the data-core was likely to be technically complicated, usually only performed by appropriate Sci-Div or Naval crew. I looked to Kaminski. He was the closest we had to a technician on the force. "We're going to be another couple of hours, at least. Are your Marines still covering the docking tube?"

"Affirmative. They're bored as shit."

"Copy. Tell them to stay frosty. We'll report when we have more. Lazarus out."

"*Colossus* out."

I turned to my team. More schematics and deck plans appeared on my wrist-comp; more decks that needed to be examined before we could draw any conclusions from this place.

"Kaminski and Mason, you go down to Data," I said. "Make an uplink with the *Colossus*, retrieve the data-core. Jenkins, sweep the Engineering Deck."

"You want me to go with her again?" James asked. "If there's nothing to fly, there's not much for me to do out here . . ."

"If he goes back, he'll need an escort," Jenkins said. "Better he comes with me."

"Fine," I said. "Martinez and I will take the Science Deck."

"Place's seen some action," said Martinez, as we explored the Science Deck.

"You always were the master of understatement."

"It's a Venusian thing," said Martinez. He was trying to sound glib, but spoke in a clipped whisper, his eyes always on the corridor, plasma rifle panning back and forth to cover the area.

Most of the laboratories had been gutted by fire. Many of the chambers still smelt of burning plastic, the odour preserved by the lifeless state of the ship. Those rooms – with their black-stained walls and upturned lab benches – seemed the most frightening. Armour-glass windows lined the main corridor, and some of those were cracked and distorted, the glass warped so that the rooms beyond appeared to ripple as we moved past them. The ship had taken on an industrial-gothic atmosphere. The glow-globes in the ceiling had been smashed, forcing us to rely on our suit-lamps for illumination.

"Fire support didn't trigger," Martinez went on.

The ship was equipped with a full halon dispenser system and yet there was no evidence that it had made any attempt to put out the fires. The labs were surely the site of a fire, perhaps more than one: in such a confined space, an intense blaze like that would be the perfect cover – eradicating evidence of whatever had actually happened in there. *They didn't want to be seen*, the voice whispered to me. *You should go from here.* Each footstep I took in the heavy battle-suit echoed a thousandfold. Anything in here would hear us coming a long way off.

"Hold up," Martinez said. "Is that a body?"

He caught something black and shrivelled on the deck ahead of us in his suit-lamps. Looked like a bundle of dark twigs at a distance, but as I advanced I realised that Martinez was right. Fire had reduced the body, made it into a mess of blackened limbs and bone. The hair had completely burnt away, but scraps of a jumpsuit still clung to the tiny shoulders, grafted to the flesh by the extreme heat.

Martinez stooped beside it. Went to touch it, but resisted

at the last moment. I understood why – the body looked like it would collapse at the slightest touch.

"No telling who this was," Martinez said. "Rest in peace, poor bastard."

Even up close, it was impossible to identify the corpse. The face was nothing more than a black mask, teeth pegs in the leathered gums.

"We need to take the body back," I said. "For identification."

It could be her. The panic took me, and I searched the jumpsuit for some ID tag – for a name, for a department – but it was too badly burnt. My medi-suite detected the change in my psychological state, and I felt a surge of combat-drugs being pumped into me. When I looked up again, stepped back from the body like I was repulsed by it, Martinez stood in front of a closed door at the end of the passage.

"Whoever it was," he said, "they came from in there . . ." A black trail linked the corpse and the hatch. "That's the Medical Deck."

"Trace it," I said.

Covering each other as we moved, Martinez and I crossed the boundary onto the Medical Deck. I stared down at my wrist-comp, at the deck plans. There were four large modules, noted as storage bays, on my maps. Ahead, the corpse's trail led to one of those hatches.

"Power is running down here," Martinez said. "That bay is locked."

"Run an override. We need to get in there."

Martinez unpacked a hacker-unit. He patched into the control panel.

I activated my communicator and switched channels. "Jenkins, you read?"

"I read," Jenkins responded. "We're at the objective."

The Engineering Deck was a good distance from Medical and Science.

"What have you got?"

Jenkins whistled. "Same. Dark, empty. Nothing on the bio-scanner, but lots of machinery down here interfering with the field. We're using the scanners on full amplification."

"You heard from Kaminski and Mason?"

"Kaminski's almost cracked the encryption. What's your sit?"

"We've got a body up on Science. About to enter Medical. Let me know when you finish your sweep."

"Affirmative. Jenkins out."

"Harris out."

Martinez's hacker-unit chimed and he cracked open the door.

Cold atmosphere hit me like a fist, punching the breath from my lungs. Blue light spilled from inside the room, cutting a rectangle across the floor outside – catching wisps of condensing cold air as it escaped from inside. This was the first active tech we'd found aboard the *Endeavour*. A spark of optimism lit within me.

"Take the left flank," I said. "I'll take the right."

"*Si, jefe.*"

As big as a warehouse or hangar bay, it was crammed full of glass-fronted capsules. Stacked floor to ceiling, vertically, back-to-back so that the occupants could be inspected. The set-up reached as far as I could see: hundreds of capsules. The entire facility produced an unpleasant bronchial wheeze – a noise that suggested the facility was about to take its last breath.

"Looks like some sort of cryogenic storage facility," Martinez said. "But it isn't a hypersleep bay . . ."

"Don't touch anything," I ordered.

"Copy that," Martinez said. The tone of his response suggested that he wouldn't want to anyway. "Watch your footing."

A shifting layer of white mist crept along the ground, concealing fat power cables and conduits. The temperature in the room was much lower than elsewhere – teetering on freezing – and I felt my skin crawling with reaction to active cryogen units.

"There are bodies in these capsules," Martinez said. "But I . . . I think that something went wrong . . . I don't like this. Not at all."

I stopped at one of the capsules. The body beyond was visible only as a vague blur – no details or features discernible – and there was no identification on the tube. Although it was frosted, the liquid inside appeared *wrong*. The preservative was gel-like, static, and some of the cables holding the body in place drifted loose. The control console set into the front of the pod flashed with error messages. I reached up, went to wipe the frost from the outer canopy—

"Shit!"

I jumped back, startled, as a dark shape loomed through the fluid. It shifted towards the canopy and silently hit the glass.

A corpse. Black and leathery; pickled, teeth bared in a death-grin, in a condition not much better than the thing in the corridor. The body involuntarily shifted in its watery prison; had perhaps been disturbed by our presence.

"You okay, *jefe*?" Martinez asked. He appeared at the end of the aisle of capsules.

"Fine," I said, irritated. I was angered at my own reaction: at how nervy this damned ship was making me. "I've got a dead one here."

"They're all dead," Martinez said. "All the same."

We were surrounded by hundreds of decayed and decaying corpses. Every capsule had a glowing red indicator on the control panel: the same flashing error message as the machine in front of me. I brushed a gloved hand along the line of capsules. Each deader than the last. Gnarled hands, formed into claws, pressed against the glass cases. Sometimes little more than skeletal remains – skins sloughed off by the cryogen.

The Endeavour's *crew, kept on ice. All long dead.*

We were too late.

"I'm sorry, Colonel," Martinez said, softly. He breathed out, producing a white plume of hot air. There was already frost on his simulated beard; forming on his eyebrows. "You want us to ship them back to the *Colossus*? Run some tests or something?"

"What good will tests do?" I barked.

I came to rest before one of the capsules. Something drew me to this one. Something indescribable.

Could it be . . .?

The inside of the tank was as murky as the others. I was glad of that: if Elena was in there somewhere, I didn't want to find her like this.

"Whatever is left of the mainframe AI," Martinez said, "it knew to keep these cargo holds powered. Someone programmed the ship to keep this deck running. I guess that it must've gone wrong somehow . . ."

I pressed a hand against the glass. Was I imagining things again? The machine felt as though it was gently vibrating, the canopy humming so very minutely that it wouldn't be detectable in a real skin. Maybe it was my sim-senses kicking in —

Not vibrating.

Beating.

A heartbeat?

The body in the tank vaulted against the glass.

My bio-scanner began to chime.

Elena Marceau stared back at me from inside the capsule.

She pushed her face against the inner canopy. Cheeks swollen as though she was bursting to breathe. Eyes – such beautiful, deep eyes – panicked. Forehead creased in anger. Mouth capped by a respirator mask.

"Elena's in this capsule!"

And she's alive . . .!

She was naked, the curve of her lower body disappearing into the workings of the tank. Her hair spread out around her, writhing like a mass of angry sea snakes. She pounded a small fist against the glass. I felt her through the canopy – *actually felt her!* – and spread my hand in reaction. Bubbles escaped from Elena's mouth, where the respirator was suctioned into place, and she thrashed. I had to get her out of there. *Think!* She was panicking; would drown on the cryogen unless I did something to get her out. I aimed with my rifle, readied to blow open the pod's outer canopy —

"Easy!" Martinez yelled. "Stop it! That's a bad idea!"

Before I had any opportunity to question whether any of this was real – why only Elena, out of the hundreds of bodies around us held in cryogenic storage, was alive – Martinez confirmed it for me. He knocked my arm down, hard, before I had a chance to loose a shot. Barged me aside, away from the capsule's control console. Armour on armour produced a startling clatter.

"What are you doing?" I asked. "She's drowning in there!"

Elena writhed some more, tangled in the web of cables

that should've fed and watered her during the sleep. Martinez jabbed the controls, muttering to himself.

"The capsule has malfunctioned," he said as he worked. "We take her out now, and there's a risk to her life."

"She's drowning!" I repeated again.

"She isn't. The imbalance – whatever killed the others – hasn't gotten to her yet."

Elena began to drift in the capsule. Her thrashing lessened, then stopped. She drifted back inside the pod, became more distant. Her eyes flickered shut again.

"See," Martinez said.

The console flushed with new data. Bars elevated to green levels, indicating correct functions.

"Is that what happened?" I asked. "These machines malfunctioned?"

"Maybe," Martinez said. Stared at the read-out. "Fuck of a way to go, but they wouldn't feel a thing. Whatever this place is, it's no hypersleep bay."

I stared at the capsule in which Elena was preserved. She was entirely still now; at rest. The gentlest rise and fall of her chest gave the lie to any suggestion that she was dead.

"Christo, Martinez . . ." I said. "She's really here. She's real."

Martinez nodded. "*Si*. She is."

I could save her. I could do this: take her home. Inside my armour, I began to shake; to feel my heart melting. Years of waiting, and it was finally happening. I would make good my promise to her, take her out of this place. The woman beyond the glass was my future – a life beyond the cycle of living and dying, beyond endless war. I turned to Martinez, wrapped an arm around him. He returned the hug, his smile broad.

"We've got work to do, *jefe*." He pointed at the machines.

"No telling how long she'll be safe in there. She needs to be defrosted with proper medical assistance."

"I . . . I know," I said. I couldn't draw my eyes from Elena's face: her gently flickering eyelids. It took me a few seconds to drag myself out of it, to focus on the mission again. As I did so, as I ordered my emotions and began to process the implications, matters took on a whole new level of urgency. "Can the capsule be dismounted?"

Martinez nodded. "I guess so. It'll be heavy, but we can carry it between us. Maybe Jenkins can search for a mule down on the hangar decks."

"No need," I said. "I've been waiting to give this strength-aug a proper run."

"*Si,*" Martinez said.

There was a sudden chime over my comm-network. Martinez got it too; frowned at the result.

Bodies in cryogenic suspension were so far under that they didn't produce registrable vitals. I'm sure that Sci-Div has produced a scanner somewhere that can read the signs of a sleeper, but that sort of tech was too delicate for Sim Ops grunt work. I held my wrist-comp to my face, watched the read-out.

Elena's bio-sign had diminished again, dipped to undetectable, but I was still getting a signal. Not from inside the room, I realised, but from the corridors around us.

"Fuck . . ." Martinez whispered.

The ship was filling with moving, hot signals.

CHAPTER SEVENTEEN

HULL BREACH

"Hull breach detected on Deck C-3," the *Endeavour*'s AI declared, suddenly – inexplicably – operational again. "Take all necessary safety precautions."

Martinez snapped his helmet back into place. I did the same, and graphic warnings projected onto my HUD.

"Whoever's out there," he said, "they're all around us, and closing fast."

Exactly *what* was closing on us was mostly irrelevant. There were far too many signals for the Legion, and the Alliance Marines were stationed klicks away aboard the *Colossus*. Possibilities cascaded through my mind. I was already working on our escape route – considering our withdrawal through the belly of the ship: across Science, through Communications, and down the main corridor into the atrium.

"Let's get this capsule free," I said.

"Copy that."

We both fell to the base of the capsule, began to unhook the power conduits. It was a standard cryogenic module:

would carry enough onboard preservative to keep Elena under for a couple of hours, at least.

My comm-net chimed. *Loeb.*

"This is *Colossus* Command," he blurted. "We have to pull out, now! We have a fast-approaching potential on the scanners!"

"Krell?"

"Can't tell, but whatever it is, it's big." The line crackled and popped, the signal deteriorating rapidly. "The quantum is on fire out there."

A ship making real-space conversion could cause quantum disturbance. It was a recognised side-effect of making a Q-jump too close to another ship. I'd seen the results, and they weren't pretty. Our scanners and comms would be fried by something coming in-system via Q-jump. *Unless*, I thought, *it's something worse than that.* The Arkonus Abyss was painfully close. There were a thousand variables at play out here.

"We're evac'ing a single survivor," I said to Loeb. "Do not – repeat *do not* – close that boarding tube."

"We have to pull out to safe distance—"

"Do not leave the *Endeavour*!" I barked. "Tell the Marines to keep the docking tube open until I order otherwise."

"I can't do that!" Loeb argued. His voice quivered with interference. "There are hardcopy soldiers—"

"I have Elena!" I roared at him. "And I'm ordering you to keep that tube open!"

Before I could formally close the communication, Jenkins' emergency channel opened.

"Wha . . . fuck . . . ship?" she started, her voice chopping.

"Cannot read, Jenkins, but if you can hear me, get back to the boarding tube. We are conducting exfil on Elena's capsule—"

"Neg . . . Bay – open—"

"I don't copy!" I yelled. I recognised the hiss of a plasma weapon firing over Jenkins' end of the comm. "What's happening down there?"

More plasma fire sounded, and lots of it. That meant multiple hostiles. James was yelling in the background.

"Jenkins! Answer the damned comm!"

The capsule came free from the base with a hiss of pressurised gas. Elena bobbed serenely inside.

"Can you manage that?" Martinez said.

"It's fine," I said. "I'll take her."

The unit was bulky, but would fit under one arm in the battle-suit; its weight was negligible with the simulant's abilities and the suit's strength-aug. I was more concerned about its fragility: the glass canopy could be easily broken. Even a fracture could lead to fatal injury – the wrinkled corpses in the tubes around me were more than enough reminder of how things could end.

"Clear us a route," I ordered.

Martinez reached the hatch. He jabbed a finger at the OPEN button. The lock began to peel apart with infuriating lethargy. Both hands on his rifle, he said, "Anything stands in our way, I'll take it."

"Jenkins!" I shouted again, over the comm. "What's happening?"

"We've got—"

The outer lock door opened, and I finally saw for myself.

A Krell primary-form stood in front of me.

Clad in a full bio-suit, and evolved for space-combat, the alien warrior was bathed in red light, ice crystals from recent exposure to vacuum still glinting off its weathered hide. The bio-helmet that the xeno wore was scarred and battered,

269

marking this particular primary as what passed for a veteran among the Krell warrior elite. As the hatch opened, it swivelled its head in response, eyes and nostrils flaring behind the mirrored face-plate, gills open. It lurched towards us, both pairs of arms up and ready to attack.

I took a step back into the bay. Elena's capsule under my left arm, I brought up my right: fired one-handed.

Commencing combat trial.

The Krell disintegrated under the hail of fire. Pulses illuminated the xeno's insides – light spilling from the exo-skeleton, revealing the tracery of veins and internal organs. The mass of writhing tendrils and bio-communication devices grafted to the Krell's back went limp, and the creature collapsed at my feet.

"How did Loeb miss this?" Martinez said in exasperation.

The question was largely rhetorical, and unanswerable in the circumstances. The Krell were here, and I needed to get Elena off the ship. Those were the facts.

I stomped the body underfoot and moved out. Martinez's suit-lamps lit beside me, catching the corridor ahead. Flashing amber security lamps had activated, and a klaxon rang out through the sector. My olfactory senses were choked with the smell of scorched Krell flesh and burning plastic: I thought-commanded my suit to switch to my internal atmosphere supply.

The *Endeavour*'s AI continued: "Hull breach on Decks C-3, B-9, A-1 through 15."

The Krell were probably using breacher-pods. They were almost invisible in the cold of space – a living, cuttlefish-like organism with a singular purpose: to propel invaders across the void of space. That would explain how Loeb had missed them.

I suddenly realised that Jenkins was back on the

com-network. She was yelling incessantly, repeating the same words over and over.

"I'm here, Jenkins," I said, cutting her off.

"We've got Krell across Engineering! Lots of them!"

"There are more boarding the ship," I said, breathing hard. "Something's incoming."

This was just the advance boarding party, meant to secure the objective. Confirming my suspicions, I felt something hit the *Endeavour*, her space frame shuddering violently. That could be more boarders, maybe a Krell shuttle.

"Where the fuck did they come from?" Jenkins asked.

"How should I know?" I barked back.

Martinez started firing again – a harsh triple-volley from his plasma rifle. Krell-shaped shadows were suddenly all over the corridor.

"Where're Mason and 'Ski?"

"Fuck knows. I'll try to reach them."

"Fall back to the docking tube," I ordered. "We can't let them get aboard the *Colossus*."

If they haven't already . . .

"Affirm—"

The link went dead. Whether it was a technical difficulty, or Jenkins had extracted, it didn't matter.

A clawed hand reached from a rent in the deck tiling, wrapped around my boot. Another Krell. It closed its claws, and despite the improved armour I felt the plating in my boot crunch. I put the target down with two shots from my rifle. More baleful alien eyes stared at me in the dark. Shrieking – Krell battle-cant – filled the chamber.

"Missiles free, Martinez," I ordered. "Collateral damage irrelevant."

"Fuck yeah!" Martinez roared.

The shoulder-mounted missile pods extended on his back.

The horde of Krell at the end of the corridor were met by a ripple of detonations. Bodies were mounting up, the kill-tally increasing.

But still it wasn't enough.

They were *everywhere*.

Clambering out of airshafts, erupting from the deck tiles, lurching down the corridor. Each weapon discharge illuminated the corridor in a flush of orange light, threw up the shadows of more inbound attackers. We were still hundreds of metres from the docking tube, and there were just as many Krell bodies between me and the way off the ship—

A Krell secondary-form stomped down the corridor, waving a rifle in my direction. A flurry of gloss-black spines slit the air. *Damned stingers.* I reflexively dodged aside – *got to protect the pod!* – moved before I'd even concluded that I was being shot at, and avoided the attack. My null-shield lit in response. Martinez put the bastard down with a volley of cluster missiles.

We reached a stretch of corridor with a view-port stretching its length. Involuntarily, I paused as I looked on space outside. A Krell bio-ship lingered on the edges of my visual, moving fast on our position. She was only a mid-sized vessel – a scoutship, designed for stealth and speed – but her hull was studded with bio-cannons, bright spines elevated along her back generating blue light. Even in the split second I had to take in the details, she had begun discharging those living weapons across near-space—

Not just one ship, either. Space warped and smeared as more vessels popped into existence: translating from the Q. Almost all scouts like the original arrival, but in numbers enough to take down the *Colossus*.

Worry about that when you need to. Stay in the now!

The missile pods mounted on my back-plate began to

pop. The smart rounds ploughed through the Krell. I pumped a grenade into my carbine underslung launcher, wishing for just *more damned firepower!* A Krell tertiary-form – massive, over-armoured – exploded as it caught an incendiary round. Shards of smoking carapace and body matter scattered across the corridor, flecked Elena's capsule.

"Keep moving!" I ordered over the general channel, to anyone left alive who could take an order.

As I started onwards again, my ear-bead chimed.

"Lazarus Actual, this is *Colossus* Command," came Loeb's voice.

"I'm busy!"

"We can't stay here any longer! That ship is firing on us!"

"Then return fire!"

Something inside the *Endeavour* exploded. I felt the deck violently shudder, felt the entire corridor shift sideways. My stomach lurched for a second as the gravity well malfunctioned. Light bloomed across the outer aspect of the ship, through the passage view-port. I had no time to check, but that had to be one of the modules cooking off; some power-bearing component going critical.

"The *Endeavour* won't be able to take much more of this," Loeb said. "From what we can see several decks are already beyond recovery – "

"I don't give a fuck about this ship any more!"

"What about *this* ship?" Loeb asked. "The *Endeavour* is going down, and when she does she's going to take surrounding space with her." I remembered what Loeb had said about the *Endeavour*'s energy core: the bluster about having fire in her belly. "The Krell are trying to board the *Colossus* too. We need to break the tether, kill any stragglers at our end, then get the hell – "

273

"No! Hold the position! That's an order! We're moving on the umbilical. We'll be gone before the ship goes down."

"We're detect—" Loeb started, but his voice was terminated by a crackle of interference.

The pipework around me started to hiss. Steam and cryogen were being vented into the corridor; the immediate predecessor to the energy core overheating. Clouds of white gas reduced visibility. The Krell made the most of the conditions, using the venting gas as cover, all six limbs moving in the tight confines. One would often leapfrog another to reach me, but my plasma rifle was always hot. I waded through the sea of corpses – the floor made slick with the blood of the fallen.

A warning appeared on my HUD: MISSILE AMMO DEPLETED. *Damn it.* I wasn't carrying reserves. Martinez's pods were pouring black smoke, the firing tubes glowing orange. Maybe the tech wasn't made for such heavy use. *Like that's going to be a complaint I'll ever get to lodge with R & D*, I thought.

A hail of plasma pulses tore up the corridor. The wave of Krell didn't exactly retreat, but were slowed by the onslaught.

Jenkins appeared at my back, James with her. They were literally bathed in Krell blood, Jenkins' camo-field flickering erratically. I nodded at them both.

"The Legion doesn't extract until I give the order," I said. "And that includes you, James."

Lieutenant James clutched the plasma pistol in both hands, the power cell indicator flashing LOW CHARGE. He could muster neither a smile nor a witty comeback.

"Got it."

"If I do go down," I nodded at the capsule under my arm, "this is the absolute priority. Elena has to get off this ship. Have the others reported in?"

"I can't reach 'Ski," Jenkins said. "Last we heard, he was pinned down with Mason in Data Processing."

"He knows what to do," Martinez said.

There was no time to worry about them; my HUD flashed with error messages, and I couldn't tell whether they were alive or not. Another, closer explosion sounded through the decks. The entire ship was now shaking, and would not stop. Around us, the shriek of encroaching Krell continued.

"Roll out," I said over the comm.

The Legion moved as one, laying down suppressing fire with plasma rifles. Another of the bulkheads began to shut on us, sliding down to seal the corridor. It was a heavy industrial hatch, made to seal the interior modules in case of catastrophic failure; a rolling vertical blast door. It would require something even heavier than a plasma rifle if we were trapped behind it.

"Get that door open!" I shouted. The alternative route would be much longer, and involve doubling back through the Communications Deck.

Jenkins ran to it, reaching the door just in time. The hatch pneumatic gears roared in protest as she caught the lower lip. She grunted over the comm-link, obviously struggling with the weight of the panel even with the improved strength-aug.

"Give me a hand with this!" she shouted at James.

James did his best, but his contribution was minimal. The door panel hovered off the ground. Both sims laboured with the task.

"Under!" Jenkins said through gritted teeth. "Now!"

I crouched beneath the door. Slid Elena's capsule under – metal clanging against the deck – and began to crawl through. The panel above me jumped erratically, eager to come down. I barely managed to get under; caught a glimpse of Elena's calm face inside the tank—

"Incoming!" James yelled.

There was activity on James' side of the door, and part of the ceiling collapsed. James went down fast and easy – no armour, soft pickings for the Krell. He disappeared beneath the alien horde, firing random plasma pulses into anything that moved. *Back*, the voice whispered to me in jeering tones, *to his twisted corpse of a body aboard your doomed ship.*

"Go!" Jenkins roared at Martinez.

The Venusian didn't need to be told twice. As he cleared the distance, the door's protest changed pitch, slamming down another half-metre. Jenkins let out a low animal shout.

"Jenkins!" I said. "We'll hold the door!"

Martinez and I went to grapple with the lower edge of the panel. Jenkins slid through to her waist.

"Hold it steady!" she yelled.

"We're trying," Martinez said.

The door bucked and slid further to the floor. I roared, felt the strength-amp working in my battle-suit. It was no good: the door was too heavy. Something grabbed Jenkins on the other side of the door and pulled her back by the lower half. She let out an agonised scream. Despite our efforts, the door panel slipped through my hands and slammed down: sliced right through Jenkins' armour, then her simulated body. I looked sideways at Martinez. He grimaced solemnly.

The door panel hit the floor with an enormous boom, almost loud enough to cut off Jenkins' scream. She was cut cleanly in half at the waist: simulated entrails and gene-factored blood smudged against the lower side of the door, guillotined. Simulants were made of tougher stuff than

276

hardcopy humans, and she wasn't dead. Not yet, but the Krell would see to that: their bodies slammed against the other side of the door, angered by the obstacle. They'd only acquired half their prize and they wanted the rest.

"Get out of here!" Jenkins ordered, scrabbling onto her stomach to haul herself upright. She was spilling guts and blood across the floor, would be gone in seconds. "I'll hold them!"

I nodded. "Solid. Martinez, on me."

Krell just *appeared* in front of us, lurching out of the gas clouds and steam emissions, claws and talons outstretched to take us down.

"It's this way," Martinez said, waving towards the next junction. "Docking tube is through the atrium—"

We had emerged into the open atrium, the concourse that someone back in the Core had decided would look good with a ceiling composed of armour-glass. Krell emerged from every open corridor, flooding the area: as though Martinez and I had walked into a chokepoint—

Space outside was filled with debris; the flickering glow of exploding warheads, energy beams igniting, and every other weapon of war that the Alliance and Krell had devised to kill one another.

From somewhere behind us, a secondary-form began to fill the area with stinger-fire. Mostly, the rounds bounced off my armour-plate, but some got through: I felt the death-kiss of poisoned flechettes across my shoulder blades. The toxin hit me immediately – sent the world around me spinning like I'd downed a bottle of Martian spirits. *Shit. Storemberg was right: they're getting better at this.* The venom was pure and fast-acting, more effective than any Krell bio-compound I'd felt so far.

Somewhere beside me, Martinez went down. He lashed

out with both arms, a flurry of wild retribution, crushing Krell bodies beneath his armoured weight. I was vaguely aware that my HUD had started to stream messages from Mason and Kaminski. Any hope I felt at that was quickly quashed: they had both extracted, swarmed by Krell on their way back through Data.

I began to slow. I stumbled, gasped with the pain. Elena's capsule slipped, collided with a wall.

Not her! I screamed. *Not like this. Not when I'm so close.*

Loeb was shouting over the comm-link, demanding an update. Ordering the bridge to *initiate maximum fucking thrust and get us the hell away from here . . .*

My simulated body was shutting down. Something big and heavy landed on my back, and I felt the slash of claws through my armour. From the mass of the attacker, it had to be a tertiary-form – rendered even more lethal by my incapacitated state. Sympathetically, another module aboard the *Endeavour* exploded behind me, showering surrounding space with frag, crumpling the deck-plates beneath me. I slammed by back to a wall: felt the weight of the tertiary-form leave me, as the fish-head was plastered across the surface. Kept moving –

Something enormous and thorn-covered and lethal smashed into me. I grappled with the xeno – *just fucking die!* – and it violently thrashed, unwilling to abandon its dedication to the Collective. I jammed my rifle into the thing's face; fired again and again. Dead or maimed, it stopped moving. Good enough, but the rifle was empty. It was useless now, anyway. Nothing mattered unless I got Elena off this damned ship.

Her capsule was under my arm again, and I was moving towards the docking tube. My medi-suite was flooding my body with drugs, counterattacking a hundred injuries that

I hadn't even realised I'd suffered. Warnings of suit breaches, impending power loss, imminent extraction, all scrolled across my HUD.

Elena's eyes were still shut, but she spoke to me. She drove me on.

You can't die out here, she said.

"I can," I said, "and I will: but I can't let *you*."

Everything became a blur.

Maybe it was the combination of drugs that my suit had administered, some added feature of the Ares armour, or perhaps my simulant was fighting off the Krell toxin. The truth didn't matter: only that I could suddenly operate again, that was all that I cared about.

The universe had slowed down, and I was moving faster than light.

I ran for the docking tube. Faster and faster. The suit was doing the work, the leg attenuators pumping. *If I died in the suit*, I wondered, *would it simply keep running?*

The Krell were just behind me.

The *Endeavour*'s airlock doors were open, and the *Colossus* awaited —

The docking tube began to warp. The deck rippled.

The *Colossus* was moving off. More of the *Endeavour* had broken up; I saw the reflected glow of muted explosions cast against the *Colossus*' hull. A Krell bio-ship spiralled past me, caught by one of the *Colossus*' counter-measures: a small victory amid the sea of defeat. Stingrays and Needlers flitted by, breacher-pods slashing space.

The Marines were at the end of the tube. Fingers on triggers of their laser carbines: panic in their hardcopy eyes.

I found my voice. "Hold the airlock!" I shouted over the open comm-network. "Get this capsule inside!"

The docking tube collapsed around me. The floor gave

way, and the walls fell in. Instinctively, I grappled for something – desperate to remain upright – but that was a
hopeless goal. Atmosphere began to suck from the tube,
venting into space. Worse yet, I felt clawed feet on my back,
my shoulders. Krell: scrabbling over me, clambering up the
tube. The Marines began to fire – ruby lances flashing by,
hitting tertiary- and primary-forms – but they were too few
in number to do any good.

From the corner of my eye, I saw the *Colossus'* thruster
engines fire. Blue against the black.

Fuck. I wasn't going to make it—

I had the capsule in both hands, ready to propel it. Elena
had slept through it all—

I reached out, threw it towards the *Colossus'* open lock
in a single underarm sweep. The muscles in my simulated
arms screamed, flooded as they were with bio-toxin.

The capsule – so, so fragile – sailed through zero-G.
Onwards towards the open airlock in the *Colossus'* hull.
The Marines were ready to receive it—

With spinning vision, I saw the *Colossus'* outer airlock
door beginning to cycle shut.

"Do you have her?" I shouted over the comm. "Report!"

The network was a wash of barked orders.

Krell scrabbled through the vacuum, lurching for me.

In dizzying, sickening zero-G, I saw the *Endeavour* and
the *Colossus* side by side; surrounded by Krell bio-ships,
opening up with everything they had.

Then the tether between the human ships was broken,
trailing alongside the enormous bulk of the *Colossus*. I
slammed my left arm against one of the now-loose deck-
plates. Felt armour and bone crack – agony shooting through
that limb. The pain was shut down almost instantly by my
combat-suit, but it was an irrelevant if merciful reaction.

I already knew that I was gone.

I cartwheeled out into space, joined by a mass of dead and dying Krell . . .

. . . a string of blue lights drew my failing eyes.

Crystals, like miniature blue stars, spinning in a line, creating a trail across space. Almost beautiful, but with dreadful implications.

Cryogenic fluid.

Oh shit.

Sometimes life – simulated or real – just wasn't fair.

Elena's capsule had been breached.

I extracted.

CHAPTER EIGHTEEN

ELENA'S ARMS

The world around me was formless chaos.

A heavy, ponderous drum beat in my ears.

Light.

Noise.

Pain.

The beating drum? It was my heart: thudding and irregular.

My brain was rebooting.

An alarm sounded in the distance. A shipboard warning.

I was in my simulator-tank. The amniotic fluid sloshed like a storm-tossed sea—

Where is Elena?

Has her capsule made it?

Are the Krell aboard the Colossus?

The SOC was in confusion. Had to be that we were trying to outrun the *Endeavour*'s blast zone. Inside my tank, my only connection with the outside world was the bead in my ear. Some Navy officers were chanting coordinates, others yelling orders.

"Bearing point nine. Null-shield holding!"

"Bio-plasma incoming."

"Hull breach on Deck A-11—"

"—engine compartment is hit!"

"Vent! Vent now!"

Then Loeb's voice cut through the discord: *"Ease off the thrust!"*

An indistinct shape appeared outside my tank. I braced against the inner canopy: felt my pulse quicken involuntarily.

The Krell—?

Something pressed against the tank. I recoiled, struggling to focus on whatever was out there.

The *Colossus'* gravity well adjusted. Began to stabilise. The part of my brain currently rebooting – where I stored the technical jargon which was largely irrelevant to my life as a soldier – whispered to me that the inertial dampeners had probably come back online; that they were countering the effects of the rapid acceleration.

The shape outside the tank became distinct, and the world snapped into sudden clarity. There was another voice in my ear.

"Confirm extraction!"

Jenkins. Naked, wrapped in an aluminium blanket, a red line cutting her neatly at the waist. The raised welt looked like a very pale reflection of the punishment she'd just endured back on the *Endeavour*, but she was also bleeding from the head. Holding a fresh wound dressing there that had already turned a pink-red colour. That must've been fresh damage, something that had happened to her hardcopy body during our retreat. Jenkins had made extraction seconds before me and would have suffered the worst of the ship's sudden evasive manoeuvring.

"Do we have her?" I asked, my voice a wet growl in my

283

throat, muffled by the respirator on my face. "Is Elena safe?"

"We have her," Jenkins said. "We have Elena, Harris."

The tank began to slough out and I collapsed against the canopy. Slammed a hand to the EMERGENCY RELEASE button, and wriggled out of the simulator. The data-cables anchored me to the machine as though threatening to pull me back inside. I tore the respirator from my face.

"I need to see her," I said.

"She's secure," Jenkins said. "And so are we, but the *Endeavour* is gone. You need medical attention—"

"I *need* to see her!" I shouted.

Loeb stormed into the SOC, scattering injured medical officers and Navy staff in his wake. His face was flushed red with what I assumed was anger.

"Can someone please shut off that Christo-damned alarm!" he shouted. He threw his arms up in the air as he paced in front of me.

"Aye, sir," an adjunct said.

The sound of shipboard and station alarms had become so common to me that I realised I'd phased it out. That, and my head was still ringing from the hard extraction. The *Colossus'* emergency routines had been in full effect, and the ship around me hadn't yet recovered from the *Endeavour*'s demise; monitors and consoles fizzled and stuttered with nervous error messages. The air stank of burning plastic and the acrid tang of halon. There had been a fire somewhere aboard the ship that had recently been put out.

"As I was saying," Loeb continued, "the Krell war-fleet has been neutralised."

That hardly got the reception that Loeb had intended.

The first and only thing I cared about right now was seeing Elena. I needed to hold her, needed to be with her.

Martinez stepped up, beside Loeb. "Leave him be, *jefe*." The rest of the Legion had dismounted their tanks too.

Loeb's eyes flared with anger. "We almost died out there!"

Jenkins nodded at Loeb. "Leave it, Admiral." To me: "You should go now."

There was a brittle edge to Jenkins' voice that I had only just noticed; a melancholy tone that I rarely heard from her. I paused, looked around at the Legion, and realised that they had closed around me in a circle, as though protecting me from Loeb's accusations.

Even James, back in a fresh next-gen simulant, stood between Loeb and me. "This can wait. The colonel should go to her."

"Is she alive?" I asked, suddenly aware that there was something very wrong with what was happening here. I struggled into my fatigues, mechanical hand twitching disobediently as it caught on my uniform.

The expression on Loeb's weathered face softened, and his eyes fell from mine. "She's in the infirmary," he said. "Dr Serova is tending to her."

Dr Serova met me at the hatch to Medical. I stormed past her, towards the infirmary, and she trailed behind me.

"Her capsule must've been breached during the rescue," she said. "Those cryogenic capsules are not made for exposure to vacuum or low pressure, Colonel. The canopy was cracked."

Medtechs and crew parted to let me through, all eyes to the floor.

"That probably wouldn't have been enough to kill her," Serova insisted, "but the patient also suffered an injury from a Krell stinger." She shook her head vigorously, despite almost running to keep up with me. "The bio-toxin is virulent, untreatable with our current medical supplies."

I stood outside the treatment room: through a large window that allowed observation of the room beyond. A Marine – maybe one of those responsible for taking the capsule aboard – ducked his head in my direction and made himself scarce. A smart move.

"We've placed her in quarantine for the time being," Serova said. She clutched a data-slate to her chest. "I'm very sorry, Colonel. There's nothing else that we can do: the toxin is rampant, self-multiplying." I watched her reflection in the plasglass window, and she gave a limp smile. "As I'm sure you know, Krell bio-weapons are unpredictable and singularly lethal."

I let the words wash over me, but I wasn't really listening. My body felt as cold as Elena's probably was; my heart a rock. This couldn't be happening again, not when I'd got so close to saving her. The cosmic injustice of it all was almost overwhelming.

Elena was the only occupant in the stark white room. She lay on her back in a bunk, her glossy dark hair spilled across the pillow, a sheet pulled up all the way to her neck, concealing her body. Her eyes were shut, but very lightly – as though she was just asleep and could awaken at any moment. Her brow was slightly creased – that characteristic frown that she wore, caught in a dream. The expression hinted that, perhaps, whatever she was experiencing was not entirely pleasant.

The rest of her presentation gave the lie to any suggestion she was sleeping. Medical dressing had been placed over her right shoulder from collar to breast, and it had turned a putrid black, contaminated by the toxin in Elena's body.

Tubes choked with the stuff were attached to her, impotently attempting to flush the poison from her system.

When did it happen? I asked myself. In truth, Elena could've been shot at any point during the rescue. The Krell had been everywhere, had infested the corridors and passage-ways. The *Endeavour* had been no place for a non-combatant. That Elena had been injured was completely explicable, likely even, although that made it no easier to accept. *She probably felt nothing*, I insisted to myself. *She probably feels nothing now.*

All I could feel was a cold surge of rage. I wanted to turn the *Colossus* into the heart of the Maelstrom; to hunt down every last fish head and destroy them once and for all—

"Are you all right?" Dr Serova asked, gingerly. "You're shaking, Colonel." She swallowed and looked down at her data-slate. Safety came from numbers – from things quan-tified and quantifiable. Serova began to reel information off to me. "I've seen your extraction report, and the numbers are worrying. We should get you checked out too—"

"It can wait," I growled. "You'll go down in Alliance history as the doctor who treated the only survivor of the *Endeavour* expedition. If there's an Alliance to go back to, of course."

Serova pulled an uncomfortable smile. "I'd rather not have the accolade, if that's all the same."

"How long does she have?" I asked, my voice breaking.

"Not long. I've run this toxin through the ship's database, and it isn't a strain we've previously encountered. The Krell are evolving so fast, it's difficult to keep track." She gave an inappropriate laugh; a nervous reaction to my anger. "That she is alive at all shows true determination, but like I said, I'm no expert on this technology."

I froze. "*Technology?*"

"Yes. It's possible that the connection is being affected."

"What connection?"

"The neural-link connection," Serova said. "I think that it what it is called. Do I have the terminology right?"

"What neural-link?"

Understanding dawned on Serova's features. Colour seemed to void from her already pale face.

"The simulant, Colonel," she said. "The woman you recovered from the *Endeavour* is a simulant. I'm sorry; I thought that you knew."

And just then, Elena – or more precisely, Elena's simulant – woke up.

The Next-Generation Simulant Project had been an attempt to create simulacra that resembled real humans as closely as possible. That had, by necessity, involved a trade-off between strength, durability and size. The next-gens were built better than a natural body, but they lacked the size and mass of combat-sims. On the other hand, they looked frighteningly similar to their donor-operator: resembled the original body, as of the date of its harvesting, in every single way. This simulant, this copy of Elena, had no protection against the Krell poison. She wore no combat-suit, wasn't equipped with a medi-suite to administer any antidote.

In itself, this moment – Elena in a hospital bed, me watching over her injured body – felt like a repeated simulation. *I've been here before*, I thought. A different world, different circumstances, but the feelings were just the same. I felt the stab of memory, a psychic backlash, as I entered the observation room.

Elena wasn't even on a proper bed. I supposed that those

had been reserved for more serious cases. Instead, she was curled up, semi-foetal, on an examination couch – an inert medical scanner on a metal arm still propped overhead. They had put her in a private chamber, just off of one of the ER corridors. The strip-lamp above flickered, waxing and waning.

Without thinking, I reached out and clutched her hand. Even if she was only simulated, I needed to know that she was here: that I hadn't constructed this entire scenario. Her skin was cool and the flesh of her hand was soft. Newborn soft. That told me that this simulant hadn't been used, hadn't been lived in.

The simulant in front of me looked to all intents like an exact replica of Elena's real body: a copy of her, as she had looked when she had left Calico. She'd been thirty-two standard years old then. Physically, she was still that woman, the only variance being the lack of data-ports. *This* Elena's arms were unmarked – the skin unbroken by the ugly black welts that pocked a sim-operator's forearms.

Elena's eyelids fluttered, as though adjusting to a bright light although the observation room was in semi-darkness. She stared ahead for a second, then at me. There was instant recognition there, but no surprise: like she had always known that I would come back for her.

"Conrad?" she asked.

The sound of her voice: it sparked so many emotions in me. Yes, there was love, desire, joy. But much more than that . . . I felt other, darker responses as well: guilt, remorse, regret. Without Elena, I was a rock. I had no need for emotions, good or bad. With her, I was fallible. She was my motivation but also my weakness. She was my vulnerability.

"It's me," I said. "I'm here."

"You came for me," she said. "You came back for me."

"I said that I would. I promised."

"Wh . . . where are we?"

Her voice was a dry rasp, and even the few words that she had spoken were an obvious struggle. The Elena-sim's lips were almost the colour of her face; her long dark hair a stark contrast to her skin tone. Her entire appearance was drained and debilitated.

"Aboard a starship," I said. "Aboard the *Colossus*."

"Your ship?"

"My ship. An Alliance ship."

"Good. That's good. What happened . . . to me?"

"We rescued you from the *Endeavour*. The ship was destroyed. There was no one else aboard. The Treaty was agreed ten years ago. You've been in the Maelstrom since then."

"Treaty . . .?" she whispered. A fleeting smile passed over her lips, but the expression was sickly. I realised that I had misunderstood her question. "Is that what . . . they told you?"

"Of course. You went into the Maelstrom to agree the Treaty, with the Krell."

"There was never a Treaty," Elena whispered.

"Yes there was," I insisted. "You're confused—"

"There was no Treaty."

"Yes," I said. "There was, and you've been gone for ten years . . ." I stumbled. Despite Elena's condition, now I was the weaker one: brought low by her words. They were wounding me in a way that a physical weapon never could. "The *Endeavour*'s mission was—"

"It was . . . always Command's plan. There never was to be a Treaty."

"That . . . that can't be right . . ."

She's ill, I told myself, *and she isn't thinking straight.*

290

Except that, as I looked into Elena's pallid face, I knew that she was telling me the truth. I couldn't dispel or ignore her words, because here she was – dying – and there was surely no reason to lie. A cold, constricting feeling clutched me and would not let go. Things that I thought I could rely upon – that were given as true, even though I hated and detested them – were suddenly slipping away from me.

"I'm sorry, Conrad . . . You have to understand: what I did was only for you . . ." She swallowed, painfully. I knew only too well what was happening to her body: cell walls bursting, organs beginning to shut down. I'd been there a hundred times before. "I traded my life for yours . . ."

Elena touched my metal hand. Her eyes swivelled in their sockets; focused on the bionics. The hand extended from my fatigues, the pseudo-muscular articulation reflecting the med-bay lights in a way that was almost malevolent. I fought the urge to withdraw it, to hide it.

"What . . . what have they done to you, Conrad?" she said.

"It's okay. I'm fine."

Tears began to fall down Elena's face, streaming across her cheeks. Her fingers probed the metalwork, moving slug-gishly, like she had less control over the simulant body than I did over the bionic.

"They have . . . hurt you . . ." she whispered. "They will hurt us all, if they have the chance . . ."

Elena's slender body was racked by a vicious shudder. I suddenly ordered my thoughts. She didn't have long left in this body, and that she was alive at all meant that her real skin hadn't been aboard the *Endeavour*. Right now, some-where, she was inside a simulator-tank. Even if she was in comparative safety, she must be in the Maelstrom.

"The *Endeavour* is gone," I said, composing myself. "I need to find you, Elena. I need to save you."

"I had a simulator . . . I went through the Damascus Rift . . . W-we used the Artefact, opened the Abyss."

I knew all of this: did not want Elena to waste her life-force explaining it to me. With my real hand, I clutched hers a little tighter. I noticed with mounting trepidation that her skin was getting colder, caused by her blood circulation slowing down. Once the death-clock had started, it could not be stopped.

"What was your mission, Elena?" I persisted. "Where did Command send you?"

"We were to do something terrible . . ." she sobbed.

"It's all right," I lied.

"It's not . . . What we found . . ."

"Where is your real body, Elena?" I said, with more force this time. "We have people aboard this ship. We can help. *I* can find you."

"The Revenant . . ." she started.

But whatever else Elena had to say was lost.

She groaned. It was a horrible, tormented sound: a death rattle. I'd seen the reaction before, and knew that she was losing control of the simulant. I could almost feel her pain. She reeked of fresh cryogen, the formaldehyde-like aroma, and her skin was stained so white that it was almost translucent at her forearms, around raised cheekbones and temples.

"We have transport," I said. "We can follow your signal. Just tell me where you are."

Elena's eyes were so much harder than I remembered. Her mouth opened to speak. I willed her on, was desperate to hear her voice one more time: drew near to her so close that I could feel her weak breath on my ear.

"Devonia," she whispered. "Planetary coordinates zero-three, delta nine . . ." Those were grid coordinates. Not precise, but enough to go on. She swallowed. "I'll be waiting."

And then it was over.

The machine beside Elena began a steady chirping. Some of her vital signs were spasming. *Shit!* I grabbed Elena's naked shoulder, clutched it as though this would stop her from leaving me. The bio-monitor gave out a loud beep. The previously jagged graphics on the holo began to flatten, indicating only one thing.

The body was still; deathly still.

Empty.

Elena had extracted.

How many times was I destined to watch the woman I loved die?

I held her hand until it had become ice, watched the guttering light in her dark eyes. Around me, the *Colossus* rang out with the occasional warning chime, and I was repeatedly summoned to the briefing room by the ship's AI. The announcements were gradually becoming more persistent, but I ignored them.

This was the horror. This was the deep hurt.

I'd lost her in Damascus, watched her fall from the Atefact's Hub, having been shot by Williams' Warfighters: a brief and terrible agony. Now I had seen her die from a Krell bio-toxin, body ravaged by alien venom. But I'd lost Elena twice even before then: once on Azure, when she had left me to join the *Endeavour*'s expedition, then again on Calico Base when she had gone into the Maelstrom. It seemed that history was destined to repeat itself indefinitely: that I was trapped in the spiral of Martinez's Nine Hells.

I leant forward and kissed Elena on the lips, reached for the bed sheet, and folded it very precisely over her. Her open eyes were the last thing I saw of her face.

"I . . . I'm sorry. We heard what happened."

I turned to see Kaminski standing at the door. I'd been so wrapped in this moment that I hadn't even heard him enter.

"Seeing her like that . . ." he said. "Next-generation sims creep me out. Too close to the real thing."

I noticed that Kaminski was doing his best to avoid looking at the outline of the body on the bed, eyes flitting between the ground and me. He had known Elena too; had been recruited by her in the early days of the Sim Ops Programme. The three of us were locked into this unholy triumvirate: we'd been there at the start, but were we going to be left standing at the end?

I stared back at Elena's body. "It's not like I haven't been here before."

Kaminski nodded. He still carried the simulation stigmata: blood-red slashes across his shaven head and, with his uniform unbuttoned at the neck, visible across his collarbone too.

"I read the Damascus debrief," he said. "She really wants you to find her, Harris. This is the second time that she's done this, and it must've taken some serious planning. Think about it for a moment: how did Elena know that we were on that ship?"

"What's your point?"

Kaminski looked pleased with himself, a big kid who had worked out a homework problem. "You're forgetting that tech is my speciality. I accessed the *Endeavour*'s mainframe from the Data Deck, before she went down. When we entered the ship, we tripped a silent alarm, and the ship's AI activated the neutrino array."

The neutrino array: the faster-than-light communications suite.

I rubbed a hand over my unshaven chin. "She knew that we were on that ship . . ."

"She knew that *someone* was on the ship. Martinez has told me that he saw bodies in cryogenic suspension. I guess that those were simulants kept in storage for too long: turned sour."

I nodded at Kaminski, felt a swell of purpose inside me. Elena had heard the signal, made transition into the new simulant body . . . Provided she was in the same galactic neighbourhood, the neutrino array would've sent a signal to her within seconds. I guessed that, alerted by the signal, she had made transition to make contact with us. It was an audacious plan, but no more so than what she had done in Damascus, and it had worked.

"Thanks 'Ski," I said. "You did good."

"I try," he said, "but I don't know where the signal was directed."

"You might not, but I do."

"Then maybe you should come tell us," Kaminski said. "The Legion is waiting for you."

The Legion, Professor Saul, Lieutenant James and Admiral Loeb all occupied the briefing room: quiet and still, awaiting my appearance.

"That must've been rough . . ." Mason said. She sighed, her slender body shivering.

That was far from an adequate description of what I was feeling, but Mason was only trying to be kind. I grimaced and nodded away the comment. I took the head of the chamber.

"Elena is gone," I said, flatly. "But we've got work to

do. Anyone want to tell me what happened out there?"

Loeb's anger from back in the SOC still simmered, though I could tell given present circumstances he wasn't going to confront me. "We should've pulled out, Harris."

"I had to save her. Surely you can see that."

Loeb nodded warily. "But that was still a very dangerous thing to do."

"We're alive," Kaminski said, coming to my aid. "Let's just be thankful for that."

"We got out of the blast radius, if that's what you mean, but only just." Loeb looked back to me: "I warned you about the *Endeavour*'s energy core. A ship that size, equipped with a goliath-pattern power module, is just about the most dangerous weapon in the galaxy."

"You got to fight some Krell," Jenkins added. "Isn't that what you've always wanted?"

"We were on top of the *Endeavour* when that damned Krell bio-ship turned up," Loeb said. "We were neutered! Our null-shields were down. The *Endeavour*'s energy core cooked off. Spilled its payload across local space, and so far as we can tell it took out the Krell war-fleet with it."

"How exactly did the Krell get the jump on us?" Martinez asked.

"That's a good question," Loeb said, "but it's one that I can't answer. They had no energy trail, and we barely saw them on the scopes until they were right in front of us."

Professor Saul leant forward across the table. "They're evolving, Colonel. Science Division has found the same thing across the Quarantine Zone. They're evolving all aspects of their bio-technology: able to respond more quickly, equipped with better stealth tech."

So turns the cycle of war . . . I thought.

"That'd explain all those tertiary-forms," Jenkins groaned.

"The bastards on that ship were bigger and faster than anything I've ever seen before."

Jenkins sat back in her seat, awkwardly and uncomfortably. She was still suffering, and her reaction reminded me that I was too: every fibre of my body ringing out with ghost-pains from the extraction.

Loeb continued the explanation. "From the CIC, we saw what was coming – saw the *Endeavour*'s drive core beginning to bleed off. We started to pull out . . ." The Buzzard's words trailed off, and though he avoided looking in my direction the criticism was implicit.

"Guess the Krell didn't see what was coming," Kaminski said, with an empty laugh. "Those stupid fishes aren't so clever after all."

"So what's the damage?" I asked Loeb.

He shoved a data-slate in my direction and I took a second to focus on the holo-projection. It showed a green wireframe schematic of the *Colossus*, populated with red icons from port to stern.

"In summary," Loeb said, "there are numerous systems damaged as a result of the operation. A munitions store was compromised; the contents are now spread across near-space. Two water tanks have been ruptured. Deck A-11 was breached; that contained our long-range communications apparatus. Our port-side thrust control has been lost."

"And the good news?" Jenkins said, with another painful wince.

Loeb glowered at her. "Our energy core is stable, Lieutenant. That's some very good news, as far as I'm concerned. That means that we aren't in danger of exploding in the immediate future."

"*Immediate?*" Mason asked.

"As in within the next few days," Loeb said. "I can't be any more specific than that. We suffered a hit on the life-support module, and we've lost climate control on most decks."

The temperature had noticeably dropped, but I had assumed that was a side-effect of my last extraction. Heating was an essential component of any starship's life-support system; necessary to protect life as we crossed the void.

"Can't we jury-rig it?" I suggested.

Loeb nodded grimly. "We can, but that'll involve suspension of all non-essential systems: something I'd rather not do in the Maelstrom."

James cleared his throat from across the room. In a fresh sim, he was about the only member of the crew in fighting shape. Everyone else, I realised, carried the stigmata of the extraction: the welts and scars that their simulated counterpart had suffered during the operation.

"But worse than any of this," he muttered, "is the fact that we've been *detected*. The Krell know that we're out here." There were rumbles of agreement across the board, even from Jenkins. "Those were scoutships, and every fish head in this quadrant is going to be out here looking for us. Based on what the Professor says we probably won't even see them coming."

James was right. Retribution might not be immediate, but by interstellar standards the Krell's reaction would be swift. That was one of the many unknowns of the Krell intelligence network: exactly how a Collective was able to share information quite so quickly. It was hypothesised that deep within the bellies of those bio-ships were Krell specialised to communicate across the vastness of space, whose only role within the wider shoal was to speak to fellow fishes. Such an advanced fish head had neither been seen nor captured, but Sci-Div were sure that they existed.

"Then we better get moving," I said. "When the fish heads get here, we'll be long gone."

"Where are we going?" Loeb said. "We can't retreat back to the Core; we've been through this already—"

"Devonia," I said.

Loeb's reaction was immediate and uncompromising. "Harris," he said, "are you out of your fucking *mind*? That's surely Krell territory!"

"We're following Elena," I said. "Before she died, she told me things." I glanced around the room at the tired faces. "Some of which weren't easy for me to accept . . ."

I told them what Elena had said: about the Treaty, and about the coordinates on Devonia. They listened with patent unease. Couldn't say that I blamed them; the disclosure sat as uncomfortably with me as it did with anyone.

"Shit . . ." Martinez said, shaking his head. "This is a lot to take onboard."

"If there was no Treaty," Mason said, "then why was the *Endeavour* still out here?"

"You're always with the questions," I said. "Look, I don't have all the answers, Mason. I didn't get that far, but Elena directed us to Devonia, so that's where we're going."

Admiral Loeb breathed out slowly, his teeth to his lip. "I was afraid that you might say that."

"Can we make the journey?" I asked.

"It's possible," Loeb said, "but it won't be easy. In our current condition, it'll take three days to reach under full thrust."

"Then that's where we're going," I repeated. I turned to Mason. "And down there we'll find the answers to those questions."

299

The room fell into an awkward silence as we all digested Elena's disclosure, and considered what it meant.

You've always had your doubts about what they were doing out here, the voice taunted. *Don't pretend that you didn't suspect that this was the case . . .*

CHAPTER NINETEEN

THE TREATY

Seven years ago

The official Alliance Command line was that the *Endeavour* mission went MIA – missing in action – a couple of years after her passing into the Maelstrom, but the timescales were never precise and it felt like the Alliance had forgotten her a long time before then. The Treaty was a success, or so the politicos claimed, and the Quarantine Zone was established. The First Krell War was at an end, and other than the occasional border dispute the whole affair looked as though it would pass into history as just another example of bloody and pointless conflict so familiar to the human species.

I didn't forget about Elena, but everyone else did.

Cassari Brooke's new article was the first time anyone had ever called me "Lazarus", and I tried my best to forget that. It was easily put out of mind but not easily forgotten. I rebuked troopers for calling me it, erased the callsign when I found it on after-mission logs. Tried to deny that which was inevitable. It was slow-burn but the name stuck.

For a while after Calico, after the *Endeavour*'s launch, I followed Cassi Brooke's news articles. I didn't hear from her, which suited me fine, but I read her stories: exposés on the military, following squads to the frontline, typical war-reporter stuff. Though she'd certainly moved on from cats up trees, the casts weren't really news to me. A couple of years after our meeting, Brooke just disappeared from the news-feeds. I guessed that she had probably got a marriage contract and a child licence; maybe retired from the dangerous business of being an investigative reporter. In real life, people did that sort of thing.

I'd learnt an important lesson – that I never trust a reporter – and I got on with existing. Living, dying, drinking. I thought that the bottom of a bottle held the only answers I was ever going to receive.

Then the strangest thing happened. I was stationed on *Liberty Point*, at a time when the outpost was still relatively new, when I received a message from her. Text-only, it was a request to meet.

Somehow, through what method I didn't know, Cassari Brooke had obtained a pass to *Liberty Point*. She was on-station and wanted to talk.

Just as she had done on Calico Base, years before, Brooke chose the meeting place. In those days, with *Liberty Point*'s firm position as the largest military outpost on the QZ, there were more than enough bars and clubs to choose from. The Civilian District brimmed with drinking holes, but Brooke chose a diner in the maintenance sector. It was a small, rundown place frequented by many of the manual workers and dock-hands – a diner that could've easily been exported to the *Point* from downtown Detroit – filled with men and women wearing ragged uniforms, with grease-stained faces. People, I realised, who were the grist that kept the mill running. They weren't heroes, and they weren't proud, but they worked hard. I almost felt out of place in my uniform, with the shiny merit badges and the holo-tag proclaiming the number of times I'd died. These people didn't care much for that, and as I entered the diner very few even bothered to look up at me.

I searched the tables, frustrated at first that I couldn't see Brooke. She'd been specific about the time and location.

Then a voice called to me from across the room, a figure emerging from one of the booths in the corner.

"Captain Harris," she said. Waved a hand. "Over here."

I paused for a moment: the recognition wasn't immediate. Cassari Brooke, formerly of Core News Network, had changed a great deal in the time since I'd last seen her. Patchy recollections of images of her from news stories I'd read came back to me, and she'd changed a lot since those as well. Somewhat reluctantly, I edged my way through the diner and sat with her.

Her red hair was faded, scruffy, and though she didn't look much older – I suspected that rejuvenation treatments had kept her objective years at bay – she looked more weathered. All glossiness had gone from her features; body shrinking into a dock-hand's duffle coverall rather than a reporter's smart-suit.

"Thanks for coming," she said.

"I could hardly miss it," I said. "I never did get a chance to thank you for that news story . . ."

She gave a pale smile. "Sorry about that. Really, I am."

"I wish that I could believe you."

"I've already ordered coffee," she said.

"I'd hoped for something a little stronger."

The smile became frosted. "I don't do that any more."

"Yeah, well, I do."

"I've read about it," she muttered. "You should rein it in. Take it easy."

"You wouldn't be the first person to tell me that," I said, "and you surely won't be the last."

The booth at which we sat was beside an open observation window, allowing an unfettered view of the comings and goings of *Liberty Point*. Lots of warships drifted past; transports and cargo tugs flitting around the larger vessels. We thought, in those days, that we were invincible – that the Krell could never take what we'd made at the *Point*. Brooke watched the window, fiddling with the wrist-strap of her coverall, biting her lip.

"Are you still looking for your girl, Conrad?" she asked me.

"Is that what this is about? Another news story?"

Brooke's eyes remained fixed on the window. I noticed that there were no lights behind them: no data-link to the mainframe any more. Had she lost that ability somehow? That was surely a news reporter's lifeblood.

In answer to my question, Brooke said, "I don't do that any more, either. At least, not via the official channels."

"I figured as much. I followed your stories on the Sierra Delta. On the war at Sigma."

"That's good," she said, although she barely sounded interested. "I worked hard on those pieces, and I hope that you enjoyed them."

"I wouldn't say enjoyed," I said, "but you did a good job covering the Sim Ops Programme involvement."

She shook her head. "They weren't real stories."

"Then what were they?"

"They were propaganda pieces," she said. "Just nice words to keep the public happy."

Sierra Delta and Sigma were both war hotspots. Sim Ops had been there, but Army line infantry – hardcopy soldiers – had spilled blood taking and holding those territories from the Krell. I was surprised to hear her describe them in such terms, having read her stories.

"Those aren't the only things I've been researching," she added. Sounded nervous. "I've been researching you, actually."

A cold feeling crept across my skin. "Really."

"Yeah. I know that your father killed himself after he was discharged from the Army." She swallowed, either aware that she had gone too far or considering whether she should go any further. "I know that your mother died during the Battle for Jupiter Outpost; that she was killed by the Directorate. I even read about your sister, though that was much harder to find."

"Someone has been busy," I said. There were no official records of my father's death. Those in higher places had done the kindness of expunging his death from the military records. "If you think that I'm letting any of that become a story—"

She shook her head, showed me her open palms. "It's not, it's not. I'm just making a point."

"Which is?"

"That there's a lot of information in the mainframe, if you go looking for it."

"So what's this about? The *Point* is an awfully long way for a not-reporter to travel, just to tell me that you've been doing research—"

"Then answer my question," she snapped. "Are you still looking for your girl?"

I poured myself some cold coffee from the glass pot on the table. Noticed a small black box beside the pot, with a series of flickering green diodes on top.

"Of course I'm still looking. Even if you aren't a reporter

305

any more, you'll know that the *Endeavour* never came back. She's lost, out there somewhere."

"That's what they say," she said. "That's what they say."

"What do you mean – 'they say'? Do you know something?"

I remembered the non-information Brooke had tried to peddle back on Calico, and given her presentation I held no hope for a genuine new lead from her now. She abruptly turned her head, avoided making eye contact with me, then tapped a fingernail – bitten to the quick – on the box beside the coffee pot.

"This is a jammer," she said. "Cost me a lot, but it should stop anyone from listening in on our conversation. Just so that you know; in case you're wearing a wire."

"Of course I'm not."

"That's good."

"Why would I be?"

"Because there are people after me, you see. Both kinds: Directorate and Alliance."

"Have you completely lost it?" I queried.

"I never had it," she said, with a weak smile. "But we should talk. I might be able to help you, Conrad. For real."

"All right," I said. "I haven't stopped looking for her. I've been across the Quarantine Zone. I've used every resource I have. But all I've ever found is closed doors. Locked doors, even."

That was all completely true. I'd fallen into a well of frustration. The rational, sober part of me had even started to believe that maybe the authorities were right. Maybe Elena, and the *Endeavour* expedition, really were lost in the Maelstrom. Perhaps she would never be coming back. That didn't stop me from looking, but I feared that – one day – it probably would.

"If the Treaty was a success," Brooke said, "then why didn't the expedition come back? Think about that for a moment. Does that make sense to you?"

"They say that the ships were probably destroyed on the way to Alliance territory," I said. I didn't believe the words, but that was the explanation. "There are more than enough ways for a ship to be destroyed in the Maelstrom."

"I know you've been in there," Brooke said. "And I also know that you don't believe what you've just said. There were sixteen ships in that fleet, Conrad. *Sixteen ships.* Were they all lost in black holes?"

"Maybe," I said.

"The Treaty was signed off years ago," Brooke said. "But do you ever wonder why the terms of the Treaty have never been publicly disclosed?"

"Not really," I said. "We know about the Quarantine Zone—"

"And whose idea was it that a Quarantine Zone should be established?" she said, speaking over me. "Surely that didn't come from the Krell. I've seen research papers. Read files. How does something like the Krell agree to a Treaty . . .?"

"I don't know. Ask Sci-Div."

"Oh, I've tried. I've been inside the Science Division mainframe."

I didn't like the turn of this conversation. Brooke was speaking fast, irrationally. Hacking into the Science Division mainframe was a high-risk venture, even for an investigative reporter. For a civilian it was probably a capital offence.

"You get caught doing that," I said, "and I don't think that anyone is going to find out about it."

Command, Sci-Div, Mili-Intel: one of those agencies would see to her. There would be no trial, no exposure of whatever she had discovered.

Brooke's face spasmed. "You don't think I already know that? That's why I have the box."

"Well, if you've been in the Sci-Div mainframe, you know more of all this than me."

"Don't be facetious. How could the *Endeavour*'s crew negotiate with the Krell?"

"They have leader-forms," I said, shrugging. "I've seen them. Maybe they can be reasoned with—"

"And another thing: this talk of the 'Collective'. Bullshit. There are several Collectives across the Maelstrom, not one singular swarm as Command would have us believe. Science Division even has names for them; knows that they aren't all the same."

I watched Brooke's face. She looked very tired and her left eyelid twisted erratically, as though a reaction to stress. When she spoke, her words came in a sudden, fast burst. She was ill, I realised, and me being here wasn't helping her.

"How do the Krell communicate, Conrad?" she asked me, again avoiding eye contact. "That's what I want to know. That's what Science Division, and Command, won't tell us. I don't think that the Krell are even interested in the Treaty. The government is keeping all of this from us. No one is ever allowed to join up the dots."

She's mad, I concluded.

"All right, Cassi. It was nice seeing you."

Brooke's hand shot across the table and she grabbed my wrist, dug her nails into the skin of my forearm. I'd often heard it said, in Sim Ops mainly, that madness gave the sufferer strength. Maybe there was some truth in that, because Cassari Brooke was much stronger than she looked.

"I'm not fucking with you, Lazarus," she said. "I don't

think that the mission was sent out there to establish a Treaty at all."

"Then why were they sent into the Maelstrom?"

Something in the woman's expression held me there: even if these were just the ramblings of an ex-news reporter.

"I don't know," she said. She released my arm. "At least not yet."

"You're mad," I said. "You should get some help."

There was a clatter behind me. Mutters from some of the patrons near the door.

Brooke moved faster than me. Shuffling papers across the table, gathering them into an open case. She scooped the black box up and put that in, too.

"You should've checked whether you were followed—!" she spat at me.

Two Military Police officers in black flak-suits approached the table. Big enough to block Brooke's exit from the booth, both carrying lit shock-batons that danced with energy.

"Cassari Brooke?" the lead trooper said. "Citizen serial code 451452, of Tau Ceti?"

"No," she said. "You've made a mistake. That's not me."

The other trooper gave a nod. "Yes, that is you. Your ID has been confirmed via surveillance cameras outside."

The game was up. Brooke's shoulders slumped.

"You're under arrest for illegal entry to the *Point*: a class-three visa violation. Get up and come with us."

Papers, case and other effects under her arm, Brooke got up from the table.

"You should be asking these questions, Conrad!" she shouted to me, as she went. "I want to know what happened out there, and unless we stand up to them we'll never find out!"

"All right, all right," one of the MPs said. "Keep it down."

"Sorry about that, sir," the other said to me. "She's lost it."

I nodded. "I thought so, too."

"Used to be on CNN, or something," he said, watching his colleague march Brooke out of the diner. "Lost her job, started being a pest to the military authorities."

"Lot of crazies got these theories," I said. Hating myself for the words, but still talking.

"Mmmm," the trooper said. "Lot of crazies. I guess Tau Ceti is a long way from the frontline. Have a nice day, sir."

The Mili-Pol officers left with Cassari Brooke, waving her arms and shouting as she went, and me with the cold pot of coffee.

The meeting quickly fell from my memory: a bizarre and pointless incident. I felt sorry for Cassari Brooke, but it never made the news-feeds, and I assumed that she was removed off-station – taken somewhere she could get some proper help.

A few months after the meet, entirely by chance, while in one of *Liberty Point*'s many bars I saw how Cassari Brooke had met her end. It was a brief and disappointing news story, relayed by a fellow reporter with a sympathetic expression. Cassi Brooke was found in a bathtub, on her native Tau Ceti, wrists slit.

Pretty clichéd stuff, I remembered thinking. The authorities had reached the same conclusion – a dried-up, burnt-out ex-reporter with too much time on her hands. Someone who wanted a taste of death, and finally got it.

CHAPTER TWENTY

DEVONIA

The journey to Devonia passed in a state of repressed anxiety, and the *Colossus* felt almost abandoned: so many empty corridors and crew modules. Those few decks left operating were populated by crewmen wearing vacuum-suits, helmets under their arms; ever ready to man the evac-pods if we got hit. There was some small irony to that, because there was nowhere to escape to out here. While the Lazarus Legion were used to suicide missions, the Navy crew weren't, and this wasn't what they had signed up for. That the starship hadn't erupted into open mutiny was probably testament to Loeb's leadership skills.

I wandered the observation decks, checked on the comms pods. The Maelstrom was unlike human territory: without the need for radio transmissions, neutrino arrays, or any of the other comms methods that polluted space with data, the void around us was remarkably quiet. I'd heard stories of sailors driven insane by the silence and for the first time in my career I almost believed them.

I spent a lot of time in the Simulant Operations Centre.

It had always been a favoured location of mine; somewhere I could imagine making transition, escaping my real body. With the depleted science team on this mission, it was mostly quiet and dark. I found simulants racked and ready for deployment, encased in cryogenic capsules just like that in which I'd found Elena's body. Beside them sat five Ares battle-suits, marked up with battle-honours and unit designations. The Lazarus Legion badge was proudly displayed on the shoulder guards, freshly painted. I sensed a hunger from each suit: a readiness to be occupied.

I checked on each simulator-tank in turn; all four tanks glowed with welcoming blue light. I ran my good hand over the outer canopies, watched the liquid inside. The machines felt warm, in contrast to the cold of the ship around me—

A reflection rippled in the canopy. Something behind me: a shape, a figure. Watching.

"Who's there?" I barked.

Elena . . .?

"Easy, sir. It's only me."

Kaminski sat in the corner of the room, half-concealed by shadow. He leant forward, into the arc of light cast by the nearest tank.

"Pull up a pew," he said, waving with affected indifference. "I was just checking on the tanks myself."

That was patently untrue: I'd activated the simulators, not Kaminski. But when he sat back, wincing again, holding his shoulder, I decided not to correct him. He was in obvious pain. I hadn't seen his most recent death aboard the *Endeavour*, but from the after-action reports I'd read that he'd been torn apart by the Krell boarders.

"Simulated wounds playing you up?" I asked.

"Yeah," he said. "Those and the rest."

"You all right?"

"I'm good," he said. "But I haven't been sleeping so well. Dr Serova thinks it's the Arkonus Abyss." He laughed. "I think it's fear of death. Maybe we're both right."

"You don't have to put a brave face on it," I said. "Truth is, 'Ski, I didn't think that the medics were going to re-certify you, back on Calico."

"I expected as much."

"It's my fault. I twisted some arms . . ."

"And I'm glad that you did," he said, sounding distant. "I guess what happened on Capa V, it's just not easy to forget. I know that it could've been worse, much worse, and I got a lucky escape . . ."

His eyes darted to the SOC doorway, in the direction of Scorpio Squadron's operations bay. The flyboys had their own room, their own dedicated facility. Somewhere in there, held in the dark and shadow, was Lieutenant James' real body. That Kaminski might've ended up like that was unthinkable. He'd never been one for soul-searching, and I could tell that this was difficult: putting his fears into words.

"Are you worried that the Directorate will come after you?" I asked, as gently as I could.

Kaminski answered my question with a question: "Do you think that we really killed the *Shanghai* at Calico?"

"I'm not sure," I said. "But I hope so."

"I saw the way that you looked at that ship," he said, "and it was more than personal."

I nodded. "Me and that ship; turns out we have history together. I didn't know until Loeb told me something about the *Shanghai*. Kyung is known as the Assassin of Thebe: responsible for the slaughter of the Alliance Navy fleet at Jupiter Outpost."

"That's right," 'Ski said. "I remember."

313

"My mother was at Jupiter Outpost. She died when I was just a kid; eight years old. I was too young to know much about how she died, who or what killed her, and it wasn't until Loeb showed me his research on Kyung that the pieces fell into place. She was captain of the *Shanghai* during the raid on Thebe, also known as Jupiter Outpost. She killed my mother."

Kaminski raised his eyebrows. "That's some heavy shit. Real heavy. You don't get much more personal than that . . ."

"I guess," I said. "So, yeah, I hope that the *Shanghai* is wasted, and I hope that Kyung went down with her."

"I'm sorry," 'Ski stumbled, almost uncomfortable. "I never knew."

"Nothing to be sorry about. It all happened a long time ago, and whether the *Shanghai* is dead or not, it doesn't much matter. She – my mother – is ancient history."

But if there was a particular turning point – a junction in my life which I could trace, which I said defined me – it was definitely her death. It meant a lot more to me than I could ever admit.

"Just another reason to hate the Directorate," Kaminski said.

I noticed that there was an opened packet of painkillers beside him, a disposable hypodermic syringe uncapped on the medical bench. I nodded at the wrappers.

"Did Dr Serova prescribe those?"

"Not exactly," he said. "That last extraction: it was rougher than anything I've felt so far." He paused, as though struggling to find the right words. "It didn't feel *right*."

He stroked the digital broach on his chest, where the holo-identifier was placed, indicating one hundred and eighty transitions. Those statistics placed him in the top strata of simulant operators, not far behind my figures. We'd been in this from the start.

"Maybe you shouldn't go back into the tanks," I offered.

"Not going to happen, boss, so don't even say it."

"Maybe it won't be the Krell, or the Directorate, or even the Shard, that'll get us in the end . . ." I said, staring absently at the blue of the functioning simulator-tank beside me. "Maybe it'll be the tanks that'll end us."

"I can think of worse ways to go," Kaminski said, "and at least it'd be clean."

"A clean death. I'd drink to that."

We sat in the darkness for a while, watching the empty tanks, counting the minutes until the next transition.

As we drew closer to Devonia, the *Colossus'* remaining functional scopes and scanners focused on our objective. Computer systems began to produce images of Devonia: renderings that became more and more detailed. Finally, I watched from the view-ports and observation windows as the planet grew to fill space, the glow of the Arkonus Abyss a baleful backdrop.

"I'm coming for you, Elena," I whispered.

When the *Colossus'* AI declared that we had arrived at our destination, I was ready.

Devonia glared back at me.

The CIC blast-shutters had been retracted, to allow the fullest possible view with the naked eye. I stepped down into the nose of the CIC, between the weapon pods and the hardwired junior officers. Loeb had summoned all essential personnel to the CIC, to plan our next course of action.

"Is this what you expected?" Loeb asked me.

"I . . . I don't know," I said, genuinely.

I'd seen Krell warzones, with and without the Lazarus Legion, and they were not *this*. They were fetid pits, worlds driven into biological overdrive by the presence of the Krell.

Devonia – in the heart of the Maelstrom, a reef world – was something else. The planet hung there, filling the port. She was apparently much smaller than Old Earth, but at this distance – without any touchstone by which to qualify her size – she appeared enormous. Wrapped in a thick layer of cloud cover, the planet was stitched into a tapestry of whites and greys. Where the cover was broken, where the clouds thinned to cotton-like consistency, the surface was a mixture of black, blue and green.

Professor Saul stood with his hands behind his back, good eye and bad eye focused on the view-ports as though the imagery enraptured him. "There are seas and jungles down there," he said, waving at the window. "Mixed with strings of volcanic mountains. We should be making recordings, conduct some remote examinations. My colleagues in the xeno-biology department would kill for an opportunity like this."

I cringed at his choice of words, but Saul didn't seem to notice. *There's a lot out here that Science Division would kill for*, I thought, as I looked out of the observation window. Beyond the arc of Devonia, the Arkonus Abyss glittered: its relationship to Devonia still unexplained.

"I've never seen a world quite like it," Mason said.

Jenkins snorted. "That's not saying much. You haven't seen many."

"Well, have you?" Mason asked.

Jenkins folded her arms. "No," she said, reluctantly. "I haven't."

"No one has," Saul said. "Not properly, anyway. The reef worlds are so deep in Krell territory that their exploration was previously thought too perilous . . ."

"But this isn't anything like what we've been told to expect," Mason said. "Of a reef world, I mean. During Basic I saw images. Vid-files, sensory simulations."

"The Krell reef worlds are second to hell," Martinez said, never taking his eyes from the shimmering planet. "That's what Science Division has always told us."

"Maybe we were wrong," Saul said. His expression spoke of the elderly professor we had grown to know in Damascus, not the war-shattered survivor of Capa.

"You're gonna need to rewrite those books, Prof," Kaminski said.

Saul nodded. "So few, even of Science Division, have actually managed to witness the Krell in their natural habitat." He waved a finger at the window. "But I have some reservations about this planet. At that mass, it shouldn't be capable of retaining an atmosphere." He shivered; it was unclear whether the response was as a result of the information or the cold. "It has an extreme density. Something doesn't sit right with me."

"That's assuming that this is their habitat," I said, "and not . . . something else."

"Whatever it is," Loeb said, "the Krell are here in force. Shower and shit, Harris. Shower and shit. You said it yourself: there's water down there, and the Krell are here en masse." He pointed to the tactical display, currently showing a tri-D rendering of space surrounding the Devonian body. "There are numerous Krell bio-ships in high orbit; a sizeable war-fleet."

"Christo . . ." Jenkins whispered, and Kaminski whistled in surprise.

I counted fifty or so ships, of varied threat designation. Easily enough to take down the *Colossus*.

"Looks like their scout reported in," Mason said.

"No," Saul said, biting his lip. "The Krell have been here far longer than that. See their orbital stations?"

On the scopes, black against the blue of Devonia's seas, were coral-like growths that orbited the planet in a wide arc. There were several of them: grown to enormous proportions, spiralling out in weird anti-symmetrical shapes. From this distance, with the scopes at full magnification, it was just possible to make out bio-ships docking in the shell-like hangar bays. Blue light spilled from the innards of the Krell station-docks, betraying any suggestion that the structures were inactive. As those scattered and battered hulks of living carapace passed in front of the electronic eyes, I caught sight of markings like deliberate brands on their outer hulls. It might've just been a trick of the light, or maybe I was just strung out, but the flesh-burns looked a lot like the markings we'd seen on the Krell prisoners from Capa V. *Are they of the same war-fleet*, I wondered, *or is this just a coincidence?* The Krell rarely carried markings, rarely differentiated one shoal from the next, and that the stations carried identifiers at all was surprising.

"To date," Loeb said, "the Krell haven't reacted to our presence. We can only assume that we're out of their sensor range."

More surprises, I thought. I knew that it wouldn't stay that way.

I pressed both hands down on the display, concentrated on the live-feeds. "What can we expect when we get down there?" I asked.

"Weather patterns will be extreme and violent," Loeb said. "It'll be hot, humid as all hell. The greenhouse effect, on a massive scale." Loeb pulled his chin. He hadn't shaved in days, and white whiskers sprouted from his rough face. "The clouds lock in surface heat, warming up the atmosphere. Barely any polar ice. That same cloud cover is acting as the best goddamned defence to our sensor-suite known to man." Loeb shrugged. "Could be some sort of natural phenomenon, or it might be a defence manufactured by the Krell. Whatever it is, it's acting as a shield and blocking our scans."

"Looks like boots on the ground are the only option," I said.

"This is getting to be a regular thing," Jenkins said. "Just leaves the decision as to how we get down there."

Martinez paced the table, muttering to himself in pigeon Spanish. "There are enough ships there to cover most approaches to the surface. Getting down there without being seen is going to be tough . . ."

It would be out of the question for the *Colossus* to make the landing. She would almost certainly be seen by the Krell en route, even with stealth systems, and even then she wouldn't be capable of planetary insertion or flight. The local gravity would tear the old warship to pieces on the way down; no one had even suggested that as a viable tactic.

I nodded. "This is where you come in, Lieutenant James."

Being skinned, and dressed in his flight-suit, James was coping with the cold better than most of the crew. He stepped up to the display. "The Dragonfly gunships will handle atmospheric flight just fine, and we have two of them in the hold." He indicated an approach vector through the high clouds. "Best window of opportunity will be in about an hour. With a low angle of descent, we can break the ionosphere there. We'll follow the coordinates given by Dr

Marceau, and that should put us down in a little place I like to call the Maze."

Devonia was unexplored territory, but James had taken the liberty of labelling some of the visible land features down on the surface. "The Maze" was a series of ravines and gullies, cast from black rock, scything Devonia's equator.

"What about the Krell?" Mason asked.

James whistled. "I'm pretty sure that we can evade the war-fleet in orbit. It's at low anchor, but a single ship straight down the pipe will be a hard target to spot."

"All right," I said, "this is it, people."

I looked at the faces of the Legion. They knew what was required, knew that this wasn't just another mission.

"The *Colossus* will retreat to a safe orbit," Loeb said. "We'll remain on-site, and try to fix the life-support module." The tactical display pulled back, to three small moons spinning around the blue and green marble of Devonia. "We'll be anchored in orbit around Devonia III; the largest moon. It should give us some decent cover from that war-fleet."

"For a while, at least," Kaminski said. "But once those fish heads come knocking . . ."

"We'll pull out," Loeb said. "In her current state, this ship won't be any good in a fight. If the mission on the surface goes wrong, there's every chance that the Krell will retaliate. We'll be going dark, and run a tight orbit around the dark side of the third moon. What with the interference caused by local debris, I'm confident that we can remain hidden until you need us. While you're on the surface, we won't be able to risk any communications. I doubt that surface to sky would work anyway – given all that cloud – but we cannot risk attracting the Collective."

"Understood."

"You want to speak to us," Loeb said, "your options will be limited."

"The Ares suits are equipped with ground-to-orbit flares," Martinez said, "but using those is going to attract a lot of attention."

"If you set off a flare, don't expect a response any time soon," Loeb said. "And don't forget that we only have those two Dragonflies."

"The fastest way to travel," I said, "will be by extracting."

Except, I thought, *if we do that, Elena and whoever else is left down there won't have a way off-world.*

"Gaia's luck be on you all," Professor Saul said.

Loeb clambered down from his command throne. He awkwardly thrust out a hand, in my direction.

"Pleasure serving with you," he said. "Just in case we don't meet again."

I shook his hand. "And you, Admiral." To the Legion: "Saddle up. I want us sim-capable in an hour."

"Affirmative," the CIC rumbled.

An hour later, in the increasing cold of the SOC, the Legion stripped and began to mount the tanks. Such a familiar process, but rendered new by the circumstances. The tanks were covered in condensation, their innards warm, blue, inviting.

I glanced around at the Legion. Strange: each of my squad had retained their extraction-stigmata. Not real injuries, but rather physical reminders of the wounds we'd suffered during the *Endeavour* operation. Jenkins was the worst, a heavy red welt across her midriff. Potent imagery rose in my memory – *Jenkins screaming as the door came down to cut her in two* – and I struggled to contain it. My own skin was lacerated with similar red marks, and I could still feel the tang of bio-toxins at the back of my throat – persisting in the fibres of my real body in a way that should not have been possible.

Dr Serova frowned at each of us as we went through the connection procedure, inspecting our bodies.

"Is that normal?" she enquired.

"Nothing is normal where the Lazarus Legion are concerned," Kaminski said. "Don't worry about a thing, Doc. We'll be back before the day's out, and maybe this whole war will be over."

"Right on," Martinez said, bumping fists with 'Ski.

"Still got your sword, eh, Mason?" Jenkins asked, as she hooked herself up. "That come all the way from Calico with you?"

Mason had hooked her sheathed mono-sword, her trophy from Damascus, beside her tank. "Never know when it might come in handy," she said.

"Things'd have to be pretty desperate before I'd trust you with a Directorate-issue mono-sword . . ." Kaminski joked.

"Desperate times," Mason said, "desperate measures. I'd rather have a sword than nothing."

I clambered into my tank. The amniotic was a grateful source of heat, and the interior of the simulator felt comforting and mundane. The various data-jacks connected to my hungry ports, and with each barb of sensation I felt closer to making transition. Finally, the respirator mask slipped over my face.

"See you on the other side," I said.

"This life or the next," Mason added.

"The simulants are loaded into the Dragonfly," Dr Serova said, her voice projected into the comms-bead in my ear. "Are the operators ready for transition?"

Kaminski banged his head against the inside of the tank. "Get us out there!"

"Transition commencing in three . . . two . . . one . . ."

In the split second it took to make transition – to establish the neural-link between the simulator-tank and my simulant – I travelled the length of the *Colossus*.

I opened my eyes in the primary hangar bay, and I was a new man. Every ache and pain in my real body was gone, replaced by the needle-sharp senses of a simulated body. *Jesus, this feel good.* The Lazarus Legion were in the passenger cabin of the Dragonfly gunship, like me all wearing Ares battle-suits and strapped in for the drop.

"Transition confirmed," I said into the communicator.

There were clipped responses from the *Colossus'* medical team, and from the CIC, but I largely filtered those out. It was difficult to focus on much more than the visuals projected onto the inside of my tactical helmet. Accompanied by a countdown from the Navy crew, the *Colossus'* hangar door yawned open, exposing the bay to hard vacuum and by degrees also revealing a first-hand visual of Devonian space. Despite being skinned, despite whatever we were about to face down there, it was still a breathtaking sight. The vibrant greens and blues swirled across the surface, almost appearing to move as I watched them. The thick jungles were so very like those I'd seen on tri-D programmes of Old Earth – back before the war, before we had turned it to shit. The impact of the visuals wasn't lost on the Legion, either. Even Kaminski was quiet, absorbing the sight.

"*You are cleared for take-off, Dragonfly One,*" declared the CIC.

Lieutenant James sat up-front in the cockpit, banks of glowing controls in front of him. He turned to us and grinned through his aviator-helmet, the visor turning transparent. Mason sat beside him, acting as co-pilot in the absence of any other flight crew.

"Let's go kill some shit," James said. "Permission to launch, Colonel?"

I slapped a hand against his flight-suit. "Affirmative."

The Dragonfly engines ignited immediately, and I was slammed back into my seat, body vibrating with the thrum of the gunship's thrusters. The world around me became a blur of light, the interior of the hangar bay replaced by the silky blackness of Devonian space.

"*Launch confirmed,*" the *Colossus*' CIC declared. "*Gaia's speed be on you. Commencing retreat pattern . . .*"

Behind us, the *Colossus* began to ponderously pull back, thrusters firing on low emission.

"Commencing atmospheric breach . . ." James said. "Here goes nothing."

CHAPTER TWENTY-ONE

THE GREEN

The Dragonfly clipped a brace of clouds, the engine pitch shifting in response to turbulence. The gunship was designed for lifting and light combat; equipped with chemical thrusters, ideal for trans-atmospheric flight.

"Apologies for the bumpy ride," James said, from the cockpit. "All this cloud cover is playing havoc with the pitch controls."

"Just keep us out of sensor range, and get us some eyes on the planet," I said.

"I'll settle for just staying in one piece," Jenkins said.

With the whole crew made up of sims, James could afford to focus on speed over comfort. We were flying fast and my medi-suite was administering a regulated cocktail of anti-sickness drugs.

The flightpath stabilised a little, and our velocity reduced.

"Should be getting some visuals any minute now," Mason said over the comm-network. "We're coming up fast on Dr Marceau's coordinates . . ."

I tapped into the exterior cameras; switched from tactical

to optical display, and watched the Dragonfly's descent. Thick cloud, rapidly clearing into wisps of mist, streaked past the cams. We emerged from the cloud bank a moment later, and the descent pattern levelled out.

"Welcome to Devonia," Mason declared.

The landscape was black and ragged, composed of what I guessed was volcanic rock. A series of tight ravines and canyons – James' Maze – etched the surface. Criss-crossing the planet in bizarre geometric shapes, they looked almost planned: swathed in a thick mist that provided perfect cover for whatever lurked inside. Where it broke, I could see alien impressions of trees – growing denser now, carpeting the ground in a thick jungle. The flora and fauna were bizarrely coloured – mostly distinct green, but also bright reds and nausea-inducing yellows.

The sky overhead was even worse. Devonia Star had burnt through the cloud cover, but some trick of the atmospherics diffused its light and gave the entire vista an unpleasant haze. The perpetual twilight was strangely disorienting. Above all of that, bright enough that it shone like a second star, was the Arkonus Abyss: a rent in space-time that seemed to hover on the horizon.

At this altitude, we were an easy target for any orbital eyes the Krell might have. It was making me nervous. I tagged one of the trenches below.

"Take us in that direction, James," I ordered. Elena's coordinates had been broad and imprecise; we had a lot of ground to cover.

"Anything you say, Lazarus."

The gunship dipped into one of the canyons, cutting the mist like a knife. The walls on either side were precariously close but James was an expert pilot, weaving among the twisting network.

"Maze is right," James said, his voice vibrating gently in time with the gunship engine. "Local conditions are a refreshing thirty-eight degrees Celsius. Gravity is slightly less than Earth-standard; you'll probably barely notice the difference."

"What about the atmospherics?" Jenkins asked.

"You want to show your pretty face to the locals?"

"Something like that."

"Then you'll be glad to know that it's breathable."

I wasn't surprised by that. The Krell had resistance to certain atmospheric vulnerabilities beyond those of a human – being able to survive in vacuum for longer, for instance, that indirectly impacted their ability to resist airborne poisons and contaminants. But the Krell were, broadly speaking, oxygen breathers like us. That was one of the many reasons, commentators liked to speculate, for the First Krell War: two species squabbling over the same real estate.

"If it comes to it," I said, "better you extract than be taken prisoner by the Krell. This is their world, and they'll be playing by their rules—"

"Hold on!" Mason interrupted.

I expected to feel the sudden impact of Krell ordnance; perhaps the chime of the Dragonfly's auto-defensive systems as we were fixed with hostile fire. The rest of the Legion braced, immediately dropped into combat mode in the same expectation.

"What have you got, Mason?" James asked.

"There's an emergency beacon down there," she said. "It's an Alliance-pattern broadcast."

Now I saw it too. Something far beneath us, deep within the Maze. The signal flickered, shifted.

"I can't get a fix," Mason said. "All this rock is making it hard to lock on . . ."

"Someone had a death wish," Martinez said. "Who'd want to set off a beacon on a Krell reef world?"

"Someone desperate to be found," I said. "Is it a signal from one of the *Endeavour*'s transports, or her fleet?"

"I don't know," Mason answered. "The pattern is definite but the signal is really weak."

My throat tightened. This was it.

"Lazarus Legion, get ready—"

A red warning – an emergency warning – flashed across my HUD.

Simultaneously, the Dragonfly pulled up sharply. James was suddenly and precisely focused on the ship controls.

"Bearing at oh-five-nine . . ." Mason said, head bobbing as she read from one station then another. "That's a confirm. That's a definite read!"

"You sure?" James yelled. "I'm not seeing anything—"

A shadow fell across us.

An enormous black structure, draining all light from the world around it, loomed through the mist.

An Artefact . . .?

James snapped in reaction. "*Applying airbrake!*"

"Pull up! You're losing roll control!" Mason shouted back over the comm-net. "We'll lose G-stabilisation on the left wing . . ."

The structure came up fast, so fast, to meet us, revealed by the shifting mists in the blink of an eye. I was powerless, completely hypnotised by the formation as it expanded to fill my field of vision . . .

Not an Artefact. Something else. Something almost as bad.

"Bio-structure!" I yelled.

It was an immense coral edifice, erupting from the side of the canyon: jutting skyward. This close – virtually bearing down on the structure – it was obvious that it was no Artefact. The surface was porous and honeycombed, unmistakably Krell. It had appeared black at a distance – because of the mist – but on closer inspection was a spattering of greens and yellows, a reflection of the jungle below.

The Dragonfly's scanners began an insistent warning, red lights across the board. The gunship banked sharply, throwing us around inside the cabin, and I grappled with an overhead safety rail to stay standing.

"We're going to hit it!" Mason declared. "Hold tight!"

The Dragonfly's wing clipped the Krell bio-structure.

It was only a glancing impact – grazing the outer shell – but the bio-tech was much stronger than it looked. From bitter experience, I knew the stuff to be about as resilient as reinforced plasteel.

"Fuck!" Jenkins screamed. "What the hell are you doing, James? You're bringing us down on a Krell nest!"

More of the Krell structures appeared around us. Some grew from the canyon sides, others from the jungle-choked trenches below, peppering the landscape. All different colours, alien and incomprehensible.

"I got signals!" Mason said. "On our six!"

The Dragonfly carried several weapons systems: a nose-mounted laser cannon, two heavy gun drones under the wings, six smart-guided Banshee warheads – capable of firing ground-to-air or air-to-air, in a pinch – and two heavy assault cannons on the door mounts.

I thought-activated my mag-locks and kicked them to the Dragonfly's cabin deck, then I rolled open one of the side-doors. The heavy cannon slaved to my suit AI – perfectly linking, as though it was one of my own weapons. The cannon was mounted on an articulated arm, braced in the open door, and I panned it back and forth, testing the targeting AI. It had a good weight to it, significantly off-set by the battle-suit's strength-aug. The ammo counter indicated a full drum. AP rounds, depleted pluto-nium core: about as anti-Krell as old-fashioned kinetics could get.

The jungle was moving so fast it was impossible to make out any detail. I squinted in the diffuse sunlight, which was still managing to create a baking warmth inside the Dragonfly.

"Jenkins, on the other cannon!" I ordered.

"Copy that," Jenkins said.

I heard her sliding the opposite door open; felt the buff of wind as it ran through the open cabin.

The automated tracking software painted potential targets across my face-plate, and in anticipation of a firefight I spun up the multi-barrelled cannon: felt the gratifying chug of the weapon as it readied. Kaminski fell into a crouch beside me, his plasma rifle aimed at the jungle. Martinez did the same at the other door, supporting Jenkins.

"You getting anything on your side?" I asked of Jenkins.

"Lot of shadows, lot of movement, but no confirmed targets."

"Maybe New Girl was wrong . . ." Kaminski offered.

No. She isn't.

I saw them first. Just blurs of light, now becoming more distinct. Three shadows skated over the green canopy, moving faster and faster. Reciprocal shapes appeared above each shadow: smears of light shaped like long, thin needles. The shadows gained speed, kept pace with the Dragonfly—

"Weapons hot!" I yelled.

I fired the assault cannon. The gun controls jumped in my hands – bounced around – but it was spray-and-pray, and a burst caught the enemy ship. Rounds sparked against the invisible armour plating, temporarily interfering with the camouflage-field.

"I see them on the feeds now!" James yelled.

"Told you!" Mason said, almost triumphantly. "Three Needlers!"

"One hella welcome party . . ." Jenkins muttered.

The Needlers, sometimes called needle-ships, were long, thin vessels, made for extreme manoeuvrability. They were usually manned by a single Krell pilot, literally grafted into the cockpit, as close to symbiosis with the living craft as you could get.

"What's our distance to the signal?" I yelled to James.

"Ten kilometres?" James shouted back. "You want me to set you down somewhere?"

"Too risky," I said. "Lose the bogeys first."

"Easier said than done," James said. Abruptly derailing any wider tactical discussion, he added: "Taking evasive manoeuvre."

Back on the door-gun, I fired again, this time a longer burst. The enemy ship veered slightly away from the Dragonfly; flickered in and out of sight as though dipping into some other dimension. The ship had an almost aquatic body and stubby protrusion along the aft that more resembled fins than wings. A circular portal opened on the flank of the craft. Krell wearing heavy armour hung inside, and in a dark mirror of the Dragonfly one of them aimed a mounted bio-cannon towards the Dragonfly's flank. A much bigger version of the stinger: a projectile-thrower.

I ducked back into the cabin, yelled "Down!"

The Krell gunner pulled the trigger.

Flechettes – fizzling with bio-electricity, probably loaded with toxins – punched through the armour plating of the Dragonfly's hull, right beside me. I fired back, without looking: kept my finger down on the firing stud of my own cannon and hoped that something would hit the attacker.

"Defensive suite online," James said. "Deploying chaffe, deploying doppler." There were thuds through the hull as the systems activated, and I saw smoke billowing from probes which launched from the rear of the Dragonfly. "Drones away!"

Two ultra-fast gun drones deployed from somewhere above the passenger cab. Equipped with low-wattage plasma carbines, they were meant to harry enemy ships that had already suffered damage. The small robots spiralled around us, keeping pace with the gunship. One of them instantly exploded, caught by bio-plasma from a pursuing Needler—

The sky overhead darkened.

"What the fuck is that?" Mason yelled.

"Stingray incoming!" I shouted. Turned my cannon on its mount to strafe the underside of the approaching ship, knowing that it would do no good.

The enormous bio-ship blotted out the light. It was moving faster and faster so that it matched us for pace. The underside of the Stingray was suddenly over us, and its belly was lined with pulsing egg-sacs, throbbing with angry, virulent life. This was the Stingray's gift. It wasn't a fighter: it was a troop-ship. There were sacs – now opening like sphincters – for a hundred passengers on the ship's belly.

A Krell suddenly leapt from the open guts of the Stingray, its talons outstretched to reach us.

"Fuck me!" Kaminski shouted, recoiling from the Dragonfly's door.

I pulled off a protracted burst from the cannon.

The Krell exploded in a green mist, falling well short of the attempted boarding. But more were launching themselves

332

out of the Stingray – kamikaze-like, sailing to the jungle below.

The remaining gun-drone registered the threat, moved to intercept, pummelling the underside of the Stingray with rounds. Krell body-parts literally rained from above.

I turned my attention to the Needler, swinging the unruly assault cannon back and forth, sweeping the Needler's flank. The xeno ship banked, too late, the volley hitting an exposed crew compartment. The gunner sprawled backwards, streaming blood from its chest, explosive rounds slashing through body armour and flesh without distinction.

"Lazarus got one!" Kaminski shouted, rallying alongside me.

"Just keep fucking firing!"

The barrel of my assault cannon spun—

"It's falling back! Left flank is breaking off!" Mason yelled.

I didn't stop firing until the gun bucked and rebelled in my hands – the red AMMO OUT warning flashing on the weapon display.

"Reload!" I shouted at Kaminski—

More bio-plasma exploded around us. Heat washed over me.

"Deploying missiles," James declared.

A missile pod on one wing flared to life, and there was a loud scream as the artificially intelligent Banshee missiles flew free. They dropped back behind the Dragonfly, searching for the damaged Needler.

It took seconds for them to find their prey. One engine went first, exploding flare-bright, and the Needler went into a spin. I watched in fascination as the gunship was hit by another missile; pouring black smoke, whining loudly like an injured animal. Then the ship clipped the jungle, and another bright explosion marked its demise.

But this was far from a victory.

The ravines around us were closing in, becoming tighter: more Krell coral blocking our route like the strands of a spider's web. We hit something, wobbling as James fought to control our flight. The Dragonfly lurched, dipping lower so that it hugged the jungle canopy. There were rapid thuds and bumps as stray branches impacted the hull.

The Needler alongside Jenkins' open door steadied, and mimicked James' course. The Krell were not giving up.

"That low enough for you?" James shouted, leaning into the flight controls. "Hold the fuck on back there!"

The upper jungle canopy thrashed against the Dragonfly's cockpit viewer—

Another shadow, now whale-big, darkened the jungle. It was coming from behind the Dragonfly, but also above us.

James' altimeter was beeping persistently, warning of a loss of altitude. Chimes and warning sirens overlapped so as to become indecipherable, save for one repeated phrase: "BRACE, BRACE, BRACE!"

The horizon shifted arbitrarily, and I was thrown back and forth inside the cabin. My simulated stomach lurched as though I was caught in zero-G. Martinez smashed into Jenkins, and she hit a wall – unconscious.

"BRACE, BRACE, BRACE!"

More Krell bio-fire raked the ship. Rounds impacted the main viewer, cracking the reinforced armour-glass canopy.

"BRACE, BRACE, BRACE!"

The engine's throb became a high-pitched wail. I hit the roof of the gunship and felt an explosion of pain in my skull as the ship banked again.

"I can outrun you, bastard!" James was shouting over and over, above the din of warnings and sirens. "I can outrun you, bastard!"

Not this time, James.

"BRACE, BRACE, BRACE!" the gunship's AI argued back.

Tree branches and trunks were hitting the hull harder now, shaking the gunship frame. And always the chatter of bio-weapons, and new shards of light appearing in the armoured roof above.

"BRACE!"

"BRACE!"

"BRACE . . . !"

The hungry jungle waited.

It swallowed us whole.

Where the fuck am I?

I woke up with a killer hangover, ten times worse than the worst ever night out in the District.

There was blue light above me, but I wasn't in a simulator-tank. It was sky, splintered through a patchwork of broken tree branches. I was on my back. I didn't know whether I'd been thrown clear of the wreckage, scrambled free, or even jumped: all were equally possible.

"Diagnostic," I barked.

Error-code and scrap messages flooded my HUD, but the thought-connection was still active.

OPERATIONAL, the suit AI insisted in my head.

Is that all you can manage?

I suddenly became alert. That had to be my suit, pumping me with adrenaline and combat-drugs – ensuring that I didn't do the natural thing and lapse back into unconsciousness. A report of my injuries flashed onto my HUD. Just bruises and sprains, luckily, but in combination enough to make me feel like hell. *Get up, trooper!* The simple act of getting to my feet sent a ripple of aches through my limbs and chest. My battle-suit was covered in numerous dinks, scrapes and deformations.

Stock taken of my condition, I took in our tac-sit. The Dragonfly had ploughed a furrow in the jungle half a kilometre long: driven a flaming, churned-up trail of destruction through the forest. Blackened branches and still-burning bushes marked the gunship's descent-path, and the scar in the landscape was testament to the speed at which the aircraft had hit the jungle floor. James would no doubt want to believe that he was responsible for fending off the assailants, but I thought that it was more likely luck. The patchwork of light threading the thick thatch above: it was probably enough to provide some cover. That, and we'd brought down at least one of the Krell ships.

"Legion!" I barked. "Sound off!"

The drugs were pumping through my system now. Our situation was precarious and the Krell were probably just behind us. We had to get moving.

"Alive!" Jenkins drawled, struggling to her feet from somewhere nearby. "Fucking hell. We got hit?"

"I'd say so," I concluded. "And we're about to get hit again."

Jenkins had Kaminski under her arm. They had fared well enough. 'Ski managed a nod at me. Behind them Martinez and Mason, covered in dirt and burn-marks, and scrapes to bodies and armour, emerged from the jungle.

"Where's James?" I asked.

"Here," the pilot growled.

James was speared, gladiator-style, with the spar of the Dragonfly cockpit: cleanly, more or less, through his stomach. Pinned, face-up, to the jungle floor. His aviator-helmet was shattered, the lower portion of his face covered in blood. That he was still alive was something.

"I'm not going anywhere," he said, struggling with gloved hands against the metal holding him in place. "But you should get out of here. Investigate the signal."

Martinez slid his plasma pistol from the holster on his thigh. Slammed a power cell into the grip, and handed it to James. The flyboy took it.

"Better to make it fast," Martinez said.

James shook his head. "There's a distress beacon in the cockpit," he said. "Activate it."

"Why?" Mason asked. "No one is coming. Loeb is under orders not to respond—"

But I understood. It wasn't about calling for help: it was about creating a diversion. Setting it off at full broadcast spectrum would call every fish head within the sector to James' position. Meanwhile, we'd be gone.

"Do it," I ordered. "Now."

"I've got twenty shots," James said, looking down at the digital read-out on the plasma pistol. He gave a weak smile: his teeth bright red. "I might even get a couple of kills before they get to me."

"It's not as easy as it looks," Jenkins said.

Martinez and Mason hauled the door of the gunship free, and were already working on the damaged control console.

"Done!" Martinez shouted from the wreck.

"The signal was a click north of here," James said. "The position should be stored in your combat-suit."

My suit was gradually coming online again, and the wrist-comp showed local directions.

James held out his fist, and we bumped knuckles. "Good hunting, Lazarus."

We fell into a forced march.

It was hard going, but we were always alert, moving as

337

rapidly as possible. Mason had a mono-knife, smaller than her trophy sword, and hacked at the undergrowth as she went, and Kaminski prodded aside enormous tree branches with his plasma rifle. The ground underfoot was sodden, swampy, and we were often knee-deep in fetid water. Stuff that looked like brilliant red reed-grass poked from mud banks. On closer inspection, those plants writhed and swarmed as though they were alive. There was mist everywhere, coiling around enormous tree boles. It was noisy too – full of chirping, burping and whistling things, animals that had vague analogues with Earth-born counterparts: disconcertingly alien.

"This place stinks," Mason moaned.

"No shower is going to get rid of that fish-stink," Jenkins agreed, "and the pollen is a killer."

"I hope," Kaminski said, "not in the literal sense."

"Use your suit's internal filters," I said.

"I am," said Mason, "but that's not helping."

Coupled with the intense heat, the smell was a double gut-punch. The deep, headache-inducing scent often defined an encounter with the Krell, but this was so much more potent. Back at the crash site, burning fuel propellant and roasting simulant flesh had cloaked the smell of the jungle. Now, there was no such perfume to the place. It smelt of rotted fish and salt – the Krell's natural odour, multiplied by ten. Not for the first time, I was intensely grateful for my battle-suit's medi-suite, pumping me with anti-sickness drugs and a regular supply of antihistamines.

"Hold!" I barked.

Hundreds of metres above us – so distant that it was barely visible – the sky shimmered. *Krell ships.* They screamed overhead, in loose formation. Less than a second later, a series of thunderclaps sounded: *boom, boom, boom.*

There was a flash on the horizon, from the direction in which we'd been marching.

"What was that?" Mason whispered.

"I'd say that they found the crash site," I said. "Stay down."

The Legionnaires were utterly still. Our reactive camo-fields mimicked the forest floor: while we were not quite invisible – outlines flickering – at range, we were close enough. That, and the thick canopy of branches and leaves, provided good enough protection, and the bombers moved on.

"At least James got a quick death," Martinez said. There was no humour to his voice. "God willing."

"God willing . . ." Mason said.

"Signal is ahead," I said. "We're almost out of the Maze." I pointed between the boles of two mutant trees, growing out of the swamp. The signal was stronger now, throbbing like a red cyst on my suit-scanner. "Half a click that way."

Visibility was still poor, but the sky was brightening, and the canyons had widened to a more open expanse of jungle. While the scenery was no more appealing, it was slightly less creepy than the network of black rock.

"Stay in cover," I ordered, "and move up by pairs."

I took point, the others moving in twos, and advanced on the objective. The jungle grew quieter – more sullen. Large ferns and thorny plants bristled, stirred by a low wind. Ahead, the trees thinned.

"This is the place," I said.

The Legion immediately assembled around me, eyes focused on the clearing.

Something cracked loudly overhead.

"Eyes up!"

An enormous piece of fabric was snagged among broken tree branches above us.

"An Alliance flag . . .?" Mason started.

Not just a flag: a parachute. It was torn and ragged, flapping in the light wind. Producing a rhythmic snapping – a sound so out of place in the chittering Krell jungle that it was instantly detectable. Snared to something much bigger, connected by a network of safety ropes and creeper vines.

"An evacuation pod," Martinez said. "It's a damned pod!"

The large spherical craft lay on the forest floor, on its side. The structure was immediately foreign to the surroundings, light playing off the soft curves of the armour plating. Much bigger than a man, emblazoned with very familiar words and logos: American and Alliance flags beneath an ID serial tag. As I got nearer, I made out words on the hull. UAS ENDEAVOUR EXPEDITIONARY FORCE.

CHAPTER TWENTY-TWO

TSUNAMI

I traced the route that the pod had taken, recreated it in my head. *Probably came through the forest canopy at a low angle*, I decided, *and made planetfall somewhere near the equator to reduce the odds of not burning up.* The decision, driven by man or AI, had also reduced the prospects of discovery by a Krell search party.

But this pod had fallen years ago.

"Elena!" I shouted.

I was surprised that anyone had survived the crash in a real skin. The pod had suffered a hell of a lot of damage on the drop. The lower half had sunk into the jungle floor, but what little I could see was crushed and deformed – crumpled like a used paper cup. Algae and barnacles had grown over the hull, and the exposed heat-shielding was stained green and black. Creeper vines, voracious and inquisitive, probed every aspect of the module. I clambered over a nearby tree root that had been severed in the crash; found the exit hatch.

The door was open, and the explosive bolts holding it in place had been blown. That almost provoked a false hope;

but I knew that once the atmospheric probes had done their work, the door would automatically fire. *It's routine, nothing more.* The remains of the door came free with a creak from rusted hinges. I braced myself, ready for the worst, and peered inside.

It was a mess. There were two crash couches with loose safety harnesses – used, but now unoccupied. The controls were damaged; the single holo-console blackened, screen shattered. My suit-lamps popped on, flickering over the battered walls. A locker, labelled FIRST AID, was open: the contents missing. Bloodstains marked the crash couches, and a handprint was smeared on one wall. *When did that happen?* I wondered. The hairs on my neck stood up and I felt a sudden rush of anger. Elena had told me, in Damascus, about the *Endeavour*'s mission becoming compromised. Had the Directorate done this? Or had the pod been shot down by the Krell? SEDATIVE, I ordered my suit. The cold rush that hit my bloodstream did little to alleviate the burn in my heart.

"You find anything, Colonel?" Jenkins asked.

"She isn't here," I said. "There's nothing here."

"No bodies?" Jenkins said.

"No nothing."

There was a clatter outside the pod. Martinez.

"*Jefe!*" he said, excitedly. "Now!"

I pulled out of the pod.

"*Aquí rápidamente!*" he babbled.

"Calm down, Martinez. What have you got—?"

"Listen!" he insisted.

Whatever he'd heard, it had sufficiently frightened Mason. She was on one knee, her rifle panning the jungle.

"Fuck me, Venus," Kaminski said, "is all this green spooking you or something?"

"Shut up!" Martinez insisted, and 'Ski fell silent.

The jungle burped and rustled; a tapestry of individual, tiny noises that were almost inseparable. Something buzzed nearby – a clutch of those alien insects that called this place home. In the distance, some unknown xeno specimen hollered . . .

"The ropes . . ." Martinez whispered, his voice barely audible.

It was such a small tell.

The ropes mooring the parachute and pod to the jungle *moved*. Vibrated just ever so softly; thrumming. Moving not with the motion of the wind, but rhythmically.

My intuition was screaming.

"Get sharp, people!" I barked.

Rifles were raised, all eyes on the jungle, back-to-back so that we formed a makeshift perimeter around the pod. My bio-scanner was chiming – a steady, resolute *beep, beep, beep* – but that was nothing new. The device was next to useless given the dense vegetation and flood of indig life-forms that populated the jungle. The jungle offered no answers. Visibility was virtually non-existent down here. The enemy would be on us before we knew it.

I needed a better vantage point. I nodded at the nearest tree.

"I'm going up there," I said. "Give me a leg up."

I picked one of the taller trees and began to climb the lower branches. The battle-suit, combined with the body-mass of my simulant, was a considerable weight, but the tree was strong enough to take it. The bark was scaled, almost reptilian, and it was like I was climbing a twenty-metre-long snake. *That wouldn't,* I decided, *be out of place among the bizarre wildlife of Devonia.* Hand over hand, I clambered up the limbs, the sense of impending danger growing with every hand-pass. The tree branches above me had started to shiver.

The Legion crowded around the base of the tree.

"I still don't see anything down here," Kaminski said. "Just jungle."

"Infrared is fucked," Jenkins said. "Everything looks the same."

"Just keep eyes on the trees," I said. "Don't let anything surprise you."

I approached the halfway point and sunlight began filtering through the broken shade of trees. A deep, basso vibration of something enormous rolling this way. A ship? I panted hard, almost at the top. Some sort of Krell vehicle? I finally broke the tree covering. The sun was low, throwing amber light across the basin, and I shaded my face-plate to look over the sector.

"What've you got, sir?" Mason called.

Just more trees. An endless carpet of green—

In the extreme distance, only perceptible because my simulant-senses were so sharp, was a ripple of movement. A shift in the treeline, moving like the waves of a sea, but in every direction.

It was a damned trick.

The Krell had been funnelling us all along.

Tsunami.

When the Krell had numbers on their side, as they often did, they reached a kind of critical mass. They became unstoppable.

"One of the many advantages of having no sense of self," a Science Division officer once told me, "is that such a creature has no parameters defining self-preservation."

I remember sitting in that hall, learning basic Krell behavioural patterns as though they were set in stone. I was barely out of Basic, only a private in the Alliance Army, stationed at Olympus Mons, Mars. Like most of the recruits, I thought that the Krell Psychology & Tactics classes were a waste of time. Most weeks they'd wheel in the same crusty old Sci-Div lecturer to bore us with diagrams and schematics: a break to a training regime that involved big guns, armoured suits and starships.

"Individually, the Krell primary-forms have little or no sense of purpose," he droned on. "They are physically imposing, but they have no tactical acumen."

"'Acu' what, sir?" someone yelled at the little man.

The intervention was met with yells of derision, aimed at the science officer.

"Tactical awareness, if you'd prefer. They follow the Collective. They follow the leader-form's directions."

"Sounds like the perfect soldier," someone else yelled.

Again, more hoots, more derision. I was still young myself; I probably joined in with the crowd. This – the theory behind it all – was surely irrelevant.

"Maybe," the officer said.

There was a holo-projector behind the science officer. He sighed, shook his head: probably pissed off that his lecture wasn't generating the interest that he felt it deserved.

"This is footage from the frontline," he said. "A video-feed recorded from Torus Siegel, where there is every chance you will shortly be deployed."

The room simmered down a little at that. Actual footage: this was far more interesting, much better than listening to the little man rambling on about Krell psychology. When he activated those files, the lecture hall had fallen into an awed silence for the first time ever.

"This," the man had said, with a grin that split his face

in two, "is a practical application of the lack of self-preservation."

We watched as the Krell attacked an Alliance Army patrol.

They moved at a frightening speed, tore ten or so soldiers apart in an assault that took barely seconds. The holo was projected all around us – fully immersive, to increase the training value, and so clear that I could almost imagine myself *there* – and the Krell crashed into us, as well as the unidentified troopers. The Sci-Div officer played the footage again and again, and every time it ended I flinched emphatically. It had come from a circling aerospace fighter, he explained: a lucky witness to the slaughter on the ground. The dead soldiers: they hadn't been so lucky.

"What is the tactic called?" someone asked, on the fifth replay.

The scientist's eyes collapsed to slits, but that smile never left his face.

"It is called the tsunami," he said. "And let us hope that none of you ever have the misfortune to experience it."

I moved down the tree in a controlled drop. Hitting every other branch to slow my fall, managing to close the distance to the ground in a fraction of the time that it had taken me to climb it.

The whispering of the jungle had now grown to a low roar. The trees were shaking, dropping leaf matter and moisture as though it was raining at the lower levels of the jungle.

"Damned Venusian intuition," I said. "You're right."

"How many have we got?" Martinez asked.

I almost laughed at that. "Too many. Probably hundreds."

"Holy fucking shit . . ." Jenkins said. "How close?"

"A few hundred metres, and closing—"

Something fast, green and deadly erupted from the

jungle: a bolt of motion, a ball of carapace and talon and fang. The Krell primary-form lurched between the branches of the nearest tree, using every limb to propel itself forward. It was well-suited to this environ: those taloned limbs on its back latching on to overhead branches, its clawed feet gaining purchase as it moved from one tree to the next.

I fired a volley of shots into the xeno and it exploded.

"Forerunner," I said. "Scouting out the best route to us."

"More will come," Martinez said, already falling back from the clearing.

"Use whatever firepower you've got," I ordered.

Make this death count, I almost added.

Plasma pulses filled the air, criss-crossing to cut the Krell to bloody ribbons. Missiles spiralled all around – smart guidance thrown off by the number of potential targets. The stink of burning flesh, of incinerated bone, was heavy in the air. Still, I kept firing on full automatic – planting my feet on the trembling ground, feeling the ebb and flow of the battle all around me.

I barely saw what the rest of the Legion were doing. It was all that I could do to concentrate on my own targets.

Primary-forms climbed through the trees, dashed over the swampland with alien agility. When we'd cut down the first rank – bodies smoking and piled in the jungle – the xenos simply clambered over the fallen. They were their own momentum, their own drive: a titanic wave of motion. Leader-forms – discernible even at this range, much bigger and more heavily armoured than their lesser counterparts – topped the tsunami, directing it onwards through the jungle.

They came from every direction.

A noose: closing on us.

The combined noise of the Krell attack wave was over-awing – a piercing, ragged blast of white noise. They were screaming as a Collective, a horde of beings combined into a single entity. The sound alone was almost disabling. Perhaps it was an intended side-effect to the attack, another method to disarm a target.

When the direct frontal assault failed, the Krell started dropping from the trees above us. One landed among the Legion, talons reaching for Mason. She shouted a warning, tossed it back into the mass of alien bodies. I put it down with a volley from my plasma rifle. The weapon flashed a LOW AMMO warning, thought-linked via my suit. I had no time to replace the power cell: could only pump the underslung launcher and send grenades out into the dark. Explosions flashed all around.

The Krell began to fire bio-weapons into the fray. Through the fallen and the living: saturating the area with rounds. My null-shield caught a pulse from a boomer in a shower of incandescent sparks. Although I couldn't see them – I couldn't see anything, beyond the immediate press of Krell bodies – there must've been secondary-forms out there too.

And then they broke through and the enemy was too close for the null-shield to be of any use. I felt Krell claws and teeth and talons against my battle-suit. Every appendage a weapon, every ounce of their being weighed against us. I smashed one attacker aside, into the bark of a nearby tree, but another was on me before I could shake the first free.

These Krell were different. Bigger, faster; their carapaces harder and thicker, covered in thorny protrusions. *Evolved.* Their bodies were up-muscled, and some were striped like enormous wasps. When before one shot would have done, now it took multiple pulses to put them down. Among the tide, there were numerous tertiary-forms: twice the size of a battle-suit. Jesus, they were *living* battle-suits.

I fell back – battered aside by a Krell claw. The blackness fended off only by another shot of combat-drugs. More of the tertiary-forms were pouring into the clearing, tossing aside Mason and Martinez now.

Jenkins was firing her incinerator, dowsing the Krell in flame; back-to-back with Kaminski.

The mission was over.

Whatever secret was down here – whatever secret the *Endeavour* had been hiding here – would be lost, and Elena with it.

Something pierced my armour – hit a spot between two armour plates at my leg – and the pain was immediate. Swearing to any god that would listen, I collapsed to my knees. My medical-alert chimed in my head, warning of mission-impairment, and I felt warm blood pooling inside my armour. *They might make it good, but it's never good enough.*

Bigger, more alien bio-forms were passing overhead. Things that not even I had seen before, that Science Division had never even considered classifying... *Quaternary-forms?* I wondered. Enormous, shadowy bio-constructions that were more tank than humanoid.

Bio-weapons began to fire a steady ordnance on our position. Secondary-forms were swathing the forest with shriekers. The weapons screamed as they discharged, catching Krell and Legion alike in the onslaught. Burning bodies surrounded us in a great arc, some still moving – claws outstretched to bring us down.

The nearest Krell secondary-form moved above me, leaping monkey-like between the trees. The shrieker bio-cannon was long-barrelled and sleek, fused to the Krell's middle arms. A fleshy sac – the weapon's fuel reserve, where the secondary-form produced the napalm that powered the gun – dangled from the base of the shrieker, underslung like an ammo-drum.

I was on my back; the combined weight of the tide passing over me.

No one seemed to be firing any more.

I guessed that the rest of the Legion were down as well, that this really was the end.

The vision above me wavered like a mirage.

"*Now!*"

The amplified voice rose about the cacophony, cut through it.

Gunfire erupted from deeper within the jungle; the bright flash of plasma weaponry, and . . .

. . . *something else* . . .

The air *whooshed* around me, and a dark beam hit the nearest Krell.

The body just wasn't there any more.

The beam weapon, whatever it was, fired again and again, throwing prisms of anti-light across the clearing. Krell bodies appeared to vanish, but as I blinked in confusion – as I began to process what was happening – I realised that the bodies were almost evaporating. The weapon was igniting the bio-matter, turning the Krell to a fine ash. I'd never seen a weapon like it.

My Ares suit responded. The null-shield reacted. Fizzled into life, throwing a protective shield in front of me. Pieces of flaming Krell carapace spattered against the barrier, sizzling hot blood and bodily fluids evaporating.

The rest of the Legion stirred.

"Report!" I said.

"I'm here," Martinez said. "*Gracia de Dios*, I'm alive . . ."

". . . although I have no idea how," Jenkins said. She looked utterly shell-shocked – an emotional response that I could seriously sympathise with.

"Nor me," Mason said.

"They . . . they've stopped," Kaminski panted. He got to his knees, grappling among the bodies for his rifle. "We're not going to survive another attack like that . . ."

The Legion were in terrible shape. Our battle-suits were pitted with stingers, scorched by boomers. Barely functional.

"Who's out there?" Mason asked.

She was answered by five shapes emerging from the jungle.

"Threat neutralised," came another voice, made genderless and anonymous by the angry buzz of a combat-suit speaker unit. "Get moving. The Krell won't wait long."

All eyes swivelled to the source of the noise, suits clattering.

"Who the fuck are these guys?" Kaminski said.

The five newcomers were clad in old-pattern combat-suits; museum-class models, equipment that was easily a decade out of date. The suits were sufficiently aged that the camo-fields had failed completely, and the troopers wore full tactical helmets concealing their faces. The armour had no insignia or other identification. The group were armed with plasma carbines, short-barrel security-issue models, and other, more esoteric weapons of black metal.

"I'd say thanks for the save," I said, "if I knew who I was thanking."

The leader kicked aside a smoking Krell carcass, weapon on hip in a way that immediately struck me as feminine, and polarised her scratched face-plate.

"It's good to see you, Conrad. If you've quite finished disturbing the wildlife, we should get out of here."

Is this real? I asked myself.

Elena stood in front of me, her lips twisted into a sardonic smile that suggested mild amusement rather than a reflection of the life-or-death situation that we faced.

We went to move towards each other, drawn like magnetics, but the jungle came alive again: that insectile rustling rising in volume.

"Another attack . . ." I said.

"Yes," Elena said. "We need to leave here, and now."

The newcomers began laying down covering fire with plasma rifles and the exotic firearms.

"How . . .?" I started, mind brimming with questions.

Something screamed low overhead. There was a blur of light.

"They have air support," one of the team said.

"There's no time to explain!" Elena said. "The Krell will regroup fast."

Elena waved her team onwards, splashing booted feet through the swampy ground. We followed through the undergrowth.

"Where are we going?" Mason said.

"You think that I would have come out here without planning the retreat?" Elena asked, her voice accented with the slightest French inflection. "We've been here for a long time. We know this place."

"Whoa!" Jenkins called, beside Kaminski. "Hold up, people!"

Maybe not so well, I thought.

The jungle fell away ahead of us.

We were at the edge of a precipice: a sheer fall that collapsed a hundred or so metres. We'd been running alongside a river, concealed by the dense vegetation, and here it dropped into a waterfall. It threw up a fine white mist all around – the air thick with moisture.

'Ski went to unshoulder his rifle, readying to fight the Krell again. "Looks like last stand time. There's nowhere left to run—"

"We're going over," Elena said. "Seal your suit. The water is deep."

"Mine is damaged—" Mason started.

"Do the best with whatever you have," Elena said. "We won't be under for long, but when we get to the other side it's important that you do exactly as I say."

"Got it," I said.

"Your team too," Elena insisted. "Even if you don't like what you see, you must trust me. I mean it!"

"You heard her," I said to the Legion. In the circumstances, they didn't have much of a choice.

"We've got hostiles incoming!" Mason declared.

A Krell primary-form burst from the jungle behind us, but it exploded in a blossom of darkness from one of the alien firearms. Elena's team rallied at the precipice, covering our retreat.

Elena remained cool, her dark hair tied back behind her head, inside her helmet. She was hardly the woman that I knew: now a survivor, a fighter. I paused, stared at her, and she caught my eye behind her helmet's face-plate.

"When we get to the other side, turn off your suits," she said.

"Why—?" Jenkins asked.

"As I said: trust me."

More Krell were coming now. More black energy discharges fired around us, but I knew that this was only delaying the inevitable. They would come again, in numbers, and this time they would take us all.

"I'm not sure that I can do this," Mason said.

"Don't tell me that you've forgotten how to swim," Kaminski said, with one of his trademark grins. He scrambled towards the edge of the waterfall.

"No rivers on Mars," Martinez said, getting ready to jump.

"But plenty of canals, eh?" said Kaminski.

I peered into the white waters at the base of the waterfall. It looked a very long way down. Amid the confusion, the bark of alien guns and the pitched hiss of plasma fire, Elena took my hand: glove to glove. Her touch, even through armour, was almost electric.

"I saw you," she said. "On Calico."

As one, we jumped over the edge.

Krell spilled from the trees and were met with a hail of plasma.

"Don't look back!" Elena shouted as we dropped. "Let the others take care of them! I'll lead the way."

She broke away from me and plunged into the water. Her armour was lighter than mine, had been adapted for use in the jungle, and she went under and into a breaststroke almost immediately. Diving deeper, into the darkened waters.

In a full battle-suit, I hit the water *hard*.

A simulant in armour doesn't float. I went under and kept going. I was vaguely aware of the rest of the Legion coming over the edge with me – falling or dropping, depending on which way you look at it, at about the same time.

The water was a brackish mix full of deposited silt and forest debris, creeper vines acting as snares for unwary jungle denizens, Christo only knows what else. As Elena had warned, it was deep, and water was entering the suit from numerous armour breaches. It wasn't made for deep-sea exploration, but using my internal oxygen supply I could breathe well enough down here. I sank immediately, the surface rapidly becoming a watery haze, a blur of light far above me. That was soon stitched with stinger-fire – bio-rounds tracing a calm, slow trajectory through the water.

I made out Elena ahead of me, waving us on. She swam rapidly through the murky water. I followed her as best I could, but I was almost plodding along the riverbed, slow motion: like combat in zero-G.

The Krell sleekly took to the water behind us. Alien bodies became knives against the river's flow: muscles rippling, limbs contorting. Their eyes shimmered darkly, perfectly adapted for this environment. Kaminski opened up his plasma rifle: soundlessly, with a flash of light. Maybe he even got one, but more were coming, diving from above. Jenkins pumped her grenade launcher, and I felt the shock-wave of an explosive going off. Debris filtered through the fast-running water, and clouds of sediment were thrown up, reducing visibility even more.

I turned back to Elena. She was far ahead now, swimming with all of her body. Unless we went with her and the team, we were going to get left behind.

"Follow Elena!" I ordered over the comm. "Leave the Krell!"

"I'm not sure that we can do that," Jenkins said. One of them had reached her, grasping at her armour, dragging her back. She slammed it aside, twisted against the flow of the river to pull after me.

There was an underwater tunnel ahead: a black hole in the wall of the riverbed. Elena disappeared inside, and as I bounced after her I saw that she had broken the surface and hauled herself out.

I fought the lactic burn in my limbs, and shrugged my body along – grappling rocks to drag myself out. I turned to haul Mason out behind me. Martinez clambered up an algae-slicked rock, then Jenkins and Kaminski did the same. The Legion collapsed to the ground, finally free of the pool.

"Remember what I told you!" Elena shouted, her voice echoing around the underwater grotto. "Do everything I say. Now, turn off your suits!"

"This is madness!" Jenkins said. "There are Krell following us—"

"*Suits off!*" Elena yelled.

Elena's team erupted from the river behind us, and proficiently rolled from the shoreline. They scattered among the rocks. Immediately went still. Instinctually, this all felt so wrong, but what could I do? I copied, and watched the rest of the Legion do the same.

"Suits power down!" I ordered.

POWER DOWN, I thought-ordered my armour. My HUD flashed with a warning, protesting against the command, but I thought-activated the override code. A confirmation message filled the interior of my face-plate as the armour became a hunk of inert metal-composite, my body locked inside a potential death-trap. I was on my back, able to see around me through the transparent face-plate—

I saw Elena moving. Dashing for the wall of the cave, scrambling over the wet rocks—

No!

A Krell broke the surface of the water behind her, using its clawed limbs to scramble up and into the cave. It would be on Elena in an instant: would rip her apart—

"Stay there!" she shouted at me, voice barely audible over the Krell's scream.

Against my better judgement, against every protective

tendency that I felt towards Elena, I did as she said. Watched as the primary-form bolted across the cave. None of Elena's team moved, and locked in our armour none of the Legion did either.

The sequence was dreamlike, nightmarish.

Elena touched the wall, fingers jabbing in sequence.

It was no wall, I realised. Blazing glyphs appeared where she met the surface. My instincts began to scream louder than the Krell. The surfaces of the walls around me were so finely etched that they were almost textured—

The Krell's talons were outstretched, virtually on Elena. She turned, her face fixed in a defiant scowl, though she didn't even have a weapon . . .

Maybe, I realised, *she doesn't need one*.

"Not here . . ." Jenkins shouted. We had no comm-link, but I could hear her voice even through our powerless suits. "Not here!"

I saw a ripple across the surface of the water, something moving above – seeping from the walls. Materialising.

Then the darkness came.

A shadow within a shadow.

Liquid darkness materialised in the centre of the room, and quickly became horrifyingly distinct. It appeared between Elena, her back to the wall now, and the primary-form.

I knew this thing. I had seen it before, seen it decimate the Lazarus Legion.

Not just kill us, but revel in the slaughter.

The Shard Reaper.

Elena turned, hands pressed to the wall.

The Krell's head jerked left, right, unsure of what threat to focus on. Strands of living oil, razor-tipped, shot from the walls: criss-crossed the cavern.

Elena hit the floor in a roll, a shadow chasing her—

Got to move! Gut-panic gripped me: it was going to catch her.

It felt like I was moving in double-gravity inside the armour; took every ounce of my strength to reach for her. My fingers clasped her shoulder, grabbed her. Then Elena's body was on top of mine – our face-plates touching, my unpowered limbs locked around her torso. She shuddered against me, her own armour powering down—

The questing tendril that had followed her suddenly broke off, darted back across the cave and found a new target. A black metal limb speared the Krell with terrible precision; hit the xeno in the sternum with enough force that the bio-armour was breached, hot innards spewing across the cave walls.

More Krell followed, leaping out of the water.

Would one Reaper be enough to take them all? I wondered.

But that question was largely irrelevant, because it soon became apparent that there was more than one.

Chrome-things, only taking shape when they needed to, poured into the chamber. They rippled over me, directing their attentions to the Krell and tossing them aside with reckless abandon.

How many did the Reapers kill? Five, ten, thirty . . . I soon lost count.

I lay very still, Elena's body pressed against mine, watching the things do their work. Flecks of alien blood hit my face-plate, and I fought the urge to wipe it clean. A claw dropped beside me, slick with ichor – still twitching as though its owner hadn't registered that it was missing. I thought of my own missing hand and the mechanical replacement lurking around Devonia's third moon aboard the *Colossus*.

It took all of my discipline to remain still. Would the

Legion react? Jenkins had seen the worst of it at Damascus. Kaminski had sworn an oath to take the Reaper on if he ever saw it again. We knew that it was futile – had seen how the Reaper had been almost impervious to our weaponry – but even so the natural reaction was to fight this thing.

Then the Krell stopped coming. Their cries echoed around the chamber; died out. The sound of a whole Collective in pain.

The Reapers prowled the water's edge. It was hard to judge how many of them there were; dipping in and out of cohesion. One moved near to Elena, spiked limbs lingering so close to her body—

Elena rolled across the floor again, pulling away from me and to the wall she had manipulated before. The symbols there still glowed a pure blue. Her hand moved to the wall. Touching the same glyphs.

The Reapers receded, limbs withering. They disappeared back into the walls in reverse of how they had appeared. It took only seconds for them to completely vanish but I breathed hard for a long moment, unwilling to accept that it had been that easy. My breath fogged the inside of my face-plate, and I scanned the chamber with my eyes: searching for some indication that the threat might return. No one around me moved, bodies remaining pinned to the floor.

"We're clear," Elena said. Her words were confident, but her voice wavered. There was fear there, I decided, and Elena had known that this plan didn't come without risk.

I thought-commanded my suit to power up again, and fresh info-feeds fluoresced over my HUD. My limbs unlocked, the suit becoming operational. The Legion were recovering just as fast.

"Did that just happen . . .?" Jenkins said, stumbling around the chamber.

But I ignored all of it.

Elena paused in front of me, watched me stand. I snapped off my helmet. Let it drop to the floor. My body had lost all strength, for the first time that I could remember in a simulant. Elena had that effect on me.

"Is it really you?" I asked.

"It's me, Conrad," Elena whispered.

She vaulted across the grotto and threw her arms around my neck. The physical response to her presence was immediate, was as though she had never left. We folded into each other and I held her for a long while. We kissed: long, passionate. Her hands reached into my simulated hair, searched through it. On some cellular level, I could tell that this was really Elena. This was no echo.

I lost myself in her for the briefest of moments. In that instant, the war didn't matter. Nothing else mattered, so long as I had Elena. We eventually parted, but Elena held on to my shoulders, looked up at me. In the simulant, wearing the battle-suit, I was enormous to her slender frame. A wistful, tragic smile played at the corners of her mouth.

This wasn't the Elena who had fled into the Maelstrom.

This wasn't even the Elena from the Artefact in Damascus, or the Elena I'd tried to rescue from the *Endeavour*. Physically, this was not the same woman who had left me all those years ago. This was the real Elena. Older, yes, but no less beautiful.

There was a cough behind me, a nervous attempt to get my attention.

"So this is Dr Marceau?" Mason asked.

She looked from Elena and her group to me, and back again. Jenkins and Martinez were silent, probably unsure of what to do.

"Good to see you, Doc," Kaminski said.

"You too, Vincent," she replied, still looking at me.

"I think I told you a long time ago not to call me that . . ." Kaminski muttered.

"Leave it out," Jenkins said.

I couldn't draw my eyes from her. This was Elena improved: Elena mark three. She had a defiant radiance to her face, her upturned cheeks. Her long dark hair was pulled back from her face, tied at her neck; a practical arrangement. She looked lean, hardened. An anger and determination lingered in her almond eyes.

"I knew that you would come," Elena said. She nodded at the rest of her team. "I told you that he would."

"I promised that I would cross time and space."

"*Merci*, Conrad. *Tu me manques mon amour*. We have waited so long for this."

The woman I'd known: she would have looked absurdly out of place in a combat-suit. This woman? She was comfortable in the battle-worn armour, dripping wet from an alien waterfall, spattered with Krell bodily fluids. She smiled at me, knowingly, as though reading my response.

"Things have changed," she said, "very much."

"I thought that I had lost you in Damascus, and then again on the *Endeavour*."

Kaminski interrupted. "Yeah, Doc. You could have made this easier . . ."

Elena shook her head. "I wish that I could have told you," she said, "but it really wasn't that simple. I had to take precautions, and I needed to know that it was you."

"It was me," I said. "And it's me now."

Elena shook her head. "Not the real you though. Always simulated."

There was truth in that. On Damascus, we had met sim to sim. I'd rescued Elena from the *Endeavour*, and met her simulant in my real skin. On Devonia, I was skinned and she was for real. I yearned to be with her in my own body, to be out of this simulant.

"It had to be this way," Elena said. "You will understand. If not now, then soon."

Although I saw a smile creeping over Jenkins' lips, the Legion stood watching us. They had the uncomfortable air of witnessing a private moment.

"Get a room, guys . . ." Kaminski sniggered.

The *Endeavour* team bristled.

"We should get back to the camp, Doctor," one of them said.

Elena nodded. "Yes. We have so much to show you."

CHAPTER TWENTY-THREE

WE CAN CHANGE THINGS

"You have questions, yes?" Elena asked, as we picked our way through the tunnels. She had taken the lead, her crew in tight formation behind her. "Ask, and I will answer them as best I can."

"How did those things – the Reapers – get here?" Jenkins said. "Did they come from Damascus?"

"No," Elena said. "We found them here, as part of this structure."

"You just, ah, controlled them," Mason said. "How is that . . .?"

"I activated them," Elena said, patiently. "They can't be controlled, but they have a limited response range. Once you understand their programming, the process is simple enough."

"Right, right," Kaminski said. "Like a computer or something."

"Exactly."

"That was risky," I said to Elena. "You could've been hurt."

Elena smiled at me. "I've been here for ten years, Conrad.

I've been hurt lots of times, and the Reapers aren't really sentient. I knew what I was doing. I can teach you how to activate them, if you'd like."

"If it's all the same," Jenkins said, "I'd rather not know, thanks."

Although I followed closely behind Elena, I regularly caught her looking back at me. It was like she was checking that I was really here; that I was not some figment of *her* imagination. Maybe I wasn't the only one seeing things.

"Watch your footing here," she said, as she navigated a rock-pool.

The tunnels were wide enough to accommodate our battles-suits, but jagged outcroppings sometimes protruded from the walls or floor. Some of the structures looked worryingly manufactured.

"This place freaks me out," Mason whispered to Jenkins, from somewhere behind me.

"You're not the only one," Jenkins said. "Shard shit . . . here . . ."

"It feels . . ." Martinez started, then paused.

"Spit it out," Kaminski said. "Unless you want to tell me in Spanish or something?"

"It feels *wrong* down here," Martinez said. "*Espíritu maligno.*"

"'Bad spirit'?" Elena suggested.

"That'd be about right," said one of the *Endeavour* group.

"What are those guns, *cuate*?" Martinez asked the same trooper. "Where'd they come from?"

The woman grinned. "You like one?"

"Maybe," Martinez said. "Don't look like they were made local."

"Sure they were," she said. "We call them prism-guns." She patted the dark stock of the rifle, slung over her shoulder with a makeshift strap of worn leather.

"We found them," Elena joined in. "Whoever made this place left them behind."

Although it was cooler, the air still cloyed with humidity. Water tumbled gently in the background, echoing through the labyrinth. It felt like we were in a different world, but though there were no Krell down here their presence was never far. A distant rumble came from somewhere far above; the thundering of a thousand clawed feet.

"Don't worry," Elena said. "They won't follow us. They'll keep looking for a while, but eventually they'll lose interest."

"How do you know that?" Mason said. Her voice was low as a whisper; as though she was concerned that the Krell overhead would hear her, despite the distance between them and us.

"Because," Elena said, pausing further down the tunnel, "they know that this is not a place for them."

We eventually emerged from a narrow tunnel mouth, set into a canyon wall. Brushing against the cold rocks we surfaced in the dull sunlight, in the jungle again.

"Fuck me . . ." Jenkins said.

A crashed starship lay on its side, half-buried in the soft earth. Less than half was visible: the ship was almost subsumed by the surrounding green. I took the lead, slowly advancing out of the caves. One eye trained on the jungle – expecting Krell scouts to appear at any moment – I assessed the ship. From the way in which the foliage had grown around it, I guessed that it had been here for years. She was undeniably of human manufacture; a small vessel, not as big or grand as the *Endeavour*. So deep was she in the jungle that I suspected she wouldn't be seen from orbital or even aerial scans: the canopy had grown thick, almost impenetrably so, and the glade in which the ship had crashed was cast in a semi-gloom.

I recognised the vessel. I'd seen it on news-casts more than enough times. Barely visible through the muck that had accumulated on the hull, the name UAS ARK ANGEL was stencilled on the ship's flank.

"This was one of your ships," I said. "This was part of the *Endeavour*'s fleet."

"It was," Elena said, with a perfunctory nod. "Other than the *Endeavour*, she was the last."

"You lost the rest of the fleet?" Mason asked. "*All* of them?"

Elena sighed. "All of them. Getting here wasn't easy."

"Must've been a hell of a crash," Martinez said.

I walked the perimeter of the ship's crash zone. She had come down at a low angle, with enough force to shatter her hull. Many of the internal modules had breached, and only the aft – where the energy core and drive cortex were located – had escaped any significant damage.

"You don't have any perimeter defences," Jenkins said. "The Krell could just roll in here at any time, Doctor."

"They could," Elena said, "but they won't."

Figures appeared from inside the ship – popping half-submerged access hatches, empty view-ports and observation windows. Men and women wearing a variety of jumpsuits and crew uniforms, but universally ragged, dirty and exhausted. Some were embellished with Krell armoured plates, others carrying improvised mêlée weapons like spears – made from metal and wood – alongside ancient sidearms. Soon, a hundred pairs of eyes were on us. They looked wary, but also elated.

One man came forward to meet us. As with the ship, I recognised his role in the expedition: Commander

Christopher Cook, captain of the UAS *Endeavour*. I remembered his image, broadcast on the vid-screens back at Calico, a decade ago. Dressed in the remains of genuine Alliance evacuation-suit, but combined with shoulder-plates and a chest-guard removed from a combat-suit. A nasty scar marked his cheek – healed, but badly so. It looked a lot like it had been caused by a Krell's talon, and had only just missed his right eye.

"By Gaia," the man said, speaking with a clipped Calican accent, "have you really come?"

Elena gave a proud smile, stood beside me. "I told you that he would."

Cook had tears in his dark eyes, and his jaw trembled.

"Hoping and seeing are two very different things," Cook said. "We have missed the world a great deal."

"Meet Major Conrad Harris," Elena said.

"Colonel now, actually," I said. "Lieutenant Colonel, at least. Only a half-bird colonel."

Elena raised an eyebrow. "And I thought that you never wanted to be an officer?"

"The decision was made for me," I said, dismissively. This seemed unreal: Elena being here, on this alien world, discussing a largely irrelevant promotion.

"Come," Cook said, waving us towards the UAS *Ark Angel*. "We have much to discuss."

"You probably landed a couple of klicks from here," said Cook.

"We tried to reach your coordinates," I explained, "but we didn't get that far. Our gunship was shot down."

"I'm sorry that I wasn't able to give you more precise information," Elena said. "I didn't have much time aboard your ship. There's a significant Krell nest east of here, but

I had hoped that you would be able to evade their defences. As you've probably seen, they have the skies covered."

Kaminski nodded. "It's a regular Krell-ville."

Elena gave him an unimpressed look. "You haven't changed, Vincent."

"Not much," Kaminski said.

We sat in what had probably once been the *Ark Angel*'s mess hall. Due to the angle at which the ship had crashed, her deck now listed to one side and the view of the jungle outside was strangely off-kilter. I'd already introduced my team, and run through the specifics of our ship's location in orbit around Devonia. The Legion had reluctantly dismounted from their Ares battle-suits, and I did the same. It made me nervous being out of the armour – dressed in only a neoprene undersuit and combat boots – and I kept looking over at the suit. *How long would it take me to mount up again if I needed it?* I wondered.

Elena had changed out of her body armour; instead now wore a crew jumpsuit that had been modified for the environment. The sleeves were torn short, and I noticed the environmental control on the collar had malfunctioned. Despite everything – where we were, the avalanche of un-answered questions, the fact that we were stranded here – I couldn't stop looking at her. The curve of her neck, the lilt of her heart-shaped face . . .

"Do you have any smokes?" she asked.

I laughed. "You haven't kicked the habit?"

"It's been a long time, but not that long."

Commander Cook hadn't stopped smiling since our arrival. "I have missed my wives and children so very much."

I hadn't the heart to tell him that Calico Base was long gone. I could only hope that his family was safe somewhere, that they had escaped the Directorate attack.

"You didn't try to communicate with the Alliance?" Jenkins probed. "If you missed everyone so much, wouldn't that have been the easiest thing to do?"

"The easiest thing," Cook said, "but not the right thing."

"I have a lot to explain," said Elena.

"You can start with how you did all of this," Kaminski said, with genuine interest. "Sending yourself to Damascus, using a simulant aboard the *Endeavour* . . .?"

"Both required some ingenuity," Elena said. "We have a Simulant Operations Centre aboard the *Ark Angel*. Even inactive, it is possible to establish a neural-link between the Arkonus Abyss and the Damascus Rift. I sent a sim back through the wormhole, waited for help. The ranges involved meant that I couldn't go any further than the Rift."

Elena had already shown me around the ship that had been her home for the last ten years. With a functional energy core, the vessel had allowed some of the basic necessities to support human life on Devonia. The ship's battery wouldn't last for ever, but by human timescales it was close enough. The *Ark Angel* had been one of Science Division's premier research vessels at the time of her departure – a support ship for the *Endeavour* fleet – and she carried an extensive Science Deck. It had been from here that Elena had operated a simulant.

Elena continued. "We detected the alarm signal when you boarded the *Endeavour*, and I made transition. Our remaining simulant stock was held aboard the *Endeavour*, but the ship's AI had become corrupted over time. Many of the skins perished."

"That's quite some plan," Kaminski said. "But I guess that it worked."

"There's a lot more to it than that . . ." Elena said.

"Start from the beginning," I said, eager to get as much information as possible from the survivor group: to start planning our escape.

And so Elena started to tell the story of the *Endeavour*.

As Elena spoke, I felt parts of my world – of a belief mechanism that had grown up around me, *justified* me – begin to slip away.

"There has never been a Treaty," she said. "It was all a lie."

As much as I'd hated and disagreed with the Treaty, it had been a constant in my life. It had explained so much: *Liberty Point*, the Sim Ops Programme, the Quarantine Zone. None of these things had meaning without the Treaty.

Elena sighed. "I know that you will be angry. I know that you will find it hard to understand, but it's the truth."

"Did Science Division know?" I asked.

I wanted something, someone, to vent my anger on. Had Professor Saul known that the Treaty was a lie?

"Some knew," Elena said, "but not many. It was a controlled disclosure; highly classified."

"Did you know before you left?"

"Not until we departed Alliance space," she said, haltingly. "And even then, not everything. It was strictly need-to-know, but as the mission progressed it became difficult to restrict."

"Why lie about it?" Mason retorted. She, too, was in disbelief: couldn't handle what we were being told. As the youngest member of the team, Mason was the least cynical.

"Stay out of this, Mason," Jenkins said. "It's not our business."

Elena answered anyway. "Because the Alliance – because Command – needed a plausible explanation for assembling a fleet of this magnitude, for sending it into the Maelstrom."

"And it was the perfect cover," Cook explained. "The Core Systems were in fear. The Krell menace loomed large. No one asked questions, because everyone wanted the war to end."

"Psych Ops at their finest," Kaminski said.

Mason still couldn't accept it. "But who were they hiding it *from*? Surely not the Krell?"

"Something much worse," Elena said "and far closer to home. The Alliance needed to cover this up, to hide it, from the Asiatic Directorate." Elena turned to me, her eyes pleading. Not just for acceptance, but for understanding. "It worked, but not completely. The Directorate were with us all the way. We were compromised."

"They infiltrated our expedition at every level," Cook said. "Many of Sergeant Stone's security forces were working with them. Gaia praise the sergeant; he died in the fighting."

Sergeant Stone had been the head of security aboard the *Endeavour*, in charge of the Army simulant operators, assigned to the mission by Command as protection detail. *Williams' Warfighters weren't the only traitors in Sim Ops*, I thought. Colonel O'Neil, head of Simulant Operations, had approved the attachment of a squad to the operation . . .

"We saw damage aboard the *Endeavour*," I said. "On the Science Deck."

"That's right," Elena said. "Many of our labs were destroyed."

"Then why didn't you come home?" Mason asked. "Why have you stayed here for so long?"

Elena pulled a tight smile. "We couldn't risk leaving what we had found to the Directorate. The *Endeavour*'s quantum drive was damaged, and the Directorate attack had cost us most of the other FTL- and Q-space-capable starships in the fleet."

Cook shook his head. "What happened here proves that the Directorate have infiltrated every strata of the Alliance. We couldn't risk communication, because to do so would risk the information being intercepted."

"But if the Treaty wasn't your mission, why send you here?" I asked. "What's so damned special about this place?"

The Legion followed Elena and Cook through the jungle, deeper into the Maze. The canyon pressed in. With each passing second that sense of *wrongness* increased. It was becoming almost unbearable. Like psychic scratching at the back of my brain, an itching over every inch of my simulated skin: uncomfortable in a way that I found difficult to explain.

There were structures around us. Half-toppled pillars of obsidian, towers that had long crumpled into the jungle. It was obvious that this had once been a grand construction: part of the cave network, something much bigger and more complex. Time had eroded the structures to little more than dust, made them a true necropolis. Shards of muted sunlight stabbed through semi-collapsed walls, the remains of a roof. That did little to illuminate the place, and it was deathly silent. Not even the wildlife was interested in probing what lay down here.

We entered a chamber inside one of the structures. Shard glyphs lined the walls, painting the room in flickering neon shades. The floor had become metal plate, etched with the tight cuneiform patterns. Glowing scripture; the madness-inducing patterns that looked like arcane circuitry.

"I . . . I can't stay in here," Jenkins stammered. Her eyes darted across every shadow. "I need my armour, now!"

"It's okay," Elena said. She patted the long-barrelled prism-gun that she held across her chest. "I have a weapon."

Jenkins didn't retreat, but she looked a lot like she was about to. The rest of the Lazarus Legion prowled the edges of the chamber with obvious apprehension. Elena lit a glow-stick, threw it into the corner of the room. Her slender figure was lit from behind by the green light, cutting a sharp silhouette.

"This is why the Krell don't come into the tunnels, to your camp," I said.

"That's right," said Elena. She spread her arms to the room around her. "This is a control centre for the original creators of this facility. What the creators called a 'memory chamber'."

"We called them the Shard . . ." Jenkins said. Her voice sounded distant, even though she was only just behind me.

"We are aware of the name," Elena said.

It felt as though the veil between real-space and the Network was thinner here than ever before. I struggled to repress the mental trauma of travelling through the Shard Network; of my brush with the Shard machine-mind. As I looked at the walls – saw the rivulets of dark water running down the textured panelling, across the densely packed hieroglyphics – I couldn't shake off the impression that they were *sweating*. It was like the whole place was alive; as though it had taken an enormous breath, and was just waiting to exhale. There were ghosts here, echoes of the machine-mind, lingering at the edge of my perception.

"We've seen similar facilities on Damascus and Helios," I insisted, trying to reassure myself as much as anyone else. "*This* is nothing new. It's just another buried wreck. Just another ruin for the Alliance and the Directorate to squabble over."

"I wish that were the case," Elena said, "but this is something much worse. It was our mission to study this site."

Cook pulled a grimace. He almost fell over as he stumbled towards Jenkins. "Stay back from there, Lieutenant!"

Cook's sudden eruption was enough to put us all on edge. As one, the Legion responded. Jenkins had reached the edge of the room and was standing close to a pedestal-like feature that erupted from the wall. In the low light, I made out a shape atop the pedestal. Something like a misshapen blob of melted rock – the afterbirth of a volcanic flow – that glistened softly.

"Cool your jets, Commander," Jenkins said, backing away from the wall.

Cook panned a glow-stick at the pedestal. The light caught the obsidian-black feature in a pool of illumination. The blob shimmered like metal, throwing out bizarre reflections.

"That," Elena said, pointing at the pedestal, "is another example of the entity you know as the Reaper."

Jenkins visibly recoiled from the edge of the chamber, her face crumpling in disgust. The chamber was peppered with pedestals: all occupied.

"They are in a dormant state," Cook said. "But I would rather not bait them."

"They won't activate unless you get too close," Elena said. "And even then, their attack patterns are limited. You've seen that, if manipulated properly, they have their purpose."

Elena's hands danced over a control console, caressing runes and impressions on the surface of the machine. At first I thought that she was activating the Reapers again, but instead the walls and structure around us began to pulse with light. The dark water that had been running across the textured surfaces coalesced, collected. Silvered metal swam across the walls: alive. I'd seen Shard tech do that before – on Helios, on the crashed ship that Dr Kellerman had shown me – but this was on a far grander scale. The atonal pulse in the background felt as though something truly massive was online, something so much bigger than the ruins at Helios or Damascus.

"This is a fully functioning Shard facility," Commander Cook said. "It was the Shard's origin, we believe, in the Maelstrom."

"But you," Elena added, looking at me, "will know it by another name. To you, it is an Artefact. The whole planet is a Master Artefact."

I wanted to question. Wanted to deny the truth of this, but the machines whispered to me. The black rock – the canyons, the ravines; the bizarre geometric terrain visible from orbit? The conclusion that those could be Shard creations was chillingly inevitable. We had been staring at the truth all along.

"The planet is artificial," Elena said. "A true feat of engineering. At one time it probably provided docking facilities for thousands of Shard warships. Can you imagine it? This place was a major node in the Machine; a device capable of altering spatial dynamics on a scale that we can barely understand.

"But over time, it fell into decline. The war was won, at least so far as the Shard were concerned, and they perhaps felt that the facility no longer needed to be garrisoned. The Krell might be responsible for Devonia's subsequent terraforming, as they made their resurgence, or it could be a natural occurrence: the result of millennia in space. Either way, the Shard were here first and this is their facility."

Cook nodded. "This is why Command sent us out here. Not to agree a Treaty, but to secure, and utilise, this Artefact."

The imagery on the walls shifted. It showed a familiar spread of stars – the former Quarantine Zone, the star systems bordering that sector.

"Science Division discovered Devonia's location from ruins found on Tysis World," Elena explained. "It was quickly identified as a location of key importance to the war effort."

That name again: Tysis World. Professor Saul had mentioned it.

"We knew that we were searching for a weapon," Cook said. "And that is exactly what we found. A world-weapon; a device capable of ending the Krell. All it required was a Shard Key. We haven't been able to find that, despite searching Devonia."

"What we did discover, however, was that contrary to Command's intelligence the Shard were not dead," Elena said. "And once we knew the reality of this weapon – the consequences of its activation – we knew that we couldn't allow the Artefact to be used."

"What consequences?" Mason asked.

Elena's face was stern. "There will be a cost," she said. "A dire cost, one that is surely not worth the gain."

"The closest human analogue to this Artefact's purpose," Cook said, "is a *summoning*. It will summon the Shard."

I watched as a pictorial formed on the wall, sketched in molten metal. Dots of light were thrown across the display. More star systems: I could even identify some of them; realised that they were systems within the same galactic neighbourhood as Devonia Star. *Far too close to home*, I thought. The display showed something moving from

Helios – from the world on which we'd found the first Artefact – to Devonia.

"The Shard were bringing the Key here," I whispered. "That was the purpose of the activation on Helios."

An icon, cast in glowing silver, moved across the Shard display: something crossing the gulf of space, moving towards our location, towards the Devonia system. The metal above us reformed at Elena's control. She zoomed in on a world now, on a single planet. Choked with vegetation and cloud cover, but the jagged black lines crossing the surface looked a lot like those banding Devonia's surface.

"We don't have all of the answers," Elena said, "but we can now understand enough of the Shard's language to decipher that if the Master Artefact is activated, the Shard Network will open. It'll allow whatever is left of the Shard to come through. It will summon the *Revenant* to Devonia."

The graphic showed the *Revenant* coming down to the surface. Then darkness spread over the world, everything scorched away, leaving only a blackened, criss-crossed husk.

Leaving only the Artefact.

Revenant. It wasn't an operation or a project: it was a starship. I had a name for the horror that had been stalking me. I had no doubt that this was the thing we'd felt in the Shard Network.

"Mass xenocide . . ." Elena whispered. "But we are all alien to the Shard."

After it had ended Devonia, the Shard graphic showed the *Revenant* moving on. Showed the ship jumping between systems, igniting worlds and stars as it went. Using the activated Shard Network, the Shard Gates, the *Revenant* travelled light-years in an instant.

"The Shard didn't just wage war against the Krell," Cook

said. "They sought to destroy all organic life in the Milky Way Galaxy. If they are summoned here, their war will start again. Neither side has forgotten what happened millennia ago."

"And they say that the fishes have short memories . . ." Kaminski said.

"The Krell, in fact, have a highly advanced species-memory," Elena said, answering 'Ski's comment as though it was a serious scientific observation. "They pass down recall of specific events, through the leader-forms. The Collectives remember this war with the Shard, and they never forget. This, we believe, is why the Krell are attracted to operational Shard technology."

They were preparing for war on Helios, I thought. *The Krell hadn't forgotten what happened there.* The same could be said of Damascus. I wondered whether this might explain their advanced evolution.

"The Shard are just as bitter," Cook said. "They are a species that has outgrown the flesh, shed it like a second skin. It's all here: recorded in these walls. The organic races of this galaxy are just a reminder of what they left behind, and an unwelcome one at that. To them, we are nothing. We are a scourge, just like the Krell."

"The Shard are a far greater enemy to the Alliance – to the Directorate, to humanity, to everything organic – than the Krell ever could be," Elena said. "And it is for that reason that this Artefact must never be activated, and it must never fall into Directorate hands."

The simulation on the walls froze. Elena manipulated the controls again, and the glowing icon representing the *Revenant* vanished.

"How do you explain the Quarantine Zone?" Mason asked Elena. "The Collective stopped fighting for a long time."

"Did they?" Elena said. "The Maelstrom is a big place. The Krell have other things to worry about, and you all talk about the Krell as though they are a single, unified race. That isn't the case at all. They panic and flee just like us, and their species-memory often dictates their actions without plan or strategy. What this place proves – what Shard tech proves – is that activation of certain devices allows us to manipulate their behaviour."

"Billions dead, and it's all some big mistake?" Martinez said.

"That isn't the way I would put it," said Elena, "but perhaps."

"Command sent us here to end the war," Mason said, more apprehensively. "Maybe they expected us to activate this weapon; to call the Shard here."

That, I had no doubt, had been General Cole's plan. But because the *Endeavour* expedition had not reported, High Command had not been in possession of the facts. They could never have known the true consequences of the Master Artefact's activation.

"They must be more desperate than we thought . . ." Kaminski said. Though Martinez and Mason were still in denial, Kaminski seemed to have accepted Elena's explanation. "But we can't mess with this Shard tech. We have to close the door, for good."

Jenkins nodded. She stood side by side with Kaminski. "I think that 'Ski's right."

"So we hide like rad-roaches until Judgement Day?" Martinez queried.

"Rather a roach than dead," Jenkins said. "That, or we make ourselves ready for when the Shard come looking for us."

"While this place still exists," Elena pushed, as though

sensing the way that my mind was working, "the Directorate will just keep coming. They'll hurt all of us until we can't hurt any more." There was no softness to her voice; only a steely dedication. "It has to end here, before any of us can leave this place."

I knew, then, that Elena was right. Whether it was the Asiatic Directorate itself, or some rogue element like Admiral Kyung, didn't much matter: this was a trove of working Shard technology, a weapon of such power that surely they would risk everything to acquire it. Once it was acquired, how could they ever resist activating it?

"Does your ship have nuclear or plasma warheads?" Elena asked. "Something big enough to kill not just the planet, but the Artefact?"

None of the Legion answered. This was my call.

"She does," I said. "We have nuclear warheads. Enough to level Devonia."

Loeb had told me about the *Colossus*'s nuclear payload when we'd fled Calico, and I'd checked on the specs myself: been able to confirm that we carried several high-yield nuclear weapons. Devonia was a surprisingly small planet, and if Elena was right about the world's purpose then there were must've been power generators somewhere beneath the surface. Breached, they would add to the planet's funeral pyre. I found myself looking at the stalled graphics on the wall; at the *Revenant* and what it represented. We were all killers of planets, in our own way.

Elena's face illuminated. "Then that is what we must do. We must blast this place from existence, and stop the Machine from coming through."

She believed in this mission – whatever it was – and the glimmer in her eyes spoke of her certainty that this was the right thing to do. Her beauty hadn't been diminished by this place, and the fire in her eyes only amplified it.

The practicalities of killing a world would have to come later.

The Legion and the remainder of the *Endeavour*'s crew set about preparations to leave. We'd discussed using the orbital flares from the Ares battle-suits, or one of the Legion making extraction, to communicate with the *Colossus*. James could send down the second Dragonfly, and the survivors would evacuate. It wasn't a plan without risk but it was a plan at least. Former Navy officers and security staff, armed with more bizarre prism-guns and plasma carbines, dressed in ill-maintained uniforms, patrolled the interior and exterior of the *Ark Angel*. I noticed, with some pride, that Elena had become the unratified leader of the survivor group. Even the Naval officers deferred to her: sometimes in preference to Commander Cook. He showed no concern at that, rather a quiet acceptance. It was as though Elena's determination to survive had driven the rest of the crew.

Elena and I walked together through the Shard ruins, through the filtered sunset. Devonia Star's light was guttering now and only occasionally breaking the jungle canopy.

"Is this really almost over?" she asked.

I thought on that for a moment. There was a hard answer – the answer that the voice in my head teased me with: that this would never be over, not after what the Lazarus Legion had seen, what we'd done. Then there was an easy answer, and the lie came to me.

"Soon," I said. "This will be finished. I'm no stranger to destroying Artefacts. I can explain to Command."

I suspected that there wouldn't be much to go back to. There would be nothing to stop the Krell's incursion into Alliance space, but I was satisfied that was the lesser risk. Better to fight the enemy we knew, than that we did not.

"If I close my eyes," I said, "I can imagine that we are back on Azure. This is exactly how things were, years ago. We could pretend that the last ten years haven't happened."

"Is that what you'd like?"

"Wouldn't you?"

She stirred, drew her long dark hair back from her face. "A lot has changed since then."

Although her body was small next to mine, this Elena wasn't fragile. Her frame had grown sinewy, muscular: forged by a decade of hardship. Her arms were stitched with old white scars. So very different from the woman I had once known. She had come out here as a shipboard psychologist, but become so much more.

"Are you angry with me?" she asked, quietly.

"No. Of course not."

"I did this for you," she said. "That was why I joined the mission, because I wanted to end the war with the Krell. It was destroying you, and I thought that I could save you by finishing things. If we had a Treaty, the war would be over, and I would have you back."

"You could've talked to me . . ."

Elena shook her head. "Not then. Not as you were on Azure."

"I'm sorry," I said. Just saying those simple words: they lifted a weight from my heart. "I've wanted to say that for so long."

"Things were not as they should have been, but it wasn't just you. I inducted you into Simulant Operations—"

"But I let it consume me," I said. "I let that happen; not you."

"The technology is addictive," Elena said. "It should never have been used as frequently as it was." She sighed. "I have tasted it too, now."

"Why didn't you tell me," I said, "that Command had made you operational?"

Elena's lips tightened. "I knew that you would find that the hardest thing to understand. Being operational, using a simulant: these are your things, not mine. I felt like this was the greatest betrayal. I ask you again: are you angry with me?"

"I'm happy," I answered, "to have found you."

Elena's expression softened, became good-humoured. "You're such a bad liar, Conrad."

"It's . . ." I said, fighting to marshal my thoughts; to present them coherently. "It's just a lot to take in, is all."

"Becoming operational was part of the mission plan," Elena said. She traced the data-ports in her forearms. They looked sadistic, cast against her slender arms. "I was activated two weeks before I left, and I hid the data-ports from you. At that time, the mission details were still classified. I wanted to tell you, but I knew that you would try to stop me. You were so obsessed with Simulant Operations, only ever interested in the next transition . . ."

"Not anymore," I said. "I've changed too. I'll give all of this up."

Elena sighed. "Could you really do that?"

"So long as I have you, I would."

"You had me before," Elena said. "And that didn't stop you."

There was a playful tone in her voice, but a sadness in her eyes. Things *had* changed. Not just in a galaxy plunged back into war, but between us. Though it had probably been a very simplistic view, I'd always imagined that when I found Elena she would immediately forgive me for letting her go, and that all of my past transgressions would be forgotten. The reality was somewhat more complex.

I nodded. "I'd leave the Army tomorrow. We can leave all of this behind, live somewhere safe. I always promised you a farm."

"I remember," Elena said. Her eyes clouded, as if she was recalling a pleasant memory. "You always said that it would be a house in Normandy. I wonder if they still have farms there."

"France hasn't been hit, so far as I know."

"This is your promise then, *mon chérie*, that you will give me my farm in old France when we get home?"

Elena smiled; an ironic, equivocal expression. I'd never known someone whose simple expressions could mean so much, whose face could convey such emotion. This smile relayed many things. Happiness, yes, but also sadness and regret, perhaps even resignation.

I nodded. "That is my promise. We'll have a farm, and get a proper child licence. You'll have everything that I promised you."

We stood there, silently, for a long while. Not quite at ease, but contented nonetheless. That was a strange reaction, given that we were aboard an alien Artefact and surrounded by Krell, but I felt more contented than I had for a very long time.

"And now the slate is clean," Elena said.

"So what's this, then? A new start?"

"It can be, if you want it to be."

"I'd like that."

"We can change things," she whispered to me. "We can change it all. Once this place is destroyed, things will be different. We can make sure that they – the Shard – can never come through." Elena nuzzled into my neck, coiled around me. "We can have that future together, Conrad. I let you go once, and I'll never let you go again."

I held her, and we kissed. She tasted salty and earthy in my mouth, the warmth of her body invigorating me.

I never wanted to break this moment—

CHAPTER TWENTY-FOUR

THEY ARE HERE

The neural-link was severed between me and my simulant, and I was back in my tank.

What the fuck is happening?

I jerked awake; reached to tear the respirator mask from my face, simultaneously blinking fluid from my eyes. There was a slight, disorienting fluctuation in gravity – between the surface of Devonia, and the artificial generator of the starship – but it wasn't this slowing me down. I was hampered by the shakes – convulsions that gripped my body.

"*This is an emergency . . .*" the AI warbled, its voice piped into my ear-bead.

Then Mason and Martinez were shouting at the same time, Martinez speaking Spanish so fast that I couldn't follow him. Younger, faster, stronger, both were probably recovering from the extraction more quickly than me. They weren't happy with whatever it was they had discovered. Bodies hurried past my tank – blue blurs through the amniotic – and an emergency bulb flashed from the ceiling of the SOC, throwing the room into amber light. I reached for the emergency evacuation button. Finally, my right hand decided to obey my command. The tank began to purge and the door control activated—

"This is an emergency . . ."

The deck rocked beneath me, violently and perilously, and the fluid in the tank shook, data-cables whipping against the canopy. Admiral Loeb stood at the door.

"Out!" he yelled, voice cutting through the other noise. "Everyone out of the damned tanks!"

I slowly complied, taking in what other details I could. *Why is Loeb carrying a service pistol?* Dr Serova was at my shoulder, her face contorted in distress. She shoved a fresh pair of fatigues in my direction.

"Get dressed and get smart!" Loeb shouted, like a drill instructor straight out of Army Basic. To one of the medtechs: "Break open the armoury and get them armed – *now!*"

The Legion had dismounted their tanks as well. Loeb stomped the SOC, waving his pistol in the air.

"This is an emergency . . ."

"What's going on?" I slurred. "You had no right to break the connection. Elena is down there – we've found them!"

"*I* didn't break it!" Loeb countered. "*They* are here!"

"Who's here? I ordered you not to extract us!"

Loeb unceremoniously grabbed the collar of my fatigue. His eyes were wild with anger and panic. "The Directorate are here, Harris. The *Shanghai* is in orbit around Devonia."

I struggled after Loeb and a cadre of his officers, all carrying peashooters, as we made haste to the CIC.

"She hit us on the way in," Loeb said, his face red with anger. "Two plasma missiles."

One of the officers gave a vociferous nod. "The first

missile was caught by our null-shield, but the second was a direct hit on the power module."

"And no one saw her coming?" I asked, incredulously.

"She's a damned assassin, just like that bitch of an admiral!" Loeb said, waving his hands around, almost ignorant of the fact that he was still carrying the M4. "Whatever stealth systems she's got, they're far more advanced than the dumbshit Proximan scanner-tech we're packing." Loeb shook his head. "I told them that this was a bad idea!"

"Damage control is online," the same officer said, "and that caused a power shortage to the simulator bay."

"Permanent?" I said.

Loeb produced a growl from the back of his throat. "Your damned simulators will still work, if that's what you want to know."

"Let me guess what we've lost . . ." I said.

"The missile launch bay is gone," Loeb said. "We've lost the nukes. No space-to-ground offensive capability at all."

The CIC was filled with officers: faces cast blue by the increasingly bright glow of the Arkonus Abyss.

Loeb, Saul and the Legion circled the tactical display. In tri-D, the tac presented an analysis of our dire situation. The Krell presence in orbit had mobilised, bio-ships darting across space at frightening speed. Their orbital stations were becoming agitated insect nests.

"Shit . . ." Martinez said. "What's happening out there?"

"They're responding to *that*," Loeb said, emphasising the last word with a stab of his finger towards the display.

The *Shanghai Remembered* hovered in near-space. Her terrible black outline was immediately recognisable, null-shield lighting as she took fire from Krell ships.

"It looks like we hurt her at Calico," Loeb said, his voice quivering with rage, "but it wasn't enough to put her down."

The *Shanghai* had seen obvious damage. One armoured flank was crumpled and pocked, a wound piercing her hide so deep that even at range I could see several decks had been vented. But she was far from out of the fight. Her railguns spat projectiles into space, while banks of point-defence lasers lanced any enemy who dared come too close. Meanwhile Interceptors and Wraiths circled her in delicate patterns, giving chase to smaller prey.

Martinez slammed a fist into the display; made the tri-D flicker. "Damn it! That was a good shot."

"I knew that we couldn't get that lucky," Jenkins muttered.

"Better luck next life, eh?" Kaminski said, without a hint of humour.

That Kyung had gone into Q-space with such a badly damaged ship spoke of her desperation. *Rogue.* That had been the word used by Command to describe her actions: *gone rogue.* Perhaps even worse than that . . .

"Why haven't you shot her?" Martinez said.

Loeb's brow remained creased, his anger star-bright. "She's faster than us," he said, "and we weren't expecting her. As well as the damage to the weapons launching array, she managed to fry our counter-measures package. We start a shooting match out here, now, and we're *both* dead."

"That isn't going to happen," I said. "Elena is down there, and now we know what the *Revenant* really is. The *Endeavour* expedition was sent here to harness the power of a weapon; a machine capable of destroying whole worlds. Ten years ago, this was Command's plan – to use the *Revenant* to destroy the Krell. If Kyung has control of that technology . . ."

Loeb paused. Glared at me through the thatch of his eyebrows. He looked very much like a predatory bird. "Christo . . ."

"Devonia is an Artefact," I explained. "The entire planet is one Master Artefact. If it's activated, it will open the entire Shard Network."

Professor Saul stirred. "Is that so?"

Kaminski nodded. "You'd love it, Prof. Except that, if Dr Marceau is right, it's the key to ending all life in the galaxy."

"I think it's a bit more complicated than that, 'Ski," Jenkins said. "But you get the idea, Professor."

"All organic life, at least," Mason added.

"Splitting hairs there, New Girl," said Kaminski. "Either way, if the Directorate has the Key, they can call the *Revenant* here."

"*Gracia de Dios* . . ." Martinez said, crossing himself. "We can't let that happen."

"They can activate the Artefact," Saul said. "This is what the Directorate have always wanted. The presence of the Key probably explains the Abyss' increased energy output."

The Arkonus Abyss seemed to have drawn closer to Devonia, and was surely responding to something. Blue light streamed from its core, polluting the dark of space: tendrils reaching for Devonia. Deep inside the rent in time-space, something dark hungered for release. I could feel data shedding from inside that space within a space, feel the cold press of the Shard Machine calling to Devonia . . .

"What exactly is happening down there?" Mason said, swallowing as she spoke. "Why is Devonia . . . *changing*?"

The clouds flashed with electrical activity, lightning playing across the globe. Even at this distance, the seas looked storm-lashed. The planet was *angry*.

Professor Saul readjusted his glasses on the bridge of his nose, still crooked from his time on Capa. "If this world really is an enormous Artefact, then perhaps Devonia is reacting to the presence of the Shard Key as well." He pointed out aspects of the planet on the display. "Already, there have been broad tectonic shifts in the northern continent. Those will lead to tidal surges planet-wide, and the bio-sphere will be significantly disturbed."

"Destroyed, more like it," Loeb said.

"But how is this happening so fast?" Martinez said. "Terraforming takes decades . . ."

"*Our* terraforming takes decades," Kaminski said. "Aren't you always saying that God made Earth in seven days? Well, it looks like the Shard can unmake a world in one."

"There's no point standing around here talking," Jenkins said. "We have to stop the Directorate from getting down there."

Loeb shook his head sharply. "It's too late for that. Almost as soon as she arrived, the *Shanghai* started deploying ships to the surface."

The sobering implications of that intel hit me immediately.

"Elena is down there!" I said. "We need to—"

But before we could plan our response any further, the communicator chimed.

"We're being hailed," an officer declared.

"Let me guess," Kaminski said: "the *Shanghai*?"

The officer nodded.

Kyung the Assassin materialised on the communications console, in jittering tri-D.

Even over the remote connection, her threat radius was palpable. Unlike before, I could not identify the location of her broadcast; whether she had accompanied the away party down to Devonia, or had remained aboard the *Shanghai*. Neither was exactly palatable – the fact that the

Assassin was in the same galaxy as me was bad enough. Such recollection as I had of my mother caressed something deep in my psyche. Fond, warm memories . . . The face glaring back at me from the holo was anything but.

"This," she said, speaking slowly and precisely, "is your first and final warning. Alliance starship *Colossus*: leave this area immediately, and desist your illegal war-efforts against the Asiatic Directorate."

The Legion bristled around me, their collective anger directed towards the creature on the tri-D.

"We aren't going anywhere, Assassin," I said, through clenched teeth. "I'm done running. You came for me, and here I am."

"You are currently irrelevant," Kyung said, evaluating me with her dead gaze. "But if you remain here, you should be prepared for the consequences. Accept this broadcast as a formal declaration of intent."

"What have you got, Kyung? Your ship is in ruins. We got you at Calico."

"Calico was nothing," she said. "But what happened in Damascus: that is unforgivable."

The various scars on Kyung's high cheekbones were thrown into relief, like valleys and craters on a lunar landscape. Little lights flashed beneath her skin, in precise etched lines, describing patterns like subcutaneous circuitry. She was in direct communication with her ship.

"On that, we can agree," I said.

"We arrive at the same conclusion via very different routes. You left me and my ships in the Maelstrom for dead."

"You attacked our fleet," I said. "You killed thousands of Alliance personnel, and caused the destruction of sixteen warships."

And that, of course, was just the start. If Command and

Loeb were right, this woman had condemned millions to death aboard the *Liberty Point* . . .

"My battlegroup had a mission," Kyung said. Her features twitched again. "I am biometrically linked to my ship. I am this ship. To feel her pain: it was devastating . . . The Krell boarded her, in number. We were . . ." She struggled to find the right word, then said, "*violated*."

The plasma burns on her face suddenly made sense. She had fought off the Krell, had been there when they were on the ship. A squirt of triumph ran through me: an abhorrent pleasure that I didn't even try to repress. The lights at her end of the connection dipped and winked, casting her image in half-darkness. Was that psychosomatic feedback, caused by Kyung's emotional reaction to the memory – bleeding over into the *Shanghai*? A little detail that I filed away.

"You shamed me," Kyung said. "You are directly responsible for the failure of my mission. I limped back to the Rim, with only a fraction of my former strength. Today, I am correcting that failure; no matter what the cost."

"I won't stand by and let you do this!" I shouted. "If you know so much about the Shard, about the Artefacts, then you will know what they mean to the Krell and us!"

"No one comes back from this," Kyung said, her face split in a smile. It was a blistering expression. "Not even you. There will be no further warning. We will not meet again, Lazarus."

The communication-link severed, and Admiral Kyung's image vanished. We all stood around the console, silent. It was all I could do to keep myself standing: to conceal the depth of my reaction.

They have the Key, and they can activate the Artefact.

"She's insane . . ." Loeb said, slowly, quietly. There was

no talk of retreat now, no suggestion that we could do anything but make a last stand against the Directorate. "Whatever happened to her ship, it's driven her to the edge."

"And over," Kaminski added.

"She'll do it," Martinez said, turning away from the communicator with his hands to his head. "*Madre de Dios*. She will do this."

"Not while I'm still standing," I said, definitively. "Can we make transition back into the simulants on Devonia?"

I thought of Elena and the survivors. When we extracted, my sim would've collapsed without explanation. There was small consolation in the fact that at least Elena knew sims and how they operated.

Loeb gave a tired shake of his head. "Dr Serova says that's not possible. Something to do with the neural-link, the exotic particulate that the Abyss is currently emitting."

The explanation didn't matter to me. Solutions: those were what I needed. "Then we go back to Devonia in new skins." I nodded over at Lieutenant James, standing at the other end of the tac. "Prep the second Dragonfly."

"I'm on it," said James.

I felt every day of my forty-five years as I stepped back from the console.

"Into the tanks," I ordered.

Minutes later, the simulants armed, the transition done, the second Dragonfly gunship scorched across Devonian space. Any pretence of stealth was now abandoned in favour of raw speed: determination to reach Devonia in as short a period as possible.

In a simulant body as new as the day it had been cloned, I thought-linked to the gunship's outer view-cams.

"I'm sure that there weren't this many ships when we

were last up here," Mason said, her face deathly serious. "Where did they all come from?"

The Krell were reaching critical mass. Immense bio-ships were undocking from the orbital stations. Shoals of Needlers and Stingrays polluted the space lanes like clouds of chaff. The flicker and flash of bio-energy discharge filled the vista.

"Out-system, I guess," Jenkins said. "Looks like the Krell are calling everything in this sector to Devonia."

Martinez grunted. "They're expecting something big, that's for sure."

"And for once," Kaminski said, his voice dipping into his native Brooklyn accent, "it ain't us."

"Then they're going to be surprised," I said, with a confidence that I didn't feel.

"You sure you want to take that in with you?" Kaminski asked Mason. "You do know that it won't be coming back."

She had the mono-sword – the weapon that she had scavenged from a dead Directorate commando, her trophy from Damascus – strapped across her back, attached to her combat-webbing. The hilt of the powered sword protruded above her tactical helmet.

"I don't care," she said. "It's back-up."

"Cut the chatter," I said. "How long until we reach the objective, James?"

The flyboy had plotted the coordinates based on our last extraction, triangulating the location of the *Ark Angel* from our rec to the surface.

"Three minutes," James said. "Provided we don't meet any resistance—"

The Dragonfly banked sharply, avoiding a tightly formed squadron of Needlers that speared our flightpath. The bone-like ships corrected their vector, adopted a descent pattern towards the surface.

"I can't let that one go," James said. "Hold tight, folks. Applying offensive measures—"

"No!" I ordered.

I thought-commanded the Dragonfly's weapons to cease-fire, applying my suit's command-override codes. James jabbed ineffectually at his fire-controls, but the gunship did not respond.

"Don't fire on the Krell," I said. "Not unless we absolutely have to."

The Needlers disappeared from our scanner-range, taking no action against us. Indeed, the Krell were ignoring us completely. The Collective's bio-ships and fighter-shoals were either heading towards the surface, or arraigned against the Abyss.

James exhaled slowly. "Affirmative, Lazarus. I hope that you know what you're doing."

"I never do, James," I said, "but winging it has got me this far. Once we're dirtside, priority is to evac those survivors." *To get Elena out of there*, I thought. I glared at the back of James' head, at his aviator-helmet. "I mean it. Don't even think of leaving them behind."

"I won't let you down," he said.

"Legion, we will deploy into the Shard ruins and track Kyung's forces." The squad nodded. I activated the comm-link back to the *Colossus*, now thousands of klicks behind us, still in orbit around the Devonian moon. "This is Lazarus Actual. Loeb, do you read me?"

"I copy," came Loeb's voice, "but your signal is weak."

"Then I'll keep this short. As soon as James has the survivors, he will lift off and return to the *Colossus*. I want you to remain on-site until I give the order."

"Affirmative," Loeb said, his voice echoing through the void.

Layered beneath the transmission, a sound within a sound, something else was present. A distant, pitched whining: a crescendo of white noise. *The Artefact's signal.* Had it already started? Had Kyung already activated the Shard transmitter? Despite the intensely uncomfortable psychic itch at the back of my hindbrain, it did not feel like that was the case. This was the preamble, the aching urge of the alien machine to make contact. What came next: that would be so much worse.

"Keep the engines hot, and ensure that the *Colossus'* AI is still live. Lazarus out."

"*Colossus* ou—" Loeb started. His voice was consumed in a poisonous squall of static.

The Dragonfly's flightpath dropped.

"Commencing atmosphere breach," James declared.

We all held tight as the Dragonfly fell to Devonia.

CHAPTER TWENTY-FIVE

THE ARTEFACT

Amid a swirl of dust and plant-matter, the Dragonfly engaged VTOL engines.

"Holy shit," James said. "This is some serious voodoo."

Unlike the last time we had dropped, now the Dragonfly skated low over the landscape. The green jungles and swamps were a desiccated brown, more of the black rock revealed beneath the seabed. Some surface features were toppling in on themselves – mountains crumbling beneath the shifting alien topography.

"Christo only knows what that is . . ." said Kaminski, pointing ahead.

The Maze – where James had originally landed – had become a network of alien glyphs: light spilling from the geometric forms out into space. Much of the rock structures, what I had assumed to be evidence of old volcanic activity, had been exposed as parts of the enormous Artefact world-engine. It was the heart of Devonia; a black cluster that formed the eye of the storm.

The Dragonfly's engines shifted in pitch as we hit turbulence, wind and rain lashing the outer hull.

"Approaching coordinates," James said. "Looks like they're expecting us."

A single red light arced across the horizon: a flare fired from somewhere inside the Maze. Military-grade – the type our battle-suits had been equipped with. It could only be Elena, using the equipment that the Legion had left behind on extraction.

"Go," I said. "Follow the flare, and put us down there."

Jenkins and Kaminski manned the door-mounted assault cannons, as James dropped the Dragonfly into the Maze. I opened the gunship's rear deployment ramp and clung to the safety rigging.

Much of the jungle had been flattened now, trees thrashing in the increasing wind, becoming a living sea. The sky strobed with lightning, reflecting off the *Ark Angel*'s tarnished hull. She had been revealed by the changed weather patterns, part of her space frame tilting as the ravine-wall into which she'd crashed had come tumbling down.

Beneath us, coming up fast, I saw the survivors emerging from the jungle.

Please let her be safe . . .

A wind-whipped figure became visible. I activated my tactical-helmet magnification, and zoomed in . . . *Elena*. Like the survivors of some great flood, she and the remaining *Endeavour* crew had climbed atop the *Angel*'s hull: an island amid the increasing chaos. They had salvaged whatever weaponry and other equipment they could.

The Dragonfly still hovering twenty metres above the ground, I leapt from the ramp. The thruster pack on my Ares suit activated and I glided to Elena's group.

Elena vaulted across the wet hull; came to greet me. She

399

carried a prism-gun and kept both hands on her the weapon, but her expression softened behind her face-plate. Our helmets touched, enabling suit-to-suit communication through the armour.

"*Mon chérie!* I thought that I had lost you."

The wind swirling around us, two impossible lovers within a universe at war, I returned her smile.

"I'm never going to let you go," I said.

"The Directorate are here," she said. "We saw their ships. I thought that they had taken you!"

"They fired on the *Colossus*, and we've suffered some damage." I paused, because saying the words made this all the more real. "The Directorate have a mothership in orbit, and she's sent dropships to the surface. They have ground forces down here."

Elena nodded. "They have invaded the Shard ruins."

"The Legion has to go after them," I said. "We're going to finish this."

There was no question of Elena coming with us, and she didn't even argue with me. "Be careful out there, Conrad. Remember that I'm waiting for you."

"I won't forget. Get aboard the transport; it will take you to the *Colossus*. Anything happens at base, pull me out. Don't try to handle it on your own."

Elena didn't answer. I knew that, if it came to it, she would risk her own life – maybe even mine – to finish what had been started out here.

"We'll be fine," she said, eventually. "The Krell are tied up with the Directorate."

"It isn't the Krell or the Directorate I'm worried about."

Elena's smile faded: became more bitter than sweet. "I know." She swallowed, uncomfortable suddenly. "Take care, *mon chérie*."

We butted heads one last time: helmet to helmet so that our faces were almost touching.

"See you on the other side," I said.

"I love you," Elena replied.

Sending out a wave of debris and heat, the Dragonfly touched down beside the *Angel*'s wreck. The Legion smoothly deployed out of the gunship. There was a changing of the guard: the survivors – ragged, tired and exhausted from a decade of guardianship of Devonia and the Artefact – began to board. James urged them on, his voice barely audible above the groan of the shifting landscape and the rising pitch of the wind. Commander Cook, also buttoned up in full armour, gave a salute as he went.

The Legion fired thruster packs to stand beside me. Covered the clutch of survivors as they mounted the gunship.

Elena clambered down the curved hull of the *Angel*, and ran for the Dragonfly. She waited as the rest of the group boarded, then tossed her prism-gun inside the waiting passenger cab. She paused at the hatch, grappling the safety rigging. The expression on her face was endlessly sorrowful.

"Like I said: I saw you on Calico. But I couldn't turn back to look at you. I couldn't bring myself to say goodbye."

I nodded. "Maybe you can now."

Elena gave a sad drop of her hand, an impression of a wave, as the Dragonfly lifted off, engines glowing blue. The ship gained speed and altitude, VTOL units snapping to the nacelles. Became a blue smear against the black.

"Good journey," Kaminski said, to no one in particular.

"I hope they make it," said Jenkins.

By now, the clouds were pressing low on the jungle: big, black, constantly shifting. There was no sun any more: only the Arkonus Abyss, charging with new life. It looked very much like one of the Shard glyphs: enormous and oppressive, claiming custody of this world. I looked towards the crumbling canyon, in the direction of the Shard ruins Elena had shown us. Like the rest of Devonia, the canyon was reconfiguring. Structures emerged from the walls at improbable angles, and it felt like gravity was throbbing all around me.

"We go in that direction," I said. "On the double, full thrust. We've got a lot of ground to cover."

"Are we going to die in there?" Mason asked me.

"Almost certainly," I said. "But it's how you die that counts."

Kaminski sucked his teeth, the sound sharp over the comm-net. "I think that Mason should stop asking so many questions."

"We can agree on that," I said.

"At least you called me Mason. It's better than New Girl."

Kaminski sniggered, and we bounced off in the direction of the Shard ruins.

"Area appears to have suffered extensive ecophagy," I whispered, into my tactical helmet. "The jungle is dying at an increasing rate. All biological material appears to be suffering from exposure to the Shard technology."

"And it's cold," Mason added, "so cold."

The armour was recording everything we said, did and saw: likely for posterity alone, as we couldn't make uplink to the *Colossus*. I doubted that anything could, with the squall of static and screaming white noise that the structures around us were generating. Every band was choked with feedback, the residue of the Artefact's song—

I paused. Held up a gloved hand, watched as tiny black dots danced across my battle-suit: things that I had mistaken for simple ash. They were so much worse than that, I realised.

The black things probed every weakness of the suit, but quickly gave up, flying off towards easier targets. The stuff was self-replicating, creating copies of itself as it consumed the world around us. That seemed to be its primary purpose.

The same as any other living organism, machine or organic.

Martinez was praying under his breath, his comm-link open so that we could all hear his ragged, detached voice.

"We can do without the Hail Marys, Venus," 'Ski muttered.

"You'll thank me later," Martinez said. "I'm doing this for all of us. It's protection."

"Leave him," Jenkins said.

Mason sighed. "Maybe it'll even help."

"Everyone stay on internal atmosphere supplies," I ordered. "The shit in the air isn't natural."

"It's the Creep," Martinez said. "It's what's killing this planet."

"But it isn't getting into our suits," Mason added. "Which has to be something."

I didn't know how long that would last. Even in a sim I knew that we were living on borrowed time. I wondered how many of the things I'd already ingested, were already trying to break down my simulated skin and bones—

A tertiary-form erupted from a dead tree. The enormous Krell was already half-consumed by the swarm; face a blackened mess of bony protrusions, one eye sagging in its socket: a victim of the ultimate anti-organic WMD. The xeno paused, looked me up and down. Instinctively, I armed the flamer on my right gauntlet. Readied to fire it at the fish head.

Two, three, four more of the xenos emerged from the nest.

The Legion fell into defensive pattern around me.

But the Krell did not attack us.

"Wait . . ." I ordered.

Rifles up and ready to shoot, the Legion did as ordered. I slowly backed away – eyes still on the Krell – and my squad copied.

"Our fight isn't with them," I said. "Not now."

The Krell twitched its head at an opening within the canyon wall, a passageway into the Artefact itself.

They know that this isn't about us any more.

The dying tertiary-form bared its teeth at me, and I saw that its hide was stitched with scars: intricate flesh-brands that looked almost ritualistic. *I've seen those before.* On Capa V, on the bodies of the Krell prisoners.

"Kyung is down there," I said. "That's where we're heading."

The entrance led further, deeper into the Shard necropolis: a corridor that ended with a portal-style hatch, much bigger than even the Ares suits. It was sealed, but light danced around the runic impressions that circled it, inviting activation.

"You ever wonder what the Shard look like?" Mason asked me. "Not the Reaper, but the real Shard?"

"I think that we might be about to find out," I said, and touched the glyphs around the door.

The portal contracted into the wall, and we entered a vast, open expanse: a chamber that demonstrated the antiquity of the Artefact, of the Shard themselves. A series of pillars stretched ahead of me, forming a processional column. Every surface was covered in Shard cuneiform that glittered with soft blue and green light: threw the space in a disorienting semi-illumination. Something enormous sat at the head of that column – a shadow rising above the floor of the chamber, reaching the distant roof above.

The Legion cautiously deployed into the chamber, weapons trained on the deep shadows around us. Strange, how this place seemed almost untouched by the chaos erupting across the rest of the planet. Targeting acquisition data fluctuated across my HUD, the AI unable to fix on a solid target. Effigies of things that I couldn't look at, couldn't even begin to describe, had been cast from black rock: grew from the walls. Everything had sharp, otherworldly angles. Crystalline structures sprouted from the centre of the chamber, and those were all aimed at the head: at the enormous shadow that was mounted there. I swallowed as I looked in that direction. The place reminded me not so much of a location with any technological purpose, more of a temple. A temple to dark and angry gods. I had the overwhelming urge to bow down to the inert creation, to worship it.

"What is that thing?" Jenkins asked.

"I don't care what it is," Martinez said. "I only need to know where Kyung is."

"I hear the man," Kaminski said. "My trigger-finger is getting tetchy—"

The structure breathed around us, and the dark exploded.

A spidery, fluid shape was on Jenkins.

It slammed into her, and over the comm-link she released a pained yelp. Before she could bring up her plasma rifle, fire at the monstrous shape, she was thrown backwards against one of the Shard pillars: pinned to the metalwork by two knife-tipped forelimbs.

In frenzied snapshots, I saw that the shape had pierced her armour at the shoulders – gone all the way through the plating. Her face, underlit by the bulb inside her helmet, was a ragged snarl, blood and spittle lining the interior of her face-plate.

"Into cover, then take it down!" I yelled over the comm-link. The network was degenerating into a hateful miasma of whispers, of voices calling out to me to *just give up*—

The spider-shape twisted about, flung Jenkins' bleeding body aside. Dead, she was a heavy weight, and her armoured corpse hit a Shard machine, shattering stonework and metal—

Four plasma rifles began to fire on full-auto.

A null-shield lit where our plasma fire hit: a blue cage of energy that threw shadows across the chamber.

This is not Shard tech, I realised. *This is something else.*

The shape moved fast. Feet skittered across the hard floor like knife-tips on metal. It was an arachnophobe's worst nightmare.

Something I know.

We chased it with plasma fire, and as the machine passed before me I caught sight of a unit badge emblazoned on the hull.

Kaminski rolled over out of cover. *Damn it.* He always was a hot-head. Maybe he'd seen the same as me, reached the same conclusion.

"You killed them all!" came a scream, hissing with static: a voice broadcast over an amplified speaker rig, driven to distortion by extreme volume.

The shape was on Kaminski next. He fired a grenade at it – scored a direct hit – and the hi-ex round exploded against the null-shield.

It was neither Krell nor Shard, but instead an adapted Spider MMR, salvaged from Calico Base. Driven by someone we had all hoped was dead, even if none of us actually believed it.

"Get down!" I ordered. "Stay in cover!"

I was sure, now, that Kaminski had seen the Spider's pilot too, because he wouldn't listen to me. He fired one-handed with his plasma rifle, pulses lighting the null-shield again and again.

The machine stomped on through the onslaught, and Captain Williams came into full view. Hunched inside the driver cab of the Spider. A machine designed for mining, this example bristled with armaments: a couple of rocket pods on the shoulders, a grenade launcher mounted on one arm, a multi-barrelled kinetic cannon on the other. Seeing as how he had tossed Jenkins' body aside, I predicted that the man-amp had been over-charged as well.

"Sweet girl," Williams said, gazing over at Jenkins' body, weathering the plasma storm. "She never could let go, though."

Kaminski lost it. He closed the distance between Williams and him lightning fast, roaring a battle cry as he went.

Williams also moved fast, into the middle of the chamber. If Williams knew fear – if he suspected that he might die in here – he hardly showed it. He leapt across the room, onto Kaminski. The MMR was a multi-ton mech; a loco-motive that would not be stopped. As the two collided – sim and Spider – I heard and saw Kaminski's armour splitting; his bio-signs plummeting. It was worse than a wasted gesture, and Kaminski was gone. Kaminski's body and rifle disap-peared beneath the Spider's bulk. There was nothing the medi-suite could do to help him.

"Then there were three . . ." Williams said.

Williams was now so close that I could see his face through the canopy, and I realised that he was not simulated this time: he was the real deal. Identifiable by the tattoos over his cheeks, the jewellery dangling at his ear . . . and those *eyes*. Madness and rage dwelt there –

THREAT DETECTED, my suit AI warned. TAKE EVASIVE ACTION.

A high-pitched whine filled the chamber; the echo of a single round being fired from somewhere above us. *Sniper rifle.* My HUD suggested possible shooter locations on the gantries or walkways, hiding places all around the room. The anti-shield round – cutting edge by Alliance standards – scythed through my shield with ease. Hit my leg, the join between armoured plates. I stumbled forward. Even with my simulated body being flooded with analgesics and endorphins, it was hard to ignore the pain.

CRITICAL DAMAGE DETECTED, my HUD told me. Impossibly, the armour hadn't breached – for now, I was still protected from the Creep – but I couldn't take another shot like that.

Suddenly the rest of the chamber became filled with threat warnings. Multiple shooters, positioned around the chamber. Some above, nestled into the bizarre Shard architecture, others well-hidden behind awakening Shard machinery.

Williams paused in his MMR. The machine heaved up and down, never at rest: like it was breathing, ready to pounce again.

"Williams . . ." I said. "So good to see you."

"This is the end of the line, Lazarus."

"No, it isn't. Not until I say so."

In hardcopy, he was leaner, wearing a black Directorate Sword uniform. Despite myself, despite the gunshot injury, that caused a stir of anger in me. An Alliance traitor, wearing the uniform of the Asiatic Directorate. His blond hair was shaved close to his scalp, which was pocked by two chemical-inducers: metal studs used to trigger drug inducements.

"You killed them," Williams repeated. He cycled up the assault cannon attached to the Spider's body, multiple-barrels spinning in readiness to fire. "You killed the Warfighters on Calico."

Directorate Sword commandos filtered into the chamber, crunching wreckage under booted feet. Ten mag-rifles were aimed at me: laser-dots dancing over my damaged armour. My suit tracked the group as they circled around behind me.

"Actually," Martinez shouted, his voice echoing around the chamber, "that was me."

Williams' face twitched. One side was claimed by a tattoo – a manic barcode that may or may not have had some purpose other than decoration.

Martinez had begun to climb among the Shard machinery, using the battle-suit's strength-aug to his advantage, his camo-field activated so that he was more difficult to track. Despite his armour, he moved fast. He fired off a volley of grenades into the room, sharp frag littering the area.

"Aim for the cabin!" I yelled.

"On it," Mason called back.

We moved as a team, plasma fire pattering against the heavy null-shield. Whatever tech the machine was carrying, it was impressive: the shield was capable of dispersing a direct plasma round, absorbing the charge.

The Spider swivelled at the waist, its heavy assault cannon indiscriminately spraying the walls. Dust and debris were thrown up into the air. The Swords' gunfire slowed, became even more erratic: panicked—

Martinez's body slid down the wall. Chewed up by assault-cannon rounds, his life-signs extinguished.

And then there were two.

Without warning, the Spider twisted about-face and lurched towards Mason. She rolled aside, flung her rifle behind her.

"Get out of its path!" I shouted, as the machine bore down on her.

"I've been saving a special something for you, Mason," he yelled. "Payback for the *Colossus*."

He fired at Mason. Her armour was taking hits at a terrifying rate.

Despite my order, she stood ground and unsheathed the mono-sword at her belt. The blade lit, blue-white lightning playing across the cutting edge, and she tested the weight.

I kept firing, moving up on the Spider. Williams seemed almost absorbed in the moment. His every attention was focused on Mason—

"Fuck you and your payback!" she shouted, running forward.

Then she was under the shield, within killing range of Williams.

He grunted in surprise as Mason's armoured body collided with his. Her blade swiped back and forth, in a frenzied arc—

The Swords closed around us. More anti-shield rounds rained down on the chamber, forced me back into cover. Something *pranged* off my armour plating.

"That's harder than it looks, isn't it?" Williams yelled at Mason.

Still beneath Williams' null-shield, dodging the Spider's many legs, she ran at him again. The blade swiped up, monofilament edge leaving a trail of sparks. Sliced against Williams' outer canopy—

And bounced off.

The armour-glass breached, fractured, but held.

Mason dropped the sword, collapsed into the waiting claws of the Spider MMR. She struggled against the machine. Williams split her face with a blow from the Spider's claw, then deployed a laser mandible from the machine's main body.

What was left of Mason, sans head, collapsed to the middle of the room.

Then there was one.

I dashed back into cover. Gunfire was everywhere: more and more of the temple collapsing around me.

Williams saw me move. I rolled aside, just a little too slowly . . .

He slammed an enormous mechanical foot down on my right hand. The walker was several tons of solid metal and weaponry; not even my battle-suit could withstand that sort of weight. The armour crunched as it took the stress. My right hand exploded with pain, my med-suite struggling to control the agony that erupted there.

"I got the other hand on the *Colossus*," Williams said, leering at me.

I was pinned to the ground.

The missile pods on my shoulders swivelled to face him, but ERROR flashed across my HUD. Something must've been damaged during the fight; the weapons wouldn't respond.

"What are you waiting for, Lazarus?" he snarled. "Aren't you going to fight back? I expected more from an old war hero."

"You're not looking so young yourself, these days," I said.

Williams' loomed over the machine's controls, bobbing inside the cabin. "I can give you their names. Every one of them a good man and woman. And you killed them, in their fucking tanks!"

"You're a lackey," I said. "Nothing more."

Williams' face was flushed red with utter, utter rage. "You've really fucked things up for me," he said. He shook his head, the machine's legs dancing restlessly like he was trying to dispel that anger. It wasn't working. "You are one big fucking pain in the ass, Harris. The op in Damascus? I was going to make out like a bandit!"

"It was your deal with the devil."

"They wanted the simulant technology, and they wanted the *Endeavour*. I could've given them both!"

Another figure advanced through the dark.

Director-Admiral Kyung stood at the head of the chamber. Shorter than the other soldiers, wearing vac-rated ghost-plate: a type of Special Operations armour that hadn't been in service for a long time. The plating was equipped with an active camo-field that swirled as she moved, reflecting the Shard glyphs around her.

Seeing this construct up close: it triggered the deep hurt.

"What are you doing here?" Kyung asked me. "You were warned to leave."

"That's what I've been asking him," Williams said. "Bastard got no right . . ."

"Shut up," Kyung said, never taking her eyes off mine.

"Of course, Admiral," Williams said. "It's your show."

The chamber began to shudder around me, but Kyung's face betrayed no emotion. Even inside the ghost-plate, she was much smaller than the surrounding troopers.

"How's the *Shanghai* doing?" I asked, as glibly as I could.

"Well enough," she said, but her words didn't match her reaction: she visibly winced.

"It wasn't last time I looked, and I think you know that, Assassin."

"You keep calling me that," Kyung said. "Did you lose someone, I wonder, on Thebe? A brother, a sister, a parent?"

I am going to kill this woman, I reassured myself. *If not in this life, then the next.*

"I take no pleasure in the name, Colonel Harris. Jupiter

Outpost – Thebe – means nothing compared to what we can achieve out here. This place: this is where real change will be made. We know what the *Revenant* is. We know what it is capable of."

"None of this is going to matter," I said, "because you're going to die out here."

She snapped her head around in Williams' direction; made a sudden decision. "Hold him."

"Of course," Williams said, raising the Spider's forelimbs. "Do I get to kill him yet? I've been dreaming about this, man. And let me tell you: since Damascus, I've been having some seriously *bad* dreams . . ."

He turned his attention on me again. Scooped my armour up with a manipulator; the two-pronged metal claw clasped around my neck guard. The Ares armour was heavy, but even that squealed and deformed under the pressure. The claw began to close on my neck . . .

Head down, Kyung marched across the chamber. Two of her troopers carried a black armoured case, the lid open. Something all too familiar sat inside: the Shard Key. It blazed with energy, glowing and pulsing and offering a universe of destruction. The Swords set it down in front of the effigy, moved back from the box as though frightened of the contents. Kyung looked up at the statue that towered over her, hands clasped behind her back.

"So this is the Shard?" she asked. "They went by many names. Some species referred to them as the 'Dwellers in the Dark', others the 'Machine-Mind'. I am quite partial to the name that Species 134 referred to them as: 'the Ones who do not Care'." More sparkling across her face: more damage to the *Shanghai* in high orbit? Or were the Shard, somehow, trying to communicate with her crippled bio-machine of a mind? "The Shard is a species that knows only war; that can claim responsibility for the extinction of hundreds of sentient races."

Williams' claw tightened some more.

Kyung inspected the control consoles. "Dr Kellerman's research was quite specific on the activation protocols," Kyung said. The room around us was buzzing with activity. "His death was a loss to the Directorate scientific mission, but the activation of the Shard technology is surprisingly simple." She lifted the Key from its case, held it up.

"You'll doom us all!" I managed.

"Just shut the fuck up," Williams said, "and let the lady work, then we can all get out of here."

Kyung stood with her back to me. "It's almost as if the machine wants to be activated . . ."

Very carefully and precisely, she inserted the Key into a throbbing portal on one of the consoles.

Time seemed to stop.

Kyung stood in front of the machine. I dangled on the end of Williams' claw, eyes darting to the control console, mere metres from my position. The Directorate troops had emerged from their hiding places and were frozen, watching the shadows around us.

"Did it work—?" Williams started.

Then the signal exploded in my mind, and an enormous wave of blue light poured from the Shard statue: the cries of a million machine-minds freed at last.

Still holding me tight around the neck, Williams' mech locked. He frowned as he tried to deliver the final twist of his claw, but the Spider did not respond.

The air was filled with data – with crackling streams of information that coursed through my mind and soul. Shard glyphs spiralled all around me, igniting the air. Machines that had not spoken for millennia, that had forgotten that they even had a voice, screamed into the void. As a human, even a simulated one, I could hear only a fraction of their cry. That was more than enough: to be in the heart of that deluge of machine-code was almost crippling.

I couldn't see it, but I knew that the Arkonus Abyss had activated.

Kyung raised a hand to her face, stumbled back from the control bank.

Shard control consoles rose from the deck, following assembly routines that had been long dormant. Vibrations spread through the artificial ground. The entire chamber quaked. Lesser components of the temple broke off, chunks of the ceiling raining down on us. Directorate troops darted to and fro, using the improved mobility of their exo-suits to escape the rockfall.

"Here we fucking go, man!" Williams yelled over his external speakers. His words sat uneasily with the tone of his voice: manic, verging on terror. "This is the *shit*!"

The roof split apart. Metal ground against metal, sending nerve-jangling echoes around the shafts. The deck beneath me was rising up, moving faster and faster. The platform on which Kyung had stood, together with her entourage, moved away from us – leaving Williams and me.

The structure rose for several seconds, like an elevator in a shaft, then the process stopped with a jolt. We were on the surface of Devonia, among the raised elements of the Maze. The sky was visible now, a billowing sheet of cloud cover, black and terrible, stretching into infinity. Searing beams of light speared the sky.

I swallowed back fear of failure: the idea that the universe was going to end on my watch . . . *How long will it take for the* Revenant *to get here?* I asked myself.

There was a terrible grandeur to what we were witnessing, and even Williams paused to take it in. The landscape around us had warped and the Maze was pocked with numerous raised platforms like that Williams and I found ourselves on. Each edifice was a hundred or so metres above the highest points of the canyons, too far for even an armoured simulant to survive the drop.

"She's done it!" Williams jeered. "This is going to end what you started a long, long time ago—"

His mech was crackling with blue energy, sending off sheets of electrical feedback. He fought to control the machine as it was subverted by Shard machine-code.

"Damn it!" he yelped.

The manipulator claw jerked open and dropped me. The platform beneath us rocked, and the Spider – Williams still struggling to control the rebellious mech – stumbled away from me. I landed on my feet. My armour was experiencing the same difficulty, but I had the strength to correct and control it. I shook my neck, released from the agony that Williams had caused.

I couldn't leave without seeing to him, without finishing him for real. I raised my right arm – extended it to arm the flamethrower – but bright warning lights flashed over my wrist-comp. The armour plating around the weapon was deformed, smashed out of shape. Williams must've damaged it in the temple.

He saw my reaction as well. Stomped towards me. I backed away. A blistering wind, powerful enough to shake even my Ares armour, scoured over me and through the Maze.

The entire weight of the Spider collided with me, and I hit one of the Shard consoles. It crumbled beneath me, but slowed my progress: I skidded to a halt mere metres from the edge of the platform. The chest panel of my armour was crumpled, and the collision was strong enough to knock the air from my lungs.

The Shard control console immediately began to repair itself. It rippled with energy as it regenerated, glyphs lighting along the various panels—

The Reapers.

I saw them from the edge of my eye: saw flickers of energy playing over them. They were still, not activated, but I sensed something about them. Williams clumsily circled me, brushing so damned close to the dark metal machines . . .

I thought fast.

Williams was gaining speed now, crossing the platform again—

I rolled sideways. Grappled with my plasma pistol, unholstered it—

—Williams swivelled, his face a mask of hate inside the machine cockpit, fingers braced on the firing studs of his assault cannon—

"Too slow, old man!" he shouted.

—I fired the plasma pistol at the nearest platform—

It hit the Reaper statue full on. Williams' leering face remained fixed, unable to comprehend anything other than my destruction. The Reaper began to ripple. Williams saw the motion too, and turned to face the activating machine.

Suddenly, there was a bigger threat out here than me. A strand of shadow suddenly shot from the nearest pedestal. Wrapped around one of the Spider's legs.

"What the fuck are you doing?" he screamed at me.

The Spider stomped to get free. Servos whined in protest.

First one, then two, then three shadows were on him. Black metal wrapped around the mech's legs, body, torso. For their size, the Reapers were immensely strong. Armour plating deformed, then ruptured, as force was applied to it.

Williams struggled with his assault cannon, tried to aim it at me. Rounds haphazardly stitched the area, impotent against the Shard machines.

I stood, watched the things taking him apart.

"I am—" I started.

"Let me guess," Williams roared, his speakers at maximum amplification. When he spoke, spittle lined the inside of the mech's canopy. "I am Lazarus?"

He raised his right arm – the mech responding in kind. There was a flamethrower attached to it, the pilot light already lit. He punched the firing stud: ignited the air in a plume of white flame. The nearest Reaper was consumed by fire, but that didn't stop it.

The Spider was crippled. It collapsed sideways, torn apart by a flurry of Reaper stabs and slashes. The pilot cabin, set into the torso, was being consumed by a mass of black metal. Any thought that Williams was safe inside was quickly dispelled. The fracture that Mason had caused with her mono-sword expanded, and the black plague began to seep inside.

The Creep had found another organic target.

"And you are dead," I completed.

The mech suit vanished beneath the tide of roiling shadow, and Captain Williams was finally finished.

The nearest shadow advanced on me, and I readied for an attack from the Reapers. But it never came. Their work done, I watched as they simply dissolved. The living metal just crumbled, was rapidly thrown to the wind. They became the nanophage: the Creep that was engulfing Devonia. All aspects of the Shard machine, working towards the same goal.

I turned, activated my EVA thruster pack.

Out there, on the horizon, was a titan-sized structure:

something so big that it almost touched the sky. A beam of light poured from the flattened tip.

Kyung is up there.

Even if I couldn't stop her, I was going to die trying.

CHAPTER TWENTY-SIX

KYUNG

Come on, come on! I urged myself. *I have to stop that beacon.*

The Krell were everywhere. The Shard were here to destroy their very habitat: there was no point in retreating, in trying to defend against the onslaught. They poured from the coral hives, from the destroyed trees. Bounded across the dead jungle.

I joined them, bouncing onwards with my battle-suit's enhanced-mobility pack firing regularly: making speed on the platform. Soon, a hundred Krell were at my back. Racing as a tide, as a bloody-minded swarm lurching up the side of the structure: crushing each other in a collective wish to reach the summit. As many Krell bodies were strewn across the jungle floor as consumed by the Shard swarm.

I looked up at the immense distance I had to clear. The range-finder on my wrist-comp – unreliable, but the best guess I had in the circumstances – suggested that the structure was already a kilometre tall, and still rising. I was never going to make it using my thruster.

Then I looked back at the Krell, at the seething mass of alien bodies moving up the side of the structure.

"I don't have a choice," I declared to myself.

I vaulted up the side of the structure, and clambered on top of the Krell assault force, joining them in the attack. If I could reach the summit, I could stop the beacon. That was the source of the transmission into Shard Space. If I could silence it, maybe I could stop this.

The Krell numbers swelled with each second. The tsunami we'd encountered in the swamp? That was nothing compared to the number of bodies gathered at the foot of the platform. Soon there were thousands of them, clambering over each other, clawing up the smooth black sides of the structure. Bodies on bodies, they were slowly but surely reaching the top. Already, some were collapsing back down to the jungle floor. Already, more were struggling to get up there. When the black tide reached them – wracked their organic bodies with phage, consumed them with shadow – more took their place.

The Krell were in a rabid state. They barely noticed me, and took no hostile action against me at all. I climbed with them, firing my thruster in short bursts, using the strength-augmentation of the Ares suit to vertically clear the distance.

I reached the tip of the Krell's attack force. The xenos there were ragged, skelctal shapes: almost completely scoured by the Shard Creep. The air at the peak was thick with nanotech; the Krell warriors were stripped rapidly, and many fell from their position in the column. I grappled onto some, but their strength was waning. More and more, I was relying on the thruster pack in my suit.

Don't look down, I insisted, as I hauled myself over the lip of the platform.

The world around me had irrevocably changed. The sky

was a bitter green glow now, the underside of the clouds skated with fire. Buffeted by winds that bore ash and phage, I stood on the edge of the structure: surveyed the dead world that had been Devonia. There were several black structures, just like the one that I was standing on, now pocking the surface of the planet. Enormous black edifices, cast of shadow, each flickering with pent-up energy.

Director-Admiral Kyung stood in front of a control console, the Shard Key in her hands, in the centre of the platform. Surrounded by a dozen or so Directorate Swords, weapons trained on the platform edges.

As I saw Kyung's ravaged condition, questions fired through my tired mind. *What did the Shard think of her?* I wondered. She was a thing both woman and machine – a cyborg entity. Organic, to be consumed, but machine, to be assimilated. She would be forever linked to the *Shanghai Remembered*. To me, the practice of mind-slaving a captain and her ship sounded despicable and inhumane, but the results spoke for themselves. She was the ship, and the ship was her. Even down on the surface, she was no doubt in regular comms with the *Shanghai*.

I wondered what state the *Shanghai* was in now. Was the ship's AI feeling her pain, struggling to interpret a plethora of new data-streams that no human mind should ever endure?

The camo-field projected by Kyung's ghost-plate had malfunctioned, and still broadcast myriad Shard symbology, glowing white-hot as though she had been branded all over. Her face-plate was damaged too, a nasty fracture webbing the plasglass, turning the plate transparent.

I unholstered my plasma pistol. Stalked towards her, close enough that I could see the hideous mess of her face. The lightshow under her skin had turned black, throbbing with new life, a crawling poison. Her lips were twisted into a grim smile; a bitter expression that suggested she had accepted that she wouldn't be getting out of this alive.

"I have done my task," she said. Her voice was distorted, just wrong. "It is finished."

I'd so far escaped discovery by the Directorate; this was my only chance. I aimed the plasma pistol at Kyung. My own suit was so badly damaged that I suspected I would end up the same way: consumed by the Shard Creep.

"We're all dead," I said, broadcasting over my battle-suit speakers. "But you're not taking her with you."

Elena. If all had gone to plan, she was in orbit around Devonia right now, planning our escape. But there could be no life for her if the *Revenant* broke through, if the Shard were allowed to spread their poisonous technology across the galaxy again—

The Directorate bodyguards closed around us, but with hesitancy. Laser sights were aimed at me, weapons trained in my direction. I flagged the Sword commandos: read their armaments and intentions. Heavy carbines. Wearing hard-suits with full exo outlays. Respirators, equipped for hostile environment ops: sealed, currently immune to the Creep. A wave of anxiety seemed to emanate from her troopers, although Kyung was oblivious. *They're scared of her.*

"I killed Williams," I said. Readied my plasma pistol, began to think about how best to do this. "He got what he deserved."

"No matter. His job was done."

When she spoke, her words resonated from the world around us: not from the twisted physical form in front of me.

I nodded at the nearest trooper. Said in Standard, "She tell you that you were going to be dying down here?"

The Sword looked back impassively. His or her helmet

423

was mirrored, only revealing the burning horizon of Devonia. But he didn't shoot, and that had to be something.

"You see now why we had to do this?" Kyung asked. "Why I *needed* to do this?"

"I don't much care," I said. "Unless you close that Gate, you'll have the blood of billions on your hands."

"It's too late for that," she said.

"No, it isn't."

Kyung's face was suddenly almost aflame with activity. The tracery of subdermal electronics flashed incandescently. She hunched over; looked like she might be sick.

One of the nearest soldiers lowered his rifle. For all their discipline, they were losing the will to fight. I couldn't say that I blamed them. They weren't sure about this.

"We can stop this," I said.

"We cannot be stopped," boomed the voice that was at once Kyung's but also something else: something that I had heard before. *Machine-code.* The Reaper's voice; the thing that had spoken to me on the Damascus Artefact. She was acting as a conduit for the Machine-Mind, for the Shard.

Shit. This was first contact. This was really happening.

The Arkonus Abyss blazed with new light overhead. The only functional sensor-suite left on my Ares suit began to chime with warnings. I was being saturated with radiation; enough that even the battle-suit was insufficient protection.

"What do you want with us?" I asked.

"This is our empire," Kyung said. "We are the Singularity."

The fracture in her face-plate had grown. From a hairline crack, it was now clearly visible. The woman inside the hard-suit had begun to look frightened, terror creeping across her features.

"If there is anything of Kyung left," I said, "know that the Directorate wouldn't want this. There is no arms race

424

here; there is no technology to be salvaged. There's only death."

I spread my arm out across the surface of Devonia, to encompass the dying world around me.

"We can use them," a voice implored, somewhat meekly. It sounded an awful lot like Kyung, fighting for escape with whatever was now occupying her armour. "They can be the ultimate ally!"

"Against who, Kyung? There won't be anyone left."

"I . . . I didn't fail at Damascus!" she implored. "Doing this – it will make everything right! I cannot leave here in failure, not again . . ."

"We have to stop this!" I yelled. Brought my plasma pistol up, aimed at the Shard console in front of her.

The commandos made their decision. Twelve rifles aimed at me: with my null-shield down, even in a battle-suit they could take me.

"It's too late," Kyung whispered, as she was consumed by the black metal: as she became whatever the Shard really were. Hesitation fled across what remained of her eyes, so fast that I almost missed it. "They are already here."

I fired.

The Kyung-thing moved faster than the real Kyung ever could.

She instantly shifted sideways, covered the console and the Key embedded into it. Caught the volley of plasma pulses that coursed the platform. I kept shooting, and a pulse hit her helmet. Her face-plate exploded outwards. The result wasn't what I was expecting: the woman staggered backwards but remained standing. Black mercury lapped at the remains of her hard-suit. She was changing—

Sim-fast, I dodged into cover, behind the nearest Shard structure.

Gunfire chased me, and hard rounds split the air, bouncing off the obsidian ground, but it was not directed at me. The Directorate Swords were firing on what Kyung had become. Their dedication had been sufficiently shaken that they would betray Kyung completely. *Crack-crack*, the rifles fired. One of the Swords hit Kyung, punched another hole through her hard-suit—

Kyung stumbled. Hands to her face. There was liquid pouring from her helmet. The stuff was also erupting from every seam of her suit, I realised, and enveloping the armour. Where the armour breached, wet metal tendrils lashed free.

Kyung rolled over. More rounds pierced her suit.

The Creep had got into her armour, had compromised her life support. Maybe she was especially prone to the contagion – being a machine-hybrid – or perhaps it was one of a hundred other possibilities. The reality was that a Reaper was birthing on the platform top – forming from the remains of Admiral Kyung.

More Directorate guns hit the body. The living metal sprayed, superheated, but instantly reformed. It threw out a spike of mercury in the direction of a Sword – effortlessly spearing the commando and tossing the corpse away, before the soldier had even considered responding – and circled another Shard structure.

The Shard control console was still operating. I could *feel* the Machine-Mind traversing Shard Space, moving to Devonia . . .

Then I saw them.

Nightmare-quiet things.

The Krell.

One by one, tertiary-forms and primary-forms were clambering onto the platform. They were wraiths: bodies destroyed by the Creep, bio-armour plating flapping wildly

426

in the wind. Individually, they were weakened and dying – such easy prey. But they were not individual.

Krell poured onto the platform, clambering over each other. A leader-form led the assault – had fared better from the storm than its brethren – and clutched at the dead and dying as cover. They fell on the Reaper with a hundred pairs of claws and talons.

As secondaries arrived at the summit bio-weapons were being fired into the thing as well. The Reaper fought back with abandon. It whirled about, moving so fast that it betrayed gravity and the rules of physics. It was a blur of activity, eviscerating Krell. Pure shadow, no shape whatsoever; then a million spikes, black fractals that were painful to look at.

And yet still they came.

A hundred on the peak one minute, then a thousand. I crept towards the edge of the platform, against the tide of bodies. *Holy Christo.* Columns of xenos had formed on every flank; were streaming from every direction.

Through the chaos of battle, I reached the console. Hands to the machine: to the Shard Key . . .

I was paralysed by the signal. It consumed me. The futility of human existence became overwhelming, disablingly apparent.

A trio of Krell Needlers passed my flank, dangerously near to the platform edge. They were flying full-throttle, nose down. I watched in a kind of hypnotic trance as the much smaller ships adopted an attack formation. Krell stinger-warheads slammed into the platform, sent bodies toppling over the edge—

Two Krell Needlers exploded, chased by silver lances.

Got to stop this!

A third Krell Needler flew closer, and began to erratically

jink. I saw the engine contrails flicker, thrusters cutting in and out. The ship was in trouble, even if the pilot didn't know it. A strand of black metal – tight and sharp as a spear – shot from the mêlée that enveloped the centre of the platform. With terrifying precision, the protrusion slammed into the Neelder's belly. It tore through bio-plating, into the guts of the ship.

I braced. Knew what was coming next. I grabbed for the Key—

The ship banked dangerously. Clipped the structure. Krell slipped, fell from the platform. The Needler was on fire, engines suddenly buzzing with the swarm—

The ship hit the platform and exploded.

My perspective shifted, and I sailed over the edge of the structure.

As I dropped, confident in the knowledge that the fall would kill me, I saw the Abyss overhead.

Reality split at the seams, and the *Revenant* came through.

CHAPTER TWENTY-SEVEN

NO COMING BACK

It would be so easy to sleep.
To sleep, and never get up.
To just let this happen.

I woke up in my simulator, surrounded by noise and activity.

The SOC was in a state of panic, but on a whole other level. The overhead lights flickered, power fluctuating, and white noise was being piped into my ear-bead. I tore that free, rested against the inside of the tank, and realised that the noise was also coming from the ship's PA: broadcast throughout the vessel.

The Shard are here.

With the noise came a cold that seared through me. Something more than just temperature: a soul-scathing chill. I struggled to breathe, forced air from the respirator into my lungs. My body shook, quaking in time with the rest of the ship, and gravity shifted around me.

Every limb burnt. Blazing welts – where the fall had just killed me – lined my body. Bright streamers of blood rose from wounds across my back, my chest, my face – wounds that should've been simulated.

Begrudgingly, the tank emptied, and as it did – in the flittering, unreal half-light – I saw Elena standing in front of me. She mashed her small fists against the outer canopy, her beautiful face stained red. The door slid open and amniotic fluid spilled onto the SOC floor.

"You're hurt!" Elena cried. "He's been injured!"

She dragged me from the tank, still trailing cables, and held me to her. Kissed me on the mouth: her lips invigorating, drawing me back to the now. I couldn't reciprocate, but then I couldn't do much. I was slick with both blood and amniotic: an adult newborn. Even the touch of her lips to mine was searing; sent ripples of pain through me. I slumped to the floor.

This was no normal extraction.

Elena sat on the deck of the SOC and cradled me in her arms. Dressed in a new *Colossus* crewsuit, deep blue now stained black by the simulator fluids.

"I . . . I made it," I said. "But I failed."

"That you made it is enough," she whispered. Her voice broke with emotion, and though it pained my eyes I focused on her face: saw tears rolling down her marble cheeks. "You tried, Conrad. You did what you could."

I felt the prick of a hypodermic on my forearm, the swell of medi-nano in my bloodstream. Dr Serova was beside me, taking readings – reeling off requests to the sci-med team. *None of this will do any good*, I thought. *Not if they are here.* Other faces swam into view around me: the Legion, Loeb, James.

"He's bleeding," Elena said. "This isn't normal! What's happening to him!"

Dr Serova shook her head. "I don't know! I've already told you people, I'm no expert on this technology!"

This was not the stigmata. This was something different, something more *real*. My data-ports – the connections in my limbs, chest, spine – were all wet with real, honest-to-god blood, and my chest was covered in lacerations. Whatever had happened to me down there on Devonia, I'd brought a little of it back with me. And a little of this pain: that was all I needed.

Hunt warned me of this.

"He's dead, and I'm not," I said, my voice garbled and defiant. "I'm fine." My vision was wavering, jumping. "Ky . . . Kyung: she did it."

"We know," Loeb said, his craggy features sullen, the weight of defeat on his brow. "It's over."

"No . . ." I insisted. I struggled to my feet, Elena's hands supporting me. That I could stand at all was a miracle. "It isn't until I say so."

A minute or so later, dressed but no more recovered from the ordeal on Devonia, we assembled in the CIC.

"This is it," Loeb declared. "Take it all in people: we're the ones here at the end."

Elena's arms were wrapped around me, keeping me upright. Her aura was like a beacon; despite our situation, her strength was somehow keeping me going. This was the first time in ten years that our real bodies had been together, I realised. So many near-misses, simulated meetings, and now here we were, watching the end of things.

"By Gaia," Saul whispered. "It's incredible."

"That's one word for it," Kaminski said.

The *Revenant* was in orbit around Devonia.

It was created from a substance so dark that it was the epitome of night – that it sucked in all available light, like the Artefacts. The Shard ship was enormous – much bigger than any of the Krell bio-ships in Devonian space, than even the *Colossus* – and only occasionally could I focus on it. The ship's outline was jagged, uncompromising: no bridge, no engine even – vaguely star-shaped, just layer upon layer of detail, sprawling and ramshackle and ancient. Reality seemed to warp around the vessel as it moved: gliding almost serenely through the destruction. A rock of calm among the madness.

The Krell had taken immediate offensive action.

Bio-ships swarmed the enormous Shard vessel, were peppering its hull with seeker missiles and more esoteric living ammunition. Occasionally, and with no regularity or frequency at all, did the underside of the ship light up with a nearby explosion. Then the ship's skin would ripple with runic impressions, as though the metal skein had a life of its own. Every surface was covered in Shard cuneiform, a billion lines of nightmarish hieroglyphics.

"I don't have any answers," Saul said.

"How can anyone answer that?" Elena said, her small shoulders sagging.

Saul nodded. "Whatever Command and Sci-Div thought they could achieve with this thing . . ." He gave a dry swallow. "They were wrong."

"What's it doing?" Mason asked.

"Always with the questions . . ." Jenkins muttered.

"It'll reap that planet," Elena said, flatly. "It'll scour Devonia until only the Artefact remains, and then it'll do what all living things do: replicate."

Professor Saul nodded, knowingly. "Yes, yes. I expect that the Creep, as Corporal Martinez calls it, will become rampant. The contagion, for want of a better word, will consume all bio-matter on the surface: tip the atmosphere into an unstoppable spiral of decline."

"How long do we have?" Mason asked. "Until the, ah, end."

"Days? Hours?" Elena said, noncommittally. "Maybe less."

"Enough time to make peace with our maker," said Martinez.

"The Krell will be dead," Jenkins said, with no pleasure whatsoever. "But so will we."

"We tried," Kaminski said. He shook his head, exhaling slowly. "This is the end, my friends. The end."

Beyond the view-port, the *Revenant* fired dark lances of energy across space. A Krell orbital-station – tiny alongside the enormous machine-ship – exploded, caught a wing of Needlers in the blast-wave. When multiple Krell ships launched at the Shard vessel, it responded with just as many lance weapons, gun-turrets forming from its hull. There seemed to be no end to the machine's capabilities.

"We should bug out . . ." Mason offered.

That's just surviving, I thought, as I looked at Elena. *And it's never going to be enough.* She grasped my trembling hands. The shadow of fear lurked behind her eyes. It struck me that it was the first time I'd seen Elena genuinely afraid since we'd come to Devonia.

I can't let her die out here.

"We have to end this," I said. "We have to stop that ship from leaving Devonia."

"That's great and all," Kaminski said, "but based on what I've just seen there's no way that we can get off this ship, let alone deal with the Shard . . ."

The communicator beside Kaminski flashed with signals; emitted a primitive beeping.

"What's that?" I asked.

Admiral Loeb tossed his head dismissively towards the

comms officer in the crew-pit. "It's the damned Directorate. They've been sending us an SOS signal since . . . well, since Kyung bought it."

Just then, the shattered remains of the *Shanghai Remembered* glided across both the tactical display and the observation window: a broken black hulk of a warship, her running lights flashing red to signal an emergency. Her hull had been breached in numerous places, with extensive new damage. She had discharged most of her evac-pods.

"They must've been desperate, if they think being lost out here is any better than staying on-ship," Kaminski said. "I've already been there."

"Kyung was slaved to the *Shanghai*," I said. "But whatever happened to her . . ."

"That ship is operational," Elena completed. "The engine is still hot."

Someone, or something, was trying to correct the ship's course vector; to stabilise her orbit. It was a hopeless and extremely optimistic manoeuvre – the *Shanghai* was going down, no matter what – but the corrections were delaying the inevitable. The ship's thrusters fired irregularly even as we watched.

Loeb glared at me. His old eyes shone with something dangerous.

Hope.

"If Kyung is dead, or neutralised," he said, "her ship will be especially vulnerable. The officers are probably slaved and there will still be crew on board . . . " He shrugged, as though unwilling to accept responsibility for the plan. "Her engines are working. Your call, Lazarus, but in our current circumstances the *Shanghai*'s energy core is be the biggest weapon we have at our disposal."

"What would the energy output on that thing be?" I said.

"Planet-killer," Loeb muttered, definitively. "Shard or otherwise: if the ship's energy core breaches down on Devonia, everything will go with it."

"Artefact and all . . ." Jenkins said, under her breath. "You don't run a whole planet without a pretty big power source, after all. And if that went up too . . ."

We'd destroyed an Artefact on Helios with plasma warheads. The *Shanghai Remembered* was probably packed with nuclear and plasma munitions: that, combined with the energy core, would make it a sizeable explosives package.

"What are you going to do?" Elena asked. "You can't go back down there!"

"I'd advise against it," Dr Serova joined in. "In your state, I don't know whether you'll survive another extraction. I've never seen anything like those readings on your last—"

I spoke over the doctor. "Is the second Dragonfly docked?"

Lieutenant James emerged from the crowd. "Yes, Lazarus. She's refuelled and ready to go."

"Back into the tanks?" Kaminski offered.

"You got it," I said.

Elena followed me all the way. Clawing at my uniform, begging me to stop, telling me not to go. Not to leave her here, among the madness. Tears and realisation mingled across her delicate features. What else could I do? I *had* to end this. Had to do something to give Elena the life that she deserved.

Back in the ravaged Simulant Operations Centre, medtechs rapidly jacked me into the tank. By the time I was hooked up, ready to make transition, Elena had calmed to a bitter acceptance.

"I'll be back," I said. "I promise."

She bit her lip, clutched my naked shoulders. "I wish that I could believe you."

"Like you said: the Directorate will never leave us alone, not while the Shard are still out there. I can't let this thing live."

"There has to be another way," she said, repeating words that she had been screaming a few moments ago.

"There isn't. It has to die, has to be finished here."

Elena knew it, too: was just desperate to say anything to stop me from getting back into the tank. She pursed her lips and backed away, arms crossed over her chest, rubbing her elbows anxiously.

"We ready to do this?" I asked.

One by one, the Legion called in.

I hooked up each data-cable in turn, fresh blood whipping about me as it polluted the amniotic. Every muscle and bone, fibre and atom of my body was aching – singing with injuries of two hundred and thirty-nine simulated deaths.

I always knew that you would get me in the end.

The Dragonfly launched through space at maximum thrust. In the cramped passenger cab, the Legion were pinned to crash couches as we made hard-burn.

"Transition confirmed," I rumbled across the comm-link.

"I hear you," came back Elena's voice, static-riddled, barely audible. "Admiral Loeb is here too."

"Elena . . ." I whispered. "I hadn't expected you to be on the CIC."

"Special concession," she said, voice brimming with emotion. "Admiral Loeb says that it's the least he could do. How are things out there?"

I watched the scene unfolding both on the tactical scanner-suite and in real-time via the Dragonfly's view-ports.

"Pretty bad," I said. "The *Revenant* is destroying anything that comes near it. Although it could just be me . . . it looks like it's getting *bigger*."

Helixes of dark matter – the Creep – spiralled from the surface of Devonia, extended like fragile space elevators to the *Revenant* in high orbit. The ship was literally sucking the world dry. The process was horrifyingly simple: a biomass to nano-mass conversion.

"It's not just you," Elena said. "The ship is gaining mass, and fast. Admiral Loeb thinks that we're still at a safe distance, but he doesn't know for how long."

The vast, monolithic *Revenant* was rapidly increasing its territory, destroying Krell vessels that trespassed too close.

"As it gains in size," Elena said, her voice sounding painfully distant now, "it'll begin to eradicate all threats within weapon-range."

"What are the range of its weapons?" I asked, rhetorically. "Tell Loeb to be ready to pull out. Tell him to leave as soon as the *Shanghai* crashes."

Elena gave a short intake of breath. Stifled a cry. "Yes."

"Not before, you hear me?" I said. "This is important. If the neural-link breaks too early, I can't guarantee that the plan will work. We need to be sure."

"I know," Elena said. "But it doesn't mean that I have to like it."

"I might be okay," I said. "I'll *probably* be okay."

Elena gave a weak laugh. "We can hope."

"Don't do anything to draw attention to the *Colossus*—" I urged.

The comm-link degenerated into a hiss of white noise, and I angrily cut the connection.

Across my HUD, green lights indicated a state of readiness for the Legion. All suits sealed for EVA, all weapons primed and ready.

"Coming up on the *Shanghai*," James declared. "She's tracking us, but she isn't firing." He swallowed. "Not yet, at least."

"All-stop," I ordered.

James applied the grav-brake. The gunship slowed, sailed closer to the Directorate destroyer. The nearer we got, the more damage I noticed. I banished the creeping doubt that she wouldn't be able to fly, that her drives were somehow compromised beyond operation.

"Get buttoned up," I said, "and open the rear access hatch."

"Solid copy," James said. "You want me to remain on-station?"

I shook my helmeted head. "Withdraw to the *Colossus*. This is a one-way ticket for us."

Kaminski stood from his crash couch, his boot-mags holding him upright in zero-G. He nodded at me, smiling like he really didn't give a shit.

"Game time, people," he said.

"On my mark."

"Ready when you are," Jenkins said.

From the rear of the Dragonfly, access ramp deployed, we fired our harpoon launchers. Left arms extended, aimed at the warship below us.

The harpoons traced a bright arc across space, active charges firing, trailing cables from our battle-suits. Simultaneously, we thought-activated our thruster packs. In normal gravity, the pack gave enhanced mobility: in micro-G, we *flew*. Almost immediately, I found myself outside the gunship – chasing the harpoon as it traced an unstoppable course to the *Shanghai*.

"Successful launch," James said, over the comm-link. "You crazy bastards."

"We're Legion," Mason replied. "It's what we do."

The Dragonfly's engines fired, and it retreated back to the *Colossus*.

Comet-like I sliced through the heavens, too small to be caught by any of the *Shanghai*'s defensive systems, or to be of interest to the sprawling *Revenant*. I breathed in short, ragged gasps; watched the reflection of laser fire and railgun munitions on the inside of my face-plate. There was a jolt as the harpoon hit the *Shanghai*'s hull – a second ahead of my arrival – and the DISTANCE TO TARGET indicator on my HUD rapidly depleted. I fired my thrusters again, readying to land.

"All clear," Jenkins declared.

The Legion were on the outer hull of the *Shanghai*. The site was a field of charcoal; barren and vast. Chino characters bigger than me marked her armour, letters in bright white. I'd landed beside a series of campaign badges – marking successful operations on the Rim, in the Sierra Gulf, and around Jupiter.

I took stock of our situation. We were fastened to the outer hull by mag-locks in our boots and gloves. We were also alone, although I knew that we wouldn't stay that way: once the Directorate realised we were out here, they would send a response team to our location.

I checked my wargear. Plasma rifle, plasma pistol, grenades. Good enough.

Ten metres along the hull sat an airlock: closed. I had no maps or schematics to assist me, but it was a way onto the ship. Also good enough. As I watched, the outer door slid open, beams of light probing from inside.

"Weapons free," I said. "Kill them."

"My pleasure," Kaminski said. "This is for Capa, you assholes."

The first soldier – wearing a vac-proof hard-suit and an exo-skeleton – disappeared in a cloud of red mist. Bored through by a volley of pulses from Kaminski's plasma rifle, sent spiralling across the cold of space. It seemed somehow appropriate that he should get the first kill.

Already, responding to the death of their comrade, the rest of the response team was moving out. My HUD flagged six of them; even in armour, their difference in temperature registered against the vacuum. Carrying mag-rifles.

I grabbed a grenade from my combat-webbing—

THIS MUNITION TYPE IS UNSAFE FOR DEPLOYMENT IN A ZERO-GRAVITY ENVIRONMENT, my HUD warned.

— primed it and tossed it in a single sweep. The Directorate had no chance to retreat; caught outside the lock. The grenade exploded: a precise sphere of fragmentation, spreading out to cover a multi-metre radius. In zero-G, the sharp debris quickly populated the area. One Directorate Sword caught a face full of shrapnel – clutching at his breached helmet, spinning away from the ship. Two more suffered suit failures, venting atmosphere from punctures in the torso and shoulders.

Before the team could rally, before the Swords could properly reply, Mason and Martinez slaughtered them with plasma fire. Two of them managed to return fire, one almost hitting 'Ski, but it was uncoordinated. A single round bounced off my face-plate – left a nasty scar on the armourglass – but I avoided a suit-breach.

"And that's how you do it," Kaminski said.

In less than five seconds, the response team was gone. Just a collection of empty armoured suits and dead bodies floating from the open lock.

"We need to get inside," I said. "And fast."

The *Revenant* was at our backs, and somewhere beyond the third moon lingered the *Colossus*. How long until she became the target for the Shard mothership?

Quickly, we clambered inside.

We smoothly breached the inner lock – whether the ship retained atmosphere was irrelevant – and got aboard the *Shanghai*.

"You ever been on a Directorate ship before?" Martinez asked me.

"Not that I know of," I said.

Let alone the ship responsible for killing my mother, I thought. *Somewhere in here, someone programmed the firing solution that killed her.*

"She's gone," I said to myself. "And there's nothing I can do to help her."

Only Elena mattered now.

"I have," 'Ski said, his expression dropping. "It didn't work out so well."

To the rest of the squad, I said, "Smooth deployment. Priority is to reach the bridge SAP."

"Affirmative," the Legion chorused.

"Blast doors shutting behind us," Martinez said, "so she still has some emergency power."

"No way back," Jenkins said, with a smile. "Same as ever."

The entire corridor was bathed in flashing emergency lights, an AI calmly reciting machine-code in the distance.

Two sailors – dressed in black Directorate Naval Force uniforms – dashed through an open door, virtually into my path. They turned to face me. Young men, scalps shaven, probably Uni-Korean stock, with respirators over their lower faces. One had a kinetic pistol, and raised it in my direction. My plasma rifle was faster: the muzzle to the shooter's chest.

The Legion brought weapons up as one.

"Stop!" I yelled.

The sailor froze. Eyes locked on mine; pools of despair. Not a Sword, just a shipboard technician. Probably brought up on stories of the mighty Lazarus Legion, of the demon that was Lazarus. Let them believe it. The gunman's friend backed away a step, stumbled.

"Bridge," I asked. "Which way?"

My suit ran the translation into Chino, and the words came out in an emotionless machine burr.

The gunman nodded towards the end of the corridor, to an open hatch that led deeper into the bowels of the ship.

"That way," he said, in perfect Standard.

I nodded. "Go," I said. "Evac-pods are down there."

Whatever the Shard had done to Kyung, whatever she had become, had polluted the *Shanghai Remembered*. Every shipboard station bleated warnings and emergency response codes, and every monitor was filled with flickering, alien gibberish: reflections of the Shard machine-code.

My HUD blinked with bio-signs all around me, running through the corridors. Gravity fluctuated, had ceased altogether on some decks. We passed through a science wing of some sort. Lots of labs, branching off a central corridor. Men and women in smocks – so similar to the officers of the Alliance's Sci-Div – fleeing in panicked droves.

An enormous explosion sent a shudder through the space frame. The deck lighting failed, and we were plunged into darkness. Mason grabbed at the wall, steadied herself, and the rest of the squad paused. If the *Shanghai* lost power in orbit, or her energy core ruptured before we hit the Artefact, this whole plan would fail—

"Hostiles!" Jenkins yelled.

"This old crate isn't as dead as we thought," Kaminski said.

Two Sword commandos wearing hard-suits bounced into view, and opened fire with mag-rifles. My null-shield failed, and I took a hit on the shoulder. Intense stabs of pain bloomed along my right side, the ablative plate cleanly penetrated by gunfire. Before they could fire again, Mason and Martinez took them down. Their smoking carcasses smashed into the wall, life-signs extinguished.

Ahead, there were words printed in glowing Chino characters.

BRIDGE, my HUD translated.

The bio-scanner flickered with hot targets, converging on our location.

Rounds sprayed the wall beside me, punched through the metal-plated walls. Something inside the bulkhead exploded and steam started venting across the corridor. I felt shots hit my back, bouncing off the Ares battle-suit. At least one got through though. ATMOSPHERIC VIABILITY NEGATIVE, my suit told me.

I flipped a grenade behind me; felt the detonation against my null-shield. Two signals disappeared from my bio-scanner – two less Swords to worry about.

Then we were on the bridge: inside the enemy camp.

"Get us sealed in," I ordered, grunting against the pain. *I can't die yet!* "Kaminski, patch us in to the mainframe."

Mason took up a spot by the door, working on the controls, Martinez watching her back. Sporadic gunfire chased us, rounds hitting equipment around the room. Jenkins covered the approach onto the bridge, while Kaminski shouldered his rifle and followed me.

The bridge didn't look so different to that of an Alliance warship – glowing terminal screens, holo-displays and posts for a dozen or so officers. The main difference was that every crewman and woman stationed here was dead.

"Shit," Kaminski said. "This is not an advert for permanently hardwiring your crew . . ."

We picked our way through the carnage, our missile pods twitching as they detected ghost-targets. The crew were all symbionts, like Kyung; bred for purpose. Probably revenants in life, rendered horrifying in death. Wide-eyed, still plugged to their stations, bleeding ears and eyes. Those were the worst – still wide, uncomprehending. Kyung had damned them all. The deck shifting beneath me again, I prodded the nearest body with the muzzle of my rifle. Gender indistinct, the officer had tried to claw his or her data-ports – to break the connection to the *Shanghai* – and had fingers wet with blood. The corpse slid from the seat, headset coming free, and a whine of static pricked my consciousness.

"Every one is the same," Kaminski said. "Every fucking one."

Every officer in this room had been listening to the Artefact – listening to the wave of psychic noise that had erupted as the Shard Gate had opened. Technical analyses of the Shard-transmission occupied every monitor—

A mag-round hit the back of my left calf. I stumbled forward. CRITICAL DAMAGE DETECTED, my HUD told me. Even with my simulated body being flooded with analgesics and endorphins, it was getting harder to ignore the pain.

"The door override isn't working!" Mason said, ducking back into cover as more rounds poured across the bridge.

"Then hold them off," I ordered. "Kaminski, get on the command terminal."

"Affirmative," 'Ski said, hurriedly moving a dead body

from the main console. He unclipped a hacking-device from his belt, began to plug it into the desk. "How long have I got?"

"A minute," Martinez broke in. "Maybe less."

Beyond the open view-port, Devonia stared at me like an unblinking eye: stripped to its black bones. Lights winked across the surface. Little acts of resistance from the Krell, whatever was left down there.

I had to speak to her.

One last time.

"*Colossus!*" I yelled, bouncing my transmission off the *Shanghai's* comms array. "Elena!"

The line was a sheet of white noise, and my heart plummeted at the thought that she wouldn't hear me, but after a second I heard her voice.

"Conrad! We're still here!"

"We're on the bridge," I said. "We're nearly there—"

The ship lurched starboard, and I was almost flung from the command throne. The inertial dampeners failed, sending loose debris scattering all around me. Every terminal filled with evacuation warnings; declarations that the ship was being abandoned. The view out of the obs windows shifted again—

"What the fuck are you playing at?" Jenkins yelled at Kaminski.

'Ski shook his armoured head, his gloved fingers guts-deep in the Directorate command station, diodes on the hacker flashing angrily. "I'm trying to reprogramme thrust control—"

The *Revenant* loomed massive. Directly in our flightpath. Swarmed by Krell bio-ships, but reaching out now. Sending energy pulses across space, finding targets. Did it know what we were going to do?

"Correcting course!" Kaminski declared, and the *Shanghai* steered port-side.

"Are you still there, Conrad?" Elena said.

"I'm here," I said. "We're going down. It's working."

As the *Shanghai* reached terminal decline, tipped into an orbit that would lead to direct impact with Devonia, I saw something beneath us.

Devonia's cloud cover had been sheared away by the devastation on the surface, and a mass of living metal spiralled out from the Maze.

Kyung.

She'd expanded, taken on mass. Become a silver monstrosity, a conglomeration of nightmare fractals, with a radius of kilometres.

"We have to do this," I said to Elena. *More will come*, I told myself. *Unless I finish it, now, more will come.* "I promise you, I will come back. Tell Loeb to be ready to activate the FTL!"

"We're ready," Elena said. "On your word."

"As soon as we're back in the tanks . . ." I said.

The ride was becoming bumpier. A bank of computers in the nose of the bridge ignited. The air was choked with smoke, and even through my suit I could feel the temperature soaring. More bodies sailed past me, and someone hit the inside of the bridge's obs window. Fractures appeared across the armour-glass.

The hull began to scream with torsion as the *Shanghai* turned towards the objective . . .

Then sudden, devastating silence.

"We've lost atmosphere," Jenkins declared over the comm. "It's working."

Only the screech of the machine-mind answered me. It dominated every frequency; flooding near-space. Out there, beyond the blast-shutters, the *Revenant* realised what we were doing. It *knew*.

"You're a day late and a dollar short, motherfucker!" Kaminski yelled at the planet below us: at the *Revenant*, too late – moving fast, but unable to intercept us.

They won't follow you any more, Elena.

Atmosphere came up to meet us fast. Outer heat-shielding was stripped away. The ship trailed black across the sky as she fell. This was the plunge of a falling comet: of an inert block thrown to earth like the fall of a hammer.

The *Revenant* fired an energy weapon, and something hit our flank. Part of the *Shanghai* sheared off, an enormous shockwave rippling through the deck.

"I couldn't think of a better bunch of assholes to die with . . ." Jenkins said.

"We are the Lazarus Legion!" Mason shouted.

The *Revenant* was beneath us.

The Kyung-Reaper atop the Artefact.

"I am Lazarus, and I decide when I—"

THE FUNERAL

Two years later

It was raining, and hard, when I arrived at the cemetery. Petrichor – the smell of rain hitting earth – lingered in the air. I've never liked the rain, but since I'd got back, things had been different. It's astounding, the little things that you miss about a lifetime spent off-world. And yes, ten years out of civilisation is a lifetime, so far as I'm concerned.

Being back on Earth was by turns exhausting and exhil-arating, exciting and depressing. The rain hung in the air and served to reinforce the dull nature of the surroundings. *They couldn't have chosen a more depressing location*, I thought. *Perhaps it was deliberate.* The only colour out here was the grid of white graves that marked the hillside. That even grass refused to grow was a reminder of the nuclear fallout that had once consumed the region. Things were different now, time being the healer and all that, but not much. The Earth I had come back to had changed immeasurably in some senses, but remained frightening similar in others.

Vincent Kaminski met me at the gate. He shirked uncomfortably, blushed a little, as he saw me. I hadn't seen him
since the debrief, since the Alliance military had given up
asking their incessant questions.

"You look handsome," I said. "The uniform suits."

Tattoos poked from the neckline of Vincent Kaminski's
dress collar, and his muscled frame strained at the shoulders
of his jacket. In truth, he looked immensely out of place in
the formal blues, and when I mentioned it he looked away
nervously. His lapels were lined with various medals, the
names of which I didn't know.

"Morning, ma'am," he said. "I . . . It's required."

"Quit the formality, Vincent. It's still me."

"It's just . . ." he said. His eyes were red-lined; his expression pained. He'd been crying, I realised.

"It's hard," I said, trying not to sound trite. "I know
that."

Since we'd got back – after the *Colossus* had limped into
port in Tau Ceti, we'd then been shipped onwards to Earth
in some military transport I'd forgotten the name of – Vincent
had changed. There was a distance between us: as though
he didn't want to look me in the eye. I'd often wondered,
in the months since our return, whether the Lazarus Legion
– the military in general – blamed me for what Conrad had
done.

"How was the flight over?" he asked. Small-talk: refuge
of the awkward male through the ages.

"Fine," I said. "Crowded."

I'd taken a sub-orbital from Paris, touched down at Wayne
County terminal; an aeroport not far from Detroit Metro.
The flight had been packed with military staff, Science Division
personnel shipping in from Europe. Thankfully, none had
recognised me. I'd slept for most of the two-hour flight.

"And how's the farm?" he asked.

"*Bien*," I said. "*Très bien*." Speaking Standard was a drag; back home we talked in French mostly. That was when I spoke with others, at least. "Thank you for asking, but we can cut through the niceties."

Vincent looked relieved, if that were possible in his ceremonial uniform.

"Help me with this," I said.

I held out a hand, and he clutched it: helped me through the wet grass.

The rest of the Lazarus Legion were already at the graveside. Keira Jenkins, Elliot Martinez, Dejah Mason. And not just them: a crowd of military personnel. Admiral Loeb, Lieutenant James. I barely knew the last two, but I'd heard that the charges had been dropped against the admiral. I was pleased about that; he was a good man. James was, quite explicably, still skinned, but the others were in their real bodies. There were so many faces that I didn't recognise, had no idea how they came to be here. Some were organised into ranks – an honour guard, was that the phrase? – but others were clustered around the open grave. It was a good turnout: a couple of hundred personnel.

"We've managed to keep the news reporters away so far," Jenkins said. She looked awfully smart in her uniform too, her hair pulled back from her face. The time since our retreat from Devonia had been kinder to her, perhaps: she looked less drawn, more together. "Figured that you wouldn't want them here."

"Thank you, Lieutenant," I said. "It means a lot to me."

"And it would've meant a lot to him," said Mason. In her formal wear, she looked even younger than in her fatigues. She, too, had been crying.

They're good, I thought. *Very good.*

"If we're all here," a po-faced priest – dressed in ridiculous robes and clutching a holy book to his chest, "let us begin the service."

Huddling under umbrellas, in the grey light of a Detroit winter's day, the service commenced.

I spied a single news-drone at the edge of my vision, flittering at the cemetery gates – watching the proceedings with its electronic eyes.

"Damn it!" Elliot Martinez muttered under his breath, starting off for the gate. The Venusian was a hot-head, and I had wondered whether he might even conduct the ceremony, but I suppose in the circumstances that would've been wrong.

I clutched his arm.

"Let them watch."

The ceremony was brief but to the point. I believe that the phrase is full military honours, or something like that.

The Lazarus Legion acted as pall bearers. One on each corner, they bore the coffin to the graveside. Sat it beside the open rectangle of earth – doorway into the great beyond. They looked as though they struggled with the weight, but that was all part of the occasion. Some of the soldiers sang a song as the coffin was lowered into the grave. It was in Spanish, and I followed only some of the lyrics. Martinez had already told me that it was called '*La muerte no es el final*'. A fitting tribute: 'Death is not the end'.

Three Hornets scrambled overhead, jet engines screeching, leaving a trail of white through the grey sky. There was a three-volley salute after that. Seven members of the Simulant Operations team fired rifles into the air, as people who had barely known Conrad Harris cried for his passing.

"He would've wanted plasma weapons," Jenkins grumbled.

"Let us bow out heads," the chaplain said, "and forget the horrors of war that Colonel Harris had to endure—"

The crowd around me did as ordered, but I didn't. I raised my head, felt the rain on my face. Damn, it felt good. It felt good to have the pull of real gravity beneath me. To be here, on Old Earth. It felt real.

"Let's not," I said, as loudly as I could. The funeral procession froze, the priest looking at me with embarrassment. "Let's remember who he was. Let's remember what he did for all of us; that he finished this mess once and for all. That he made the ultimate sacrifice."

That he destroyed the Revenant.

"This is highly unorthodox, ma'am . . ." the chaplain said.

"Let's remember him for who he was," I said, searching the faces of the gathered mourners. "The man that I loved. The man known as Lazarus."

A hint of a smile tugged at the corners of Jenkins' lips.

"Couldn't agree more," she said.

The military contingent were slow to dispel after the funeral, and lingered at the graveside. Several officers – men and women whom I was sure Conrad hadn't known, and probably wouldn't have liked even if he had – threw flowers into the grave. I was choked a little at that. *He'd hate flowers*, I wanted to say. But I bit my tongue; played on as the grieving partner. *It's better that way*, I told myself.

By the time the proceedings were finished, several news-drones had gathered at the gates. Their privacy-intrusion settings were restricted, and despite the annoyance they caused they did not reach into the actual cemetery. Flashes went off as they captured vid-feeds and still images of the party, of the Legion leaving the grounds. Two reporters lingered there as well – a glossy-faced woman and a slick-looking man – and their attitudes to privacy were not quite so fixed. They wandered between the rows of stark white graves, waving microphone wands under my nose. *Are machines sometimes better than flesh?* I'd been asking myself that a lot since I'd come back from the front, since I'd left Devonia.

"Dr Marceau!" the woman implored. "I realise that this is difficult, but can you spare a moment of your time?"

"Chester Sinclair," the man introduced himself. "With Core News Network. I'd love to hear your views on the latest developments with the Krell. Was Colonel Harris' sacrifice worth it?"

I waved a hand at the reporter, dismissing him. "He died doing what he loved doing."

"But he hated the Krell, didn't he?" the man probed. "How would he feel, do you think, hearing that the – ah, fish heads – are to be our allies?"

"I have no idea," I said. "You'd have to ask him."

"Was his loss worth the founding of the Second Treaty?" the woman persisted. "I mean, he ended the war; but what about for you? We're looking for a personal angle on this story, and as his closest kin what better person to give us an insight—?"

"He died in the tanks," I said. "Exactly as he would've wanted."

"No comment!" came Martinez's growl behind me. He was stockier, broader of chest than the others in his real body. He looked quite imposing. "Now fuck off!"

The reporters looked suitably startled. They pushed back from the gate, taking their news-drones with them.

"They would've left," I said to Martinez. "You didn't need to do that."

He was the moody one, the soldier that I found most difficult to read.

"Parasites," he said. "After all you've been through, can't they just leave you alone?"

"I'm fine, Corporal," I said. "Really, I am."

"I'll walk you to the car," Jenkins said.

The Lazarus Legion dispersed, kept watchful eyes on the reporters across the street. I was surprised, actually, that there were only two.

"My car is at the end of the road," I said. It was a rental job; an air-car with false plates.

"Okay," the lieutenant said.

"I've heard that you're going back," I said, abruptly. "To the front, I mean."

Jenkins paused before answering. "There isn't a front any more. Not after what Harris did."

"That's a lie, and we both know it. I've heard that you're getting a squad of your own."

"Will he be disappointed if I go?"

"I doubt it," I said. "It's what he'd always expected of you, isn't it?"

Jenkins shrugged. "I'm Lazarus Legion."

"Without a Lazarus, is there really a Legion?"

Jenkins didn't answer.

We had reached the end of the street, and the reporters were long gone now. I knew that it would roll over, that they would lose interest. It was already happening: with fantastic stories of the new enemy, of the advances that were being made as a result of our new friendship with the Krell Empire. I doubted that much of it was true – I'd already seen and heard the Alliance propaganda machine at its best – but I was glad of the shift in attention.

"This is my car," I said. It was a basic Sedan with

blacked-out windows. That had been my only requirement. "Thanks for walking me."

Jenkins nodded, turned back towards the cemetery. But she paused a few steps away from me; looked back.

"Does it have to be this way?" she asked.

"Yes," I said. "It does. It really does."

She bit her lower lip. Thought on it for a second, then nodded at me.

"Maybe I can drop by the farm one day," she said.

"He'd like that," I said. "It's a short flight from any of the off-world terminals."

"Be seeing you, Dr Marceau."

She turned and left.

The flight back was less crowded. I slept again.

Paris wasn't much better than Detroit, but at least it was French. Almost as soon as I left the orbital, I shed Standard and dropped into my native tongue. The terminal was quieter than it was on the way out, and I was confident that I hadn't been followed. I took an autocab downtown, under the shadow of the ruined Eiffel Tower: a ragged, skeletal reminder of the war.

I found the cafe in one of the less-frequented suburbs, a district occupied by many ex-Army vets. None of them knew me: I was just another face among the crowd. I'd been dead for years. But I smiled as I took up a seat, because it wasn't me that needed to avoid being recognised. I ordered a cappuccino.

"How'd it go?" he asked.

Voice like gravel, dripping in animosity. Such an angry man.

"You'd have liked it," I said. "There was a good turnout."

He grumbled into the newspaper. "Can't they print this in Standard?"

I laughed. "You could've gone, you know. Maybe worn a disguise."

"They'd have seen me," he said. "That's the whole point of this; of going underground." Conrad folded the newspaper and slid it across the table. "I don't want to put you in any danger. Lazarus is dead, and now there's a body in a casket in prove it."

The body was next-gen, just a simulant. But if any one cared to examine it, the corpse would pass rudimentary analysis: Sci-Div were getting better all the time. The soil out Detroit way was so radioactive that the simulant would degrade quickly. Soon, Lazarus would be gone for ever, leaving just his legacy.

"I did it for you," he said.

"And I've already told you: I can look after myself."

I half-turned in my seat. Conrad always seemed uncomfortable in civilian attire. He might look healthier, but he was constantly on edge. There was a lot of pent-up energy in the man. Beside him, attached to the cafe table, sat a jamming device: the reader indicating that it was functioning, that it was cloaking both our conversation and disrupting communications signals in the vicinity.

"Did the Legion go?" he asked. Metal hand resting in his lap, polished through manual labour back on the farm. "How are they?"

"Of course they went," I said. "And they are well, all of them. Lieutenant Jenkins is going back."

The Legion knew that Harris was alive. They'd played their roles at the ceremony, done their part to make this seem real.

"They're better actors that you give them credit for," I said.

"Figures," he grunted.

I laughed. "Not even death changes you, Conrad."

"Not any more, it won't," he said.

There was some truth in that. Conrad's sleeves were pulled up, revealing his swollen, muscular arms. Naked arms, scarred by the absence of the data-ports. Barring the well-worn metal hand, mine were just the same.

"Do you miss it?" I asked.

"All the fucking time," he said. "But that's a whole other story."

ACKNOWLEDGEMENTS

They say that writing is a solitary process, and to a degree that's true, but I couldn't have written *Origins* without the support of a network of people. *Origins* is the third book in the Lazarus War series (well, the fourth if you include *Redemption*), and I've come to rely on these people to get me through the process.

More than ever, my wife Louise has helped me with ideas and proofreading. I really couldn't have done this without her. We got there in the end! The rest of my family deserve credit too: they have to put up with me when I'm "in the zone" and getting that next scene written is all that matters...

My agent Robert Dinsdale provided essential feedback and encouragement throughout. His views on the Lazarus War universe have helped it become what it is.

I'd also like to say a big thank you to my editor Anna Jackson. Anna took a chance on a debut author; she's edited all of my books to date. Her editorial input has been vital, and she too has shaped the direction of the series. Everyone at Orbit has gone above and beyond, and I'm privileged to be supported by such a great team.

extras

www.orbitbooks.net

about the author

Jamie Sawyer was born in 1979 in Newbury, Berkshire. He studied law at the University of East Anglia, Norwich, acquiring a Master's degree in human rights and surveillance law. Jamie is a full-time barrister, practising in criminal law. When he isn't working in law or writing, Jamie enjoys spending time with his family in Essex. He is an enthusiastic reader of all types of SF, especially classic authors such as Heinlein and Haldeman.

Find out more about Jamie Sawyer and other Orbit authors by registering for the free monthly newsletter at www.orbitbooks.net.

if you enjoyed
THE LAZARUS WAR: ORIGINS
look out for

LEVIATHAN WAKES

The Expanse: Book One

by

James S. A. Corey

Prologue: Julie

The *Scopuli* had been taken eight days ago, and Julie Mao was finally ready to be shot.

It had taken all eight days trapped in a storage locker for her to get to that point. For the first two she'd remained motionless, sure that the armored men who'd put her there had been serious. For the first hours, the ship she'd been taken aboard wasn't under thrust, so she floated in the locker, using gentle touches to keep herself from bumping into the walls or the atmosphere suit she shared the space with. When the ship began to move, thrust giving her weight, she'd stood silently until her legs cramped, then sat down slowly into a fetal position. She'd peed in her jumpsuit, not caring about the warm itchy wetness, or the smell, worrying only that she might slip and fall in the wet spot it left on the floor. She couldn't make noise. They'd shoot her.

On the third day, thirst had forced her into action. The noise of the ship was all around her. The faint subsonic rumble of the reactor and drive. The constant hiss and thud of hydraulics and steel bolts as the pressure doors between decks opened and closed. The clump of heavy boots walking on metal decking. She waited until all the noise she could hear sounded distant, then pulled the environment suit off its hooks and onto the locker floor. Listening for any approaching sound, she slowly disassembled the suit and took out the water supply. It was old and stale; the suit obviously hadn't been used or serviced in ages. But she hadn't had a sip in days, and the warm loamy water in the suit's reservoir bag was the best thing she had ever tasted. She had to work hard not to gulp it down and make herself vomit.

When the urge to urinate returned, she pulled the catheter bag out of the suit and relieved herself into it. She sat on the floor, now cushioned by the padded suit and almost comfortable, and wondered who her captors were — Coalition Navy, pirates, something worse. Sometimes she slept.

On day four, isolation, hunger, boredom, and the diminishing number of places to store her piss finally pushed her to make contact with them. She'd heard muffled cries of pain. Somewhere nearby, her shipmates were being beaten or tortured. If she got the attention of the kidnappers, maybe they would just take her to the others. That was okay. Beatings, she could handle. It seemed like a small price to pay if it meant seeing people again.

The locker sat beside the inner airlock door. During flight, that usually wasn't a high-traffic area, though she didn't know anything about the layout of this particular ship. She thought about what to say, how to present herself. When she finally heard someone moving toward her, she just tried to yell that she wanted out. The dry rasp that came out of her throat surprised her. She swallowed, working her tongue to try to create some saliva, and tried again. Another faint rattle in the throat.

The people were right outside her locker door. A voice was talking quietly. Julie had pulled back a fist to bang on the door when she heard what it was saying.

No. Please no. Please don't.

Dave. Her ship's mechanic. Dave, who collected clips from old cartoons and knew a million jokes, begging in a small broken voice.

No, please no, please don't, he said.

Hydraulics and locking bolts clicked as the inner airlock door opened. A meaty thud as something was thrown inside. Another click as the airlock closed. A hiss of evacuating air.

When the airlock cycle had finished, the people outside her door walked away. She didn't bang to get their attention.

They'd scrubbed the ship. Detainment by the inner planet navies was a bad scenario, but they'd all trained on how to deal with it. Sensitive OPA data was scrubbed and overwritten with innocuous-looking logs with false time stamps. Anything too sensitive to trust to a computer, the captain destroyed. When the attackers came aboard, they could play innocent.

It hadn't mattered.

There weren't the questions about cargo or permits. The invaders had come in like they owned the place, and Captain Darren had rolled over like a dog. Everyone else — Mike, Dave, Wan Li — they'd all just thrown up their hands and gone along quietly. The pirates or slavers or whatever they were had dragged them off the little transport ship that had been her home, and down a docking tube without even minimal environment suits. The tube's thin layer of Mylar was the only thing between them and hard nothing: hope it didn't rip; goodbye lungs if it did.

Julie had gone along too, but then the bastards had tried to lay their hands on her, strip her clothes off.

Five years of low-gravity jiu jitsu training and them in a confined space with no gravity. She'd done a lot of damage. She'd almost started to think she might win when from nowhere a gauntleted fist smashed into her face. Things got fuzzy after that. Then the locker, and *Shoot her if she makes a noise.* Four days of not making noise while they beat her friends down below and then threw one of them out an airlock.

After six days, everything went quiet.

Shifting between bouts of consciousness and fragmented dreams, she was only vaguely aware as the sounds of walking, talking, and pressure doors and the subsonic rumble of the reactor and the drive faded away a little at a time. When the drive stopped, so did gravity, and Julie woke from a dream of racing her old pinnace to find herself floating while her muscles screamed in protest and then slowly relaxed.

She pulled herself to the door and pressed her ear to the cold metal. Panic shot through her until she caught the quiet sound of the air recyclers. The ship still had power and air, but the drive wasn't on and no one was opening a door or walking or talking. Maybe it was a crew meeting. Or a party on another deck. Or everyone was in engineering, fixing a serious problem.

She spent a day listening and waiting.

By day seven, her last sip of water was gone. No one on the ship had moved within range of her hearing for twenty-four hours. She sucked on a plastic tab she'd ripped off the environment suit until she worked up some saliva; then she started yelling. She yelled herself hoarse.

No one came.

By day eight, she was ready to be shot. She'd been out

of water for two days, and her waste bag had been full for four. She put her shoulders against the back wall of the locker and planted her hands against the side walls. Then she kicked out with both legs as hard as she could. The cramps that followed the first kick almost made her pass out. She screamed instead.

Stupid girl, she told herself. She was dehydrated. Eight days without activity was more than enough to start atrophy. At least she should have stretched out.

She massaged her stiff muscles until the knots were gone, then stretched, focusing her mind like she was back in dojo. When she was in control of her body, she kicked again. And again. And again, until light started to show through the edges of the locker. And again, until the door was so bent that the three hinges and the locking bolt were the only points of contact between it and the frame.

And one last time, so that it bent far enough that the bolt was no longer seated in the hasp and the door swung free.

Julie shot from the locker, hands half raised and ready to look either threatening or terrified, depending on which seemed more useful.

There was no one on the whole deck: the airlock, the suit storage room where she'd spent the last eight days, a half dozen other storage rooms. All empty. She plucked a magnetized pipe wrench of suitable size for skull cracking out of an EVA kit, then went down the crew ladder to the deck below.

And then the one below that, and then the one below that. Personnel cabins in crisp, almost military order. Commissary, where there were signs of a struggle. Medical bay, empty. Torpedo bay. No one. The comm station was unmanned, powered down, and locked. The few sensor logs that still streamed showed no sign of the *Scopuli.* A new dread knotted her gut. Deck after deck and room after room empty of life. Something had happened. A radiation leak. Poison in the air. Something that had forced an evacuation. She wondered if she'd be able to fly the ship by herself.

But if they'd evacuated, she'd have heard them going out the airlock, wouldn't she?

She reached the final deck hatch, the one that led into engineering, and stopped when the hatch didn't open automatically. A red light on the lock panel showed that the room had been sealed from the inside. She thought again about radiation and major failures. But if either of those was the case, why lock the door from the inside? And she had passed wall panel after wall panel. None of them had been flashing warnings of any kind. No, not radiation, something else.

There was more disruption here. Blood. Tools and containers in disarray. Whatever had happened, it had happened here. No, it had started here. And it had ended behind that locked door.

It took two hours with a torch and prying tools from the machine shop to cut through the hatch to engineering. With the hydraulics compromised, she had to crank it open by hand. A gust of warm wet air blew out, carrying a hospital scent without the antiseptic. A coppery, nauseating smell. The torture chamber, then. Her friends would be inside, beaten or cut to pieces. Julie hefted her wrench and prepared to bust open at least one head before they killed her. She floated down.

The engineering deck was huge, vaulted like a cathedral. The fusion reactor dominated the central space. Something was wrong with it. Where she expected to see readouts, shielding, and monitors, a layer of something like mud seemed to flow over the reactor core. Slowly, Julie floated toward it, one hand still on the ladder. The strange smell became overpowering.

The mud caked around the reactor had structure to it like nothing she'd seen before. Tubes ran through it like veins or airways. Parts of it pulsed. Not mud, then.

Flesh.

An outcropping of the thing shifted toward her. Compared to the whole, it seemed no larger than a toe, a little finger. It was Captain Darren's head.

"Help me," it said.